LAST CALL

"Witty dialogue, engaging scenes and the ever-present smoking-hot chemistry once again prove that Clayton is a master at her trade."

—*RT Book Reviews*

"The hilarious conclusion to a series that made me laugh until I cried, swoon until I sighed, and reminded us all that there's always time for one *Last Call*."

—*New York Times* bestselling author Colleen Hoover

MAI TAI'D UP

"Clayton's trademark charm and comical wit saturate the storyline, which features engaging dialogue, eccentric characters and a couple who defines the word 'adorable.'"

—*RT Book Reviews*

"Alice Clayton is a genius! *Mai Tai'd Up* is sexy, steamy, and totally hilarious! A must read that I didn't want to end."

—*New York Times* and *USA Today* bestselling author Emma Chase

SCREWDRIVERED

"Cheers to Alice Clayton! *Screwdrivered* is a hilarious cocktail of crackling banter, heady sexual tension, and pop-your-cork love scenes. The heroine is brisk and lively (can we be friends, Viv?) and the hot librarian hero seduced me with his barely restrained sensuality. I've never wanted a nerd more."

—*New York Times* and *USA Today* bestselling author Kresley Cole

"*Screwdrivered* has sexual tension, romantic longing, and fantastic chemistry."

—*Fresh Fiction*

RUSTY NAILED

"We want to bask in the afterglow: giddy, blushing, and utterly in love with this book."

—*New York Times* and *USA Today* bestselling author Christina Lauren

"Clayton's trademark wit and general zaniness shine through in abundance as readers get an intimate view of the insecurities one faces while in a serious relationship. Steamy playful sex scenes and incorrigible friends make this a wonderful continuation of Wallbanger and Nightie Girl's journey to their happily ever after."

—*RT Book Reviews*

"For fun, sex, and strudel, make sure to spend some time with these wallbangers."

—*Heroes and Heartbreakers*

"A great follow up to *Wallbanger* . . . just as funny and HOT as the first!"

—*Schmexy Girl Book Blog*

"Humorous, sizzling hot, romantic, and not missing dramatics. If you weren't a fan before, you certainly will be after reading *Rusty Nailed*."

—*Love Between the Sheets*

"Excuse me, I need to catch my breath. Either from panting or cracking up. Because I was always doing one of the two while reading *Rusty Nailed*. Alice Clayton, you never disappoint."

—*Book Bumblings*

WALLBANGER

"Sultry, seXXXy, super-awesome . . . we LOVE it!"

—Perez Hilton

"An instant classic, with plenty of laugh-out-loud moments and riveting characters."

—Jennifer Probst, *New York Times* bestselling author of
Searching for Perfect

"Fun and frothy, with a bawdy undercurrent and a hero guaranteed to make your knees wobbly . . . The perfect blend of sex, romance, and baked goods."

—Ruthie Knox, bestselling author of
About Last Night

"Alice Clayton strikes again, seducing me with her real-woman sex appeal, unparalleled wit and addicting snark; leaving me laughing, blushing, and craving knock-all-the-paintings-off-the-wall sex of my very own."

—Humor blogger Brittany Gibbons

"A funny, madcap, smexy romantic contemporary. . . . Fast pacing and a smooth-flowing storyline will keep you in stitches. . . ."

—*Smexy Books*

And for her acclaimed Redhead Series

"Zany and smoking-hot romance [that] will keep readers in stitches. . . ."
—*RT Book Reviews*

"I adore Grace and Jack. They have such amazing chemistry. The love that flows between them scorches the pages."

—*Smexy Books*

"Steamy romance, witty characters and a barrel full of laughs. . . ."
—*The Book Vixen*

"Laugh out loud funny."

—*Smokin Hot Books*

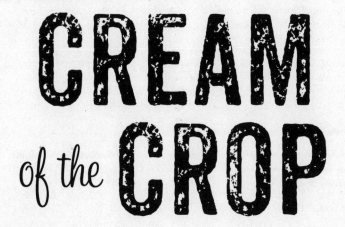

CREAM of the CROP

Alice Clayton

GALLERY BOOKS

NEW YORK   LONDON   TORONTO   SYDNEY   NEW DELHI

G

Gallery Books
An Imprint of Simon & Schuster, Inc.
1230 Avenue of the Americas
New York, NY 10020

First Gallery Books trade paperback edition July 2016

GALLERY BOOKS and colophon are registered trademarks of Simon & Schuster, Inc.

For information about special discounts for bulk purchases, please contact Simon & Schuster Special Sales at 1-866-506-1949 or business@simonandschuster.com.

The Simon & Schuster Speakers Bureau can bring authors to your live event. For more information or to book an event, contact the Simon & Schuster Speakers Bureau at 1-866-248-3049 or visit our website at www.simonspeakers.com.

Manufactured in the United States of America

10 9 8 7 6 5 4 3 2 1

Library of Congress Cataloging-in-Publication Data

Names: Clayton, Alice, author.
Title: Cream of the crop / Alice Clayton.
Description: First Gallery Books trade paperback edition. | New York : Gallery Books, 2016. | Series: Hudson Valley series ; 2
Identifiers: LCCN 2016010533 (print) | LCCN 2016017343 (ebook) | ISBN 9781501118159 (softcover) | ISBN 9781501118166 (ebook)
Subjects: LCSH: Women executives—Fiction. | Man-woman relationships—Fiction. | BISAC: FICTION / Romance / Contemporary. | FICTION / Contemporary Women. | GSAFD: Love stories.
Classification: LCC PS3603.L3968 C74 2016 (print) | LCC PS3603.L3968 (ebook) | DDC 813/.6—dc23
LC record available at https://lccn.loc.gov/2016010533

ISBN 978-1-5011-1815-9
ISBN 978-1-5011-1816-6 (ebook)

To Neens, Lolo, and PQ.
I'll meet you at Tower of Terror.

Acknowledgments

So many people go into bringing these books to life. The usual suspects like Nina Bocci, Jessica Royer-Ocken, Kristin Dwyer, Christina Hogrebe . . . these are the gals that make this possible. You the Reader and me the Writer, we decide together what we like and what we love, and hopefully that'll happen within these pages all over again.

This book specifically was important to me because I've always wanted to write a story with a truly plus-size heroine. And plus-size in All Ways. Not just the thighs and the bum, but in personality, in lifestyle, in mannerisms . . . BUT the key is here that her being plus-size is *not* the central point of the story. I just wanted a beautiful woman, who just happened to be a little rounder than the normal romance novel heroine, to get hers. Natalie is Too Much and Not Enough wrapped up together and set down in her city of Manhattan. I love her, and I hope you do too.

This story also has special meaning to me now because it marks the end of a little era in The Story of Alice. A little over three years ago a wonderful woman dropped out of the sky and changed my life: Micki Nuding, senior editor at Gallery Books.

Somewhere in the universe, tiny things shifted in exactly the right way at exactly the right time and a copy of *Wallbanger* made its way onto her desk, and *poof* . . . here we are today. She is sassy and clever, smart and witty, hopeless with a cell phone, and will sell her soul for a glass of good red wine.

Micki has literally walked through fire to help craft my new trajectory, from patiently waiting through deadline after deadline, to sitting with me in stolen conference rooms to wrangle plotlines out of my stuffy head, to letting me cry on the phone when I'd lost all confidence in my ability to tell my ridiculous. She's been with me every step of the way the last few years, even flying to St. Louis and being there when I walked down the aisle to my very own Prince Awesome.

She's the best cheerleader I've ever had, she's made me a better writer in a thousand ways, and I will miss her telling me every single time I turn in a new manuscript (always around 11:57 p.m.) that THIS book is her new favorite.

Micki Nuding is my favorite. Big fat sloppy kisses.

Alice
XOXO

CREAM of the CROP

Chapter 1

"Can you raise the blinds a little bit? The sun is setting; it makes for a nice view," I directed.

"While you reel them in?" Liz teased, letting the soft afternoon sun into the conference room.

Forty-seven floors up, you got a helluva nice sunset across the Hudson River. It made the room seem warm and inviting, and with the powerful backdrop of Manhattan behind me, what client would dream of saying no? Especially when a ray of sunlight landed directly on my cleavage like some divine sign.

I heard the gasp of a guy crushing on me; the intern was clearly looking at my boobs again.

"Hey, junior, eyes up here," I instructed. I felt the teeniest bit sorry for him as he blushed and stammered his way out of the room, promising to return with the bound copies of the proposal I'd asked for. He was mostly able to keep his eyes redirected. Mostly.

"Poor pup, he's totally enamored." Liz chuckled, adjusting one of the pie charts that were propped up along the wall. Even in the days of easy-to-use PowerPoint presentations and glossy, slick color printouts, there was nothing like a giant pie chart hung on the wall to make a client feel like you'd done your homework.

And I had. I was pitching a new ad campaign to T&T Sanitation, one of the biggest distributors of Porta-Potties in the Northeast. Make all the jokes you want, but this business was incredibly lucrative. And incredibly competitive. T&T sanitation was the second-largest distributor; they'd been chasing Mr. John's Portaloo for years, always coming in second in sales. They were determined to outdo them this year. That's where I came in.

I started unpacking twenty-by-twenty-four-inch pictures mounted on foam core and kept the images facedown as I arranged easel stands all around the conference room. Once they were distributed, I began to flip them over. Liz came back in with an armful of handouts, and nearly tripped right out of her Jimmy Choos.

"Holy shit."

"Exactly," I replied, grinning broadly. I'd literally covered the entire room in pictures of T&T potties, stationed around some of the toniest locations in town. The Bronx Zoo, the Brooklyn Botanical Gardens, even one on the lawn of Gracie Mansion.

"Wow, their outhouses certainly have gotten around," Liz said, walking the room and taking in all the images. "Has Dan seen these?"

"Dan has not seen these," an incredulous voice boomed from just inside the door. "Dan has not seen these, but would love to know why his walls are covered in Porta-Potties." My boss stood in the doorway, jaw ticking as he realized his conference room had been taken over by something most unusual.

"You knew I was leading off with this, Dan," I said, quickly walking to his side and handing him one of the proposals. "The cornerstone of this new campaign is bringing up the one thing no one wants to talk about when discussing their product, and the one thing people really want to know about."

"Pictures of portable toilets," he stated, eyes widened. He had faith in me, sure, but this much faith?

I nodded reassuringly. "Pictures of their product placed all around town, pictures of exactly what you get when you hire T&T: a high-quality portable sanitation unit that's not nearly as tacky as you might think. It's designed to make the customer think about all the different reasons you might need one of these, and how much nicer they look than the ones we typically think of. These are updated, clean, pretty, even. This"—I pointed to a particularly fetching picture of a mint-green one juxtaposed against the skyline of Central Park West—"is what you want for your daughter's wedding, for the Fourth of July picnic. Even the mayor uses this one when they're doing renovations on the official residence."

Rob, the intern, hurried back in, eyes steadfastly fixed on the exact spot in between my eyes. "They're here," he said in a hushed tone, then realized what he was surrounded by. "Wow, that's a lot of Porta-Potties."

"It most assuredly is," Dan replied, his tone measured as he met my eyes across the room. *This had better work,* they said to me.

Message received and acknowledged, my own look sent back to him.

Liz tried unsuccessfully to suppress a giggle, and we gathered around each other in the conference room.

At least no one was looking at my boobs anymore. Which, to be fair, was a first.

In the end, it was the pictures that did the trick. Mr.

Caldwell, president of T&T Sanitation, walked into the conference room, and while his marketing team stared in horrified silence, he walked up to a picture taken outside the Trump Tower on Fifth Avenue featuring a prominently displayed unit and burst out laughing. "I'm already in love with this idea," he pronounced on his way to the seat with his name on it. He and I were already on the same wavelength. It was time to bring the rest of them around.

I spent the better part of an hour describing in detail exactly the campaign I was proposing, buying ad space on television, radio, and the Internet. I'd put together a plan that made his product something people would be talking about, and would stay in a consumer's mind long after the initial promotional push had ended. Every question asked by his team was answered efficiently, either by myself or by a member of my own team. We'd covered every base, we'd thought around every corner, and we were confident that we were presenting something very different from what any other advertising firm had created to sell portable outhouses.

Dan sat in on the pitch as he always did, occasionally commenting, but letting me take the lead as usual. He'd been surprised to see the display I'd created, sure, but once the clients were in the room he was 100 percent supportive. And now he watched me bring it on home with a secret smile on his face, a smile that told me I'd nailed it.

"In the end, I think you'll see that no one else will be able to deliver such a unique, specifically crafted campaign as we can here at Manhattan Creative Group." I leaned across the table a little bit with a twinkle in my eye, looking straight at Mr. Caldwell. "This is the one occasion where we here at MCG think it makes perfect sense to talk shit about the competition."

The room was silent and still. I could feel every set of eyes on me, including Intern Rob. His were about ten inches below my eyeballs. Eh.

Mr. Caldwell leaned across the table, mimicking my posture. "I do love a pie chart." His eyes twinkled back.

The call came in two hours later. T&T Sanitation could now officially be counted as a client of MCG.

❦

There is nothing more glorious in the entire world than Manhattan in October. I sighed happily to myself as I walked up the steps of the Fourteenth Street station along with everyone else heading downtown on a Friday afternoon, anxious to get the weekend started. After the smell of stale air and countless bodies, when I emerged into the sunlight and the crisp autumn air, it felt like a little bit of heaven. With only a six-block walk to my apartment, I slowed my pace a bit, lingering as I often did at the windows along the shops, nodding to some of the shopkeepers I'd come to know. Some by face, but more than a few names in the shops I frequented often.

I didn't understand people being scared to come to New York. Being born and raised here, I tried to see my city as others might. Loud, noisy, brash, full of concrete. I saw excitement, lively, vibrant, architecturally magnificent. A college friend had once asked me, "It's only thirteen miles long, two miles wide. Don't you get bored of seeing the same things every single day?"

I'd drawn myself up and told him, "It's 13.4 miles long, and 2.3 miles at its widest part near Fourteenth Street. And anyone who could get bored in Manhattan doesn't deserve Manhattan." I'm not friends with fools.

I walked along the street, noticing for the thousandth time how charming my neighborhood was. Anyone who thought New York was endless blocks of cement and concrete high-rises had never spent any time downtown. Or in Midtown for that matter. Or the Upper West Side. Or the Upper East Side. Regardless of where you plunk yourself down on my island, I can guarantee you that you're within a few blocks of a park. A green space. An old beautiful brownstone. A hundred-year-old pub. There are pocket neighborhoods and incredible history literally around every single corner. And in a city made up of corners and right angles and hard turns, I lived in the pocket that was all wonky angles and soft turns, winding streets and impossible-to-follow street signs. Off the city grid, in a neighborhood built before the city laid out its easy-on-the-eyes pattern. The West Village.

And it was in this Village that my favorite cheese shop on the entire planet lived, this cheese shop that I walked three blocks south of my normal route to stare at. And quite possibly drool at.

Cheese. *Cheeeeeese.* What a thin, flat, nasal-sounding word for such a luscious, rich, gorgeous thing. Hard. Soft. Ripe. Grainy. Creamy. Often stinky. I'd yet to find a cheese I didn't adore.

My love affair with cheese went back to childhood, when I'd sit in our kitchen with a dish of ricotta sprinkled with sugar. My mother, a world-renowned artist, would work on her sketches; there were countless sketches in every room of our brownstone. I'd eat scoop after scoop of the decadent cheese, and we'd talk about anything and everything. As I got older, my palate developed further, and I continued my love of all things dairy. If I ever developed lactose intolerance, I'd throw myself into the East River.

I'd often wondered if the size of my considerable posterior

was directly related to my love of Gorgonzola. If the size of my thighs was exacerbated by my craving for Edam. Probably. But I could live with big thighs and a grabbable ass. Live without Roquefort? Perish the thought!

As I approached La Belle Fromage, I felt the fontina sending out a tendril or two. *Come here, Natalie, lay your gentle head down on these pillows of Camembert, or cradle a chèvre against your lovely bosom. And here, Natalie—come sit by this English cheddar, a cheeky bastard but strong and capable, willing to prop you up if you are tired from your long journey underground . . .*

"Never skip lunch again," I muttered to myself as I pushed open the heavy oak and lead-glass door.

"There she is!" a voice sang out, and my favorite cheese monger, Philippe, came around the counter.

"My beautiful Natalie. I worried when I didn't see you! It's almost six o'clock, I was almost ready to close up!"

"Had to work a little late." I smiled, leaning in for the double kiss but with a curious look. "How'd you know I'd be stopping by?"

He rolled his eyes in a way that only a Frenchman could get away with without seeming rude. "*Être vénère.* You think I don't know the habits of my best customer? Always on Friday, always on your way home. 'How'd you know I'd be stopping by' indeed . . ." He walked around the counter muttering, knowing I'd follow. The shop was almost empty, just one other customer. Younger guy, knit cap, with a few blond curls escaping. Bottle-green eyes that met mine in the mirror behind the case. I let the tiniest smile creep over my face as I checked out a display just to his left, making sure to make eye contact once more.

Good boy, come this way. He grinned at me in the mirror, and I pretended to not see it. I played with the edge of my coat, letting my fingers do their lingering along my collarbone. He put down his Gouda, picked up a cheese log, and from the way he was holding it, I knew I'd hit pay dirt.

Mmm, start out the weekend with a quickie? Good goddamn I'm good.

Knowing that I had the pup right where I wanted him, I headed over to the counter where Philippe was still going on and on about how well he knew me and how I alone appreciated his perfect palate. I paid attention, but mostly my eyes were on the Cheese Mecca that beckoned.

Philippe prided himself not only on having one of the most complete selections of French cheeses, of course, but on finding the most interesting and wonderful local cheeses from all over the Northeast. He knew my favorites, he knew what I liked, and he knew what I *loved*.

"Now then, you must try this. I've been sold out of it all week, but I just got more in for the weekend business. Taste this!"

I tasted this and that, a little here and a little there, my toes curling inside my shoes as he placed slice after slice of heaven in my hand, where it quickly disappeared into my nearly panting mouth.

"Now then, this one is really going to knock your shoes off," he cried, pulling a new round from the case with a look of delight.

"Socks, not shoes."

"*Oui*, of course." He leaned across the counter with a spoonful of something rich and dense.

I opened my mouth, he slid it in, and the second it hit my tongue, I moaned.

I knew that taste. I dreamed of that taste. I moaned again.

I heard a small cough from behind me, and I knew Knit Cap Quickie Guy was very aware of the sounds I was making. I didn't even bother blushing; I was enjoying this too much. To be clear, I was enjoying what was in my mouth.

I opened my eyes to find Philippe standing there, grinning widely, delighted that he'd picked exactly the right one. This cheese was killing me.

"Where did that come from?" I asked, delicately licking my lips, already knowing the answer.

"It's brand-new, from a small dairy in the Hudson Valley. Bailey Falls—"

"—Creamery," I said, the word *creamery* falling from my lips like a caress.

I knew the man who had made this. Strike that. I was aching to know the man who had made this. Know him, and *know* him.

"I'll take it," I told Philippe, my voice breathy. I looked left and saw the other customer, the guy who just moments ago I was considering bringing home for a Friday Night Special. He now paled in comparison to—

Long tanned fingers

Beautiful strong hands

No no. Save it until you get home and can enjoy. No mental pictures right now, get home before you—

Ink. Up one forearm and down the other. At least as far as one could tell—the ink disappeared via biceps covered by a thin cotton tee. Did the ink go all the way up? Circle around his neck and back? Did the ink go all the way down? Cutting along his torso, snaking around his hip to—

Get. Out.

"I'll take all three, Philippe. Can you wrap those up for me?" I said, dabbing at my brow. Pulse racing, I handed over my money, collected my delectables, bestowed a "sorry, it's not happening tonight" smile on Former Mr. Wonderful, who was looking so hopeful it was almost pitiful.

I hurried out of the shop, fifty dollars' worth of cheese under my arm, and headed home. Needing something to change the images in my head, I turned on the mental soundtrack that I almost always had playing.

Cue "Fireball" by Dev.

What, you don't have a running mental soundtrack?

As I walked quickly down the street, I was aware of the glances I was getting from men. I didn't need to look in the reflection of the windows to know what I looked like. Long, bouncy strawberry-blond hair, pale Irish skin, likely still flushed from my heated imagination. Deep-blue eyes, almost indigo, set off by an array of freckles across my nose and cheeks.

My body was poured into a deep-green wrap dress, accentuating my true hourglass figure. Rather than slouch my tall body around town, I kicked it up even higher by wearing ridiculously high heels, the higher the better. I'd learned to walk across the old cobblestones of Lower Manhattan, and I could walk in heels almost better than in sneakers. These golden peep-toe pumps weren't practical at all, unless you wanted to make sure your legs looked fantastic. Which I did.

Size-eighteen women weren't supposed to show off their legs, which I did. They weren't supposed to show off their cleavage, which I did. Size-eighteen women were supposed to wear trench coats in the winter, long sleeves in the summer, and somebody better cancel Christmas if they wore a dress that showed off some cleavage. Size-eighteen women were supposed to dress like they were apologizing for taking up too much space. Fuck all that noise. I took up space. I took up space in a city where space was at a premium, and I never apologized for it. And right now, I knew exactly how much space I was taking up, strutting down Fourteenth Street to the song playing in my head, with a bag full of delicious and already fantasizing about my favorite pastime.

Oscar the Dairy Farmer.

∽

I made the last turn onto my street, feeling the smile that broke over my face every time I did. I was incredibly blessed to be able to live where I did, the way that I did. Most gals in their twenties in this city were lucky if they shared an apartment with only two other girls, and I knew plenty who shared with more than that. I lived alone, a luxury, in an apartment I owned, an unheard-of luxury.

Well, technically my father owned it. But it was in my name. So according to my own version of the rules, I owned it . . .

I grinned back at the pumpkins and gourds that peeked merrily over the brownstone stoops. Halloween was only a few weeks away, and decorations were going up all over town. As I clicked up the stairs to my own home, a gaggle of white Lumina pumpkins glowed in the twinkle of the streetlights. Juggling my purse and bags, I unlocked the front door, then paused to gaze up at my building. Three stories with an attic, it was three separate apartments, with my own on the first floor, or parlor floor. The other tenants had been here for years, and helped me take great care of the building. We shared the garden out back, and the fourth-floor attic was a shared storage space.

It was converted from a single-family residence back in the fifties, and much of the original woodwork and detail was still intact. The main central staircase had been preserved when it was closed in, making each apartment a self-contained unit sharing the same stairs. Beautiful honeyed wood shone brightly in the entryway, with an original period mirror poised just inside.

A bronze umbrella stand, complete with antique parrot-head parasol, stood proudly in the corner, another shared item.

I let myself in my own front door, which had been rescued from a salvage yard when my father renovated the building years ago. The original renovation had been done on the cheap, with ugly flat steel doors. My father had scoured antique shops and architectural salvage dumps until he found beautiful mahogany doors, likely pulled out of another brownstone in the city. Replacing them throughout the building made it feel more homey, and certainly more fitting for a house built in the late 1870s.

I carried my bags through the living room with its shiny pocket doors and eighteen inches of intricately carved crown molding, in through the dining room and its waist-high chestnut wainscoting, on into the galley kitchen with its marble tiling and butcher-block counters. Setting my bags down as I slipped out of my shoes, I listened to the relative quiet. Relative because it was never truly quiet. Cars honking over on Bleecker, a faraway siren, and the ever-present background hum of 1.6 million people living in twenty-two square miles.

It had been a great day. I'd landed a great account based on my unconventional yet killer pitch. I had the entire weekend to look forward to. I had a bagful of luscious cheese to indulge in. And I had a headful of luscious images to indulge in. Pouring a glass of red wine, I let my mind run wild . . .

Oscar. His name was Oscar. I know this because my best friend, Roxie, had clued me in, knowing him from the small hometown she had recently moved back to. Her boyfriend lived on the farm next to Oscar's. Before I knew this, I only knew him as The Hot Dairy Farmer I Crushed On at the Union Square Farmers' Market.

I had it bad for Oscar. I'd lived most of my adult life able to date pretty much whomever I chose. A late bloomer, I'd spent much of my teen years hiding my ample body under big sweatshirts and a loud mouth, never letting boys close and certainly never letting anyone under the big sweatshirts. My freshman year at culinary school (a disastrous decision considering I could burn water, but a great decision considering I met my two best friends, Roxie and Clara), I embraced my curves, my natural good looks, and realized that confidence went much further than a small ass in tight jeans.

I'd spent the first part of my life as an observer, watching the world as it went by instead of participating, particularly when it came to men. I'd watched my girlfriends fumble through relationships, watched guys run circles around them, especially when the girl lacked confidence. I learned things about how men and women operate by listening and watching and remembering.

I'd had one boyfriend, just the one, and when it ended, it ended badly. It nearly broke me, in fact, and when I came out the other side of it I was determined to never let a man define me again. Moving across the country and enrolling in culinary school on a whim, I found a new family of friends that welcomed me with open arms.

No one knew me. No one knew my story. No one knew I was the ugly duckling, and in a school where everyone was as in love with duck fat as I was, no one blinked an eye at a pretty (which was news to me), chubby girl who was finally finding her way back out of the dark.

When I finally found my own confidence, I took my sharp tongue (honed from years of defense humor) and my surprisingly good looks (a mother with gorgeous Celtic genes mixed with a Viking-like father) and used every trick of the trade I'd observed over the years on the opposite sex.

I found a certain kind of power in walking into a room

where I knew no one, and figuring out how everyone ticked. Narrowing in on the best-looking guy in any room, and going on the offense. Size-eighteen women were supposed to be timid. Size-eighteen women were supposed to be shy. Size-eighteen women were supposed to be grateful for any male attention, and to feel especially honored if a good-looking man paid attention to them.

Fuck all that noise. I took the best-looking guy home with me whenever and however I pleased. Confidence went a long way. You walk into a room armed with the knowledge that you can have anyone you want? You can literally have anyone you want.

Plus I had a sweet rack. Which always helped.

I made up for lost time, dating as much as I could, discovering what men liked and what men loved. And when it became apparent that a career in the culinary arts was not in the cards for me, I said good-bye to my new best friends, packed my bags, and headed east. I crashed back onto the scene in Manhattan, unpacking confidence and a touch of cheeky along with my new sexy clothes, determined to keep the party going New York style.

Enrolling at Columbia, where I'd had been accepted my senior year of high school but deferred while I played line cook in Santa Barbara, I discovered a newly untapped talent for writing quick and edgy copy. I spent four years pursuing an advertising degree, dating almost nonstop the entire time, and when I graduated at the top of my class, I had my pick of junior copy editor positions at several New York advertising firms.

Mmm, professional men. I loved it.

I loved men, and I didn't apologize for enjoying them. I wasn't looking to get married, I wasn't looking for someone to take care of me, and I certainly wasn't looking for a man to take me home and stick me in an apron. But I did enjoy myself.

Did I run into jerks? Sure, that was par for the course. Are there great-looking guys out there who are also assholes? Of course. But instead of shying away, I went crashing right on through, making them want me, making them need me, making sure the thought of sleeping with a big girl as a pity fuck was a thought they'd never have again.

I was confident around men of all sizes, shapes, colors, and political persuasions. I prided myself on being a connoisseur of the opposite sex, and never felt "lucky" or "grateful" when a man dated me.

I overheard a beautiful man once say that fat chicks give great blow jobs, because they needed to make sure a guy kept coming around. That same man gave me incredible head three times a day for a solid week, and I never once sucked his dick. *He* was lucky. *He* was grateful. *I* was grinning.

I dedicated my days to becoming one of the youngest advertising executives in the business. I dedicated my nights to indulgence in all the things I never thought I could have, figuring out what made a man tick and then taking him home with me.

Yet there was one guy who reduced me to mush every time I saw his gorgeous face and heard his gorgeous voice say that one gorgeous word to me, every week at the farmers' market.

The first moment I'd laid eyes on him, I'd been dying to lay thighs on him. My thighs. On his shoulders. I'd been hit with an instant wave of lust. Months ago I'd been visiting my favorite farmers' market, visiting my favorite stalls, chatting with some of the producers I'd come to know, as I was here almost every Saturday. A new stall caught my eye: Bailey Falls Creamery, Hudson Valley, NY. Thinking I might have stumbled onto a new source for yummy local dairy treats, I headed over, drawn by the chalkboard sign advertising butter, milk, cream, and . . . oh!

Behind the counter was the best-looking man I'd ever seen. Six feet six inches of stunning. His skin was a deep golden color, tan but swirled through with the lightest caramel. Thick chestnut brown hair was caught back in what looked like a leather tie, but a few wavy pieces had escaped and were strewn about a chiseled face. That perfectly tousled pony would have cost forty dollars at any decent blow-dry bar, but you know he just tugged it back in the morning and ran with it.

The hair framed a sinful face, deeply set gray-blue eyes shone out from under heavy brows, one of which had a slashing scar through the middle. Very Dylan McKay. Except this guy could have broken Dylan McKay with his ponytail alone.

His features were dark and, coupled with the golden skin, hinted at sun-swept island beaches and South Seas waves. I'd ride those waves.

But the ink! Sweet mother of needles, the ink. From across the market I could see the swirls of red, green, orange, and black coating him in full sleeves, stopping just above his wrists.

I'd dated bad boys, and I'd fucked my share. But this guy was like . . . hmm. Cross a bad boy with a supermodel, add a dash of linebacker with a big scoop of Polynesian love, and then you might, just *might,* have an appreciation for the wet dream across the market from me.

And then he—oh lordy—he pulled a tall bottle of purest white milk from the cold case, twisted the cap, and drank deeply, wiping his mouth with the back of his hand.

"Sweet—"

"—Christ," I finished for the woman next to me, standing there with her mouth hanging open, who'd been lucky enough to witness the same glory I had.

"Almighty," a third slack-jawed bystander added to the mix,

this time a tall stockbroker-looking type, his own mouth falling open in worship.

I immediately pinched myself, certain I'd fallen asleep somewhere and was experiencing some kind of wonderful, but imaginary, dream.

Ouch. Not dreaming.

I began looking around, trying to find the hidden camera, as this was surely a prank show of some kind. The city of New York would never let someone this beautiful just walk around loose like this; it could start a panic.

The two people I'd been staring with had already gotten in line, so it was time to strike, before someone else claimed him.

I straightened myself up to my full height, glad I'd worn something casually sexy this morning. A silky summer shift, it was a little like a bathing suit cover-up, a little like a nightie, and a lot like sexy. I threw my hair back over my shoulder, breathed in deeply, and strutted over to his stall.

I waited in line. I looked over his wares. I was convinced we'd be horizontal before noon. I tasted a few of the samples he'd thoughtfully provided for his customers. I tasted sweet grassy clover in the buttery Camembert, deliciously twisted dark in the Stilton, and was bowled over by his strong cheddar, finally selecting a lovely Brie. I was convinced we'd be *vertical* before midnight.

I watched and listened as he interacted with his customers, picking up little hints here and there about the man. He was commanding, forceful, short on words but long on brooding, and the furthest thing from a natural-born salesman. His products must be good enough to stand alone, because clearly this guy wasn't winning anyone over with his conversational skills. Would I go in strong, and knock him down a few pegs? Or soft and demure, thinking he liked a soft, sweet girl who turned into a crazy one in bed?

Didn't matter. Because the closer I got to him, the strang-est thing happened. My skin flushed, my knees wobbled, and my heartbeat got all fluttery. It was my turn in line next—what would I say? I tried to will my racing heart to calm down, to tell the butterflies inside me to shut it, it was time to snag this guy. But when his eyes fell on me, those beautiful blue piercing eyes, and they traveled the length of my body and back up again, the eyebrow with the scar rising in (Appreciation? Admiration? Carnal frustration?) question, he merely said one word.

"Brie?"

"Oh. Yes," I whispered, not trusting my voice to go any louder. He nodded, wrapped up a package, and handed it to me. For one instant, one glorious fireworks-filled instant, his finger brushed mine.

I mentally placed an order for wedding invitations.

"You pay the cashier down there," he said, jerking his chin toward the cashier.

As he looked past me to the next customer, I suddenly re-membered I had legs. And boobs. And a lovely round bottom. I remembered how to regain control and get us back on the hori-zontal schedule. But he afforded me only one more glance, and while it was clearly at my legs, he was done with me.

I shook my head to clear it, somehow made my way to the cashier, and paid for my Brie.

I mean. This *guy*.

I stole one more look over my shoulder, and saw his gray-blue eyes flash once more toward me, feeling it all over my body.

But I was left holding his Brie, and nothing else.

Back at home I started plotting for next Saturday. And the Saturday after that. And . . . you guessed it. Because week after week, cheese after cheese, I'd lose all my nerve and all my strut the second those eyes looked at me, looked through me.

"Brie?" he'd ask, and I'd answer, "Oh yes." He'd wrap it up, I'd walk away on shaky legs, and our time together was over, but for the exquisitely lustful fantasies that ran through my head every day as I counted down how many more days I had to go before seeing him again.

This was beyond a crush. This was beyond a quick naked tussle behind the dairy truck. This was maddening.

And I'd see him tomorrow morning!

I fell onto the couch, squealing, kicking my legs into the air like a cricket.

Chapter 2

Saturday mornings were set in stone. I always got up early, went to Bar Method class (half ballet, half yoga, all hard-core), picked up my dry cleaning and a smoothie, then went home to shower. And dress. And strut. And Brie. But somewhere between the shower and the Brie, there was Roxie.

"Girl. How're the sticks?" I asked, sinking down onto the couch with my berry-banana concoction.

"How're the sirens?" she shot back, her answer every week. My best friend for years, we'd fallen into the habit of chatting more often now that she was back on the correct coast and only a ninety-minute train ride away up in the Hudson Valley. We'd always stayed close, but something about living closer to each other had kicked our friendship up a notch, and now I looked forward to our weekly Saturday-morning chats. I spent a similar hour each Sunday morning on the phone with our other best friend, Clara, whenever she was in the same time zone. A branding specialist for luxury hotels, she was frequently out of the country on business.

"How come you haven't shipped me one of your coconut cakes yet? My doorstep is suspiciously devoid of Zombie Cakes care packages . . . who should I talk to about that?" I teased, slipping out of my sneakers and examining my pedicure. I might need to pop over this afternoon for a shine-up.

"You can talk to the lady in accounts receivable, which is me. As soon as you buy a cake, you'll get a cake, it's that simple," she said with a laugh. "I'm starting a business here; I can't be giving away the profits."

"Can I get it at cost?"

"Sure. It costs fifty-five dollars, plus shipping."

I rolled my eyes. Roxie had recently started a food truck in her hometown of Bailey Falls, using her grandfather's old Airstream trailer. She was already making a name for herself in the Hudson Valley and had even brought the whole show into the city on a few occasions. It took time to start a business, naturally, but she was doing it in exactly the right way. She'd started small, and with a little guidance from me in terms of marketing, she was kicking some ass. Her cakes were wonderfully rich and nostalgically old-fashioned, a great combination. "How was your week?" she asked, snapping me back from my thoughts.

"It was good; brought in a new client, assisted on a few other campaigns, nothing too exciting. How about you?"

"It's crazy here right now with the harvest; Leo is going nuts. You'll be proud of me, though; I learned how to make a plaster-of-paris town hall."

"For Polly's class?" I grinned, thinking about how upside down Roxie's life had become within one summer. She'd come home to help her mother out with the family diner, and ended up falling in love with a local farmer who had a seven-year-old daughter. She was head-over-heels in love with her new life.

"Yeah, they're making a mock-up of Bailey Falls, and we were in charge of the executive branch."

"Sounds exciting," I said drily.

"I'm glad she didn't get assigned the water tower; that would have been difficult."

And just like that, the life around you begins to change. We were growing up.

"Leo ruined the first town hall. It was all finished and ready to go to school the next morning, when he got all twisted up in my panties, tripped us both, and fell, sending me ass first into the cupola. We had to stay up all night making a new one."

And just like that, you realize nothing ever really changes.

"Enough with the Mayberry. You planning any trips into the city anytime soon?" I asked, dangling the city carrot every week.

"Nothing on the books right now. You planning on coming up here for a visit anytime soon?" she asked, already knowing the answer.

"You're adorable," I said, chuckling, finishing my smoothie and rising off the couch to throw it away in the kitchen. "There's a big foodie festival here the first week of November; you should try and get your cakes into it; lots of gourmet eyeballs there."

"Send me the details and I'll see what I can do. Speaking of food, are you gonna talk to Oscar this week?"

"Shush."

"Explain this to me again, please," she said, her voice incredulous. "I've seen you get a guy to literally eat out of the palm of your hand, and you can't talk to Oscar the Grouch?"

"He wasn't eating out of the palm of my hand."

"He ate olives off your fingertips, and he kneeled down to do it. In a bar, for God's sake."

I giggled. He did. Yuri. He'd said he was a Russian mafia guy, but he wasn't so tough. I stuck my tongue in his ear, whispered what he could do to me if he played his cards right, and . . . wow. He really *was* eating out of the palm of my hand.

"I don't understand why this guy makes you so googly! I

mean, he's obviously got that brooding bad-boy sex god thing going on, and—"

"You can stop there; that's enough to make me go googly," I interrupted, my eyes crossing.

"You know, if you came up here for a visit, I could easily arrange a meetup . . ." Her voice trailed off, plotting.

"No! I can't, no!"

"Why in the world not?"

It was a good question. Why *wasn't* I jumping all over this?

"If I come there and I see him, and we talk, about cheese or whatever else might come up, then it's like . . . I don't know. Something changes."

"Yeah. We get this shit moving past the scrambled-brain phase," she replied.

"Exactly! What if, once we start talking, he no longer scrambles my brain? What if, once I get to know him, there's no *grrr* behind the golden? What if"—and I had to sit down to even say this out loud—"what if he's got a teeny weenie?"

I could hear her intake of breath.

"Well then, Clara would take the train down and we would get. You. Through!" It almost sounded like she'd choked.

"Are you laughing at me?" I asked, narrowing my eyes.

"No. Not at all," she insisted, and coughed strangely.

"You are totally laughing at me, asshole!" I exclaimed.

"I can't believe you're actually serious! A teeny weenie? I'm pretty sure Oscar is packing a giant milk can . . ."

"Oooh, you think?" I asked, relaxing back onto the couch and curling up like a cat, my teeny-weenie terror momentarily subsiding.

"You're certifiable," she said, undoubtedly shaking her head. "Seriously, though, you should think about coming up here and taking this thing to the next level."

"I like this level. I know this level," I said, chewing on my ponytail.

"But it doesn't make any sense! You should own this guy, *destroy* this guy—and you can't even talk to him? Make this make sense to me."

I thought for a minute. She asked me this almost every weekend, and every weekend I said I don't know. I didn't know, and that was the truth.

"I wish I knew, Roxie. Somehow, everything I know about guys goes out the window when I see him. There's just something about him."

"Well, what are you wearing this week?" she asked, the browbeating done and the girl-talk planning now beginning.

Once off the phone, I wandered around in my apartment, restless. I folded some laundry, I spot-cleaned a few shoes, but mostly I paced. I'd circled the kitchen a few times, finally landing next to a cupboard that was almost hidden behind the trash can.

Inside that cupboard was my secret little world, one that I rarely shared with anyone. This city girl . . . loved the country.

Scratch that. Loved the *idea* of the country.

I'd been collecting pictures out of magazines for years, always depicting small-town Americana at its best. Town squares complete with duck ponds and hitching posts. Hayrides, wash hanging on the line, kitchen gardens, and homemade cobbler.

I had this idea that one day, far off into the future, I might leave it all behind and live in the country. Wild and free, wearing comfortable overalls and broken-in old work boots, picking blueberries by the side of a dirt road with a country dog by my side. I even knew the song that would be playing on this little blueberry adventure, "Dust Down a Country Road," by John Hiatt.

I really did have a soundtrack for everything.

Even more specifically, I secretly dreamed about one day giving up my advertising career to chuck it all and start making cheese for a living. It's true. I knew nothing at all about the actual process, but in my head it was very romantic and sweet, just me and my cows and rows of tidy little cheese rounds.

I'd devoted an entire cupboard to this very 3-D version of a vision board, one that I'd visit when particularly daydreamy or when the city had been especially tough.

Ten minutes spent gazing into my cupboard was worth an hour of therapy, even if officially I'd never acknowledge my love of never-actually-visited-but-often-imagined all things country.

I looked at the clock, my heart jumping a bit when I saw it was almost time to go see my dairy god.

✑

Strutting, strutting. Just strutting along, not a care in the world. Here I go. In fact:

Here I go again, on my own . . .

As Whitesnake's classic song played in my head, I could see myself doing front walkovers across a car, or riding through a tunnel halfway hanging out of the passenger-side window while Oscar drove, reaching over with his long, tanned fingers to caress the inside of my black thigh-highs.

I Tawny Kitaen'ed myself through the farmers' market, stopping whenever I saw something interesting, just doing my normal Saturday shopping.

Oh look, farm-fresh eggs. I'll take a dozen. Speckled brown? Fabulous. Into the linen bag they go; it'll be my contribution to the family brunch tomorrow.

Mmm, my favorite flower stall. Look, beautiful deep-red dahlias. I'll take a few bundles for some color in my living room.

Just shopping, not noticing at all that there's a stall now just twenty feet away that contains the most beautiful thing ever created on this earth.

There he was.

Come on, strut it out, girl.

No use. Those gray-blue eyes laser locked on me across the pavement, and the entire world stopped. Usually I didn't see him until I made it up to the counter. He said his line, I said my line, and that was it for the rest of the week. Sometimes, if I was lucky, the wind would blow a few wisps of that thick, wavy hair around his face. And then angels would sing . . .

But today, something was different. He spotted me way before it was time, and he held my gaze. His eyes were piercing, cutting through the crisp autumn-morning air.

And as the wind blew, I realized there was no tie in his hair today. The chestnut was mixed with mahogany and copper and all the other sexy brown crayons. It was thick and a little curly, and cropped just above his shoulders. As I watched he ran his hand through the length, pushing it up and away from his face.

Today was different, I could feel it. I forced my feet to move toward him, using muscle memory to make things that should bounce, bounce. He noticed. He dropped his gaze from my face and it rolled down my body, his stare heavy enough that I could feel it.

There was no one else in line—another first. I walked right up to him, slowing my pace at the end to make sure that when I revisited this later in my dreams (day, sleeping, and wet varieties) I could truly savor it.

Now, standing in front of him, glorious in his simple godlike jeans and T-shirt, I took a moment to breathe. This time, I got a hit of him. Peppery, clean, with a hint of sweet butter. It made sense: the man owned a dairy.

I would kill someone with my bare hands to see him hold his churn.

The mere thought of this nearly knocked me off my feet, but as it was, I was already feeling the telltale signs of going googly, as Roxie called it. Thank goodness, he knew the drill.

"Brie?" he asked.

"Oh. Yes," I answered. He wrapped it up, handed it to me, and this time, instead of what simply could be called an accidental brush of a finger, he held onto it for exactly two seconds longer than he needed to. And in those two seconds, he reached out with his thumb and stroked the inside of my palm. For two seconds, he thumb-stroked me.

I held my breath for an eternal two seconds, thumb-stroked so good that I saw stars. And when we finally let go, I knew I'd never be the same.

If he could make me that stupid with his thumb, what would happen if he—

My body was threatening to blow out every circuit, so I stepped away as he looked over my shoulder to the line that had formed. I walked up to the cashier, handed her the package, and fumbled in my linen bag for my—

Where's my money? I peered into the bag, seeing the eggs and the flowers, but no small coin purse holding my cash for the day. I looked behind me, looked on the ground, and for pockets that I didn't have.

"Shit," I breathed, wondering where it had gone. "I'm so sorry, I think I lost my money," I told the cashier, confused and still rattled by the thumb porn.

"Sorry, cash only," she said, taking my cheese and setting it back onto the display. "Next!"

"It's on me," a deep voice interrupted, and I looked up to see Oscar handing me back the cheese.

"On *you*?" I repeated, and for the first time, he grinned.

"Mm-hmm." He raised that scarred eyebrow in a knowing way. "On. Me."

Yeah, today was different.

∽

If Saturday morning had a ritualized feel to it, then Sunday was etched into stone tablets and mounted on the wall.

You will have brunch with thy mother and father. So it is written. So it is done.

Brunch with my family meant a lazy morning reading different sections of the *Times,* consuming platters of food from Zabar's, and recapping the week's events over incredible coffee. An unstated rule was that, barring anyone being out of town, Sunday mornings were nonnegotiable. Even hangovers were not an excuse for no-showing. You got your ass out of bed, and nursed it with one of my mother's patented Bloody Marys, supplemented by extra onion on your bagel and schmear with belly lox.

Once when I was home on summer break from college, I developed a terrible case of mono and could barely walk. My father carried me downstairs on Sunday mornings and my mother would push on my jaw to make sure I ate my chicken soup.

If you were breathing, you were brunching, my mother would say. And for the most part, with the exception of Great Aunt Helen's untimely demise in our front room one Sunday, the rule was rock solid.

The other rule, equally unstated, was that you don't bring someone home with you on Sunday morning unless there's a sparkling ring in your very near future. My brother, Todd, once brought over a Dakota or a Cheyenne or some such, who giggled and pranced and preened, and kept referring to my brother as Tad. He never made that mistake again. Sundays were for family.

This particular Sunday I was lounging at my end of the dining room table, croissant in one hand, fashion pages in the other, trying to concentrate on what I was reading. But my eyes kept wandering to the travel section that my father was reading, to the story on the back page with the picture of a small farm in upstate New York.

Its claim to fame was a flock of imported Scottish sheep that were not only delightful to look at, all snowy white and puffy, but apparently gave some of the most delicious milk around. The farmer made incredible sheep's milk cheese likened to a Spanish Manchego, salty and perfect. A husband and wife, living in the country, making things with their actual hands!

I wondered if the wife was happy, if she loved her life. I bet she was adorable, all sunshiny and strong hands and cute cardigans. To bed early, up when the cock crows—I bet she lived her life according to the natural circadian rhythm of the earth; not segmented around fashion week and art gallery parties.

I got all that from the back of the travel section in the Sunday *Times* that I was sneak-reading instead of reading my own section. I bit down hard on the croissant.

I thought about my secret dream, the one that only Roxie and Clara knew about, which was to one day venture off my island and into the wild. To live on a farm and collect eggs and make gorgeous handcrafted cheese in sweet packaging from smiling sheep. And if there was someone sharing my bed who woke me with *his* crowing cock . . . well, that would be very okay.

I sighed, thinking about cheese and the simple life and simple yet intense sex. I wondered if Oscar liked cardigans. I wondered if he'd like me in *only* a cardigan, the edges barely covering my breasts, one large button barely keeping it closed somewhere around my navel, crossing my legs just so as I perched on a hay bale to keep him from seeing my country kitty. His eyes would shine, his shirt would disappear, displaying all of that wonderful ink as he stalked across the barn toward me, his hands flexing as he ached to take hold of me, flip me over the hay bale and—

"Natalie."

"Hmmmm?"

"Natalie," I heard again, and I blinked. My mother, father, and brother were looking at me with amusement, my croissant squished in one hand.

My forehead was damp and I was hot all over, my pulse pounding. Good lord, I'd been daydream-fucking Oscar at Sunday brunch?

"Excuse me," I said, heading into the kitchen.

My mother was close on my heels. "We lost you there for a minute. Where'd you go?"

"Nowhere special." I sighed, quickly drinking a cold glass of water. The chill spiked through my haze, bringing me back down to earth.

"Sure looked special, from the dreamy look on your face." She started slicing more bagels for round two. "Anything going on that I should I know about?"

I've imagined an entirely separate life for myself based on the word Brie . . .

I haven't been able to concentrate on one guy for more than an hour at a time ever since I saw the Cheese Man . . .

There was a moment yesterday where I thought thumb-stroking could quite possibly be my new favorite thing ever . . .

"Nope. Same old, same old," I said. "But I landed a new account on Friday."

"Sweetheart, that's wonderful! Did you tell your father?" An artist by trade, my mother was tall, like me, but even more fair-skinned, which she took great pains to maintain. She kept the wide-brimmed-hat business hopping. Her long, thick red hair was usually worn in a lazy bun.

"Go tell your father, I'll bring this along in a moment. Ask your brother if he ate all the olives already . . . I could have sworn there were some for the platter . . ." As she looked for the lost olives, I smiled and headed back into the dining room.

My father had begun the crossword puzzle, so before he got too far into it, I sat down next to him and plucked the pen from his hand. "I'm supposed to tell you I landed a new account on Friday," I announced.

Todd peeked over the top of his newspaper. "Congratulations!"

"Thanks. And I'm supposed to ask *you* where all the olives are. Mom's going crazy trying to find them."

My brother grinned. "Olives? Never heard of 'em."

"She'll kill you," I said with a knowing look.

My father took off his glasses and cleaned them with the edge of his shirt, looking at my brother. "If you've hidden them somewhere, I'd strongly recommend that you go put her out of her misery."

Todd headed into the kitchen with a grin, and a moment later we heard, "Stop teasing your poor mother!"

"So, tell me about this new account," my father said, giving me his full attention. I told him everything, from how I'd come up with the pitch, to the research I'd done into past campaigns and how effective they'd been in the marketplace. He listened and nodded, asking a few questions as I went along.

"I know Mike Caldwell, the guy you pitched to. He's tough," my father said, a look of pride on his face.

My father was head of Grayson Development, a real estate

development company operating in the five boroughs. He'd moved into Brooklyn ahead of the renovation curve twenty years ago, and could have retired long ago based on that building boom alone. He developed some commercial, but he mostly concentrated on residential. Occasionally high-rises, but mostly prewar conversions in the smaller buildings. He loved a brownstone.

"You could have asked me for an introduction, Natalie. I would have been happy to put in a good word for you and MCG," he said.

"I know that." And while he would have called up this client in a heartbeat, he also knew that I didn't need him to. Which made him even more proud. Which in turn made me all preeny. From the beginning, my father had instilled in my brother and me that you carve the path you wanted, and then you work like hell until you get it. Not that he'd ever be opposed to offering a helping hand, as in introducing me to Mr. Caldwell. But I was proud knowing that I'd gotten where I was in life on my own. "I did kind of kill it in the pitch," I said with a quiet smile.

"Of course you did!"

My mother came into the dining room with the bagel platter then, and all shop talk ceased as brunch continued. Where my father instilled the "get where you need to go on your own" mentality, my mother instilled the other half of my "take no prisoners" attitude. Family first, but never sacrifice yourself in the process. She was already an up-and-coming artist when she met my father, and in the middle of their whirlwind romance they had an unexpected surprise: my brother. She could have set her own life aside to make a home for my father, but they were equals in every way and they made sure neither sacrificed more than the other.

As I watched them move around our dining room, each

perfectly complementing the other, I sighed in contentment, knowing that no matter what happened outside these walls, my mother and father would be inside, keeping it together.

Brunch continued, plans were discussed for the upcoming week, and other than an occasional look from my mother that told me she definitely knew something was up but was biding her time, I managed to keep my dairy fantasies to myself until I got home.

When I got in bed that night, however, I let them fly.

Chapter 3

"Okay, team, did everyone bring their agenda with them?" Dan asked the assembled group, and was greeted with the usual acknowledgments. Monday-morning meetings were early, they were efficient, and they were murder without coffee.

One of the reasons I chose Manhattan Creative to begin my career was their fine reputation, their wide network of colleagues across the country—the globe, really—and their barista-like coffee bar on the forty-fourth floor.

The president of MCG worked his way through college at a tiny old-fashioned coffee shop, and prided himself on having only the finest coffee products for his hardworking team. It was a perk, pardon the pun, to an already incredible job.

Over the weekend, a burst water pipe on the forty-fifth floor meant the coffee bar was no longer. They'd found beans down on twenty-seven, or at least that was the word on the street. Intern Rob had been sent down to bring back Starbucks for everyone, but until he arrived, those not smart enough to bring their own brew from home were struggling this morning.

Not Dan. Dan was one of those herbal-tea people. He brought

his own bags with him to work, even had a teakettle in his corner office, and therefore felt none of our pain this morning.

"Let's have another round of applause for Natalie's team. Ms. Grayson managed to bring in the T&T Sanitation business with an . . . let's say interesting . . . presentation late Friday evening. For those of you who didn't check their email over the weekend, it was a success; we are now officially peddling shit!"

"Hear! Hear!" a voice called out, and I stood to curtsy and wave à la prom queen.

"Also, for those of you who didn't check their email over the weekend, I'll need your resignation on my desk by 5 p.m. today," he finished, the twinkle in his eye missed by the very green and very young Edward, a junior copywriter who wore a look of panic and was slinking lower in his chair by the minute.

"Easy, Eddie, he's teasing," I whispered, nudging him back up higher into his chair. "But way to call yourself out. Nice poker face."

"But I—"

I shook my head at him, motioning for him to keep his eyes on Dan.

"So, page one as always is new business. Let's go through what's in the hopper this week," Dan continued, and we all read along with him as he outlined potential jobs on the horizon. A cat food brand, not too exciting but lucrative and great visibility potential. A small chain of boutique hotels was looking to go global next year, and wanted to raise some green quickly to look more favorable to investors. To raise the funds they needed, they were willing to spend some money to strengthen their brand. I immediately thought of Clara, and wondered if this might be an opportunity to work together. I put a checkmark next to that section, waiting until he finished going through every item on the agenda to formally put in for the job.

Dan ran a very tight ship, with an impeccably tight team. If you brought a client to the firm, then that was your client. But when someone solicited us on their own? It was up for grabs. Each account executive made a case for how they would be the best point person on each project, and then he and the partners would select who got what gig.

Due to my recent success, and the fact that I'd closed more accounts than any other account exec over the past eighteen months, I could essentially pick and choose the jobs I wanted. Like T&T Sanitation. Now, most didn't want it, thinking it would just end up as a joke campaign. But I saw the potential to go out on a limb with new clients and really make something out of nothing. And, more often than not, the gamble paid off, and I made the partners and myself a nice signing bonus.

I half listened to the rest of the agenda, waiting until it was time to officially throw my hat into the ring on the hotel chain. Might get some nice travel out of it, might get to work with one of my best friends if I could swing bringing in a consultant on this job, and, most important, it could be what finally made me a partner.

A partner before thirty. That had always been the goal.

My father ran his own real estate developing company. My mother was a famous artist. I needed this feather in my cap to keep the name Grayson held with the same distinction that my parents had, and I needed to do it on my own. I could have gone into business with my father; he'd have been thrilled. But other than taking him up on his offer to live in one of his fabulous brownstones, I managed my life on my own.

I scanned ahead on the agenda and realized that Dan was almost through with the new business, and it would be time to formally ask to be considered for the hotel chain pitch. I began to rehearse in my head exactly what strategy to use when I heard him say, very clearly, Bailey Falls.

"Wait, Bailey Falls?" I asked, interrupting Dan and causing the entire room to look at me strangely. "Did I hear you say Bailey Falls?"

"Bailey Falls, yes you did. Looks like someone better hope Rob gets back with coffee soon," Dan chuckled, and light laughter rang out through the group. "The Bailey Falls tourism pitch, it's on your agenda there, almost at the bottom."

I quickly scanned toward the bottom, and right there were the words BAILEY FALLS, HUDSON VALLEY, NY.

It seemed that Roxie's small town was looking for some big-city direction.

"I'll take it!" I shouted, surprising everyone in the meeting, including yours truly.

"Natalie, I admire your enthusiasm, but it can wait until the end of this, yes?"

"Yes," I answered back, a little embarrassed and more than a little confused by my outburst. I quickly rallied, listening to everything he had to say.

Bailey Falls, like most small towns in the Hudson Valley, relied heavily on tourism as a source of income. But with the rise of cheaper flights to Europe again, they'd seen a drop in their tourist business, especially noticing that not nearly as many New Yorkers and New Jerseyans were as interested in weekending there as they were even ten years ago.

People were gun-shy now about buying; they wanted the freedom of renting a summer house, a lake house, a winter camp. They wanted to rent and come and go and not suffer like an owner when the roof leaked or the plumbing broke, or a family of owls set up shop in the attic, which apparently was a common occurrence up in the sticks.

Therefore, some of these smaller towns that featured a slice of Americana as their very bread and butter were not doing so well. And rather than wait, the town council of little Bailey

Falls had pooled its town's resources and decided to hire a big-shot New York advertising firm to put its town back on the tourist map.

Huh. Roxie had just been saying she thought I should come up for a visit. Then Saturday, for the first time ever, something new happened with the dairy farmer, who just happened to live in Bailey Falls.

Could be . . .

Who knows . . .

As I tuned out the last bit of my boss's new-business speech, I heard the words of *West Side Story: something's coming, something good.*

When selecting a soundtrack for your life, it's always good to throw a little Sondheim into the mix.

New business was concluded. I took a deep breath. But before I could make a play for the Bailey Falls pitch, Dan looked straight at Didn't Check His Email Over the Weekend and said, "Hey, Edward, how'd you like to work on the Bailey Falls pitch?"

I fumed.

I was still fuming when Intern Rob came through the door with hot coffee and I burned the back of my throat downing my venti double with three extra shots.

Ouch.

ᗞᗞ

Throat crackly, I stormed down the hall to Dan's office, practically dragging Edward by the collar. He knew better than to protest.

"Dan. What the *hell*?"

"*You're* asking that question? I'm not the one who's trying to hang Edward up like a trench coat. And stop doing that, by the way," he said, sitting down behind his desk with a curious look in his eyes. No doubt wondering why his usually easy-breezy employee was foaming at the mouth over something like—

"Bailey Falls?" I asked, settling Edward into a chair and beginning to pace in front of Dan's desk. Edward just looked relieved to be off his feet. "You gave junior here that account without even asking if anyone else was interested. When did that become standard practice?" I gave Edward the side-eye. "No offense."

"None taken?" he said.

"It's not standard practice, but I decided to switch things up a bit. I knew Edward here would never step up to the plate unless I put the bat in his hand. No offense, Edward."

"None—"

"None taken, we know," I interrupted, resisting the urge to pat him on the head.

"Besides, why in the world would you be interested in working on a campaign like this anyway? It's not your usual kind of job," Dan continued, like Edward wasn't even there. "What's in this for you?"

Orgasms. Endless orgasms. Brought forth into the world by a man who used his mouth and lips and tongue for something way more important than hooking up silly words and phrases and clauses. But not the kind of thing you could explain to your boss, and expect to keep your job . . .

"What's *always* in it for me, Dan. A chance to create something truly incredible, to elevate, to illuminate, to take something no one is talking about, and make it the thing that *everyone* is talking about."

Edward applauded. I smiled graciously. Dan was having none of it.

"I have no idea what's actually going on here, but I'm not buying any of it. You realize where Bailey Falls is, right?"

I blinked innocently. "Hudson River Valley, upstate."

"In the country."

"Yes." I blinked innocently.

"Natalie."

"Yes, Dan."

"You once commuted three hours a day when working on a job in Paramus because you refused to, and I quote, "sleep in this godforsaken state.""

"Well that's entirely different," I stated matter-of-factly.

"Why is that different?" he asked.

"That was New Jersey," I said just as matter-of-factly. Dan groaned and buried his head in his hands, scrubbing at his face. "Look, Dan, before you go working yourself over here, this isn't such a big deal. It's something new, something different, and aren't you always saying it would do me good to get off my island occasionally?"

"You have an island?" Edward asked, looking impressed.

"I do, you're sitting on it right now," I replied, no longer resisting the patting-on-the-head urge. I looked at Dan as if to say, *See, this is exactly the reason you need me on this job.*

He shot me back a look that said, *I agree with you on that point, but I still think you're up to something.*

I acknowledged with a *"Trust me, I got this."*

"Okay, Edward, we'll find something else for you to work on. Ms. Grayson is taking on the Bailey Falls account."

Pleased, I turned to the junior copywriter, who looked positively relieved. "Come on, Edward, I'll buy you a pretzel." I grinned at Dan, who no doubt still wondered what I was up to, but was letting it go for now.

"I'll forward you everything the Bailey Falls councilman sent over this afternoon," Dan said, and I chirped a thank-you as I escorted Edward out of the office.

"You don't really, like, own Manhattan, do you?" he asked quietly, pretty sure of my answer but green enough to ask it anyway.

"Depends on the day, sweetie, depends on the day," I answered, strutting off down the hall, Edward in tow.

⁃⟨◎⟩⁃

I spent the afternoon doing research on the town of Bailey Falls. Founded in the early 1800s, it had once been an artists' colony and still maintained a vibrant and supportive art scene. Bryant Mountain House was located there, an old Catskills mountain resort that had survived remarkably past the sixties and seventies, when so many of those beautiful old resorts had been torn down. And with the Culinary Institute of America just up the road in Hyde Park, it had what looked to be an impressive selection of restaurant and dining options for such a small town.

So what gives?

I reread the last part of the email that had been submitted to MCG.

So you can see, our town has everything to offer the weekending couple or family that just wants to get out of the city and into the country for a while. But while other towns in the Hudson Valley seem to have flourished in recent years, our little hamlet has remained off the beaten path. We like to consider Bailey Falls upstate New York's best-kept secret. I think we're ready to let everyone else in on it now. With your help.

Looking forward to hearing what your firm might be able to do for us,

Councilman Chad Bowman

Chad Bowman. Chad Bowman. Why did that name sound familiar? On impulse I called Roxie.

"Do you know a Chad Bowman?" I asked when she chirped a hello.

"Are you talking about The Chad Bowman?" she asked.

I frowned and reread the email. "I'm talking about Councilman Chad Bowman; is that the same thing?"

"Ha! Councilman! Shit, that's right, I never heard him referred to that way, all fancy and everything. But yes, I am familiar. He was my all-time favorite high school crush, I mean, of all fucking time. Wait, why are you asking me about him?" she asked.

"He wrote to us here at the firm about drumming up business in your wee village."

"Oh, that's fantastic! He'd be the guy to do it, too; he's on this kick to make Bailey Falls the next hot spot. He's got this idea that—" She stopped cold. "Wait. Wait a damn minute. Your firm is working on this?"

"Yep."

"Are you working on this?"

"Yep."

"So you're coming to the sticks?"

"Yep. Got a guest room?"

She shrieked so loud my ears were ringing for the rest of the day.

Chapter 4

That week was spent researching, making calls, and packing. I had Liz already started on working with the people over at T&T Sanitation, revising the budgets and beginning the early stages of that campaign. This wasn't the first time I'd juggled multiple campaigns, and it certainly wouldn't be the last.

I talked endlessly with Roxie that week, making plans for my trip and deciding exactly how many high jinks we'd have time for in addition to both of us keeping our jobs.

"We can go apple picking, and hiking, and white-water rafting, and sailing on the Hudson. And then on Saturday—"

"Natalie! Slow it down, how much time do you think there is in a day?"

"If I'm coming to the sticks, then I'm coming to the sticks. Nature me up, sister," I said into the phone one night.

"We couldn't do that much if you were here for an entire week, much less a weekend when you're technically working. And so am I."

"We don't have to do it all, but we can at least go apple picking, right?"

"I have an arrangement with the bees that live in the orchard. I agreed not to go into the orchard." She gave a horrid little shudder that I could imagine even over the phone.

"And what did the bees agree to?" I asked when she didn't finish the statement.

"They also agreed that I was not to go into the orchard."

"Oh boy."

"But Leo will be happy to take you; there's always an orchard tour on the weekends this time of year." Her voice dipped down low and secretive. "Or I can ask someone else to take you apple picking . . ."

"Stop it; I'll combust if I think about being in the woods with that man! I'd likely climb him instead of the tree!"

"You'll have to talk to him if you go into the woods, though," she reminded me. "Don't you think we better get you talking first?"

"Talk schmalk, I'm hoping his mouth is otherwise occupied," I said with a sigh, and could hear her eyes rolling all the way from upstate.

Since Roxie was essentially going to be my tour guide for everything I was officially working on this weekend, I'd finally told Dan that my best friend lived in Bailey Falls, which kept him from looking for any other reason why I was heading up north on the Hudson River Line.

Once I'd made the decision to take on this project, I couldn't get Oscar off my mind. I thought about him while I was making my coffee in the morning and adding a splash of cream. I thought about him at lunch when I was taking my nosh outside and eating his Brie in the park across from the office. And at night . . . my brain was full of thoughts of a decidedly different nature.

But I was also being a responsible adult about all this. I already had lots of ideas for boosting the tourism in that little town, starting with Roxie's boyfriend. Leo Maxwell ran one of the Northeast's most innovative organic farms, with teams of apprentices coming from around the country to work and learn. Based on what I'd gleaned from Roxie and the Internet, it could be a wonderful draw for people who were very much into their home gardens and being as sustainable as possible. Sustainable. Local. Homegrown. All current buzzwords that generated Internet clicks and tourism dollars that could potentially be spent in Bailey Falls.

It also didn't hurt that Leo came from a very well-known and wealthy New York family, and looked like a Greek god from the island of Hipsteropia. Was I planning to exploit his natural good looks?

Hey, if his farm was featured in a possible future magazine spread encouraging Connecticut housewives to bring their family to the wholesome town of Bailey Falls for a weekend visit, and his smiling face was dead center? It couldn't hurt.

I never turned over a stone that didn't want to be flipped over, but if I thought it might give, I always started pushing. The stone usually let me know.

I also packed. As a rule, I didn't leave Manhattan for any reason unless I was going somewhere fabulous. I'm sure Bailey Falls was charming and all, but it was definitely different from my normal business trip to somewhere with tall buildings and round-the-clock deliveries. How did I pack for the country?

I headed to REI. I explained to an oddly confused saleswoman that I was headed into the wilderness and needed to make sure I had the necessities. I was going on an adventure, and didn't want to be caught without something that might come in handy and save my life. She led me to the survival gear, which I was surprised to realize didn't include anything cashmere. Purification tablets, sure, but no cardigans?

I always found great sweaters at Barneys, so I'd head there

next, but before leaving REI I did manage to procure a great pair of subzero hiking pants, a puppy tent with an optional starry-night ceiling, and several packages of something called gorp.

I also visited the salon for my regularly scheduled waxing (everywhere, thank you) and picked up a few last-minute glam packs to make sure that even in the sticks, I was highlighted, primed, and perfectly dewy. Should the need arise.

I was in the office Thursday morning finishing up some last-minute details when Dan stopped by to check in one last time.

"When is your train?"

"I'm gonna jump on the 1:43. That puts me in at Poughkeepsie around 3:30."

"Sounds good. When are you meeting with the client?"

"I'm scheduled with the councilman who reached out to us tomorrow at 9 a.m. I figured I'd start with him first, get a feel for what he wants. Then I'm supposed to meet with the rest of the council over the weekend, after my official tour." I packed up my laptop. "And apparently there's a barn dance. Can you believe that?"

"Hope you packed your petticoat," he said, chuckling along with me.

I patted my second suitcase. "You bet your ass I did."

"You didn't," he said, blinking at me.

"Dan. When am I ever going to get the chance to go to a barn dance again? You should see the boots I got to wear with my dress!"

"Please promise me that someone will be taking pictures. I just need one," he said, shaking his head. "I still can't believe you're going up there. Best friend or no best friend, this just isn't like you."

As I stood in the perfectly modern office in a high-rise with a view people would kill for, a slow smile spread across my face.

"I know."

∽

When I was ten years old, my family and I took a weekend trip up to Lake Erie to stay with an old friend of my mother's. We got a late start out of the city, broke an axle on a lonely country road after dark, and ended up spending the night, and the better part of the next day, in a little town in the literal middle of nowhere, waiting for the one body shop in town to get the part it needed to fix my dad's car.

We spent the night at the Greenwood Inn, an old hotel that had seen better days. But while my mother and father complained about the size of the bathroom and the thread count of the sheets, I was fascinated with the bell on the counter downstairs and the fact that there was a potbelly stove in the corner. The next day, while my father dickered with the owner of the body shop, my mother and my brother and I spent the day in town, walking the town square, playing in the little park in the center of town, and feeding the ducks in the duck pond. I watched the little town bustle around me, locals coming into town to pick up some groceries from the mom-and-pop grocery store on the corner, to visit with each other at the café over a slice of pie, or to shop for new school clothes at the one clothing store, over which was Miss Lucy's Dance Studio.

My brother was bored. My mother was frustrated. I was enthralled. The little town—and still to this day I have no idea where exactly it was—came alive in front of my eyes, like a walking, talking picture book. We spent exactly seventeen hours in this town, and it forever changed my view of small-town America . . . and was the spark that lit the secret never-to-be-spoken-of-out-loud desire to one day live in one.

As the train sped along the Hudson, I watched as the little river towns flew by. I took pictures as we zoomed by, the river, the stations, the hills, everything. The train made many stops, and I watched the people getting off. These were people who worked in my city, but chose to live just up the river, in an entirely different world.

Huh.

I snuggled down into my seat, wrapping my cashmere cardigan more firmly around my shoulders, marveling at the world that existed beyond the magical land that is New York City. And before I knew it, we were at the end of the line.

Poughkeepsie Station.

Chapter 5

"Wow. It's bigger than I thought it would be."

"See now, that's exactly what I said the first time I saw Leo naked."

"Nice." I slid my hand over for a low five. She slapped it, keeping her left hand on the steering wheel.

"Actually, that's not true," she admitted, a blush creeping into her cheeks. "I totally knew it would be big."

I laughed. "Atta boy, Leo! Its always nice when beautiful boys are not only economically blessed, but blessed down below as well. I can't wait to meet him and congratulate him on his big dick."

She cackled, clapping her hand on the side of her thigh. "Yes, please say exactly that."

"Done." She knew I totally would. "Not that I don't enjoy all the junk talk here, but what I actually meant was *Poughkeepsie* is bigger than I thought." We'd pulled out of the station a few minutes ago, and I'd expected to be in the country almost immediately.

"Poughkeepsie is decent sized, Bailey Falls is positively minuscule. You sure you're up to this?"

"I'm not that citified, am I?"

"Sweetie. There's no Starbucks. No blow-dry bars. We have one cab, driven by a man named Earl, who wears glasses as thick as Coke bottles. I'm not entirely sure they're *not* actual Coke bottles."

"I'll be fine," I answered, settling back against the seat. "I see you're still driving this beast."

"It's not a beast, it's a Jeep Wagoneer, a classic. They literally don't make them like this anymore."

"That's true, you don't see much wood paneling these days, at least not on the outside of the car," I replied, smoothing my hand across the side panel. My hand was resting on the window ledge, the air blowing in off the river, and with it a strange scent. "What am I smelling?"

"Country." She grinned and turned off onto a wooded two-lane highway.

"Perfect." I smiled back. "When's the barn dance?"

"The what?"

"Barn dance. Councilman Bowman said there'd be a barn dance. I bought a petticoat." I was confused when she burst out laughing.

"Oh sweetie," she said, slapping her hand on the steering wheel. "He must have been teasing you, there's no barn dance."

"It's not a real thing?" I asked, disappointed.

"Oh, it's a thing; just not this weekend. But I'll look at the calendar and see when the next one is."

"But my petticoat," I said, sniffing.

She just patted my hand and snickered once more.

As we drove, she began to point out landmarks, some designated as actual landmarks, and some Roxie landmarks.

"Here's the spot where my Jeep broke down when I was in high school, and I had to walk two miles to the nearest house.

Aaaand there's the Lightning Tree, gets struck by lightning at least once every summer, but the damn thing just never gives up and falls over. And here's the turnoff to The Tube, best swimming hole for miles."

"A swimming hole? Explain please," I said, not understanding. Sure, I'd watched old TV shows where people were swimming in, well, swimming holes, but that couldn't be what she actually meant. Wait, right?

"A swimming hole. You've never gone to a swimming hole?"

"I once went swimming at a YMCA in the Bronx, does that count?" I asked.

"Oh honey, you're so pretty," she said, shaking her head at me.

"I know," I answered promptly. "Continue."

"Well, it's like a pond but it's spring-fed, and it's always moving, not stagnant."

"Can you see the bottom?"

"Mostly."

"It's not squishy and muddy?"

"A little bit, but it's mostly just rocky."

"That'd freak me out. Who knows what the hell might be lurking in there." I shuddered.

"You swim in the ocean," she said.

"Sure, but it's the ocean. It's not a hole in the ground."

"You come back next summer, and I'll take you to a swimming hole."

"I feel like I should say thank you."

She gave me the side-eye. "You're the one that wanted to come up here and learn all about Bailey Falls."

I nodded my head. "Sorry, was my Manhattan showing?"

"No, but your city snob attitude was." She pretended to glare at me.

"Oh good, I was afraid I was losing my edge," I replied, then dodged her smack.

"I'll smack you properly when we get out of the car. But now, while we drive down Main Street, it'll cause too much gossip."

"Main Street?"

"Here we are." She grinned and turned down a new street, heading right into town.

It truly was like a picture out of a magazine—one printed in 1935. It was darling.

The light was beginning to march west, but it was still golden. Main Street was lined with tall and full maple trees, flashing crimson and poppy. A breeze ruffled through, sending a few leaves to the ground, where they joined thousands of their cousins. Scuttling through the thousands of leaves were children, many children, all in a line holding hands with a few teachers herding at the front and back, all of them laughing and kicking through the crunch. More of that country air blew through, sending a few leaves into the street, where we rolled through them pleasantly.

Lining the sides of Main Street, in between the leaves and the adorable kids, were rows of shops. In front of most, shopkeepers had mounded pumpkins, funky little gourds, hay bales, stalks of corn, and one rakish-looking scarecrow with a straw hat to guard them all. People walked along the street, darting in and out of shops with bundles and bags full of what they needed to have this beautiful fall day. And above it all, an impossibly blue sky soared. Not at all hazy or smudged, just gorgeous blue for miles and miles, dotted with white puffy clouds.

"Oh my," I breathed out, practically hanging out of the window like an old hound dog. Snap snap snap went my camera, capturing everything I could for later inspiration.

While I would go to my grave saying there is nothing prettier than a fall sunset in New York City, Bailey Falls might be a close second.

And right smack-dab in the middle of Main Street was Callahan's. The diner had been in Roxie's family for years, and was the reason she'd moved back home. Running the diner for the summer while her mother competed on *The Amazing Race* had been the last thing she wanted to do, but it ended up being the very best thing she could have done. Now she had a burgeoning business, a hot guy, and this darling town in her life every single day.

I admired the large picture window, the tidy brick steps, the green-and-white-striped awning. It looked old but well-kept, with exactly the kind of nostalgia that weekenders ate up in droves. A peek of the good old life, the way things used to be—a life that was likely not nearly as interesting while actually in it, but that in hindsight was just peachy perfect. This diner had that in spades. And I hadn't even made it inside yet.

"You're meeting Chad for breakfast tomorrow morning, right?"

"Nine o'clock, bright and early," I answered.

"Perfect. I've got to come into town for supplies, so I'll drop you off." She turned off the main street and into the town square. "Thought I'd give you the driving tour before we head back to my place."

"Oh I'd love it!" I exclaimed as she turned onto the first corner. Drugstore, candy shop, one-screen movie theater, even the Laundromat was cute. Turning the corner, we drove by a few antique shops, a butcher, and oh, there we go, the cheese shop. Another corner, and even more adorableness. Kids' clothing store, a coffee shop (no competition for the diner, thank you very much), a gourmet food shop next door to a good old-fashioned dive bar. And on the last street we turned onto, what looked to be city hall.

Four streets, four corners, with a sweet little park in the center with a duck pond, a summery-looking gazebo, and some early Halloween ghosts flying through the fall oak trees. And here and there, on the edge of town, a peek of the Hudson.

"Honestly, could this town be any cuter?" I marveled, already beginning to frame out shots for the photo shoot I'd be doing to capture the essence of this charming village.

I could see instantly the magazine ads, the copy I'd write, the perfection of making this place a must-see for weekend tourists. I'd bring New Yorkers here in droves.

"You think it's cute now, but wait until wintertime."

"Oh, God, I bet it's darling at Christmas!"

"Sure, sure. And when there's snowdrifts packed higher than my head and it's below zero for days on end, then it's positively idyllic."

Though her tone was teasing, she was clearly enamored with her hometown in a way I hadn't seen her in years.

"I'm glad you moved home. It's nice having you back east," I said.

She rolled her eyes. "I need to get you away from all this Norman Rockwell shit, its making you schmaltzy," she said.

"Okay, so take me back to your farmhouse and cook me some of your allegedly fantastic food."

"Driving tour over," she announced, and we left the town square behind.

"I'll see the rest of the town tomorrow; I'll get Chad to show me around," I teased.

"Don't you be flirting with my high school crush! And sweetie, you've seen the rest of the town."

"That's it?" I exclaimed, looking behind me to see the town square fading away in the distance.

Roxie just laughed as she drove me into the wild . . .

✑

I lay on the iron bed, which squeaked just from the movement of my breathing. I drew in a breath. *Creak.* I let it out. *Squeak.* Good lord, how do country people fuck without waking up the entire town?

I rolled over onto my stomach, smiling at the thoughtful touches here and there. Comfortable-looking extra blankets piled onto the antique chest in the corner. A few bottles of water on the nightstand. A stack of fresh towels. And my very own pumpkin on top of the dresser, facing out into the front yard. It hadn't been jack-o'-lanterned, but was still a nice touch to an already homey room.

When Roxie had told me she'd found an old farmhouse, I wasn't sure what to expect. It was small, but that was okay. It was just her here, and it was nice and cozy. I got the impression that she and Leo had discussed moving in together, into his very nice house over on the Maxwell property, but I also got the sense she was pretty happy where she was, setting up shop on her own in her hometown. The house was clean, simple, and a bit old-fashioned, but in a nice way. It was a very Roxie-style house.

She was downstairs getting started on dinner, and had encouraged me to head up to the guest room and get comfortable. I'd opened up the windows, smelling more of that bracingly clean air. It smelled funny, but I could tell my lungs were appreciating it. Situated at the end of a road, almost hidden in the trees, the house was a world away from my townhouse in the East Village. And quiet! Oh my goodness, so quiet. Other than the creaky squeaks.

I got up off the old bed and started unpacking. I always pack too many clothes, since you never know when a wardrobe change might be necessary. I pulled out a few dresses and hung them in the closet, thinking about what I wanted to wear tonight. It was my first time meeting Leo and his daughter, Polly. Hmm, what does one wear to meet your best friend's farmer boyfriend and his seven-year-old?

Obviously a coral jumpsuit with three-inch snakeskin peep-toe heels.

When I arrived in the kitchen, Roxie took one look at me and burst out laughing. "This is you in the sticks?"

"The sticks is no excuse not to kill it," I said, strutting across the plank floor. "And coral is very autumnal." I leaned over the counter, looking for anything I could pilfer. Aha! Cherry tomatoes. Snagging a few, I headed over to the table.

"Of course, how silly of me. I'd ask you to help with dinner, but—"

"But you remember how culinary school turned out for me," I finished, popping in a tomato.

She laughed, chopping garlic and throwing it into a pan. Instantly the room smelled incredible.

"Mmm, what are we having? Your famous cioppino? Saffron risotto with peas and asparagus? That's always been one of my favorites. No no, wait, don't tell me. You're making that incredible blue cheese soufflé that smells like feet and tastes like heaven?"

She shrugged. "Nope—spaghetti and meatballs. It's Polly's favorite."

I smiled. "How stinking cute are you, making her favorite dinner."

"Oh hush."

I poured myself a glass of wine from the open bottle on the table. "Listen, if *you're* making spaghetti and meatballs, it'll be the best spaghetti and meatballs ever made."

"You're so sweet. I know you were expecting something a little fancier."

I waved her off. "Please, I can have fancy anytime I want it. I'm just excited to meet your fella and this meatball kid who sounds smarter than I am."

"She's so fucking smart it's a bit scary." Roxie chuckled, stirring onions and garlic together. "Grab me that basil, will you?"

I walked to the windowsill where she had pots of herbs growing and grabbed a handful. "Do you still add sugar to your sauce?"

"Sometimes I do, if I'm using really fresh tomatoes, but not usually. I'm amazed you still remember that trick."

"Girl. I did retain a few tidbits of information here and there. And I still have my knives."

She rolled her eyes. "Which you never use."

"But they look impressive as hell in my kitchen." I perched on a stool in the window, watching her add a little pinch of this here, a little dollop of that there.

"I will never understand why the hell you were there in the first place. Especially since you love Manhattan so much—there are incredible culinary schools there, too." She'd turned around, giving me a pointed look.

I gave her a little smile. "This is good wine."

"Natalie Grayson, what are you not telling me?"

I felt color rise up into my cheeks, wondering how this conversation had arisen when I'd successfully avoided it for all these years. "I just wanted something different from what I knew."

"Different how?"

"Different from Thomas," I said, my voice unexpectedly hollow. I took a breath, took a sip of wine, and saw the reflection of headlights coming up the drive to her farmhouse.

A dusty Jeep came around a bend in the driveway and pulled up beside the house, an enthusiastic ponytail wearer already bounding out of the backseat, calling Roxie's name.

"Hey, I think your farmer's here," I said, feeling my heart rate begin to return to normal.

My best friend stared me down. "We'll come back to this later," she said, wiping her hands on her apron and throwing open the back door. I let out a sigh, downed the rest of my wine, and watched as she hopped down the back stairs and right into the arms of her Leo.

She caught Polly into a close hug, too, then the three of them headed for the house. I smiled broadly, happy to meet them—and wondering, not for the first time, if there would ever be someone that glad to see me at the end of the day.

☙◉❧

I'd seen Leo out and about in the city in the past, before he'd beat feet upstate for the simple life. But I'd never met him, and I could see why this guy was such a player. Tall, broad shoul-dered, and strong, but with an easy look about him. There was a warmth in his smile that I hadn't seen before. Most of the city had been worn off, revealing a kindness, a quick laugh. It was easy to see that these two females hung the moon for him, and this guy loved his life.

"I've heard a lot about you," he said, grinning as he shook my hand.

"Likewise." I grinned back, tugging on his hand until I got close enough to hug him. "You've been putting it to my best friend for months now, so you're required to hug me." Surprised but willing, he hugged me back, wrapping his strong arms around me.

"Watch it, that's my guy," Roxie warned from the corner.

"Nice," I replied, slipping out of the hug but still keeping hands-on. I squeezed his biceps a bit. "Very nice." Leo's eyes twinkled down at me, and I just shook my head. "You're lucky I didn't meet you first."

"Seriously, still in the room," Roxie repeated, and I finally released Leo. "And this munchkin is Polly."

I stuck out my hand for Polly to shake. "As in Pollyanna?"

"Well, I wasn't named after a polynomial," the kid said, her eyes as green as Leo's but much more appraising.

I laughed. "It's nice to meet you, Not a Polynomial."

Polly grinned up at me. "Smells good in here, what's for dinner?"

"Polly, we just got here. Maybe ask Roxie if she needs any help?" Leo said, ruffling up her hair. "It *does* smell really good."

"Do you need any help, and what's for dinner?" Polly asked, and I retreated to my kitchen stool, hands raised, knowing full well that the person who was actually in charge had just arrived. I was just hoping she'd let me have some of her spaghetti and meatballs . . .

~⁄∽

"So you're here to figure out how to get more people to Bailey Falls, right?" Leo asked, buttering a piece of bread for Polly and putting it on the side of her plate. She was trying to twirl her pasta on a spoon, just like Roxie. Her little tongue poked out of the side of her mouth while she concentrated.

"Kind of. I'm here to get the lay of the land, so to speak. My firm got an email from Chad Bowman—you know him?" I forked up my own bite of pasta, and my goodness was it good. My girl could *cook*.

"I do. He and his husband are members of the farmshare program we offer to locals; they're great guys." Leo smothered a laugh when Polly's spoonful nearly went flying. "Want me to cut it up for you, make it easier to get on the fork?"

"Roxie says to never cut pasta," Polly said with a serious look on her face. "It disrupts the integrity of the noodle."

"That seems like exactly something she would say," I agreed. Roxie was coughing into her napkin in a very timely fashion. "So tell me about the farmshare program."

As Leo talked, I began to get a better sense of what he'd created over at Maxwell Farms. The more I heard about it, the more eager I was to see it. "This seems exactly the kind of thing that could make this town even more inviting. Norman Rockwell charm meets local sustainable agriculture, which everyone is interested in now. You give tours at the farm, right?"

"Every day," Leo said, "Two on Saturdays."

"Perfect. Can I come by tomorrow?"

"You got it. We're moving some of the animals tomorrow for rotational pasture grazing, so it's a good day to come by. Lots of activity," he answered.

Roxie turned from helping Polly with twirling her pasta. "Moving any dairy cows tomorrow?" she asked, trying to sound nonchalant but failing. I looked hard at her, but she seemed very interested suddenly in a loose string on the end of Leo's T-shirt.

"Yep, we're moving them up onto the east pasture. Why, what's up?" Leo asked, tucking into another meatball. "Watch what you're doing there, Sugar Snap, don't unravel one of my favorite tees. I only saw the Pixies play live once."

"I was just thinking it might be fun for Natalie to see that, to watch you moving the cows," Roxie answered, still picking at his T-shirt. Leo absently put a hand over hers, stopping her from unraveling the whole thing. I couldn't blame her; what a grand sight that'd be.

"Sure thing, you want to come tomorrow around noon?"

"And get the opportunity to say I literally saw the cows come home? I wouldn't miss it." I turned toward Polly. "I'm going to meet a moo cow tomorrow, want to come along?"

"They're not moo cows, they're Guernseys and Brown Swiss." She blinked. "And I have school tomorrow."

"Ah. Of course," I replied. Speaking of schooled . . . "Okay, so tomorrow I'll swing by the farm after my meeting with Chad. Sounds like a plan."

"Sounds great," Roxie said, grinning broadly.

Chapter 6

Anyone who tells you a good night's sleep in the country is a cure for all ills has never actually slept in the country.

Between the crickets, the owls, the wind howling, the trees scraping against the windows, and the creakiest, squeakiest bed in America, I barely slept a wink.

And just when I'd gotten the tiniest bit used to the cacophony of sound going on outside in the Wild Kingdom, everything stopped. The wind died down, the trees stopped scraping, the crickets and owls agreed with each other that it was time to take five, and it was like the world outside went on permanent mute.

The world inside dwindled down to the occasional creak from my bed, the ticktock of a grandfather clock downstairs, and my breathing, which sounded loud in the silent room.

Where was the hustle? Where was the bustle? Where were the sirens and the horns honking and the *people,* for Christ's sake, that you could always count on for background noise at all hours of the day and night?

Silence pressed in on me from every direction, convincing me that Roxie had faded away and it was just me left alone to battle the shadows from a thousand nearly empty trees outside, silhouetted by an angry pumpkin moon gazing down on this land that time forgot.

When it's quiet in the country, it's all too easy to imagine a man in a plaid shirt striding out of the woods. Peering at your farmhouse from across the field, wondering if there was a buxom city girl curled up in a squeaky bed upstairs, too pretty to be killed off at the beginning of a horror movie, but kept alive for something truly terrible somewhere near the end of the third act.

Yeah, sleeping in the country isn't all it's cracked up to be.

❧

"How'd you sleep?" Roxie asked brightly as I staggered downstairs the next morning, following the smell of coffee that beckoned like an olfactory pied piper.

"I hate you," I muttered, pushing my hair back from my bleary face. She rolled her eyes and handed me a cup of coffee, which I grasped like a talisman. "I love you."

"You're so dramatic."

"I agree." I sighed, sinking into a chair at her table. "How long did it take you to get used to sleeping with all that racket?"

"What racket? I didn't hear a peep."

"Yeah, that's the other thing. It's either as loud as Mardi Gras out there, or the sound of silence. What's up with that?"

"I grew up with it so I barely notice it anymore. Of course, I don't sleep much anyway."

Roxie had had insomnia since she was a kid. "That getting any better?"

A content look crossed her face. "It's funny, but ever since Leo and I, you know . . ."

"Started fucking?"

"Started seeing each other is what I was going to say," she said, her cheeks pinking. "I've been sleeping better. I mean, I'm never going to get eight hours, but I'm definitely getting more sleep than I ever used to."

I sipped at my coffee, nodding. "It's all that fucking."

"It's more than the fucking," she insisted, hooking a chair over with her foot and sinking down next to me. "It's the before and the after, you know?"

"Ah yes, the sweet nothings and the afterglow." I picked a stray yarn on my sweater. "I'm usually wondering when the fucking will be starting back up again."

"Oh, the fucking starts back up again," she said, her blush deepening. "But there's just something about sleeping next to him. It's . . ." She paused, searching for a word.

"Amazing? Incredible? Out of this world?"

"Nice."

"Nice?" I asked, shaking my head. "That's all you got, is nice?"

"It *is* nice. It's *so* nice," she replied with the most perfect sense of peace and contentment I'd ever seen. "I don't get to sleep with Leo every night; some weeks there's only one or two nights we can have an actual overnight due to Polly's schedule. So when we're together, of course it's full of slap and tickle, but then, when that's through, and it's just him and me and the quiet—that's the nice." Her eyes looked right through me; she was in her own world now. "He always drifts off first, of course, so I get this time with him to just . . . be with him. Watch him sleep, listen to him breathe, listen to him snore, for God's sake, and just feel this big, warm man next to me, his body wrapped around me, those big callused hands on my hip or on my belly, and it's honestly the best feeling ever. It's just . . ." She trailed off, dreamy and faraway.

"Nice," I breathed, understanding.

"Yeah," she replied.

I'd had nice. Once. But then it was so very *not* nice.

We both mooned for a moment, lost in our own thoughts, and then I broke the spell by telling her I was off to meet her high school crush.

"Tell him I'm still waiting for direction on Logan's birthday cake. I don't know what I'm making, but if he doesn't tell me soon it'll involve Walmart fruit cocktail," she called out to me as I headed down the stairs and off to the Jeep.

"I'll do my best, but I'm sure with all the flirting going on, it'll be hard to remember," I teased, knowing how she felt about her high school crush.

"I loved that man since puberty; you better watch your ass, city girl," floated out to me through the open kitchen window. As I turned back I could see the curtains fluttering, and I pantomimed my finger doing something inappropriate to the hole my other hand was making.

I couldn't wait to meet this guy . . .

∽

"How adorable are you?"

"Excuse me?"

"Excuse *me,* but you're the second beautiful man I've seen in this town since arriving last night. What is in the water upstate?"

"You must be Natalie," replied the beautiful man who was exactly as Roxie had described The Chad Bowman to be. Tall, handsome, confident but not cocky, the guy was worthy of many a high school crush.

"And you are definitely Chad Bowman. You're as gorgeous as Roxie described."

"Back at you—she gave me the lowdown on you as well. As soon as you strutted through the door, I knew it was you," he said, pulling out a stool for me.

"I don't strut." I gracefully lowered myself onto the seat. Adjusting, I winked. "Okay, maybe a little. I prefer to think of it as sashaying."

"Either or, you're killing me with the shoes," he said, gesturing to my heels. "How many accidents did you cause walking in here this morning?"

I thought back to the two blocks I walked after parking the Jeep. A couple of dropped jaws from some teenage guys, one shy wave from the little old man at the barbershop I sauntered past, and a whistle from the gentleman who was walking out of the butcher, right before he dropped his pork loin. Nothing crass like I'd get in the city, no hoots or hollers—but definitely some nice, respectable ogling. "A few near misses, but no fender benders."

"I can imagine." He ordered up two coffees and I pulled out my things to get started.

I studied him while he interacted with the server, talking *to* her, not *at* her. Something that I made a mental note of. He was handsome in that "is he real?" sort of way that all high school crushes are made from. I imagined him and Roxie back in the day, her fawning all over this godlike creature, and him causing heart failure everywhere he went.

The diner was packed with a steady breakfast crowd; everything from singles to couples, moms and babies, and a pair of grumpy old men who sidled up to the counter looking so old that the town was probably built on their backs.

Ideas had started swirling late last night when I was flipping through local commercials. You learn a lot from the ads that small towns create. From the small fifteen seconds of Karla's Klip 'n' Kurl to the robust ads that the Bryant Mountain House put out to court the weekender, this town had a little bit for everyone. The plan was coming together.

"So tell me, what do you think of our little Bailey Falls?" Chad said, blowing on his hot coffee before taking a sip.

"It's darling, but you know that," I started, eyeing up the pie case. There was a slice of awesome that would go just right with my diner coffee. "I don't mean that in a condescending way, either. It's truly a little spot of perfect, nestled in the mountains. The scenery on the train ride up is worth any price of admission."

Chad beamed, much like Roxie did when she got all moony and pie-eyed talking about the town. Having been away from it for so long, she'd been convinced that she'd hate it when she'd returned for the summer. Get in and get out was her goal, but it hooked her and didn't let go. It wouldn't be for everyone in long doses—but in short?

More of the puzzle pieces were falling into place.

"I'm glad you see the potential. The town is a huge part of our lives. My husband, Logan, comes from a small town, so when I brought him home for the first time he absolutely fell in love with Bailey Falls, and we immediately started making plans to move our business here.

"We brought you in to show everyone why this is a great weekend destination or summer hot spot. I see it. The town sees it. But you saying that *you* see it is really very validating."

My heart pitter-pattered, the way it always did when I was excited about a project. "Things are percolating, but I need to see more of what I'm working with first," I said, waving over the waitress. "We'll take two slices of whatever your best dessert is, please."

With a quick nod, she examined the full glass case. Choosing two slices, she plated them and hustled over. "Hummingbird Cake. Roxie's specialty."

"They feature Zombie Cakes here, too? I'm surprised Callahan's didn't try to put a lock-down on sharing the family love with the competitor," I mused. Roxie's mom must have had a fit when her daughter started plying her wares around town and not just within the confines of Callahan's Diner.

I didn't just moan around the fork. I eye-rolled, legs-clenched, and obscenely licked every last stitch of frosting from the fork. Poor, adorable Chad Bowman looked like I just asked him to motorboat my lady bits in front of his husband.

"Good goddamn, that woman can bake a fucking cake," I moaned around another mouthful.

Chad shifted in his seat, smothering a laugh. "Yes, yes she can."

I finished the cake without further embarrassing poor Chad, who couldn't stop staring at my mouth after seeing me defile the fork. I made a mental note to have Roxie start shipping me Hummingbird Cakes once a week in the city.

We chatted a bit longer about the hopes for the town. He explained that the town council was trusting him with this venture to take Bailey Falls in a new direction in terms of advertising, and that he'd do damn near anything to make sure it worked.

"You're in good hands, Chad. I've landed more accounts for Manhattan Creative this year, or the last three years, than any other account executive. My initial approach is simple: get to know Bailey Falls in and out. Top to bottom and everything in between. I want to know what makes this town tick, and why it should be *the* destination for city dwellers, retirees, and families. This place seems to have it all, and we just need to make sure that everyone knows it."

Chad thought for a moment, then smiled big at me. "Normally I'd just shake your hand and tell you to get to work, but because of the Roxie connection, I feel like I want to hug you."

"It's been at least twelve hours since a gorgeous man has had his hands on me, and technically that was Leo, so get over here," I said, waving him off his stool. "The Roxie Connection— that has a nice ring to it, doesn't it?"

"Very eighties-dating-show-meets-Agatha-Christie-novel." He laughed, pulling out his wallet and settling the bill. "So what sort of crazy plans does Roxie have planned for you this weekend?"

I laughed. "I think a shorter list is what she *doesn't* have planned for me. She's got the whole weekend packed in an effort to make me fall in love with Bailey Falls."

He slid from the stool and smiled. "I selfishly have to say that I hope it works and that you never leave. We need some more badass women up here to shake things up."

"Oh, I don't know," I said, feeling the heat rise to my cheeks. I had a farmer fantasy, for sure, but long term? I belonged in the city. "You may have converted me into a weekend transplant." I swiped the last bit of frosting on the plate with my thumb and sucked it off while I thought about someone who might be able to make me visit Bailey Falls more often.

Sucked it off indeed . . .

∾

What I "know" about living on a farm comes from picture books and movies. I also have a tendency to embellish and gild images that I revisit in my mind, coloring and shading things until I can get it just right, until I believe *that's exactly how it is*.

Two things happened at Maxwell Farms.

One, I realized I had no idea how an actual farm works. It's not some idealized place where an overalled farmer pats pretty cows while his wife, an extra from *The Donna Reed Show*, skips through the pasture at lunchtime with a chicken pot pie tucked in a basket under a red handkerchief, after which they *shtup* each other silly under the blue sky. A farm is dirty, kind of smelly, and a lot of really hard work.

Two, Maxwell Farms *is* an idealized place, where people work hard and make something beautiful out of a few acres and serious sweat. I saw chickens laying eggs, picked a pumpkin from a vine, and scratched a pig on his actual pork belly. It was a riot of smells, sights, sounds, and tastes as well, since Roxie made us sample everything in the kitchen garden, some still with dirt clinging to it. I laughed as she dusted everything off on her farm jeans, telling me to just go with it and let my country out a bit. It really was a magical place.

When I'd shown up at the big stone barn, she took one look at my high-heeled boots and made me put on a pair of Leo's galoshes, which were like canoes on my feet. But after stepping in crap for the fifth time, I was grateful for them.

I took pictures everywhere, sneaking in a few of Leo with his land in the background, dirt on his hands, a smile on his face, and the love for what he did shining through with everything. I wasn't sure exactly what I had yet with the pictures I'd taken, but I knew they'd lead me where I needed to go with this campaign.

Leo moved the animals around the farm to keep things trimmed down, and to provide a kick-ass place for the chickens to relax all day. I'd already seen the chickens and their charming coop-on-wheels get moved onto a freshly sheep-mown pasture. Then we went to see the sheep on the next field, fluffy and white and bleating away as the wind ruffled their coats. Now we were finally moving on to the moo cows, which I'd fight to my death to call them despite Polly's disdain.

I wondered if Leo had any idea how much trouble he was going to be in when that very smart girl turned into a teenager. I grinned to myself.

And speaking of grinning, Roxie looked like the Cheshire cat, even bouncing a little in the front seat as Leo drove his Jeep to the cow pasture.

"What's with the grin?" I asked her, leaning forward.

"Who, me?" she asked with a wide smile. "I'm just having a great day. I've got my best friend here, I'm sleeping with the hottest farmer since Almanzo Wilder—"

"Don't let her fool you, Natalie. She'd throw me over in a second if the actual Almanzo was available," Leo interjected.

"—and the sun is shining. What more could anyone ask for?" Roxie finished, brushing a few pieces of my hair back away from my face and fussing with my headband.

"A dirty martini and couple of nudie magazines?" I asked brightly, earning a high five from Leo.

"Dirty, I can manage," Roxie said suggestively.

And just as I turned to ask her what she meant, I saw Oscar. In the field, surrounded by moo cows.

"Fuck me," I breathed as we pulled up to the gate. Behind him was a parade of fall colors, rich browns and bright reds and oranges. Around him, pretty-looking cattle, deep red and silky brown, with big, gentle eyes. And in the middle of it all, this golden man.

Vaguely in the background, where my internal soundtrack plays, I could hear the opening riff of "Here Comes Your Man" by the Pixies . . .

He looked up from the herd to our Jeep, and waved to Leo. Chestnut hair as always tucked back with a tie, black T-shirt with flannel shirt tied around his waist, faded blue jeans wrapped around long legs. Seeing him here, in his natural element, was even more striking than seeing him at the market in the city.

And speaking of striking . . .

I leaned forward and whispered to Roxie, "I can't *believe* you!"

"What?"

"Don't *what* me, lady! What are you up to?"

Oscar was cutting across the field, his big, long strides taking up probably twenty yards at a clip. Fucking Paul Bunyan, this guy. I was pre–panic attack and getting over the pre- pretty quick.

Leo, beautiful and oblivious, just grinned and pointed. "That's my neighbor Oscar; I let his cows graze on my land sometimes."

"You don't say." My smile felt like it had a lot of teeth. "We'll be right over."

Oscar was almost to the fence now. Just another few steps and he'd be here!

I slid low into the backseat. "Roxie, you're on my list. Scratch that, you *are* the list." Was it possible to call a cab to a field? I started looking for an Uber signal.

"Oh, list schmist, I'll go back to favorite-person status the minute he gets here with that hair, which is glorious by the way," she said, undoing her seat belt. "I wonder what kind of conditioner he uses for— What the hell are you doing?" She stared down at me.

"Hiding. Which you should try, since once the shock wears off, I'm going to choke you." I slid down onto the floor. "Is there a trapdoor in here?"

"Oh, stop being so silly about this guy! It's time to actually meet, without cheese!"

I tugged on her shoulder frantically. "Keep your voice down! He'll hear you!"

"You're being ridiculous."

My pulse was racing. What *was* it with this guy? And not for nothing, if I was going to meet him this weekend, which I knew was a possibility, I had an outfit and a scenario picked out to boot. Something low-cut, a low-lit bar, some witty repartee, and then hours and hours of sweet sweet fucking. Nowhere in this possible meeting was I wearing a trendy turtleneck, velvet riding jodhpurs, and another man's poopy galoshes!

I could hear his deep voice coming closer, answering Leo's questions with words like "Yeah," and "Uh-huh," and "About ten inches."

I could die.

Roxie argued with me right up until Leo and Oscar were maybe ten feet away from the Jeep. I wasn't ready to face him yet, not yet. He existed in another space and time, a space called The Market and a time called The Best Ten Minutes of My Saturday Morning, and seeing him here and now was threatening to unravel the continuum that held our fragile universe together!

I couldn't stand him being real yet. So I handled things like any grown-up, professional, adult woman.

I pulled my turtleneck up and over my face and hid inside my sweater. I could see through the weave two very distinct shadows appear over the back of the Jeep, one impossibly tall.

I could perceive Leo looking back and forth between me and Roxie, her own shadowy figure shaking her head.

"Um, Sugar Snap?" I heard Leo say.

No use. I couldn't stay inside my sweater forever. I took a deep breath, inhaling a hit of confidence from the perfumed cashmere, and peeked over the top.

Staring down at me with a curious look was Oscar. His gray-blue eyes had a touch of amusement mixed in with the what-the-hell. And as I pulled the sweater further down my face, his eyes changed from confusion to recognition. And as realization dawned, a flare of heat flashed through them.

"Brie," he breathed, placing the face and my order at the same time.

"Oh. Yes."

∽

Roxie was shaking her head back and forth so quickly she was going to give herself whiplash. "I gave you the perfect opportunity, and I mean the *perfect* opportunity, to talk to him, to turn on the old Natalie charm and make him want you. You were trapped in a field, in a Jeep, surrounded by cows, *his* cows, mind you. You literally had nowhere to go, nowhere to run. And what did you do?"

"I ran," I answered, laying my head down on the dashboard. "I. Ran."

"Across a field."

"Covered in cows."

"*Totally* covered in cows!" Roxie exploded.

I turned my face toward her, keeping my head on the dashboard. I'd retreated back into my turtleneck, but my eyes were still peeping out, watching Roxie for any sign that I might still be bordering on charming and not psychotic. "To be fair, I didn't run very far," I pointed out. "I turned around."

"Because a cow was chasing you."

I went ahead and pulled the turtleneck up and over my entire head. It was true, it was all true. When he'd realized it was me, and we'd completed our Three-Word Waltz, I hadn't waited around to see what he would say. Because like a flash, I jumped my size-eighteen ass up and over the side of the Jeep, and took off in a shuffle-hop-step across the field, one of Leo's galoshes hanging halfway off my foot.

Turns out gentle sweet dairy cows get startled when someone comes running, and they don't always take too kindly to a shuffle-hop-step. One of them came after me, and although it was likely at a pace of about a mile per hour, it looked very fast in my head. I panicked, turned back around, and headed for the Jeep again, while Leo, Roxie, and a beautiful but semifuming Oscar tried to call out alternate directions to me.

"Stop!"

"Keep going!"

"Turn around!"

"Over here!"

"Over there!"

"What the hell are you doing to my cows?"

Luckily, by the time I'd made it back to the Jeep, the men were in the herd, calming down the Bessies, while Roxie was left to calm down this Bessie. And this Bessie directed her to get us the fuck out of there right the fuck fucking now.

And so here we sat, a half mile away from the cow pasture, and I was wondering if there was a one o'clock train back to the city.

"What in the world, Natalie? Really, what's going on?" Roxie asked, and I groaned inside my turtleneck.

"If I knew, I'd tell you. I just go to pieces around this guy." I pulled down my turtleneck to just above my nose. "When I see him, I literally lose my mind. I can't talk to him when I see that face, and those eyes, and those lips, and all that gorgeous ink, and those hands—did you see those hands? And—"

"Okay, I got it. So, what if you *couldn't* see him?"

"How can you *not* see him? How can you not see that face, and those eyes, and those—"

She held up her hand. "I'm not going to sit here while you go through another round of Sexual Head, Shoulders, Knees, and Toes."

"Knees and Toes," I sang back. Which made her smile, which made me smile. A little.

She sighed. "I need to get back to the barn to make lunch."

"Great! I'm starved!" I announced, tugging down my turtle-neck, anxious to sweep this whole thing under the Jeep.

"A lunch that Oscar is attending."

"I'm actually still full from breakfast." Up went the turtle-neck.

Roxie's hands tugged it from my face. "You're going. This ends today, one way or another." She started the Jeep and pointed it toward the farm.

I sat on my hands the entire way back to the barn to stop my-self going full turtle. And as I sat on my hands, I thought about every time I'd seen Oscar, and how I'd reacted. I was fine when I was in the market, I was fine when I was in line, I was even fine when I was paying for my Brie. It was when we were full frontal, his eyes all over me and the force of him turned up to eleven, that reduced me to mush.

And an idea began to take shape . . .

Chapter 7

Roxie chopped.

I paced.

Roxie stirred.

I paced.

She sautéed.

Still . . . I paced.

I was making her nervous. I knew this because every three or four minutes, she'd set down her knife/spoon/ladle/grinder and say, "You're making me nervous, dammit."

I kept an eye on the road. Leo had texted to let Roxie know they were coming for lunch soon—*they* being the key word. *They* were on their way, *they* included Oscar, the tattooed god-like creature that I'd humiliated myself in front of for the last time.

I chewed on a piece of celery, gnawing almost angrily as Roxie told me again that she thought I should go easy on this one, let things happen naturally, cool my jets and maintain my composure, and simply remember that I was a knockout who could have any man I wanted. But while I placated her with a few "yeses" and "you got its" and "shit yeahs," I knew that I'd be using a different tactic when the milkman cameth.

And just over the ridge, here he came, thundering down the road on a shit-yeah motorcycle. I almost couldn't take it. Hair flying in the wind, sunglasses on like an ad for Ray-Ban, Oscar came to rest just outside the kitchen door, kicking up dust. Leo followed in his old Jeep, the two of them almost overkill.

Just as my skin tingled and my thighs clenched, Roxie's voice brought me back from the brink of a public orgasm.

"Remember, Nat, be cool," she said, flipping the chicken cutlets.

Be cool? Tell that to my clitoris . . .

Time to nip this in the bud.

I nodded as I stood, my eyes locked on the tall drink of gorgeous as I went to the door and strode purposefully toward the man on the motorcycle. Leo took one look at me and wisely beat feet toward the kitchen, where I could see Roxie peeping through the flour-sack curtains.

"Oscar, right?" I said, keeping my eyes focused on the pastoral scene just above and beyond his left shoulder. Powerful muscles, beautiful golden skin, swirled with enticing ink.

I let my eyes run down toward his hand, which I grabbed before I could lose my nerve. Avoiding eye contact, I headed toward the unrenovated part of the barn, where Roxie had shown me the old milking stalls. I could feel the heat of his hand as he held my fingers tightly in his grip, making me fully aware that he was along for the ride.

I could also feel that his gaze was firmly on my backside. A smile crept over my face as I felt Normal Natalie show herself for the first time around this guy.

Sweet-smelling hay crunched underfoot and the sun fell through the space between the rafters as I led him toward the stalls in the back of the barn.

Reaching the end of the aisle, I turned to face him, keeping my eyes straight ahead. He was so close behind I nearly crashed into his chest. I noticed, not for the first time, how very tall he was. I was used to men being only a few inches taller than me, the same height when I was wearing my heels. Which I almost always was. But this guy's collarbone was exactly the same height as my mouth.

Oh.

I released his hand and placed both of mine on his warm, broad chest. Inhaling, I got an intoxicating noseful of Oscar. My eyes were drawn up past the sight of my hands on him, which made me shiver, to the sliver of skin above his T-shirt with just the barest hint of ink. Licking my lips, I lightly pushed him backward toward the side of the stall. And when we were there, I ran around the wall to the adjoining stall.

Where I couldn't see him.

Where I could finally talk to him.

I took a deep breath, then opened my mouth to speak.

"So here's the thing, Oscar. Can I call you Oscar?"

"My name *is* Oscar," he said, sounding a little amused.

"Right," I nodded, screwing up my eyes in frustration. Hmm. That was actually even better. I couldn't see him, and now I couldn't see anything. Much better. I reached out, catching hold of a wooden slat, rough under my fingertips, yet grounding somehow. "Here's the thing, Oscar," I repeated. "You're fucking incredible to look at, and when I see you, I turn stupid. Weirdly, oddly stupid, because normally I can talk to any guy. But with you, it's like all I can say is what I always say. *Oh. Yes.* Which believe me, I've thought about all the different ways that I could say that. And obviously your cheese is amazing, but it's not all about the cheese for me. What I mean to say, is . . ." I bit down on my lower lip. Should I just come out with it? "I think about you all the time, naked all the time, with me, and I'm naked and I'm doing things to you, and holy shit are you doing things to me, and it's *so* very very good, and if you were any *other* guy we'd already be doing the naked very good things, but you're not, it's like you've got some kind of mysterious hold over me—speaking of which, I've thought about you over me, and under me, and behind me." I laughed out loud, realizing that my brain had clearly decided to *just come out with it.* "So—I needed to say this, and you needed to hear this, and now maybe I can be in the same room with you and actually have eye contact and not turn stupid anymore, because it's out there now. We're both aware of it, and now when I come to see you in the city and you ring up my order, you'll know and I'll know that while I definitely want your Brie, I'm also imagining banging the ever-loving fuck out of you."

There.

Said it.

And he wasn't saying anything. Not good.

"You know who I am, right?"

Still nothing from his side of the stall.

I climbed up one rung, then the second. Was he still there? I made it to the top, peered over—but the stall was empty.

"I know exactly who you are," a deep voice said behind me.

I startled, then realized Oscar was exactly where I wanted him to be. Behind me, getting a great view of my exceptional—

"You're the Brie girl with the great big ass."

I turned slowly on my precarious perch, a slow burn building toward the top of my head.

As I turned, his eyes flickered up from my ass to my face, and he blinked in surprise when he saw my expression. Springing lightly to the ground—a feat I'm sure someone with all this *great big* ballast wasn't supposed to be able to do—I poked him squarely in the chest and looked him dead in those beautiful gray-blue eyes. "You want to say that again? To my face?"

A slow grin spread across his face. "Which part?"

"You know exactly which part."

He moved closer. "Oh, the part about your great big ass?"

I blinked in total surprise. "I can't believe you have the balls to say that out loud."

"What, that you've got a great ass?"

"Come again?" I asked, confused.

He took a step closer to me. Which made me take a step backward from him. "Seeing you standing in my line is the second-best part of my Saturday," he said, taking another step.

I was up against the wooden wall with nowhere to go. "What's the first-best part?"

"Watching you walk away." He placed his hands on either side of my head and leaned in. "I love watching your great big ass."

"Hold up," I said, placing one hand on his chest and slowing his roll. "Are you saying great big ass? Or great *comma* big ass?"

He looked at me quizzically. "Great *comma* big ass?"

This was going to be harder than I thought. "Okay, I'm confused. So you're not saying that I have a *great big* . . . *ass*, you're saying that I have a *great* . . . *big ass*. Meaning—"

"Your ass *is* big. And it's great." He dipped down to bring his face to within inches of mine. "How is that confusing?"

"You're not supposed to say something like that to a woman," I said, narrowing my eyes and trying not to notice that he'd just licked his lips, making them look even more delicious. I lifted my chin. "Luckily for you, I'm aware that it's a great ass. And yes, it's big."

He studied me. "You sure talk a lot. If you're going to talk this much, say more about the naked stuff you want us doing."

"Oh, you mean like the—"

Oscar grabbed me by my hips, his giant hands wrapping around my look-how-tiny-he-makes-it-look waist, and pulled me against him. Before I could even take a breath, he kissed me. Intense heat burned against my lips, crushing, twisting, slanting this way and that as he consumed me.

My breasts were pressed against his chest as he moved impossibly closer, and I slid my hands up his arms and around his neck, tangling into the hair that I'd been dying to touch. I wrapped my fingers around the thick, coarse strands as I tugged his head down toward mine while he kissed me again and again. My feet slipped on the hay, but he held me against the stall with the strength of his body.

From the back of his throat came a rumbling sound halfway between a groan and a moan, and I reveled in the knowledge that he was as lost as I was. But just as his tongue swept out to lick my lips and scramble the very last part of my brain, he pulled away abruptly, leaving both of us panting.

He ran his hands through the hair mussed by my roving hands, then scrubbed at his face as though trying to get his bearings. His eyes burned as he took me in again, messy and still glued to the back of the stall, wondering where all the heat had gone. He reached out to run one thumb across my swollen lips, which I quickly took into my mouth ever so slightly and nipped.

There was the heat again, flaring in his eyes, and I could see him weighing his options of whether to pursue once more (yes yes and a little more yes) or back away and save some for later (also a fan of this).

"Those naked very good times you mentioned?"

I dropped a kiss on his thumb. "Mm-hmm?"

His eyes raked over me, thrilling every inch. When those eyes focused once more on mine, I was on fire. "I'm in."

And then I heard a metal triangle being clanged, and Roxie's voice calling that lunch was ready.

Now what?

I smoothed my shirt, shaking out my hair and trying to make myself look like I hadn't just mouth-fucked a god.

Oscar stood aside, suddenly a gentleman with a devastatingly ungentlemanly grin, allowing me to go first. And as I walked past, I heard that same rough, rumbly sound from Oscar.

So I put some extra sway in my great . . . big ass.

Internal soundtrack picked up the cue and immediately hit Play on the Commodores' "Brick House" . . .

Chapter 8

$\mathcal{I}$'d just been kissed within an inch of my life, and now I was expected to eat prawns in a reduced fig and chili demi-glace over a bed of mustard greens and baby bok choy?

Apparently, yes. And the prawns were delicious. But sitting across from Oscar, watching him lick a bit of errant sauce from his lower lip after he was licking *my* lower lip only moments before? Pure, sweet torture.

And during this sweet torture, no one said a word. But as I watched everyone's faces, I could read their minds. Roxie was scheming, her eyes darting from Oscar to me, trying to work out what had happened and how she could further things along. Leo was oblivious, enjoying the exquisite meal his girlfriend had prepared for him. Oscar was eating as well, but his eyes were fixed solidly on me, watching every move I made. I could feel the heat of his gaze as I lifted a bite of bok choy to my mouth, and most especially when my lips parted to take it in. I was getting eyefucked, and how. How scandalous.

Eventually the silence became too much to bear, and Roxie jumped right in.

"So, Oscar, did you know that Natalie is here to help put Bailey Falls on the map? From an advertising perspective, that is."

"Your name's Natalie?" he asked, once again conveying an entire world of words in a simple three. He'd had his thigh between mine, his hands on my hips, and his mouth all over my face earlier, and only now is he realizing he doesn't even know my name? Mmm, how scandalous!

"It is," I answered, brushing my strawberry-blond hair over my shoulder, revealing the full power of my bosom. His eyes flared. Naturally. "Your town councilman Chad Bowman wrote to our firm in the city asking for some help. They want to bring more money into your adorable town, more tourists."

"Tourists." He chuffed like a horse. Go back to the part where his thigh was pressed between mine, and I can attest that his chuffing wasn't the only resemblance to a horse. Hung like a . . . "Why do we need tourists?"

"They can add significant income to any small town—especially one that not only captures the natural beauty of the landscape, but also has something that I haven't seen featured in any other travel publication regarding the Hudson Valley." I popped in a prawn.

"What's that?" Leo asked, as Oscar continued his laser lock on me.

I chewed, thought about how to phrase this, and then decided on the direct approach. "Hot fucking farmers, that's what." Leo's eyes grew to the size of Oreos. "I mean, you two are ridiculous—how do the women in this town get any work done?"

"There's a reason why Leo and I don't work together," Roxie snorted as Leo looked at her in surprise. "What? It's true. I don't know exactly where Natalie's going with this, but I have to agree with her assessment." She then turned to me. "Where *are* you going with this?"

"You've got Leo Maxwell here, heir to the Maxwell banking fortune, who gives it all up to run upstate and raise organically produced eggplants—you don't think there's a great story there?

Before you say anything, I'm not talking about exploiting anyone here—but think about it. It's interesting, right? When the entire country is starting to really consider where their food is coming from, and who is growing it, it's a perfect fit. Show New Yorkers how coming to the country and touring that gorgeous farm is a great way to not only do something good, but bring new eyeballs to this fantastic town."

Leo was shaking his head, unsure.

Undaunted, I prattled on, working on the pitch out loud as I ran with it. "I'm not talking about a Men of Bailey Falls calendar—just a few key stories placed in exactly the right magazines, exactly the right social media platforms, all about getting back to nature and experiencing a quieter way of life. Brought to you by these hot fucking farmers. All very tasteful of course, no one would even have to take their shirt off. No beefcake. Just implied gorgeous. Accidental hotness. And this guy," I said, pointing at Oscar. "I don't know the story here yet, but I know there must be one. A hot dairy farmer? The copy writes itself."

Everyone had stopped eating. Leo's forkful of prawns was poised a few inches from his mouth, frozen there as he listened to me position this in the worst possible way. Oscar gave me a long, hard look, then shrugged and returned his attention to his plate. "There's no story here."

Hmmm. No one without a story has ever said there's no story here. But this wasn't the time to dig.

"You know what, let's table this for now. Let me finish touring the town, get to know the DNA a bit more, before we start thinking about anything concrete." I turned to Oscar. "So, I hear you've got a huge barn. Care to show it me sometime?"

Roxie started coughing, and Leo handed her a glass of water and patted her on the back. "You okay there, Sugar Snap?"

I just grinned at Oscar. Who actually grinned back. Now that I'd talked to him, and been kissed by him, my old confidence had returned. He'd be putty in my hands soon enough—they always were.

Oscar leaned forward, planting his elbows on the table. "My barn is enormous."

My internal soundtrack immediately began to play Salt-N-Pepa's "Shoop," but it was hard to hear over Roxie's coughing.

After lunch was over, Roxie and Leo left to clean up, leaving me alone with Oscar.

"So, all kidding aside, I did really hear about your barn. Roxie said it's over two hundred years old?"

"Two hundred and seven, built out of local fieldstone."

"And has the farm been in your family all that time?"

"Nope."

"Let me guess: two hundred and six?"

"Nope." He didn't say much, but the corner of his mouth lifted.

I snorted. "You really do have a knack for scintillating conversation, as I'm sure you've been told."

"Says the girl who, until today, only knew two words," he said, lifting an eyebrow as well.

As a blush came into my cheeks, his warm hands closed around mine. "I say plenty." His voice was low and soothing. "When the mood strikes."

All the air left the room. And then thirty seconds later, so did he. When Roxie and Leo came back into the room, I was grinning like a schoolgirl. Or an idiot.

"How do you always manage to con me into doing dishes, Callahan?"

"You do the dishes because your cooking sucks, Grayson."

I nodded at the suds in the sink. "Not to put too fine a point on it."

"Hey, They Might Be Giants, you're slacking." Roxie set down a stack of plates she'd just cleared from the table. "Get your ass in gear or I'll make you come down to the diner and prep potatoes."

"This isn't culinary school; you can't pretend to boss me around anymore," I said, taking the plates. "You boss Leo around like this?"

"Only when he wants me to." She winked and went back to clearing the table. "Believe me, Leo is happy to do the dishes if he knows I'll keep cooking for him."

"Well look at you, little miss I'll Never Fall in Love, cooking for her man and happy to do it. Not to mention his rug rat."

"I'm getting soft in my old age, what can I say?" she said, wiping the table. "Is it terrible to admit that there are nights when I look across at the two of them, enjoying my fried chicken or meat loaf or stuffed peppers and I think, why the hell did I wait so long to give over to this?"

"You did it when you were supposed to," I replied, rinsing the last dish. "And who the hell makes stuffed peppers for a kid? You should be reported; that's just wrong."

"It did feel very fated—coming back home after all these years, stumbling into Leo and his nuts . . . maybe it was supposed to happen." Dreamily she came to rest next to me at the sink. "Think Oscar might stumble into you with his nuts?"

"He's a dairy farmer," I said, laughing. "I've been more focused on his milk can."

Roxie snorted. "He is ridiculously good-looking."

"I know!" I cried, turning to face her and leaning against the sink. "He kissed me."

"Shut up."

"I sure won't. He kissed me in the barn. And he told me I had a great big ass."

"Whoa, what?" She looked around for a torch and a pitchfork.

"Easy, stand down. He put a comma in exactly the right place."

"He didn't put anything else in the right place, did he?"

I smiled. "Not yet."

"Well, thank God. It's been messing with my head to think that there was a man out there that Natalie Grayson couldn't snare. It was, like, a whole new world order."

"Oh stop it."

"Seriously, there's never been a guy that you couldn't figure out, sort out, wrap around your finger, and make him move heaven and earth just to be with you."

I swallowed. "Come on, Rox." I turned back to the sink, rinsing out the final bit of suds as she prattled on behind me.

"You've always been the Dude Whisperer. You can see right through them, decide what makes them tick, then relax and enjoy, knowing that they're yours for as long as you want. No man stands a chance with Natalie Grayson."

I turned the water on full blast and added the disposal to further muffle her words. I knew my way around men, it was true. But that hadn't always been the case.

Not in the least.

Chapter 9

Sundays in Bailey Falls are the thing that small-town dreams are made of, especially in the fall. I snuggled into a gray cashmere sweater, skinny jeans, and my Chanel black leather thigh-high boots and practically danced down the front steps of Roxie's farmhouse that morning, bound for another breakfast meeting with Chad Bowman.

Doesn't everyone wear thigh-high boots to a pancake breakfast?

Roxie was sleeping in. The diner was closed on Sundays, her food truck was closed as well, and she usually spent the afternoon over at Leo's.

Which meant I had the day, and her old Wagoneer, to myself. I prided myself on being a city girl who could actually drive, something that not all native Manhattanites can do. Between the subway, cabs, and town cars, there was no need to drive oneself, so many city girls never learned.

I learned to drive in this very car, Roxie's old Jeep Grand Wagoneer, in California, so I was quite at home behind the wheel of the giant old boat.

As I drove into town, I took the time to enjoy being alone.

In the wild. Crimson trees danced overhead, their leaves begging off and rioting to the earth below. The air was crisp, clean, and even though there was a constant tickle in the back of my throat (the smog perhaps finally giving up and making way for the clean?), it tasted glorious. I felt so good it almost made me forget how I'd tossed and turned the night before.

Equal parts woodland symphony followed by crushing spooky silence, accented with a side of reliving that incredible kiss over and over again, meant I'd been unable to sleep until way past two in the morning. I'd sleep well tonight back in the city, where I belonged.

But I had to admit that despite the inherent sleeping problems, there definitely was something about this little town. As I drove through the downtown area, all six blocks, I watched as families and kids made their way in their Sunday best to the three churches on their busy street corners. Everyone was laughing, everyone was smiling, as if there were some kind of Mayberry addiction. I had to admit, I'd like a taste. People waved at each other—they actually waved! Calling out greetings, shaking hands, and patting each other on the back—there was such an air of conviviality, a friendliness that seemed woven into the very fabric of Bailey Falls.

I parked the car diagonally along Main Street, only a block away from the town square and the coffee shop where I was meeting Chad. As I walked, I pondered.

Were all small towns like this? If I lived here, would I become as friendly? Would I smile and nod and greet everyone cheerfully? Would a stranger patting me on the back become commonplace, or would I have to stifle the urge to mace, knee, and run?

As the coffee and pastry shop's overhead bell jingled, I sighed and breathed in deeply. A Whole Latte Love was a gorgeous brick building situated on a corner of Main Street, occupying a great slice of real estate. It boasted magnificently high ceilings capped off with bronze tin tiles. The walls were peppered with seventies music posters that were framed and lit like the best art in the museum.

Now *this* place was what I'd pictured the Hudson Valley to be. It was hipster chic down to the mosaic flooring.

It even had its own hipster barista working the massive chrome machine like he had eight arms. I spied Chad in the back, tapping away on his laptop and sipping on a large coffee, with two tiny scones ready for nibbling.

"What's good?" I asked, pulling out the antique chair. Nothing in the place matched. Everything was deliciously eclectic and just the right amount of odd.

"It's all good. You can't order anything bad here. They were just featured in some café magazine for best East Coast spots. Homemade scones and muffins, and Sumatran, Italian, and French coffee blends that wake you up just by smelling it from the street. I'm not kidding, go easy on the coffee here. It'll knock you on your very stylish ass."

"I think I can take it," I said, grinning, and he raised his eyebrows with a "you've been warned" expression.

The stunning young waitress came over. "What can I get you?" she asked, flicking her tongue ring against her teeth.

"I'll take whatever a person orders when they need a swift kick in the ass to wake up. Plus a few of those chocolate biscotti I saw in the jar."

Nodding, she scribbled it down and took off.

Chad Bowman shook his head and muttered, "You'll see."

She brought the coffee over in a dainty teacup. "This is how you serve this hard-core coffee?" I tittered, waving a hand at Chad.

It was the most out-of-place thing in the shop. Here I was

among the requisite musical memorabilia and antique chairs, not to mention a cozy stage for slam poetry night—this place was right out of a CW teen drama—and I was being served in fine china.

But when she set it down, it wasn't the beautiful rose pattern or the gold rim that made me laugh. It was the pitch-black tar goop that filled the cup.

Oh boy.

Never one to shirk a challenge, I thanked her and took the cup in a shaky hand. Eyeing it, I could already feel the jitters running through me, and I hadn't even taken a sip.

"Go on, it's not going to drink itself," he teased.

The sludge in the cup didn't even move.

"What the hell is this?" I asked, watching to see if it bubbled.

"Your kick in the ass," the waitress said over her shoulder, with a wink in Chad's direction.

"It's like a coffee-scented Blob," I said, tipping the cup. The "coffee" didn't slosh—it crept up the side.

With a deep breath, I lifted it to my lips. After one sip, I was done. My eyes watered, my throat burned, and I'm pretty sure you're not supposed to have to *chew* coffee.

"It's really good," I mumbled around it, setting it down. Note to self: country folk like their coffee *strong*.

Well, pride wasn't going to come between me and my morning joe, I thought, coughing and calling out for an ice water. Chad laughed and sipped his beautiful, nontoxic-looking cappuccino.

When the waitress came over, Chad pushed the ooze to her and ordered me a kinder, gentler cappuccino, too. I'd have ordered it . . . but I was still chewing.

"How was yesterday? You get a better feel for what makes Bailey Falls tick?" he asked, a hopeful twinkle in his eye.

I nibbled on the biscotti. The crumbly bits of cookie mixed with chocolate nibs melted in my mouth. It was no wonder this place was regionally featured. I made a mental note to search for the article to include in my proposal.

"Yesterday was very informative. You've got a gem here, Chad. You know it, this town knows it, and now I know it. It's just a matter of harnessing it into a campaign that appeals to everyone," I said, popping another bite of biscotti into my mouth. I wondered what other flavors they had, and made another mental note to pick some up before I left today.

As I toyed with the napkin and listened to Chad, tinier pieces of the grand puzzle fell into place for how I would be able to help each of these businesses. For me, this wasn't just a huge-scale project to sell the whole of Bailey Falls to a grand audience. I was also taking the time to understand each owner's business model. From the menu, I learned these biscotti were homemade every morning. And they packaged the coffee and sold it at the counter and local grocery store.

"Have these owners ever thought of turning an extra profit by selling their goods en masse? Open up a little bakery/factory/coffee-roaster-thingie? People lose their minds over locally sourced treats like this," I said, scribbling a quick note on the napkin.

"I don't know. We could ask."

"I will. After I finish this, I may want to circle back. Plant some seeds to help them grow the business, and not just in town. I'm thinking big market picture here. Later, though." I told myself, *One thing at a time, Nat.*

"We have a gorgeous office building in town that was just renovated."

"You think the coffee shop could expand there?"

"No. I was just thinking that the whole top floor is open, and in need of a sharp city mind with a keen eye for marketing," he answered with a small smile.

"Uh-huh."

"Just saying . . ." He paid the bill and we ventured out in the warm sun and into the busy intersection of pedestrians, kids on bikes, and joggers.

"Target marketing is up first," I said, typing a quick note into my phone. I've drafted entire campaigns in the note section. "I want to chat with more of the business owners to create a slick sheet of quotes and blurbs about each of them. I'll need to get a photographer up here next weekend probably. The sooner the better. Then I— What?"

I turned to see Chad smiling at me. "I'm just wondering if you're talking to me, or just yourself."

"Oh, myself. It's how I take mental notes. I ramble and it all falls into place. Feel free to pay attention, though. This is all marketing gold for the taking."

❦

Chad and I walked back in the direction of our cars, taking the scenic route around the town square. In the center was the requisite gazebo and duck pond, but not so requisite were the thirty or so eight- and nine-year-olds dressed in football uniforms proudly bearing the name BF Lions while moms and dads praised and cheered on from the sidelines. And in the middle of all these kids, tackling each other left and right, was Oscar. Once again, like the tallest sequoia in a sea of reedy pines, he stood out from the crowd, as I imagine he would in any crowd. What caught my special attention, however, and what made me more than my usual swoony, was the clipboard he was carrying and the whistle he was wearing.

He fucking coached kids' football. I can't even.

Without missing a beat, in my head I began to hear Smashing Pumpkins: "Today."

Chad noticed that I was slowing down as we neared the football game. To be clear, when I said slowing down I meant full stop. Because seriously, I needed to stop or I'd likely wander into traffic, unable to stop staring at this guy.

"Pretty, right?" Chad asked.

"Pretty. Right," I breathed back.

"Sometimes he runs with the kids, and oh man, is it something to watch."

"If he runs, I run."

"How very *Titanic* of you," Chad snorted, slipping an arm through mine and tugging me in the direction of the game.

"For the record, I'd drown Jack Dawson myself if it meant that I could get in Oscar's lifeboat."

"For the record, I'd drown Rose and take them both. But I get what you're saying."

The two of us walked down to the edge of the game, taking a seat on the end of one of the benches. We weren't in the middle of the parents and kids, per se; we could have been just watching the ducks. In that duck pond about fifty yards away. And speaking of fifty yards . . .

I watched as Oscar pulled a kid off the bench, squatted down in front of him, and spoke into the kid's helmet. I could see the helmet nodding. It was obvious that some kind of sports play was being discussed, perhaps a go long or a forty-seven scooparound.

Never watched a football game in my life . . .

He sent the kid into the game with a smack on the helmet and an encouraging, "Go get him, Benjamin!"

Benjamin was "bagged" within ten seconds. I learned a new term. *Bagged* is when the quarterback gets tackled. Apparently Chad played high school football. Learning new things is fun.

"So what's his story?" I asked, leaning closer to the councilman.

"Benjamin? Good kid, wants to be a pirate when he grows up. Tells terrible jokes on Halloween, though—"

"I realize we just met, and I am really hoping to get to know you better, Chad; you do seem delightful. But spill it or I'll cut you."

"Ah yes, the story of Oscar. It's all coming back, it's coming back to me now," he said.

"Can it, Céline," I warned. "Dish."

He glared at me slightly. "For someone that *I* hired, you are frighteningly bossy. Not to mention a bit rude."

I blinked back at him, not saying anything.

"Although anyone who can pull off those boots can be bossy and rude, I suppose."

"Thank you. Dish, please."

"There is surprisingly little dish. He moved to town a few years ago, before I came back. As far as I know he keeps to himself mostly, works on his farm, makes his cheese, and sells it in the city on Saturdays."

"This I know," I said with a sigh.

"Other than that, I don't know too much. He started coming to the cooking class Roxie teaches. Hey! That'd be a fun class to come to. It started out as just a few of us, and now there's a waiting list to get in. Oscar doesn't always come, but often enough. Other than that, he's not what you'd call . . . communicative."

"You almost don't have to be when you look like that," I thought out loud, watching him from across the field.

"He's crushworthy for sure," Chad said dreamily. As we sat there, in the fall sunshine, watching tiny football players running here and there, I had another flash to what it must have been like to go to high school in a town like this. Hayrides, apple picking, Friday-night football games, and crepe paper homecoming floats.

A homecoming float has nothing on the balloon inflation party that takes place at Seventy-seventh and Columbus the night before Thanksgiving.

True. Grass is always greener.

Or concrete's always grayer. People would kill to live where you live.

Also true. But as I thought of grass versus concrete, I suddenly felt tingles all over. I looked up, across the huddle and the tackle, and saw Oscar staring at me. I wiggled my fingers hello, he lifted his chin back.

And grinned.

"I feel like you might be adding a chapter to Oscar's nonexistent story," Chad murmured.

"Everybody has a story," I murmured back, and set off across the field toward him, determined to elicit that chapter.

❦

"Hi," I said, a little breathlessly. That hike across the field had been murder on my boots. Heels made for concrete and cobblestone didn't fare as well in ankle-deep leaves and mushy soil. But I'd made it.

"Hi," Oscar said, glancing down at me. "Great turtleneck."

"Thanks." I laughed, delighted that it'd only been five seconds and I was up to three words already. "Great footballs."

He arched an eyebrow at me, but said nothing, eyes on the field and intently following the action. "Right, so, I was thinking, maybe after the game I could stop by? See that barn you're so proud of?"

"You're inviting yourself over?" he asked, eyes still scanning the scrillage. Another football term I'd picked up from Chad. A scrillage is more than a practice, not quite a game. "Toby! Get your head down, or number seventeen is gonna take it right off!"

An enthusiastic "Okay, Coach," floated back to us on the magical autumnal breeze as I considered what he'd said. I *was* inviting myself over. Somewhere between putting him in his own stall, and him invading my stall and kissing me so hard my lips could still feel it, I'd lost my uncharacteristic shyness. I was getting back on sure footing with this guy, back to where I knew what I was doing.

"I feel no qualms about inviting myself over. Especially when I'll be there on official research purposes only. Scouting locations for publicity shots, you know. Checking out that barn, which could be featured in the Bailey Falls campaign. Maybe even the money shot."

Even though he was trying like hell to keep his eye on the ball, he was also trying like hell not to smile. He covered the smile with a whistle, blew it, and yelled out, "Okay, team, that's enough for the day. Huddle up!"

"Wow, you must really want me all to yourself, to call off your scrillage just to take me up on my offer," I purred in a husky voice I knew drove men crazy.

He pulled something off from around his neck, underneath the whistle. A stopwatch. "The *scrimmage* was over—see?" He showed me the countdown, then took off toward the huddle of boys, turning around as he jogged backward. "Don't go anywhere," he called back.

Several of the mothers on the benches stared at me, half of them adding a side of nasty to their stare. Chad was nodding proudly, my own personal cheerleader. Inside my head, I fist-pumped.

Chapter 10

I bounced along the country roads, following Oscar's truck as he led me to his farm.

A phrase never before thought, much less uttered, by this city girl. *He put me in his town car and rubbed my feet on the way back to his townhouse?* Yes, that sounded like me. *He went down on me while I sprawled across the back of an Uber Escalade while we drove through the Bowery?* Mmm, nice memory. But *being led to his farm?* Not in my wheelhouse.

For the record, I had an entire cupboard back home devoted to this exact wheelhouse: chickens and woods and hayrides and a farmer with a truck and a big barn he seemed willing to show me. This was the secret dream, the secret wish.

Bam! The Wagoneer slalomed around rut after rut, pothole after pothole. Say what you want about city driving, they were consistently fixing the streets. Out here, in the sticks, I didn't get the sense that the roads were repaved very often.

Oscar turned off the country highway and onto a road that was dirt mixed with the teensiest bit of gravel that led up a steep hill. I bet this was a bitch in the winter. I also bet that if this were a horror movie, this would be where the audience would begin yelling at me to turn back, turn around, don't be so stupid, and why are you following this man into the woods.

It *was* a rather creepy dirt road. But waiting for me at the end of it was a gorgeous dairy farmer, the aforementioned barn, and hopefully more of that kissing.

I continued to bump along behind Oscar's red truck, rusty in places, dented in others, and entirely covered in a fine white dust that was being kicked up on the road. As it made a final turn, I saw an ancient wooden mailbox marked Bailey Falls Creamery, with a smaller name underneath, Mendoza.

A moment later I was pulling into a clearing, surrounded by enormous trees covered in reds, oranges, rusts, and yellows. In the center stood a white clapboard farmhouse, complete with large wraparound porch, green shutters, and a stone chimney. An old tire swing hung from the oak nearest the house. Late-autumn chrysanthemums were planted in pots all along the porch, spilling out into the yard and lining the beginning of the drive. Huh. Oscar sure had a green thumb . . .

In the field beyond the house was the barn. I could see why he was so stinking proud of the thing; it was indeed massive. Huge stone stacks made the walls, while a red-painted roof soared high above, arching up to the skyline cupola.

A cupola is the tiny structure found atop some barn roofs, particularly those constructed back in the 1800s. When barns housed not just hay but animals as well, extra ventilation was necessary to regulate the temperature, particularly in the winter months, when the animals spent much of their time indoors. Newer barns that housed only equipment still sometimes added cupolas just for their aesthetic value.

Yes, I read up on barns.

And in the field above the house and barn were the bread and literal butter of Oscar's operation: the cows. What looked like some of the same kind of cows I'd seen the other day over at Maxwell Farms, the pretty red and brown animals giving their gentle calls welcoming Oscar home in direct opposition to what I now knew was their true nature . . . that of an angry horde determined to one day trample me.

Oscar climbed down out of his truck, and after taking one last glance in the rearview mirror to assure myself that yes, I was indeed as cute as I'd remembered, I pushed open the door to the Wagoneer and stepped out into the dooryard.

Into a huge puddle of mud.

Arms flailed while boots sank, then stuck, and as I pinwheeled to stay vertical, gravity took a moment to assert itself. Down I went, vaguely aware of Oscar running toward me, reaching to snatch me up out of the mud. But I zigged when he zagged, and landed squarely on my ass.

Mud splattered everywhere, soaking into my jeans. My thigh-high boots were thoroughly soaked as well, making me swear loud and long.

Oscar came to the rescue, kneeling down next to where I sat, covered in mud. "You better quit that yelling, the cows will come see what's wrong."

"I'm *covered* in mud!"

"I'm aware of that," he said, smothering a laugh. "Come on, I'll help you up."

I let him scoop under my arms and put me on my feet, bringing me close to all that flannel and thermal . . . mmm. Touching and feeling all that cotton made me quite sure it could very well be the fabric of my life. I inhaled deeply, breathing in all that cottony softness, all that crisp outdoor air, edged with a touch of burning leaves.

Once I was on my feet again, all I wanted to be was down on the ground, rolling around with this guy. Though I could feel the earth under my feet, I still felt light, airy, weightless. I wanted more weightless. I wanted more of that suspension with him, that heady feeling that I could feel crowding in and making me a bit dizzy.

"Look at you, dirty girl," he murmured, showing me his now mud-covered hand.

"You have no idea," I murmured, tilting my head back and gazing up at him. Backlit by Mother Nature, he was stunning. And I was in his arms. I let my own hands come up, sliding along that red plaid flannel shirt and up around his neck, sinking once more into that decadent hair. "Now put that hand back where it belongs."

Oscar should grin more often. Because when he does, birds sing and angels weep. And holy shit, cows moo.

He bent me backward a bit, very old-school Hollywood, but instead of kissing me like I hoped, he dipped lower, nuzzling along the column of my neck, nipping gently at the sensitive skin there, settling right along the pulse point just underneath my jaw. "It's really a shame about those boots. They're sexy as fuck," he said. I squealed a little as the scruff below his lips tickled at my skin. "I hope they're not ruined."

"No worries. I've got a guy who works on all my leather."

"How much leather do you have?" he asked, and I could feel him smiling at my collarbone.

"Not like that." I giggled. "I just meant I've got someone who can clean them."

"Good, that's good."

"It's nice of you to be concerned, though, since they are Chanel."

"Maybe next time you'll wear the boots," he said and, with a gentleness a man so large shouldn't possess, lightly plucked a fallen leaf from my hair.

"Next time I'll wear the boots, I promise."

"You didn't let me finish," he said, crunching the leaf in his hand. "Maybe next time you'll wear the boots . . . and nothing else."

His gaze burned into mine and I crushed my lips to his fiercely, my entire body going up in flames of lust.

He ended the kiss by wrenching his lips from mine, both of us breathing heavily. Emotions warred in his face: keep kissing me stupid in the mud, or clean me up? Chivalry triumphed over ribaldry.

"You still want to see my barn?" he asked, dipping his head down for one more kiss, sweeter this time but still white-hot.

I gulped. "I can say with all sincerity that I'm literally dying to see your barn."

He laughed, slipped his arm around my shoulders, and took me and my muddy boots across the yard.

This man, this man right here, was going to be the death of me.

∽

The barn truly was an engineering marvel. In an age of steel beams and corrugated metal siding, this thing was built to last. The outside was gorgeous of course, all that stacked fieldstone and cheery painted wood, and the inside was dim and cozy.

It was amazing that over two hundred years ago, someone took the time to design style into a building that was made for necessity. A turned post here, an embellished cornice there. Nothing fussy or fancy, but the workmanship that went into this structure was fascinating.

And it was huge! How it could also be cozy was beyond me, but even though there must have been fifty stalls set into the long side walls, each spread thickly with soft-looking hay and big enough for a cow to lie down, spread out, and even read the Sunday *Times,* the barn was segmented into several sections, making it feel less huge.

"And this is where all the cows sleep?"

"Not so much in the summer, but always in the winter." He walked just behind me as I explored, running my fingers along the smooth beams and weathered wood. "When it's nice out they like to be outdoors as much as possible, but when it snows? My girls like a warm bed."

"Who doesn't?" I murmured, looking back at him over my shoulder. "This original structure is incredible, and the repairs and additions look almost flawless—they blend beautifully."

"Additions?" he said.

"Run your gaze along the ceiling, and you can see where the wood dovetails," I said. "It's a different wood—oak, likely— where the original part is chestnut. It's really rare to find a barn made of chestnut."

"It is?"

"Oh yeah. New York State, and eventually the entire country, was hit with a huge blight in the early 1900s that killed nearly all of the native chestnut. American chestnut is essentially non-existent these days."

"You don't say," he mused as he walked behind me. "And how does an advertising executive know about chestnut?"

"My dad's in construction in the city, doing renovations. I lived on his job sites when I was a kid, practically grew up surrounded by architectural salvage. Some kids had dolls; I loved to line up staircase spindles like little toy soldiers. Except I couldn't ever play with anything made out of chestnut. It's so hard to find, people pay top dollar to have it added back into their brownstone." I turned in a full circle, marveling once again at the detail, stopping when I caught his gaze.

"What?"

"You surprise me," he said, his eyes sharp and assessing.

His expression unnerved me a little, almost as though he could see right through me, seeing more than I usually reveal. I changed the subject. "Do you know much about the family that built the barn?"

"A little. The previous owners told me some." He shrugged. "And people in town love to talk about their shared history, so I've picked up some bits and pieces here and there."

"They are a chatty bunch, aren't they?" I laughed, thinking about how many people stopped by this morning over pancakes to talk to a "new face in town." "You, however, not so much."

"Nope."

He grinned at me, a teasing expression on his face.

"Did you grow up here?"

"Nope."

Hmmm. "Are we playing twenty questions?"

"I don't play games." He took a step. "At all." He took another step.

"Games can be fun," I answered, standing my ground. Dating was a game, sex was a game, life was a game, for those who looked at it that way. Make your own rules, try not to run over anyone on the board, or at least make them think they *wanted* to be run over when it happened.

"You sure talk a lot for a girl who only said *oh* and *yes* forty-eight hours ago." He took another step. So did I. *Toward* him.

Aaaaand cue soundtrack: "Simple Things," by Miguel.

"You make me nervous," I admitted, naming the feeling that had taken root deep in my tummy. The butterflies, the racing pulse, the tingling in my fingers and toes.

"I do?"

"Mm-hmm." I nodded, taking that last step to just in front of him, my toes nudging at his. Other feelings were beginning to take over. A slow warmth was starting to spread, moving those nervous tingles further through my body. "But right now you make me . . . other things." And then I stepped forward again, driving him backward, step by step, into one of the stalls. His hands came up, and I mirrored his, like that game of shadows you played when you were a kid in dance class, except here our hands touched. Fingers tangled. I ran my thumb down the center of his palm, and I could see his breathing change. He lightly pinched the skin between my ring and pinky fingers, and why this made me shudder, I don't know . . . but I did.

I moved forward again, and suddenly I'm in charge, and I'm running this crazy train, and he was up against the back of the stall, and I pressed into his body. On tiptoes, I opened his arms and wrapped them around me, closing them tight around my hips, the way I already knew he liked to hold me.

Did he always like to hold women this way, gripping tightly? Or was it just me? Did he like the control, or did he just love the feel of a woman under his fingertips? Did I feel different from most women he'd been with, with actual curves to hold on to? I breathed through another shuddery shiver as I imagined him holding on to those very curves, his hands tightening as he guided me up and down on his . . .

Time to stop imagining what he was like and actually enjoy it. Still on my toes, I leaned in, inhaling that autumnal scent that was concentrated in this lovely warm spot in the exact center of his throat, where I could see his pulse beating.

I kissed it. He moaned. I licked it. He groaned. His pulse sped under my tongue. I allowed myself a secret smile, enjoying my effect on him. I pulled his head down to mine, and whispered, "You're too tall. Get down here."

He did, but whispered back, "You really do talk too much."

But then no talking, because we were finally kissing. Again. I love kissing this guy.

Every Saturday at the farmers' market, as I'd walked away, I'd fantasized what it would be like to kiss Oscar. To feel those lips on mine. Would he be soft and gentle? Would he be strong and forceful? Would he lick my lower lip until I opened up, then slide his tongue against mine sensually? Or would he put his perfect hands on my face, turn it how he wanted it, and fuck my mouth with his own?

Yes. Yes. Yes. And fucking hell, yes.

Because while Oscar didn't talk much, when he's focused on something, he's all in. Fully present. This kiss, these kisses, they are lazy and unhurried, frantic and frenzied. How can they be both?

My hands left the perfection of his hair and slid down his incredibly strong chest, and I could feel his muscles through his thermal shirt.

While guys I'd dated ranged from tall to short, lean to not, white to brown to black, I tended to gravitate toward tall and lean; not so much muscle-bound.

This guy might change my mind forever. Feeling his innate strength beneath my fingertips, feeling the actual striations of his individual muscles, knowing that if I knew more about anatomy I'd be able to tell a pec from a delt to a tri-something; Oscar had them all. Tri-something. Great idea.

I snuck my hands down while the rest of the entire planet was watching him devote himself to sucking gently on my lower lip, and lifted just the edge of his shirt.

My fingers danced across the skin of his abdomen. His intake of breath stole my own right out of my mouth. Frozen for mere seconds, the entire world stopped once more as we panted. And then the world began to spin again, faster than before, as he spun me in a flash and had me pinned once more up against the side of a stall, my fingers scrambling for purchase as he held my arms out, away from my body, absolutely at his mercy and thrilled to be there.

His eyes were on fire as he stared me down. Then he dipped his head once more and licked up the column of my throat. When he looked into my eyes again, I saw hunger. Need. Absolute desire. The kind I knew was mirrored in my own expression. He licked me once more, primal, pushing the fabric of my turtleneck away with his nose.

"Yes," I said, panting, not entirely sure exactly whether I was asking for permission or granting it. He released my arms, and as my hands tangled into his hair once more, he knelt down in the hay, his mouth still coming halfway up my torso. Dragging his lips down my skin, he left in his wake sweet little kisses, soft and wet. My back arched, pushing my skin closer to his mouth, wanting more, needing more of this man. Leaning his forehead against my breasts, his hands ran down the length of my boots, still thigh high, still muddy, still on.

Then he lifted his head, and with his gaze fixed solidly on me, he ran his hands up the backs of my thighs. The sound of twin Chanel zippers cut through the charged silence. That, and the sound of my heart beating so hard that I feared for my ribs.

"Your jeans are pretty muddy, too," he murmured, raising one foot, then the next, onto his knee, slipping the boots down and off.

"Isn't that terrible?" I asked. His eyes were asking me, how far did I want this to go?

Further.

I nodded, offering a smile as I added another zipper to the mix. As he removed my boots, he watched as I thumbed open the button on my jeans and wiggled my hips a little, just barely pushing them down.

"Hold on there." His hands covered mine, his fingers slipping inside the edge of my jeans and tugging slightly. "Mmm, there we go."

There had been a time in my life where just the idea of standing naked in front of a man would have made me break out into a cold sweat and would have covered my staying-completely-clothed body with gooseflesh. Naked? And worse yet, in the daytime?

He'd see! He'd see it all! The dimples in my skin, the not-perfectly-smooth thighs, the way my legs pressed together in the middle and likely always would, the way my panties would never just casually sit on my hips, but band inward, denting the soft skin there. Everything so damn soft and squishy.

All true. Every bit of it. And every inch, no matter how soft or squishy, made up me, made up Natalie. But then I learned something important about men; something that almost without fail was always true.

Men love a naked woman. But more than that, they love a confident naked woman. Now, everyone has a type, of course, and preferences about how tall or short, athletic or voluptuous, and there's no discounting that. But a woman who loves her body, and knows what she wants? There's nothing sexier than that.

To a real man.

And once I realized this, realized that this exact version of Natalie was how I was supposed to be, and that my body could make a man literally fall to his knees . . . things got a lot more fun for me.

I was standing in the middle of a barn with an almost-stranger, and he was taking my jeans off. And I was encouraging it. Willing it. I didn't have many rules when it came to dating; I was all equal opportunity when it came to getting mine. But getting naked on the first date? Not typically my scene.

Then again, this wasn't a date. This was a barn, and I was in it with the man I'd been crushing on for months. Technically, we'd been seeing each other for a long time . . .

Let this happen, I urged myself, and I gave in to everything I was feeling. Which at the moment was supreme satisfaction, watching as his face changed, taking in my lacy panties, emerald green with black scallops.

"Did you wear those for me?" he asked.

"You mean when I woke up this morning thinking all I had on the agenda was a pancake breakfast with councilman Chad Bowman?" Once again, he picked up each foot and placed it on his knee, his fingertips dragging gently along the back of my thigh, teasing and slow.

"So you wore these for pancakes?"

"I wore these for *me,* you big caveman." I sighed, then giggled as he tickled at the sensitive skin behind my knee. "Girls mostly buy lingerie for themselves. Guys are usually happy with white cotton panties, as long as they get to see them."

"I like the lace," he said, tugging the last of the denim from my leg, easing it over my heel. "But you're right, your ass would look incredible in white cotton panties."

He looked equal parts dangerous and sweet, kneeling at my feet with the cockiest grin imaginable. He looked down at my toes, painted bubble-gum pink with teeny red polka dots, my left foot still resting on his knee.

His gaze followed his hands as he ran them slowly back up my leg, wrapping his long, tanned fingers around my calf, kneading the muscle there. Coaxing my leg to butterfly out slightly, he slid his hands higher up my leg, one holding on to my knee while the other spanned across my thigh, my fair Irish skin a strong contrast to his darker hands. Some of his knuckles looked like they'd been broken before. Imperfectly perfect, and I let out the softest sigh when I saw how incredible they looked on my leg.

He leaned down, dropped a wet kiss on the top of my knee-cap, his finger tracing the edge of a scar there. "A brawl?"

"Yeah." I smiled. "With my brother. I was seven; he was nine. I'd stolen Darth Vader. He had every right to try and retake it with his lightsaber." He smiled into my skin as I continued, dropping kisses all around. "Scars are like a map, you know? They're little clues, hints about the person who wears them."

"Maybe I'll learn something about this gorgeous girl with the great"—he paused for effect—"big ass."

For someone who didn't talk much, when he did, he chose his words well. But before I could ask him anything else, the kisses he'd been languishing across my knee began to move farther up my thigh. His breath was warm on my skin, making it pebble, and that same low sound came from the back of his throat, making me shiver once more. He gripped my leg harder, seeming to ground himself in the touch.

He looked up at me, and now I was the one sweeping his hair back from his face.

"Are we really doing this?" he asked, his voice the slightest bit shaky. Was he thinking the same things I was a moment before? Too fast, too soon, too perfect, too yes exactly we *are* doing this?

As I looked into his eyes, I knew I wanted this, right now.

"Some girls would say no, it's too soon, will he respect me tomorrow, what will he think of me . . . all thoughts that should be going through my head right now."

"What *is* going through your head right now?" he asked, grasping my bottom in his hands. He tugged me closer to him, one hand spread across the small of my back. I moved my foot to the ground, feeling the hay slipping between my toes. He planted two kisses at the tops of my thighs, high up where any thigh gap had bid bye-bye a million years ago.

"Honestly?"

"I think now would be the perfect time for honesty, don't you?" he asked, nudging me closer, his nose tickling at my lace.

"So honesty means I've got to admit that I've daydreamed about exactly this—with you on your knees in front of me."

His deep chuckle signaled that I was right on track.

"And I'm thinking that in that daydream, you're telling me that I'm beautiful."

He bit me, hard, on the inside of my left thigh.

"You *are* beautiful." He pushed my legs apart with his broad shoulders. "Especially now, with your hair all messed and you in your panties and that turtleneck, looking all fifties pinup girl."

"That was the last time a girl with curves had it so good." I sighed, throwing my arms over my head and arching my back, stretching and feeling my body beginning to go all gooey and boneless.

"You better tell me the rest of that daydream," he said into my skin.

I closed my eyes, overwhelmed with the sensations running wild. A sharp smack to my behind brought me back.

"Ah-ah, Pinup Girl, don't go getting lazy on me." My head snapped back to look at him in surprise. He reached up and brought my hands down to my hips. "Take your panties off."

Oh.

Chapter 11

Covering my hands with his, we both slipped them down down down until they were at my feet, and once more he gently lifted each foot in turn, sliding my panties off and laying them carefully to the side. A gentleman. His eyes following the action, only now did he look at me. And I watched as his eyes took on an even deeper tone, narrowing, lids heavy. His mouth parted, and his tongue snuck out to dab carefully at his lower lip, literally licking his lips as he watched me standing there, bare. The slowest of grins appeared, breaking across his face like a sunrise, the happiest, lustiest sunrise I'd ever seen.

And then his gaze found mine once more, and he rose, slowly standing until he was positively towering over me. My back to the stall, I stared up at him, his frame crowding me against the slats, and I could feel my turtleneck snag on the rough wood. He tugged me against him, all strong hands and entangling arms and then his lips were on mine again, and I had to hold my breath, it was so fiery, so fierce, so fantastically frantic.

A switch had been thrown, and now we both scrambled at each other, my hands digging in, trying to find purchase on his ridiculous shoulders. As he kissed me, he explored, his fingertips dancing up and under my sweater, then back down again, knees pushing my own wide.

I tugged my head back, my lips leaving his in a wrench that made him growl, but I wanted to see his face as he touched me for the first time and . . . oh, there it was.

He growled again as I groaned, his fingers finding me already slippery and wet and ready for him. I tugged at his shirt, needing to see him, needing to see more of him, but his hands, his hands! Those rough, callused fingers were gentle and strong at the same time, swirling and twirling and finding the spot that would spiral me out of my head.

But if I was going out of my head, I needed to see him first. I pulled at his shirt, and he finally left me long enough to tug it over his head, and my eyes widened as I took him in.

Those tattoos—the ones I'd been staring at for weeks at the farmers' market, the ones that peeked out from under his T-shirts and trailed down his arms—were just the tip of the iceberg. Because underneath it all, where it was just Oscar and skin, was a world of paint. Bright, angry colors bloomed across his chest, each pectoral its own canvas for the art that had been exquisitely inked onto his skin. Bold lines, panels of images and symbols and here and there a word. A moon. The stars. An enormous oak tree stretched across his abdomen and curled upward over his heart, the branches curving in, surrounding a bloodred sun.

Beautiful. But before I could admire him properly, he picked me up, wrapped my legs around his waist, and pressed me up against the stall once more. Holding my weight entirely in one hand, he slipped the other down in between us again and began to circle my clit, low and slow and maddeningly perfect. I slapped at the slats, he circled faster. I cried out, he dipped lower. One finger, then two, slid inside me, driving me, my hips beginning to thrust, riding his hand as his thumb pressed down . . .

"Oh. Yes," I said, sparks of light beginning to crackle at the edge of my vision, which was focused entirely on this man, this man who was groaning while he watched me begin to come undone, thrashing, undulating, so very close.

"There she is," he murmured, and I came. Came hard and fast, pushing him away and pulling him closer at the same time.

When I opened my eyes, he was watching me, head cocked slightly to the side, a slow, sexy grin creeping across his face.

More. I needed more.

"My jeans," I managed to say.

"Your jeans?"

"Condom. Back pocket."

"Yeah?"

"Immediately."

He untangled my legs and set me gently on my feet, and was in my jeans and back again with the condom before I could say hey, this hay is slippery.

He wrapped his arms around me again, pulling me fully against him, and I relished barely coming up to his collarbone. He was so tall, so very tall, that I felt dainty and small and entirely surrounded by this man. Plus, I was eye level to the most beautiful collarbone ever imagined. I kissed that collarbone, planting kisses all along the swirls of ink there, while he held me tight, both hands firmly on my bottom, pressing me against him.

"Aren't you glad I came to your scrimmage thingie today?" I asked, sneaking one hand down and finding his zipper.

"Any other time I'd tell you why it's not a thingie, but yes," he replied, eyes widening when I reached inside. "Not really going to argue with you right now."

"What *do* you want to be doing with me right now?" I purred, using my other hand to push down the edges of his jeans, watching as his abdomen flexed and that wonderful V appeared, delineating his hips, and sweet Christ, this man was a work of art.

"I want you on top of me," he said, kneeling once more and pulling me along with him, tearing at the condom wrapper with his teeth and coaxing me to straddle his legs. He pulled himself forward from his jeans and gave one long stroke, rubbing the head with this thumb, the same thumb that had just sent me over the moon and back again, and I rolled my hips reflexively. "I want you all over me."

Rolling the condom on, he grasped me once more, positioning me over his body, holding himself at the base with one lucky hand while he looked up at me through heavy lids. "What's your last name?"

"Hmm?" I murmured, lost at the sight of him in his own hand.

"Your last name?" he repeated, his eyes full of mischief.

"Grayson." I was almost shaking with need as he ran his other hand up and over my bottom, poised just above him.

"Nice to officially meet you, Natalie Grayson," he whispered, and thrust up inside me.

I threw back my head, my eyes clamped shut as I slid down, taking him into me, stretching to allow him to fit, because he was big, so big, proportionate to the rest of him. Crazy hot, crazy thick, and my back arched to allow me to push down more, harder, faster—I wanted it all from him.

His groan was as big as he was, powerful and echoing through the quiet barn, full of want and need, exactly the way I felt after lusting after this man for so long, wondering and wishing—and now here he was, perfectly inside.

But now . . . he was moving. Sliding, slipping, guiding my hips as he retreated, then thrust deep once more. I cried out, my muscles slick but swollen and so very tight against him.

Lifting my head once more I stared down into his eyes,

the gray receding and the blue taking over, intense and focused, the same wonder that was no doubt in my eyes reflected in his.

This felt amazing. This felt incredible. This felt different.

I rocked, he rolled. I circled my hips, he circled his. In sync, wonderfully in sync we were, and I gasped when I could feel him, so strong underneath me, inside me, filling me up and making me shiver-shake.

His hands clutched at my hips, tight on my bottom, lifting and guiding me as I rode him hard, impossibly hard. But he was so very strong that I could let myself go, really let him feel all of me.

"Beautiful," he groaned as I sank down once more, all the breath in my body leaving at once. "So fucking beautiful."

I already loved that he thought I was beautiful.

He fucked me frantic on the floor, legs and arms tangled and grasping, and he said my name over and over again as his hips sped up, thrusting harder and faster now, his fingertips digging into my skin so hard it brought tears to my eyes. Good burning tears, the sheer strength that he possessed and the way he knew exactly how much I could take, like we'd been doing this *for years*.

And I knew in that moment, when he threw his head back and came with a roar that made the walls shake and the veins pop out on his neck, raw and needy, that I could do this *for years* and never, ever get enough.

Because then, when he came down and I leaned forward, he wrapped me in those same strong arms, cuddling me close to him, no space between us.

His hand, so rough and worn, tenderly caressed my cheek and I nuzzled into it as he held me.

"Where did you come from?" His voice was gruff, raw.

I blew on a strand of hair that had fallen in my eyes and gave him a tired, extremely satisfied smile. "The West Village."

∾

"Ridiculous," I said.

"Hmm?"

"This is ridiculous."

"I still don't get it," Oscar said, raising an eyebrow in question.

I was standing just inside the barn door, wearing nothing but his red plaid flannel shirt and a pair of his work boots, waiting for the cows to come home. Literally. We'd spent the better part of the afternoon messing around in the barn like teenagers in heat, and now it was time for the moo cows' dinner. As they lined up in fairly orderly fashion and came trotting down their path toward the barn, I watched as Oscar, wearing his thermal shirt and half-buttoned jeans, waved them on down.

"Who gets fucked in a barn, then brings the cows in from the meadow?"

"The pasture," he corrected, and I rolled my eyes while I rerolled the sleeves of his flannel. I quite liked the feel of that worn-so-thin-it-was-silky flannel against my naked skin. I also liked how delicate his extra-extra-large shirt made my wrists look.

"I'm just saying it was warm in the barn." I shivered a little, the setting sun taking the warmth of the day with it.

"The house is warm, too. Go on inside and I'll be right behind you."

"Promise?" I winked naughtily, and he looked back at me just as naughtily. I danced across the yard, taking care to avoid all the puddles. It was hard to swish and sway wearing size-fourteen work boots, but I did my best. And it worked—by the time I made it to the back porch, there was a dairy farmer plastered to my backside.

"I thought you had cows to tend to."

"That's the thing about cows," he said, giving my bottom a swat that made me jump, and in the process, lose one of the boots. "Leave the door open, and they know their way home."

I stuck my foot out. "See that? That's what happens when you smack my ass. I lose your stupid boot and get my foot all muddy."

"Something else happens when I smack that ass."

I made a show of looking directly at his dick.

He reached out and pulled me against him once more, holding my bottom in both hands and squeezing tightly. "I knew the first time I saw you walking away from me at the farmers' market with that great big ass, how much it would jiggle when I smacked it."

From any other guy, that statement would have earned its own reciprocal smack. But the way his eyes lit up, and the way he ran his enormous hands over my behind like he was just happy to finally have his hands on it—my tough city girl shield melted a little. Also, let's not discount what he said about thinking about it and wanting it from the beginning.

However, he wasn't walking away completely unscathed.

"We need to talk about your phraseology," I said, bumping him back with my hips.

His hands, restless on my body, twisted into my hair as he tipped me backward once again. "Is that a fancy word for my dick?"

My burst of laughter caught him off guard, and he grinned, waggling his eyebrows.

"Seriously, Oscar, you can't just say things like that. You're gonna get punched one day for saying shit like that to a girl."

"Are we back to that comma nonsense again?" he asked, then blew a raspberry between my breasts. "You have a great ass. You have a big ass. You have a great"—he paused for effect . . . pausing . . . pausing . . . still pausing—"big ass, and I can't wait to see it bouncing on my dick."

"You really *are* a fucking caveman," I said, eyes wide.

"One caveman, coming up," he replied, spinning me like a top and placing my hands on the porch railing. One of his hands slipped between my legs, and my back arched without thought. I giggled, feeling the warmth of his body against my back, wondering how long it would take before I was screaming out his name again—when I heard footsteps coming up the other side of the porch, and then an unmistakable gasp. And it wasn't me gasping this time, which was a testament to how surprised I was, considering where Oscar's hand was.

"Oscar?" a female voice said, and we both turned.

Standing on the end of the porch in a buttoned-up trench coat was the cutest little brunette I'd ever seen. She'd unwound her scarf and now stood there like a statue, one hand full of striped wool, and the other full of . . . aluminum foil–covered dishes?

"Ah shit," Oscar muttered, tucking me behind him, giving me the barest hint of privacy. "Whoops." I heard his zipper go up.

"What on earth is going on here?" she asked, and as I tried to quickly button up my shirt—his shirt—I peeked over his shoulder on tiptoes. She was really cute in a Girl Scout jamboree kind of way. And she was clearly furious.

"You're early."

"Not that early."

"I didn't realize it had gotten so late—sorry about that. Um, Missy, this is . . . umm . . . this is . . . ."

"Natalie," I supplied, squeezing his bicep and digging in with my nails. "I'm Natalie."

"Yes, sorry. Natalie, this is Missy."

The brunette seethed. "His wife."

I dug in deeper with my fingernails.

"Ouch! Stop that!" Oscar looked back over his shoulder at me, then turned to Missy. "You always forget the *ex* in *ex-wife*."

I retracted my nails. A millimeter.

"I'll just put these on the table," she said, so angry her lips were pinched white. He nodded to her almost nonchalantly, still keeping me tucked behind him. She walked inside through the back door, and I could see her bustling about in a kitchen she was clearly at home in, setting down her dishes, starting to take things like lettuce and carrots out of a grocery bag.

Oscar and I watched her for a moment, then he turned to me. He didn't go back to what he was doing before, of course, but he didn't make any effort to hurry me off the porch, either. I wrinkled my brow. "*Ex*-wife?"

"Ex," he confirmed.

"Does she know that?"

He shrugged, easily. "She likes to bring me casseroles on Sundays."

I could hear casserole dishes being set down on counters— and they sounded like they were being set down from ten feet above. Oh boy. Time to go.

"I'm going to go ahead and split." I looked at his watch. "Wow, I didn't realize how late it had gotten, either; I was planning to catch that last train back to the city tonight. Gotta be at work tomorrow morning, you know . . ."

My ramble was cut off by a searing, toe-curling, tongue-tangling kiss. When his mouth released mine, I continued. "So . . . yeah. Bye."

I left with as much grace as I could muster, pulling his work boots back on for my trip across the yard to retrieve my own. He'd folded my muddy clothes and piled them neatly on a chair just outside the barn earlier, so it was a quick snatch-and-grab. I was all elbows and knees and flashes of bum as I slid my jeans on, wincing at the cold and the wet. I gave up trying to wrestle with my muddy Chanel boots, and finally ran, still half dressed, across the yard to the Wagoneer. Avoiding the mud puddle, I went around to the other side and climbed across. I started the car, tossed a wave to a grinning Oscar on the porch, a second wave to a white pinched face glaring at me through the kitchen window, and took off, the rear tires spitting mud and gravel back toward the house.

On the way home, every single pothole and rut in the road made me bounce, and I felt each bounce all over my body, reminding me of the good kind of sore I felt, and Oscar's words about bouncing on his dick.

When I pulled into Roxie's driveway, she and Leo came out to watch me hop out, half dressed, clothes in my arms and hay in my hair, smiling like a lunatic.

"Gotta catch that train," I singsonged as I skipped up the porch steps and into the house, past their curious eyes. I popped my head back around the doorframe. "Is that your famous Sunday chicken I smell? I'm starving!"

Chapter 12

$\mathcal{I}$ caught the last train back into the city with only three minutes to spare. There'd been an earlier train, but that would have meant missing out on Roxie's Sunday chicken.

As I sat in the last car with a take-out container full of leftover chicken, buttermilk mashed potatoes, and garlic and shallot green beans, I thought back over the weekend, balancing the pluses and minuses.

Plus: The town was adorable.
Minus: The air was almost too clean.
Plus: The scenery was lovely.
Minus: It was too quiet, especially at night. No horns.
Minus: It was too loud, especially at night. Fucking crickets.
  Fucking wind. Fucking scary scraping trees everywhere . . .
Plus: The dicks were large . . .
Plus: And in charge.
Plus. Plus. Plus.

I shivered from the excitement my body still felt whenever I thought about that mouth, those lips, that tongue . . .

That *ex.*

Hmm. What was the story there? I'd spent half a year fanta-sizing about this guy, and half a day letting him get me off twelve ways from Sunday. And I didn't even have his phone number.

I waited for some part of me to feel guilty about that, to *tsk-tsk* me and shake an admonishing finger and make me feel the teeniest bit shameful for spending naked time with a man I barely knew. But it never came.

I wanted to know more about him, not because I should, but because he fascinated me. I wanted to know the story that was there, because while he occasionally had these wonderful verbal treasure nuggets, for the most part he still responded to every question with *yep, nope,* or *great big ass.*

He also responded with *beautiful, pinup,* and *you taste in-credible,* but that's beside the point.

I still should've gotten his phone number. At least then we could send dirty texts . . .

And as the train ran down the tracks, heading back to my city life, I started pulling up train schedules . . .

✑

It's funny how visiting a place just once can imprint it on your psyche. The first time I traveled to Prague, I fell in love with the smoky red-brick-topped roofs, the black-and-white-tiled side-walks, the sound of a foreign language hopelessly unrecogniz-able to my American ears, all hard Z's and clucking K's. The first time I visited Dubai, I was captured by the skyline and the hard-driving sand that coated even the enormous shopping malls, and the oppressive heat that weighted every move.

Now, all week long I found myself thinking about the color of the fall trees on Main Street in Bailey Falls, the scent of burning leaves in the air, and the slip and slide of hay underneath my bare feet. My bare *everything,* to be exact.

But with all this daydreaming, work was still center stage. The T&T project was coming along very nicely. We'd begun casting for the commercials we were shooting, as well as for the print advertisement.

For the Bailey Falls campaign, I was still kicking around the idea of using the local-farmer angle, how to position it to show these wonderful local farms in exactly the right light. Not to mention lighting those farmers to look irresistible to any woman on the East Coast with a pulse and an overnight bag . . .

I wondered how Oscar would feel about being photographed for the campaign. I wondered if Casserole Missy would object. I further wondered why I'd taken to referring to her as Casserole Missy, since I was just having some fun, getting a taste of some local flavor, as it were . . .

I'd resisted the impulse all week to call up Roxie and ask if she had Oscar's phone number. I wondered if Oscar had called her and asked for mine. Or maybe he'd ask Leo to ask Roxie to ask me if it was okay for him to call me—like a game of high school telephone, the kind with the windy knotted cord that I'd twine around one hand while holding the phone to my ear, giggling late at night on the phone with my girlfriend, talking about how he'd held my hand during lunch and asked me to the dance after the big game Friday night.

And how he'd told me how satiny soft the inside of my thigh was on his tongue.

I pulled myself out of Bailey Falls and thoughts of phone numbers. Something told me I needed to play this one easy, casual, and not crowd him. And since my instincts were unfailing in this area, I literally sat on my hands more than once to stop from texting Roxie. But I wondered what he was up to this week, and if he was thinking of me.

I was giddy. And giddy plus Natalie can equal dangerous territory.

When I was walking home after work and saw Bailey Falls Creamery cheese in the window of La Belle Fromage, my heart raced. When I saw a red flannel shirt in the window at Barneys, in a display of fashionable lumberjacks, my skin tingled. And when I saw a salami in the window of Zabar's, it was almost more than I could bear.

I was stopping by to pick up a few things to have sent over to my parents' house, since I'd missed brunch the previous Sunday. Work-related issues were an acceptable excuse for missing brunch, but only when cleared in advance and only when it was career enhancing. I usually adhered to this rule, but in the haste to get out of town last week I'd forgotten to call my mother, thus beginning the biggest case of recorded guilt the city had seen since my neighbor Francis Applebaum had forgotten to call his mother on Rosh Hashanah. That he'd been having an emergency appendectomy was usually overlooked in the relaying of this story, but the entire block had taken sides.

It was Wednesday night, and though I'd originally planned to have the treats delivered, it was a nice night out and I wasn't quite ready to go home yet. I felt a little out of sorts, twitchy, perhaps a little restless? And wondering how in the world I was going to tell my mother I'd be missing brunch again *this* Sunday . . .

I was planning on taking the train up to Bailey Falls again on Thursday afternoon. I had a breakfast planned for Friday morning at Callahan's with the chamber of commerce and some of the local business owners. I wanted to chat with them about what they wanted, how they saw their town, and how they'd like others to see it. Chad was helping me organize the meeting, making sure the key players were there. Roxie had already been tasked with making the cakes that would follow the meeting. If it went well, cake to celebrate. If it went not so well, then every-one would hopefully just remember the cake . . .

"You're heading up there again? This weekend?" Dan had asked when I gave him my expense report for the week before.

"Yeah, this weekend I get to hobnob with the elite of Bailey Falls, including the mayor's wife. You know how it is, mingling with the upper crust." Perched on the edge of his desk, I men-tally ran through my wardrobe and wondered if there'd be time to get another pair of thigh-high Chanel boots before the week-end. Sadly, the extended vacation they'd taken in the mud and the water had ruined them. Twenty-two hundred dollars, down the drain.

Oscar did say he'd like me in the boots, though, and only the boots . . .

"You'll be back Monday?" Dan asked, interrupting my day-dream.

"That's the plan. I'll take the train back home on Sunday."

"Staying up there the entire weekend *again*? Two Saturday nights in a row, this town has been deprived of Natalie Grayson. I'm surprised the lights didn't dim on Broadway," he teased.

"I'm dedicated, what can I say?" I laughed, snatching back the expense reports after he signed them and running them down to accounting before he could ask me any more questions.

And speaking of questions . . .

"I just don't understand. What in the world could possibly be so interesting upstate that would keep you away from brunch? I mean, it's brunch, for God's sake, Natalie," my mother was say-ing, walking from the kitchen to the dining room with a tray to arrange the cookies I'd brought. "Explain this to me like I'm an idiot."

"You're not an idiot, Mom," I said, biting into one of the cookies.

"I must be, since I'm not understanding this. Two Sundays in a row, Natalie. Two!"

"Ma! It's for work, okay? New campaign. I'm working with out-of-town clients, and I'm still collecting information. Its research that I need to do, and it helps when I'm in the place I'm actually supposed to be selling to everyone, you know?"

"I understand that, but—"

"And Roxie's there. It's great to see her, and meet her new boyfriend and her friends, and it's a great little town. It's . . . I don't know . . . it's nice," I muffled my voice with a cookie, "spending some time out of the city."

She blinked several times. "Who is he?"

"Who is who?"

"Who's the he that's making you miss brunch all the time."

"All the time?" I laughed. "Two brunches is hardly 'all the time.'"

"Quit deflecting," she said, sitting down across from me at the table. She'd been in her studio today; she had paint under her nails. She had a new show coming up soon, her first in a few years. "You've met someone."

"You're psychotic."

"That's twice now you've changed the subject or not answered me directly."

"Maybe because you're being psychotic," I said through the cookie.

"You always tell me about the guys you're dating. Why aren't you telling me about this one?"

"Because there's nothing to tell! Jeez, what's with the third degree?"

She settled back into her chair and appraised me the way only a mother can. "You look me in the eye and tell me there's not a guy involved in this, and I'll drop it."

I leaned across the table, keeping my face as composed as I could. "There is not a guy involved in this."

She paused a moment, her eyes searching. "Okay. Enough. I won't say another word."

I let out my breath. "Thank you. Now, if you'll excuse me, I need to pack some things for my trip tomorrow. Did you know that there's a town literally five minutes up the Hudson where you can't even see the city?"

"It's called Yonkers, sweetie. It's been there a long time. I think we might have kept you in Manhattan too long."

"Perish the thought." I grinned and dropped a kiss on her head. "I'll call you on Sunday, how's that?"

"I'll be reading the *Times,* don't interrupt me."

"Duly noted. Love you." As I walked past her, she reached out and patted my arm.

"You'll tell me about this guy when you're ready."

That woman has X-ray vision.

~

Thursday morning went by in a blur, and before I knew it, I was on the train and heading north once again along the Hudson. It was a gorgeous sunny day, the sun shining down and reflecting off the water so brightly it was almost blinding. But not so blinding that I wasn't able to enjoy the view. Normally a train for me meant sardine-packed between a thousand other commuters, or don't fall asleep or you'll miss your stop.

But I found myself once again watching the little towns go flashing by, wondering at the lives led behind those front doors. I got a quick snapshot into a life that I'd never know anything about, but it was fun imagining what might being going on behind those closed doors. My train was merely a background sound to them, a train that had rattled by twelve times a day (twenty-four if you count the other direction), a sound they'd no doubt tuned out long ago. Or a train they'd taken themselves on a sunny Saturday, to head into the city to watch the Yankees play. All these little snapshots of a life led on the Hudson River Line, and today I was once more part of that background noise—albeit a very excited part, as I was nearly bouncing out of my seat to get back to Bailey Falls.

I had all my research and notes for the Friday-morning meeting, to talk about how they wanted their town presented. I had a date set up with Chad Bowman to get a more specific glimpse into some of the businesses and sights that I might feature.

But I certainly wasn't bouncing out of my seat because I'd be meeting with Myra Davis, owner of the Klip 'n' Kurl, a third-generation beautician and proprietor of the town's hottest beauty spot. Or with Homer Albano, owner of the hardware store on Main Street, who'd been handing out homemade popcorn along with his wrenches and hammers since 1957.

I was bouncing and humming and practically climbing out of my skin because I was going to hopefully, probably see Oscar again. And the thought was driving me mad.

I wasn't unfamiliar with the one-night stand; I'd indulged a time or two or several. The term implied, "Hey, let's scratch this itch and then go our separate ways, but thanks for the orgasm." Or multiple orgasms, if you were lucky.

But I was coming back to the scene of the one-night stand. The *one-afternoon-getting-thoroughly-worked-over-in-the-barn* stand. And I wanted more.

I craved him, simple as that. When I just saw him at the farmers' market, I was free to make up any backstory I wanted about him. Now he was real. Now I knew enough to know I wanted to know more.

Had he thought about me this week? Had he been at work concentrating on something really boring but necessary, and then an image of my naked body shot across his imagination?

I squeezed my hands into fists, channeling the tension I could feel running through my body. It had been ages since I'd been this worked up about a man, and I needed to keep it in check.

∾

I spent another near-sleepless night tossing and turning at Roxie's. I appreciated the guest room; I appreciated the comfortable bed even with the squeaks and creaks. But honestly, how the hell did anyone sleep in this town with all that racket outside? I was finding some earplugs while I was in town today.

Friday morning in Bailey Falls dawned clear and crisp, and before I could say howdy-do I was bouncing along the rutted country roads next to Roxie, eating one of her cinnamon biscuits and marveling at how blue the sky was when you could actually see the sky. Not that there was anything wrong with the sky behind the Chrysler Building, but it just wasn't the same.

"Did you tell Trudy thanks for letting us host the meeting at the diner?" I asked, sipping from a travel mug of my special-roast coffee. After the disaster at the coffee shop last weekend, I came prepared this weekend, getting off the train last night with a smile and two pounds of Colombian gold coffee.

"You can tell her yourself, my mom can't wait to see you. She's officially pissed that you didn't stop by last weekend to see her. She said, and I quote, 'Tell that city snot to get her ass in to my diner or I'll send Bert after her.'"

"Who the hell is Bert?"

As we turned onto Main Street, Roxie pointed to an ancient cop car sitting in front of city hall. "Bert. Chief of police, coach of the women's bowling team, champion Scrabble player eleven years running, and unofficial number-one flunky willing to do anything my mother asks, on account of the giant crush he's had on her since they were paired together for square dancing in seventh-grade physical education."

"Wow, that's specific," I said, peering out the window at the grizzled-looking old man in the cop car peering back at me. "Did he just wave at me?"

"Looks like my mom has already alerted him about the new girl in town. Nice of her, wasn't it?"

"Fucking Mayberry," I muttered, while Roxie laughed. We pulled into a spot right in front of Callahan's, the diner that had been in Roxie's family for three generations. When Roxie was running the diner last summer she'd made a few updates to the menu, most of which Trudy kept when she returned home from her world tour and realized that even the oldest recipes can be tweaked and brought into the new century.

I hopped down from the Jeep, pausing a moment to straighten out my black pencil skirt and make sure that my button-down had the correct number of buttons *un*buttoned. I didn't know if Oscar would be making an appearance at the town meeting this morning, but my cleavage and I wanted to be prepared.

"Natalie Grayson, get your sweet buns in here and give me a hug," I heard booming from the behind the counter before I'd even made it inside the front door. All eyes swiveled to me as Trudy Callahan—grown-up hippie and Salisbury steak dynamo—came barreling across the linoleum to hug me tightly.

"Hiya, Trudy, how are you?" I asked, wondering how someone so small could be so powerful.

"We are just *so* excited you're here! A big-shot city ad lady coming to talk to us about our little town? Couldn't be more tickled! Now you sit over here. I cleared the corner booth for you; what can I bring you? Cuppa joe? Eggs? Slice of ham? Slice of pie?" Trudy would have given me the entire menu, but by now Roxie had caught up with us and was leading her back behind the counter.

The two of them were knee-deep in an argument about why the sign Featuring Zombie Cakes had been moved from the front window when Chad Bowman appeared, radiant in North Face fleece and perfectly pressed jeans. "Hi, how's it going?"

"Good, really good, just wanted to get here a few minutes early and get some things set up. Are you expecting people to be on time this morning?" I started stacking some notepads and pens on the table, getting a few of my graphs together that I'd pulled from the local census about who and what comprised the town.

"Are you kidding? They're all here already," he replied, helping me pop up my easel. "Nice charts, by the way."

"I don't see anyone," I said, looking over my shoulder and just seeing a crowd full of diner customers.

"Trudy closed down the diner this morning to everyone but chamber of commerce members. Everyone here is a business owner, here to see what the woman from New York is going to tell us about how to generate business for our little town."

"Wait, what?" I asked, now seeing the diner customers for what they really were. In between coffee sips and breakfast eats, they were already assessing, calculating, wondering what I might have up my sleeve.

I could handle this. I'd faced down boardrooms filled with the toughest sharks the advertising world had to offer. Titans of industry. Masters of the universe.

Turns out they were nothing compared to Myra, the owner of the Klip 'n' Kurl.

∞

I spent the better part of the morning asking and answering questions from a group of townspeople as excited and fired up as I'd ever seen. They all had very specific ideas about what needed to happen in order to make Bailey Falls a destination town. They were open to new ideas, but they wanted to make sure they retained the small-town atmosphere that had been created over the years, that no new weekenders were going to ruin a good thing. But of course money talks, and the possible new streams of revenue that could be brought into the town by some new blood was attractive to all.

I'd printed some of the photos I'd taken the weekend before and displayed them around the diner, giving them a taste of what a Natalie Grayson campaign would look and feel like. I went through possible layouts in regional and national magazines, showed them examples of featured columns I'd orchestrated for other clients in newspapers like the *New York Times,* the *Boston Globe,* the *Philadelphia Inquirer,* and the *Washington Post.*

I'd brought my iPad and was able to screen a few of the commercials I'd put together to give them an idea of what I was capable of. And when the people of Bailey Falls began to realize that some of them could be featured in a commercial just like the ones I showed them, they began to get excited.

So excited, in fact, that Norma from the florist and Arnold from the pizza place suggested that Bailey Falls host a screening party the night of the premiere.

"Um, what premiere exactly are they talking about?" I whispered to Chad, who'd been passing out pencils for the question-naire I'd just circulated.

"Oh, they're pretty sure that if there's a commercial they'll need to have a premiere party, just to make sure everyone knows how fabulous they are."

"Usually the screening takes place in my office, and the client Skypes in," I said, listening as the chatter grew louder and more excited.

"Yeah, no. Eugene from the firehouse just offered up the barn at the end of Main Street. You just planned a barn dance and you didn't even know it."

I laughed, loving that they'd gotten so carried away. "I take it I'm officially hired, then?"

"You brought charts. They love charts. You're hired." He nodded, draping an arm around me and tucking me into his side. And as I watched, I could feel a sense of belonging, feeling a part of something even though I'd been here only twice.

If I could capture that feeling, I'd be able to sell this place to even the most cynical.

While I was woolgathering, Chad had waved someone over and was waiting to introduce me.

"Natalie Grayson, this is Archie Bryant, of the Bryant Mountain House."

"Ms. Grayson, nice to meet you. I'm sorry I missed the beginning of your presentation, but I'd love to talk to you about your plans for bringing additional tourist revenue into the town, and hopefully up to our mountain, as well."

"Nice to meet you, too, Mr. Bryant. I've heard wonderful things about your resort; I can't wait to come for a tour." I shook his hand, looking up into deep indigo eyes. Paired with wavy auburn hair and a handsome face, Archie Bryant was good-looking in an almost old-fashioned way. "I've done a bit of research already on your hotel. It's been in your family for five generations, right?"

"I'm the fifth," he replied, an expression of pride crossing his strong, elegant features. "Call my office anytime; I'm happy to arrange a tour for you when you're able to come up."

"That'd be wonderful," I agreed, thanking him for coming and wondering again what the hell was in the water that made these men so damn good-looking.

"I hope you can drive some traffic up there," Chad said as Archie began shaking hands and chatting with some of the other business owners from town. He seemed to know everyone, seemed friendly enough, but there was something a bit reserved about him. Not quite chilly, but certainly on the cool side.

"Oh, have they been slow?"

"Yep, my niece works the phones in their reservations department, and they're having some trouble keeping the rooms filled."

"Are you kidding? The pictures I've seen are gorgeous!" I'd Googled Bryant Mountain House while doing my initial information gathering on tourist destinations in and around Bailey Falls, and this place was stunning. Perched on a glacial lake and cut into the side of a mountain, it was epic.

And built in a different time, for a different era, when people vacationed differently.

Hmm . . . I wondered if I could bring in my friend Clara to consult . . .

The meeting went on for another hour or so, with me fielding questions about this and that, me asking questions about this and that, getting a feel for the pulse of this town and its DNA. And as things finally wound down and Trudy began ushering everyone out so she could get going on the lunch service, I felt the air change in the room. Every molecule in my body froze, then turned toward the front door.

Oscar had arrived.

I'd wondered if he was going to show up. He was a business owner, he had a stake in how things went in this town, and he was a responsible and upstanding, if somewhat grouchy, member of this community, so it made sense that he should be here.

Plus I'd worn a pencil skirt just for him. And since he'd been inside me only a week before and chanting my name, wasn't it only natural he'd want to show up and see how cute I looked?

People waved when they saw him, others slapped him on the back as they left. His eyes never left mine. It was unlike any other feeling, having those deep gray-blue eyes fixated solely on me. I could tell he appreciated the heels and the way they shaped my calves. The skirt alone earned a tick from that scarred eyebrow. His nostrils flared as I knew they would when he spied the carefully unbuttoned button-down, and I could feel down to my toes how much he was thinking about popping the rest of those buttons and going to town.

He walked toward me, and the diner disappeared. I couldn't hear the waitresses cackling with Roxie's mom, I couldn't hear the orders being called out. I was vaguely aware of "I Can't Get Next to You" playing on the jukebox, and my brain granted me exactly one second of mental clarity to acknowledge that the song was perfect for this moment before slipping back into appreciation for a slow-walking Oscar.

He walked like he was in a Michael Bay film, striding across the tarmac to save the world from a rogue asteroid or kamikaze fighter planes. I could only stop and watch and admire the pretty.

Wearing faded jeans, scuffed work boots, a holey old off-white Irish sweater with big cable knits, just the edge of a white T-shirt peeking out of the collar, he was right off the pages of *Fuck Off He's Beautiful* monthly. He *could* have been wearing clown shoes and a sandwich board that said Eat at Joe's for all I cared, because what really made me gulp in air faster than I could actually breathe it was his face.

He might be the best-looking man on the planet. On any planet. His hair was tied back in his usual leather wrap, which accentuated the cheekbones, the jaw, the strong brow, the full, kissable lips. But what was most striking today was the measured joy. He was obviously happy to see me, but he was working to hide it somewhat, allowing only bits and pieces of it to show through. Wanting to hold something back, perhaps? I could understand that. It was early in whatever this was, to be showing every card. But I enjoyed the fact that he was happy to see me.

And once more, he surprised me. Before I could say hello or ask what he thought of the meeting, he slung one big arm around my shoulder, grabbed my bag and put it over his other shoulder, and said, "Let's go make some cheese."

In the history of romantic opening lines, it probably wouldn't make anyone's top-ten list, but it was music to my ears.

Chapter 13

He opened the passenger door to his truck, and once he had me tucked inside, he went around to his own door. Score another point for being a gentleman. Inside, he turned the key in the ignition, pulled out of the parking lot, and headed in the direction of his place. All of this he did with his right hand firmly on my thigh, which he'd exposed almost immediately by pushing up my black tweed pencil skirt. It was luxurious, the ease he had with touching my body so freely, and the slightest bit possessively? Hmm . . . caveman.

"So, hi," I offered.

He shot me a brief side glance. "Hi."

Silence. Driving. Silence.

"Good week?"

"Good week," he stated.

I was unable to take my eyes from the sight of his hand on my leg. Had I planned this when I picked out a skirt this morning? Not purposefully. Had I wondered, however, when I was standing in front of my overnight bag this morning and looking at the black peep-toe Manolos with the sparkly jewels, if I did happen to see Oscar today, would they drive him crazy?

You bet your sweet ass . . .

"So you had a good week. That's great. I did, too. So . . . thanks for asking."

"I didn't ask," he said, keeping his eyes on the road, but his fingers slid half an inch higher on my thigh—his caramel skin on my Irish cream—and I felt myself growing more and more excited. I was also growing more and more irritated that he wasn't at all interested in having even the most cursory of conversations with me, when he finally looked my way. "But I'm glad to hear it."

My ears pinked up, I could feel it.

He continued. "I was distracted all week. I thought about you, thought about when I might see you again."

"You did?" I asked, trying like hell not to squeak out the words but failing miserably. My cheeks pinked up, I could feel it.

"Mmm-hmm," he said, sliding that hand north another inch. "Thought about those sounds you made, how sexy you looked." He stopped at a railroad crossing and looked me straight in the eye. "In the barn."

"Oh," I managed, not even bothering to squelch the squeak. Something else pinked up, I could *feel* it.

"You here till Sunday again?" he asked, the railroad light flashing. Vaguely, I could hear a *ding-dong ding-dong* from the signal . . .

"Uh-huh." This time I sounded like I smoked eight packs of cigarettes a day.

The lights stopped flashing. The dinger quit donging. And I was lost in those smoldering eyes, which were touched by a bit of happy. "Good," he said, all heat and smooth and sweet and rough at the same time.

"Good," I repeated, reaching down and sliding his hand up another inch.

"Holy shit, you weren't kidding."

"What did you think I meant, when I said let's go make some cheese?"

"I thought we'd be wrapping those cute little Bries that I buy from you, in the sweet blue and white gingham paper?"

Oscar had driven me back to his farm. Over the hill and beyond some of the pastures was a large secondary barn proudly bearing the name Bailey Falls Creamery over the entryway.

"No way, Pinup. We're making cheddar today."

This was it! This was my dream, the secret dream tucked away in the back of a kitchen cupboard in the form of cutout pictures of sweet cows and rolling hills and cardigans.

"I'm not really dressed for cheese making, am I?"

He popped out of his side and made his way to the passenger door. Tugging it open, he held out his hand and I slid on out, landing close enough to him that he'd be required to catch me. He lifted his eyebrows, knowing full well what I'd done as he caught me around the waist and set me right.

"Doesn't matter. You seemed to do okay in my boots last weekend, didn't you?" He winked and led me around toward the back of the truck. By my hand! "Besides, we've always got smocks and hairnets for visitors."

Hairnets?

Oh yeah, hairnets. Within fifteen minutes of my arrival at Bailey Falls Creamery, which had always sounded quaint and darling and maybe just the tiniest bit Dickensian, I was beginning to realize that cheese making, even artisanal hipster made-by-the-hottest-man-imaginable cheese making, was an industrialized kind of operation with sterile, stainless-steel troughs, drains in the floors, and tables that looked right out of the movie *Saw*.

The "shed" that I'd observed was huge! Room after room of all kinds of equipment, not to mention several "caves," where the cheese was aged. Another concept I'd Disneyfied in my mind. Although an actual French Roquefort would only be called a Roquefort if aged in the actual caves where the bacteria is naturally present to create its beautiful, pungent beauty, most cheeses these days apparently are aged in noncave caves: climate- and humidity-controlled environments where cheeses can age and mellow over time, and be turned occasionally by the cheese maker.

And my personal cheese maker had an entire team of cheese makers. A few full-timers, some part-timers that looked like local high school kids, and interns from the Culinary Institute up the road in Hyde Park. Bailey Falls Creamery was quite the operation.

I was given a fifty-cent tour, basically a brisk walk-through end to end, before being brought back to the first room. The enormous stainless-steel trough was waiting for milk, which I'd learned was not only from Oscar's herd, but from several other dairy farms in the area. Only pasture-raised, only organic, only happy, humanely treated cows got to bring their milk to his creamery.

He watched happily as the milk spilled into the trough. Three women stood at the ready, stainless-steel paddles in hand, waiting for the milk to get to the right temperature.

"Fantastic, I can't wait to see how the magic happens!" I cried, clapping my hands. I looked around and saw a low bench over by the window. "Should I go ahead and sit over there? Don't want to get in the way," I said, starting for the bench.

"Natalie," a low voice called out softly, and I turned to see Oscar. Holding his paddle. Ungh.

"Yes?" I asked, just as softly.

"Here's your hairnet," he said, throwing me what looked like a handful of old hosiery.

"You're adorable." I laughed and began to turn away once more when I felt a hand on my shoulder.

"Put on the hairnet, and the smock, and the boots, and meet me back here in five minutes."

I blinked back at him. "You're kidding."

"You better get a move on," he warned, not at all kidding. But just when I was about to tell him where he could stick his paddle, I saw the twinkle in his eye.

Country boy tries to show the city girl she can't cut the mustard. Hmph.

I snatched the smock, and the boots, and the godforsaken hairnet, and met his challenging gaze with a toss of my hair. I'd call his bluff, no problem. "Should I take everything off and just wear the smock, or . . . ?" I looked at him innocently, opening the top button on my fitted black oxford.

"Over your clothes is fine," he replied through clenched teeth.

I heard the women over by the tub giggle.

"Be right back," I sang out, heading for the restroom. Inside, I stared at the hairnet.

I'd better get to take home some cheddar . . .

It turns out I look fucking fantastic in a hairnet. I piled all my hair up on top of my head, popped the net on, but off to the side in a jaunty fashion, touched up my siren-red lipstick, and I was ready to paddle some cheddar. I plodded out in my shapeless smock and Oscar's boots, with a grand smile, and was pleased when I saw him scan the length of my leg now visible beneath the smock.

I had, in fact, taken off the clothes underneath. Because I was hot . . .

"Okay, Caveman, show me how you make your wares," I announced, rolling up my sleeves and trying to take the paddle away from him.

"Not so fast. You'll watch first, then you can go to work on that tub over there."

"Whatever," I replied, playing along. I stood off to the side with Oscar and watched as the three women worked on the first trough.

"So when the milk is the right temperature, they add the rennet. In this tub over here, they've already done that. See how when she slices into it, it almost looks like it's set up a bit? Now it's ready for the next step."

"Which is?" I asked, conscious of his elbow touching mine. He was, too, because he bumped me with his.

"Remember Little Miss Muffet?"

"I should probably tell you now that if you're going to call a spider over to sit down beside me, you're also going to want to hold tight to your balls, because—"

"Good lord, woman," he interrupted, furrowing his brow—while also surreptitiously dropping his hands protectively. "What the hell kind of fairy tales did you read when you were a kid? They're separating the curds from the whey."

"Oh! Sure, sure, that part." I sighed, relaxing back once more. And as we watched, the woman walked up and down the length of the tub, pulling along a steel contraption that almost looked a little like a small handheld rake, except with only a few teeth. Almost immediately, you could see that when it cut into the jiggly white mass, tiny pieces began to form, suddenly floating in a sea of yellowish-white liquid.

I wasn't aware that I was crinkling my nose until he bumped

me once more with his elbow. "What's the matter, not quite what you were expecting?"

"No." I sniffed. "It's quite interesting. Very much so." It looked disgusting. And now that it looked disgusting, I became aware of a somewhat strange odor in the air. It wasn't rancid or spoiled; the place was spotless, for goodness' sake. But there was a definite . . . funk. Funk I liked, especially when I was enjoying a really good piece of Maytag blue at the end of a long day with a few figs and some honey. But this funk was all around me, and I wasn't really liking it.

"Okay, your turn!" Oscar said, tugging me by the elbow to the untouched third tub, obviously my introduction to the world of cheese making.

"Fabulous," I said, smiling wide as I approached the milky-white substance. Not at all what cheese making had represented in my head for so many years. Where were the artfully scarred wooden tables, the crooked yet charming slate floor, the barn cats cleaning their faces prettily in the window while waiting for a bowlful of cream?

Not here. But Oscar was still smiling, and looked so proud. "Go ahead, see if it's ready. If it is, when you slice into it, it'll give, but it won't be mushy. You'll be able to make a clean slice, but it'll still fall back on itself," Oscar said, handing me a little curved spatula.

"Fabulous," I repeated, the smell stronger here. I'd once gone to Coney Island when I was a kid and eaten three Nathan's hot dogs followed by a tall glass of milk. Two spins on the Wonder Wheel later and I'd honked it all up. I wasn't really a fan of hot dogs or milk after that, and this . . . precheese . . . had a similar warm smell. But when I looked over at Oscar, he seemed curious to see what I'd do, so I tried to remember what they'd done at the tub we'd just watched.

Initially, before slicing it, she'd poked it. So I poked it. It jiggled slightly. I poked it again. Same thing. It sort of sprang back, almost like a panna cotta or flan texture.

Now I never wanted either of those desserts again.

I started to poke it a third time, when Oscar leaned in behind me, and with his mouth right beneath my ear, and my hairnet, said, "Are you going to poke it all day, or are you going to do something with it?"

Stifling every witty retort I had flying through my brain in that instant, I took a deep breath and stuck in my little spatula. He was right, it wasn't mushy, and a clean slice fell back from the blade.

"Looks like it's ready to go," I said, handing it back to him and starting to turn for the door.

"Whoa whoa whoa, city girl, we've still got a ton of work to do," he called.

"We do?" I asked, silently begging for fresh air, any air, any air sans funk.

"Unless you're too soft to do a country day's work," he said, his voice literally dripping with challenge.

I turned on my heel and marched straight back to him, poking my spatula in his chest. "Bring it, Caveman," I whispered, then stuck my empty hand straight out to the side. Picking up her cue perfectly, one of the other women tossed a rake thingie and I caught it in midair.

I worked hard that day. I raked cheese, I salted, I paddled, I pounded, I flipped, I shaped, and I hooped. I washed rinds, flipped rounds, scraped mold, injected mold, rotated molds, and damn near threw up about a hundred times. And through it all, sassing and teasing me, but also educating me, was Oscar. He knew every aspect of his little cheese world, and he was free with both knowledge and comebacks.

I laughed my ass off all day, but I must admit, nothing smelled as good as the clean fresh air at the end of the day, when he finally let me go outside to scruff around a bit.

"Sweet, sweet air, let me eat you," I shouted, running past him when he finally pronounced it was quitting time.

"You'll get used to the funk," he teased, taking off his own hairnet (which looked almost as good on him as it did on me) and scratched at his hair, extra curly after cooking under the nylon all day.

"I wouldn't count on it. I'll be lucky to ever eat Comté again! You may have ruined me." I sighed, sucking in big gulps of the fresh air. I was feeling a little queasy. Cheese making was long, backbreaking work, and I'd never take it for granted again.

I also might need to modify my Dream Cupboard to reflect less cheese making and more cheese eating. Fingers crossed. Because right now, the last thing I wanted was—

"Oh, I almost forgot. Since I can't really pay you for today, I've got a surprise." From behind his back, he pulled out a paper bag with Bailey Falls Creamery stamped on the outside, with the signature blue and white gingham wrapping peeking out from inside. "Your favorite Brie."

I threw up on his boots. The ones *I* was wearing, luckily . . .

❧

"I threw up on your boots."

"You sure did."

"I mean, my God, I threw up on your boots! For fuck's sake, how embarrassing!" I moaned, covering my face with the damp towel he'd brought me. One thought about Brie, the tiniest whiff, and out came the pancakes from earlier that morning. I could just die.

After making sure I wasn't about to barf again, he'd driven me to his house, and tucked me into a rocking chair on the front porch with a glass of water and the cool towel.

"I don't even know what happened! It was just, like, no more funk."

"It happens."

He said everything in that matter-of-fact, easygoing way. I'd thrown up all over the place, and he took it in stride as though I'd just dropped a bag of pretzels or something.

Was that his game? Acting like nothing bothered him, no skin off my nose, nothing was a big deal? Was not playing games his game?

Before I could ruminate on this for very long, the wind shifted and I got a strong whiff of . . .

"P to the U," I groaned, pinching my nose.

"You get used to it. They're just cows."

I shook my head. "No, it's me. I'm downwind of me, and all I can smell is vomit. I need to get back to Roxie's so I can shower."

He rocked back and forth on his heels, seeming to ruminate on something himself. "I've got a shower here. I've even got some flowery soap that girls like."

"Oh, you do, do you?" I asked. Was it left over from Missy? Hell, who gives a shit? "What kind of soap do *you* use?"

"Lava."

"Of course you do." I sighed, stretching out in the rocking chair, not feeling sick at all anymore. "I suppose I *could* shower here. It does present a problem, though."

"Problem?"

"Mmm-hmm. I'll be naked. And you won't be."

He shook his head. "I must not have been clear. If you're showering, I'm showering."

My skin tingled. "That makes sense. Water conservation, being a good host—all those things."

"Plus, you'll be naked. And wet."

I blinked. "Why are we still talking about this, instead of doing it?"

∾

I stood in his bathroom, letting the water warm up while brushing my teeth with my finger and then swishing with half a bottle of Scope I'd found in the medicine chest. I rinsed once more, just as the steam was starting to fog up the mirror. It was an old-fashioned bathroom, with a makeshift shower suspended over a claw-foot tub, which I'd bet someone's last dollar was original to the house.

I never bet with my own money.

He knocked at the door just as I was slipping out of my clothes, and I turned to look at him over my shoulder as he peeked his head around, his eyes covered with his hands.

"You decent?"

"Far from it," I replied.

His answering grin was slow and sweet. He uncovered his eyes just as I let my smock hit the floor, and I loved the way they lit up at the sight of me, naked and ready for the shower.

"Nice," he murmured.

I did love how he said exactly what was on his mind.

"Did you have this in mind when you asked me over here today?" I asked.

He closed the door, stepped toward me, then pulled his shirt off over his head. "You mean, when I invited you over to teach you how to make cheese only so you could vomit on me? All in the hopes of getting you naked and wet in my shower?"

I narrowed my eyes at him. "I knew it."

He unzipped his jeans, pushed them down, and stepped out of them, leaving him as naked as I was, but with one beautiful difference.

"You're hard." I gulped.

"I've been hard all damn day." And with that he lifted me straight up and over the edge of the tub, under the spray of the water.

"That must have been terrible," I teased as he closed the pink rose shower curtain around us. "I like the flowers, by the way."

"What flowers?"

"On the curtain?" I shook my head as he gathered up handfuls of my hair and dipped them under the water. "We're kind of surrounded by them."

"I don't see anything but you right now, Pinup." And then his mouth was on me, leaning down and pressing kisses all along my neck, my throat, my jaw, as the water spilled down over both of us. I could feel him against my stomach, hard and thick. And he'd been hard all day?

It got me hot because the idea that someone like Oscar, all giant Paul Bunyan guy, was thinking about me all day, was intoxicating. "Did you really think about me today?"

"Mm-hm," he said, his voice hot on my skin. I could feel his breath moving across my skin. "I thought about you all week."

"You could have called me."

"I didn't have your number." He tipped my head back under the water, saturating my hair. Filling his hands with shampoo, he began to work up a lather.

"Roxie would have given it to you."

"True," he said, massaging my head with strong and sure fingertips. "But then you would have known I was gonna call you."

"And that's bad?" I sputtered, just as he thrust his hips against mine.

"I knew you'd be back."

Humph. Cheeky.

"Now close your eyes." He brought my hands to my hair, encouraging me to rinse the bubbles out.

I did, leaning back and feeling the suds wash away, smoothing my long hair back and making sure there were no tangles. He knew I'd be back. How cocky was this guy? How did he know that—

He put his mouth on me. *Ohhhh.*

He put his mouth on me *there*.

My eyes flew open to look down, down between my legs, where a beautifully wet Oscar was kneeling, kissing, licking my sensitive skin. His tongue delved deep and I shivered, slapping at the shower tile, slapping at his shoulders, trying to get purchase on anything that could ground me while his mouth surrounded me with the sweetest kind of torture there is.

One hand slid up the back of my leg, opening me further, snaking around my knee and lifting it to the edge of the tub, exposing me fully to him, to whatever he wanted to see or touch or taste.

"Oh. Yes," I cried out, as he flicked his tongue against my clit, his shoulder pushing my legs wider as he panted against me, his mouth open and wet and hot and . . .

there

there

there

right

exactly

there . . .

"Oscar," I groaned, feeling his late-afternoon stubble scrape

against my sensitive skin, too much and not enough all at once
and wrapped together and

there

there

there

fuck

there

oh

yes

there.

And I exploded.

"There she is," he moaned, licking and sucking and letting
me ride it out as he held me up. And as soon as I was boneless
and noodly, he scooped me up, wet and slippery, and carried me
to his bed.

I tried to wrap my arms around him, tried to get them to
work, but I was still shaking, still shivering as he rose over me.
Dimly I saw him rolling the condom on. Dimly I saw him wrapping my legs around his waist. Dimly I heard him grunt as he
twisted, pushing into me with words like *so tight* and *so beautiful*
and *fuck that's good.*

Finally I lifted my hips to meet his thrusts, wild and rough.
He hovered over me, stretching his glorious body across me,
those colors on his chest and arms flashing as he gazed down at
me, all eyebrow scar and biting down on his lower lip and spilling down those gorgeous words all over me.

He held my hip in one hand, my breasts in the other, running his fingertips over the taut peaks and teasing. Then his
mouth was on me again, on my breasts, using that same tongue
and those same teeth that had coaxed that wild orgasm from me
just moments ago to make me scream again at the exquisite feel
of him sucking at me.

Sucking and fucking and biting and scratching as my nails scored his back, determined to bring him deeper into me, which was impossible, as his thrusts alone were ready to split me in two and it was *still not enough*.

"You. Again." His brief words spoke volumes as he dragged one hand down between us, licking his fingers, then sliding them against me, knowing already exactly how I liked to be touched.

My back bowed off the bed as I came again, ridiculously loud and long and fierce, him following only a moment after, his own groans filthy and primal.

He collapsed onto me, his head on my breast, my arms and legs wrapped around him as I held him to me. And we panted heavily, a shuddering pile of "sweet fuck, that was good."

∽∾

Oscar's house was old and rustic, with wide-plank floors, wainscoting, beadboard—all the architectural details you'd look for in such an old farmhouse. He'd told me it wasn't nearly as old as the barn but still from the last century, and had been in the family he'd purchased the farm from for generations. It had the requisite farmhouse sink, the farmhouse kitchen table, the Franklin stove in the corner, and even an old outhouse hidden behind a stand of old trees.

And there were things all over the place that just didn't look like Oscar. A series of framed pictures depicting black-and-white-spotted cows shopping for groceries, mowing the lawn, and look, here's one of the cows playing poker. In the hallway bathroom there were tiny cow figurines dancing down the counter, black-and-white-cow-printed wallpaper, and little paper Dixie cups with—you guessed it—black-and-white cows.

And hung over every single doorway were sprays of dried

flowers. You know the kind: dusty eucalyptus, big sunflowers, mauve roses; gathered together with raffia, and tied into a big floppy bow.

None of these things looked like something Oscar would have paid money for, much less walked around his house and deliberated which he'd put where.

They looked suspiciously Missy-like.

∽

We'd returned downstairs after the shower, and I'd made a bee-line for the giant comfy couch in the family room. Wrapped in a fluffy blanket from the back of the couch, I'd made a little nest for myself. Once I was settled, Oscar tucked himself behind me, his head pillowed on my behind. His sigh of contentment made me smile broadly.

There was something good about a guy who liked a big, comfy butt.

"Hungry?" Oscar asked, his voice a bit muffled.

My stomach rumbled. "I'm famished." I'd texted Roxie earlier, letting her know where I was and not to worry. She texted me back that the key was under the mat, to have fun, and to use a condom. That's a good friend.

"I don't have much to eat in the house," he said, running his hand absently along my bum. "Want to go into town? There's a great pizza place on Main Street."

"Great pizza, huh? I'm from New York, sweetie. You can't say such things to me."

"We're in New York," he said, lifting his head.

"You're adorable," I replied, patting it sweetly. "Gimme a few minutes to get dressed, and you can take me out for pretty good pizza."

"I'll make you eat those words, City Girl," he growled as I

jumped off the couch and danced out of reach of his grabby hands.

"I'll make you eat something else," I teased, relishing the look I got in return. Then I gasped when I saw how fast he could move—he was already halfway across the room with a devilish expression.

His playful attack stopped when his phone rang. Like any new "friend that was a girl," I motioned to him that I was heading into the kitchen for my purse . . . and then I stood right around the corner and listened in.

Though I could only hear his side of the conversation, I could make out most of what was going on.

"What's up? . . . Again? . . . I'm telling you, that thing needs to be replaced . . . no, not a problem . . . nope, nothing that can't be postponed . . . sure . . . twenty minutes . . . no, I'll pick something up on the way . . . yep . . . yep . . . on my way."

By the time he walked into the kitchen, I was nonchalantly sitting at the farmhouse table, twisting my damp hair up into a bun and admiring his black-and-white cow-shaped salt and pepper shakers.

"Gotta take a rain check on pizza, is that okay?"

"Sure, everything okay?" I replied, swiping on a coat of fresh red lipstick and looking unconcerned.

"Yeah, just gotta go take care of something," he said, reaching for his coat and shrugging it on. "Can I drop you back at Roxie's?"

"That'd be great," I said lightly, and meant it. This was new and exciting, sure, but *new* was the operative word. Play this one too clingy, and it could crumble before it even became anything.

But as he held my jacket open and helped me put it on, I

planted a surprise deep, searing kiss on him, letting myself get lost in our combined warm scent.

"Oops, look at that!" I pulled away, leaving him panting and looking a bit wild. "I got some lipstick on you—let me fix that." I took a tissue from my purse and quickly dabbed it around with a laugh. He chuckled along with me, clearly grateful that I'd cleaned him up.

Which I did—a bit.

When he dropped me off at Roxie's, I made him call me so I'd have his number.

"Now I can text you dirty words whenever I want to," I teased as he held open my door once more, catching me on the way down.

"Don't send me anything too dirty until midmorning. I'm driving in for the farmers' market," he explained, his hands lingering on my waist. "And if I'm thinking about you, I'm liable to drive right off the highway."

"Of course," I replied, reaching down to tangle my fingers with his.

"When are you heading back home?"

"Not until Sunday."

"I'll text you when I get back tomorrow, see what you're up to?"

I wanted more than anything else to say *That sounds great, and then maybe we can have more of the naked.*

But what I said was, "I've got a pretty full day, sightseeing with Chad and Logan, and meeting some more business owners who couldn't make it this morning." All true, and all decidedly *un*clingy.

I didn't kiss him again when he dropped me off at Roxie's, making a joke about my red lipstick. But he kissed me; on my neck, under my ear, on my nose, on each eyelid, and the center of my collarbone, his breath tickling at my skin as it bloomed frosty and white in the chilly air.

When I said good-bye and waved him back into the car, breathless and silly, I snuck a last glance at his lips, and checked that there was still a noticeable lipstick stain . . .

Rain check, indeed.

Chapter 14

"I love that *that* is what you're wearing for a walking tour," Logan said when I opened Roxie's front door. He laughed, motioning to my wedge-heeled boots.

"What? Chad said boots," I rebuffed, pointing a toe forward. I waved a hand at his getup. "Are we stopping by Lands' End for a catalogue shoot?"

"Har-har. Let's get moving."

"Where's your equally gorgeous other half?" I asked, looking around him to see the porch and car empty of Chad. Logan smoothed his hair back, giving me a view of those damn cheekbones. Good Lord. I'd only seen them together, as some kind of Gorgeous Team. But Logan was the kind of good-looking that stood on its own. "He's ordering at the coffee shop while I fetched you."

With Oscar in the city, selling his wares and getting his swoon on (I was under no illusion that I was the only one in his line swooning), I was heading out with Chad and Logan to see the must-sees and -do's of Bailey Falls. It was something that I'd been meaning to do, but when given the choice between spending free time being pranced through town or being bundled up in warm dairy farmer . . . not so much of a choice.

The tour would afford me incredible insider information—and not to mention uninterrupted time with my two new favorite guys.

By the time we pulled in front of the café, I was as in love with Logan as I was with his husband. We parked and were joined by Chad, carrying a few bags and a tray of coffee.

"Is it coffee or tar?" I asked warily, sniffing the cup, grateful when he assured me that it was the former.

We air-kissed quickly before he planted a solid one on his husband. In the middle of the town square on a Saturday morning, while families of all kinds passed by on the crowded sidewalk. Another mark in the plus column for Bailey Falls, and one worth mentioning. Having a place city couples could escape to in the country, and still enjoy their lifestyle without scorn and scuffle, was something I felt very happy to be selling.

"So, where are we off to first?" I asked around a mouthful of banana nut muffin.

Chad handed his coffee to his husband and pulled out a list from his pocket.

1. Stroll through town
2. Bryant Mountain House
3. The Tube

"The Tube?" I asked, raising an eyebrow.

"Swimming hole."

"I don't have a suit. And it's a bit nippy." I thrust my chest out to further cement the idea.

"Trust me," Chad insisted.

"And we're doing this by foot?" I asked, seriously rethinking my choice of footwear.

"Mostly," Logan said knowingly. "We've got a carriage taking us up to Bryant."

Oh, thank God.

"Where are we starting?"

Chad pulled out his keys and unlocked his car. Grabbing a camera bag, he said, "We're getting more of those photos that you wanted for the campaign around town first. Then heading up to Bryant to tour the grounds."

We finished our quick breakfast and started out. The town was just opening up its shutters on a lazy, cool Saturday morning. Chad and Logan walked beside me, answering any questions I had about a business or a townsperson. With the sunlight coloring the town just right, we stopped every few feet to take a photo. Some were just signs; others were of the owners in the doorways. Anything to illustrate just how special this town was.

By the time we reached the pickup spot for the carriage, I was happy to sit.

Bryant Mountain House was as much a part of this community as anything else around here. One of the original Catskills resorts, it was built back in the mid-1800s when city folk were beginning to realize the benefit of traveling out to the country and "taking the air." Built into the mountain, the place had every amenity that a vacationing New Yorker would need. I took notes in my phone as they gave me its history, and I sent myself a text to make a reservation for a few nights to see what the fuss was all about.

On the way back down the mountain, we stopped so I could change my shoes before heading over to The Tube.

"It's a little cold for us to skinny-dip. Or are you two going to hop in and give me a show while I stay warm on the shore watching?"

Logan laughed. "You wish."

It didn't hurt to ask.

We traversed the hill down to the swimming hole, following

the voices. We found a few groups of people situated around the water, picnicking. It wasn't until I was at the shoreline that I realized just how big this place was. I'd assumed that the "swimming hole" was going to be an actual tiny hole, but I couldn't have been more wrong. It was an oasis, canopied by trees, shielded from everything man-made.

Chad pulled out a blanket large enough for eight people and spread it on an empty patch of grass. Then we sat and just stared out into the water.

"This is great," I murmured, turning my face up to the sun. The area was large enough that despite the other people, it was quiet and peaceful. "What is it about trickling water that makes you just want to curl up and take a nap?" I asked, closing my eyes and leaning back. It was soothing. I could almost feel the water sliding over me.

I opened my eyes when I heard the first click and saw Chad standing over me, taking my picture. "Oh no, mister. I'm not going to be in the campaign. Let me take one of you two snuggled up by that big ol' tree."

"Are you kidding? You looked gorgeous. Very Zen. What better sales pitch for crazy busy New Yorkers than to see one of their own totally zoned out?"

He had a point.

I let him click away while I soaked up the autumnal sun, happy to be in the middle of nowhere.

This town was killing me.

∽∽

The day was very fruitful but long, and by the time we finished up at the swimming hole, I was plumb tuckered out. So the boys took me back to their place for tea and cookies.

"Your home is beautiful," I remarked, sitting in their warm and cozy kitchen as they bustled about.

"Thank you! It took some work, but it was worth it," Logan said.

"Some work? It took a shit ton of work," Chad exclaimed by the stove, waiting for the teakettle to whistle. "But yes, totally worth it."

I could tell. On the main drag in town, it was a restored Victorian complete with a turret and widow's walk. Inside, several of the walls had been removed and doorways widened, creating a much more open, livable space. Painted in creamy whites and muted grays, with pops of teal and aquamarine scattered throughout, it was a very sweet home. And big!

"How many bedrooms do you have here?" I asked as Chad poured water into a teapot.

"Five, but one is an office," he answered.

"And the turret room is a second office, on the third floor," Logan chimed in.

"A big house for just two boys. Planning a family?" I asked as the first swirls of chamomile came wafting through the air. The two exchanged glances. "Sorry, too personal? Feel free to tell me to shut it—I always stick my nose in where I probably shouldn't."

"No, no, it's not that. We're trying to make some decisions about exactly that. Lots of pressure, you know," Logan said, setting down a plate of shortbread. "Everyone has an opinion on when and how."

"Don't talk to my mother, then," I said, leaning over and grabbing my own cookie. "If she had her way, everyone would have kids—several of them. The gays, the straights, the singles, the mingles, everyone breeding round the clock."

"That's exactly like my mom!" Chad rolled his eyes. "You buy a house, and as soon as the housewarming presents stop, the baby talk begins.

"When exactly *is* that happening, by the way?" Logan asked, slapping at Chad's hand as he tried to snatch a cookie.

"Longer than you think, if you keep trying to bogart the shortbread," Chad answered promptly, dodging another slap successfully and biting into butter heaven. "Fuck me, these are good. Roxie?" he asked, little shortbread crumbs puffing out.

"Roxie," Logan said, nodding. "You went through all the trouble to get that cookie, you should consider keeping some of it in your mouth." He leaned across and immediately began wiping up Chad's puffs.

"Quiet, you," Chad warned, lifting the lid off the teapot and calling it good. Pouring a round for all three of us, he carried a tray loaded down with cream and sugar, and more of the shortbread cookies, into the living room at the front of the house.

From that vantage point, nearly all of Maple Street, only a block south of Main, was visible. Pumpkins on every porch, leaves raked into tidy but very jumpable piles in every front lawn, golden retrievers being walked by adorable children as far as the eye could see.

"Was that a good sigh or a bad sigh?" Logan asked.

"Hmm?"

"You sighed. Good or bad?"

"Good sigh. For sure, a good sigh."

"Pleasantly tired, perhaps?" Logan asked. Both of them leaned forward slightly, and I got the vaguest impression of two mountain lions fixing on their prey, just before they jumped.

"Well, you two did drag me all over creation and back," I said.

"Of course, a busy day with us. But any . . . other reason you might be feeling a little . . . tired?" Chad asked.

Hmm, maybe mountain lion was the wrong spirit animal here. Vultures perhaps? Really sexy vultures? "Ask what you want to ask, I have no secrets," I replied, sipping at the good hot tea.

"Word on the street is you've been seen coming and going from Bailey Falls Creamery, usually wearing boots belonging to a certain kids' football coach. Care to comment?" Logan asked.

"I do like boots." I grinned, extending my current kicks for inspection. New Manolos, slouchy suede, Alaska gray. Paired with black cashmere leggings and a fluffy pink Mohair sweater I'd found in a Chelsea vintage store—I felt extra cute today.

"Oh, she's as bad as Roxie was when she and Leo started *shtupping*," Chad said, giving me a firm look. "Okay, it's like this. If we guess the dish, then it's not really dish—got it?"

"I haven't the foggiest idea what you're talking about," I said innocently, giving him my best Cheshire cat.

"Fair enough," Logan said, eyes twinkling. "If you don't take another cookie, that means you really did just borrow a pair of Oscar's dirty work boots—boring, boring, boring. But if you *do* take another cookie, that means that you've been . . . well . . . wearing Oscar's boots, if you know what I'm saying."

He held out the plate of cookies, looking innocent.

I waited a few seconds, then a few more, as they watched me with bated breath. Then I finally . . . reached out for a cookie.

Which I never got, because Logan was so excited that he threw his hands over his head with a roar of victory, forgetting that he was holding the shortbread.

"Oh for fuck's sake," I exclaimed, cookies raining down everywhere. "You guys need some new gossip around here!"

"You have no idea how long we have watched that poor boy

slouch around this town, speaking only in grunts and occasional one-word answers—"

"But you don't care, because he's so much fun to look at," Chad interrupted as Logan nodded vigorously.

"He is fun to look at," I admitted. "I'm still getting the one-word answers, although he's opening up. Some."

"Met the ex yet?" Chad asked.

"Yes," I said, now leaning forward in my chair. "Let's talk about that. What's going on there?"

Chad and Logan told me everything they could, which wasn't much. They'd only been married a short time when they moved into town, and they divorced within a year of that. Still appeared to be on friendly terms, based on the few times they'd been seen out in public together. And because he was as untalk-ative as he was nonsocial, no one knew much at all about Missy, or their past, or why they'd divorced. She lived in the next town over, was very sweet and nice and kind and quiet, and that was literally all they knew.

"So you've seen her?" Logan asked.

"You could say that. She came over a few Sundays back when we were there on the porch, and . . . she saw some things she probably shouldn't have."

"Details are not only appreciated, they are coveted, revered, and possibly typed up and framed. So go slow, and make it worth it," Chad instructed as they sat back to listen.

"Sorry." I liked to talk a good game in the abstract, but I rarely gave up the goods on anyone I was involved with beyond a one-nighter. And even then, names were usually changed to protect the satisfied . . .

"Okay, if you're not going to give us any tawdry tidbits about you and the dairy god, then at least tell us more about you," Logan said, determined to glean some information.

"Me? What do you want to know?"

"Start with how you got to be so fabulous, and go from there," Chad said.

"Honey, we don't have *nearly* enough time for how I got to be so fabulous. And even then, my story isn't really the kind you tell over tea, for God's sake."

A frosty bottle of vodka quickly appeared from the freezer, along with a pitcher of Bloody Mary mix and a jar of olives.

"You're like the cocktail Boy Scouts, always prepared." I chuckled, watching as three drinks were quickly assembled.

"And they'll actually let us lead a troop now!" Chad quipped, then pointed at me. "Fabulous. Go."

"I'm fabulous now, it's true." I paused to take a long sip of my cocktail. "But the perfectly pulled-together awesomeness that you see here today was not always the case. Not even *remotely* the case in junior high."

"We were all in bad shape back then," Chad said.

"Not true. Roxie has shown me her yearbooks, and you were ridiculously good-looking," I corrected.

His cheeks colored slightly. "I might have made it look easy, but believe me, there was some shit going on inside."

"It was junior high. We all had shit going on inside, and most of us were assholes sometimes." Logan moved closer on the couch to Chad.

"I don't know if I was an asshole, but I sure went to school with a bunch of them."

"Bullies?" Chad asked sympathetically.

"No, just normal kids picking on each other. Imagine this lush body"—I slid my hands down my ample frame—"on a thirteen-year-old. Now add braces, a healthy sprinkling of acne, and this smart-ass mouth."

"Recipe for junior high disaster," Logan said.

"Yes, one that extended all through high school. Though I had friends, I certainly didn't have any boyfriends."

"Me, neither," they said in tandem, making me smile.

Then my smile faded. "I'd never kissed a boy until I met Thomas." I closed my eyes, thinking back to the first time I saw him, how beautiful he was. I was waiting outside St. Francis, the private school I attended up on Seventy-fourth. My parents had hired a driver to pick me up after school, even though by my senior year I was tugging at that leash, wanting more freedom, like all teenagers do. I'd grown up in the city and knew the subway system like the back of my hand, but families like mine didn't let their kids travel around unattended—so I sat in the back of a town car like everyone else in my class, to and from school.

But traffic that day had slowed everything to an almost standstill, and as I waited around the corner, I saw him across the street, coming out of the park.

Tall, and a little bit on the gangly side, he was dressed in that simple carefree way that guys can get away with sometimes, open button-down, white undershirt, jeans that sat low on his hips, scuffed sneakers. It was the hipster beanie that got me. I had a soft spot for guys in those knit caps, their hair all messy and casual and sticking out from under like they'd just come from a warm bed.

He stood on one corner, and I on the other, and just like in the movies, our eyes met. And I couldn't pull away, even though everything about me at that time in my life was looking down, or looking away, or pulling my hair lower across my face. I rarely made eye contact with anyone for long, unless I knew them well, and even then I tended to duck and cover. But there was something about this guy; I couldn't take my eyes off him.

And then, wonder of all wonders, he actually crossed the street. Toward me! One foot in front of the other, eyes still locked with mine, and all I was aware of was that face and my heart, which was pounding in my ears. Sometime between him crossing the street at arriving at my figurative doorstep, a furtive grin crept across his face, as though he could hardly believe it himself, that this was happening, that this was occurring, that this moment was real.

"Hi," he said.

I gulped. He grinned and made it okay, made it seem perfectly natural that someone that looked like him would be talking to someone who looked like me. I tugged at my shirt, pulling at it in that way I was always forever tugging at it, to cover, to hide, to somehow trick myself into thinking that if I had an extra half inch of cotton Lycra blend pulled down lower on my hips I'd magically be pretty, instantly be thinner, finally be less than. Because I was always more than enough, and not in the good way.

He started to walk with me, not away from me, and I started to walk with him, somehow sensing that I was supposed to do that, that this beautiful guy actually wanted to walk with me.

We walked a block. Another block. By the third block, I'd said hello. By the fourth block, I knew his name. Thomas. By the sixth block, I knew he was a student at NYU, had just come from meeting some friends in the park, and did I want a Frappuccino? He knew my name, that I was a senior, that I didn't live in the neighborhood but lived downtown, and that yes, I'd love a Frappuccino.

By the time my driver called my phone for the fourth time, in a panic over what my father would do to him if he didn't pick me up immediately, I was over the moon.

As I climbed into my town car, he'd caught the edge of my shirt, tugging me back slightly. "I'd really love to call you sometime. Would that be okay? Natalie?"

He'd said my name like he was happy to know it. And as I nodded, still not quite believing this was happening, he slipped my phone out of my back pocket and quickly dialed his own number.

"Save that number, okay? That way, you'll know it's me calling." And he pushed my phone back into my pocket, slowly and deliberately, as though it was his hand caressing my too-big behind. Too big for pretty clothes, too big for the old wooden desks in the oldest part of the school, too big for anything other than ridicule and shame . . . Never a part of my body that was beautiful, or desirable.

"Bye," I whispered, and into that one word, that one whisper, I put all of my young love angst, my "never been considered, much less kissed," my "if I can make them laugh they'll hopefully never notice that I'm red-eyed and lower-lip trembly when it's prom and homecoming time"—all of that, squashed into one terribly hopeful "Bye . . . Thomas."

"Oh my," Chad said, and I blinked in surprise, brought back to the present, where Chad and Logan were clasping hands and biting their lips, dying to know what happened next.

My heart racing the way it had that day, and without even thinking, I began tugging at my sweater, pulling it down farther on my hips, shrinking inward. "Sorry," I said, shocked to hear how shaky my voice sounded even to my own ears. "I don't talk about this very often." I went to slurp my drink, and found it just ice and melted water, with the saddest little red rim around the lip.

"Another?" Logan asked, and I nodded gratefully. "For the record, I can relate to the never-been-kissed. Casanova over there was super-popular in high school, was covered in tits and pussy from the moment he hit puberty—"

"It's true. I knew I wasn't a hundred percent sure I liked guys, but I also knew that anything hot, wet, and warm felt pretty fucking great," Chad said.

I could easily imagine what a big swinging dick he was back then.

Then he looked toward the kitchen, where his equally handsome partner was fixing another round. "I've seen *your* high school yearbook, and you were smoking hot. The only reason you weren't covered in tits and pussy as well is—"

"—because I was scared to death of it. Though to be fair, I was scared of dicks, too. But I got over that pretty quickly at lifeguard camp, the summer before senior year. Stephen Tyler . . . mmmm." Logan trailed off, his eyes going all faraway.

"From *Aerosmith*?" I asked.

"From Appleton, Wisconsin. I spent the summer up there, and holy shit, could that guy use his mouth."

Chad waved him over with the drinks. "No more 'blow jobs from Stephen Tyler' stories right now—but feel free to tell me about it later, with more details. Right now I want to hear more about Natalie, and her very own *Sex and the City* stories."

I smiled ruefully. "It was more like a bad CW show than it was *Sex and the City*. But it does have the sex. And we were in the city."

And the city came alive in the company of Thomas Murray, who knew more trivia bits and factoids about Manhattan than anyone I'd ever met. One day we walked up Broadway from Fourteenth Street all the way to Columbus Circle, and he literally guided me through the history of our city as told through architecture. Thomas was planning to be an architect when he completed his master's program at NYU. In the early days of our . . . whatever it was quickly becoming, I'd spend my days pining my way through calculus and AP English composition, mentally comparing every high school boy in my class to Thomas the College Man and finding them coming up woefully short. He got to study exciting things, fields of interest that would actually lead to something, a career, a real grown-up career, while I was stuck still in high school, spinning my wheels and doodling his name all over everything that would stand still. I'd always been an A student, but for the first time ever, my grades took a dip. And if it wasn't for it being my senior year and being accepted into all three schools I'd applied to, I probably wouldn't have been allowed to see him as much.

Although my parents had no idea how much I really *was* seeing him.

The first time he kissed me was on the third floor of a townhouse my father was renovating. I'd brought him there once after school, after hearing him talk on the phone the other night for what seemed like hours about pocket doors and the architectural significance of them. I'd stolen the master key ring my father always kept inside his briefcase, told my parents I was going to study at the library (not an unheard-of thing on a Friday night, thank you very much), and told him to meet me on Seventy-sixth and Madison.

I'd never done something like this before. But I'd grown up on my dad's job sites, I knew the codes, I knew exactly how to execute this sneak attack. And when I walked Thomas inside, and he saw the breadth of the renovation my father was taking on, he was in awe.

Looking back now, it was easy to see that not only was he in awe of the townhouse, he was likely also in awe at the ease with which he'd managed to sweep the chubby and slightly lonely daughter of one of New York's prime real estate developers off her Crocs.

I certainly didn't feel lonely when he pressed me up against one of those very pocket doors I'd seduced him with, and kissed me until I was seeing stars.

And when his hands slipped around my waist, and I instinctively shrank from his hands on that part of my body, a part that no one ever touched, he tugged me tight against his torso and broke that first kiss. "You're beautiful, do you know that?"

My heart soared.

"I know most guys mind a little extra padding, but not me."

My heart soared higher.

His lips kissed a path down my jaw, stopping just below my ear, where he whispered, "Though not too much more, right?"

"Right," I answered breathlessly.

He kissed me right out of my head, and when he pushed his hand under my shirt and grazed the underside of my breast, I was certain that if he'd asked that night, I would have let him do anything he wanted to me.

But he waited. A gentleman? Sure, let's go with that.

The rest of that spring I spent with Thomas. If I wasn't physically with him, I was thinking about him, dreaming about him, mooning over him. He couldn't always be with me, of course; he had studying to do, projects to work on, and I would never think of interrupting him when he was working on his master's thesis. But when he had a break, I dropped whatever it was that I was doing to be with him. After all, as he'd pointed out numerous times, I was a senior, and really didn't need to spend as much time on my studies as he did. Last semester senior year was just a formality, right?

Until my midterm grades came in, and my B's had fallen to C's, D's, and one very upsetting F.

My parents had met Thomas by now, and while they liked him, and liked that their daughter had a boyfriend (I had a boyfriend!), they weren't crazy about me spending so much time with him. Especially after my grades came out.

A war was waged in our brownstone that day, a war that had been waging between teenagers and their parents since the dawn of time. And I was going to fight to the death to be allowed to continue to see Thomas.

For a girl whose world had been mostly observing the world happen to other people, now I was actually experiencing things, doing things, wanting and being wanted. It was intoxicating, and nothing could have stopped me from what I wanted, what I needed.

And what I needed, more than anything, was Thomas. Never mind the fact that I never once met his friends (*it's not the same as silly high school parties; my friends are all busy either studying or working their two to three jobs because not all of us were lucky enough to be born into wealthy families*), never once met his parents (*they live in New Jersey and I don't have a car, and no, you can't just take a town car everywhere*), or even went out to a nice dinner (*if we stay in, you can practice your cooking skills. I mean, really, Natalie, how can you not even know how to make toast?*).

The first time he put his hands on me, he told me how pretty I was, how soft I was, and how I should never feel bad about my body, that I just wasn't meant to look like most girls my age.

The first time he put his mouth on me, with his head between my thighs and a serious expression on his face, he told me it was natural for women to love this, and if I didn't love it, too, that maybe I should think about how lucky I was that someone was willing to do this, considering the obvious. And that even though he personally thought I had a pretty cunt, perhaps

I should visit a spa and have some of that au naturel look taken care of.

The first time he let me put my mouth on him, he told me how perfect I looked on my knees, and that he was so very glad that I'd never done this before, because he wouldn't have any bad habits to break. And for fuck's sake, he wasn't an ear of corn, to control my teeth and the urge to not gobble like I hadn't eaten in a month, which of course would never happen to someone like me.

The first time he was inside of me it didn't matter if it hurt, because that's what love was, it was supposed to hurt a little so that you knew it was true and real and worth having, and that don't worry, it will get better, and if I could figure out how to finally have an orgasm like regular girls, it wouldn't be something I'd have to think about anymore.

Looking back now, how fucking stupid was I not to see what was going on? But when you were in it, you didn't know it, and when your life had finally started to happen, it didn't matter what else you were giving up for that life. It only mattered that you were special—to someone—and that you were very lucky indeed to have that someone. And everything else should just fade away and become background noise.

Background noise like prom, which I could have finally gone to because, hello, boyfriend! But, hello, college guy, and why the hell would he go to some stupid high school prom with other stupid uppity rich kids?

Background noise like college essays, because even though I'd been preaccepted, I still had to go through the formality of being actually accepted into the schools I'd been dreaming of attending since I was in junior high and beginning to plan out my life carefully and methodically.

Background noise like my high school paper, of which I'd

been the editor, but now was lucky to get an article in every other month

. . . like my brother's birthday

. . . like my parents' anniversary

. . . like my graduation.

I missed my high school graduation, spending it naked on a mattress on my hands and knees, getting fucked in the ass by someone who told me I would absolutely love it, and if I didn't, then there must be more wrong with me than he originally thought, and that it was only because he loved me so much that he hadn't dumped me weeks ago.

If someone had told me that I would have moved out of my parents' home to go and live in a fourth-floor walk-up in the Bronx with my boyfriend, to say fuck off to my mother when she told me this was a terrible mistake, and tell my father he was an asshole when he told me college was off the table if I did this, I'd have said they were nuts.

And yet that September, when everyone I'd known since elementary school was off at Brown and Wellesley, I was standing in front of a two-burner stove, trying like hell not to burn toast because I'd never hear the end of it, wearing nothing but a plaid skirt and bra because that's how he liked me best, and wondering how much it would cost to get a new air-conditioning unit for this piece-of-crap apartment, because ours had died last night and it was *stifling* hot.

I'd never spent August in the city. We had a house in Bridge-hampton, natch. I'm not trying to play poor little rich girl, but the city was murder in the heat. And the excitement of walking away from my life to play house with Thomas was beginning to wear a little thin.

What wasn't thin was my body, something that was the center of almost every conversation I had with him. Where he used to tell me how much he loved my curves, he now told me how flabby I'd gotten, and how much everything jiggled when he was pounding into me. Which was almost every night, and every day, pounding and thrusting and thrashing and hair pulling and *get up on top like this* and *arch your back like that* and *why the hell can't you figure this out for God's sake why do I have to do everything?*

I'd been picked *on,* but I'd never been picked *apart* like this. Not by someone with love in their words, but not in their heart. I was beginning to see some cracks in his charm, in his words, in the promise of what it would be like, could be like, when it was just the two of us against the world.

Any hope he might have had of working for my father someday was gone the second my grades went in the toilet. And any hope he might have had of building great things, huge things, in the city where my father knew literally everyone at every architectural firm, every construction company, every everything that had to do with building in this incredible city of architectural beauty, was gone the second I missed my father's fiftieth birthday party to bring my boyfriend chicken soup because he was feeling under the weather, and I thought that was more important than anything.

And with his world beginning to crumble when his thesis fell apart and his advisor told him he was way off base and in danger of not getting his master's, *my* world was going to shit right along with it.

The veiled hints that I might stand to drop a few pounds here and there had become aggressively rude and crude, with handfuls of fat grabbed during angry sex. Red fingerprints on white skin that folded and crumpled when forced to sit naked, hunched over in order to see just how many rolls there were.

Do I really think that when he saw me across the street, those many months ago, that this was his plan? Maybe not. Regardless, he very likely already knew what he'd be able to get away with, considering who I was back then.

When I saw my mother for the first time since I'd moved out, she burst into tears. I couldn't cry, and not just because I was emotionally shut down, but because I literally didn't have enough water in my body to do so. I'd lost sixty pounds in four months, and was so exhausted I could barely meet her eyes.

I'd gone shopping downtown, taking the subway when Thomas was teaching his undergraduate class one afternoon and I actually had some time to myself. He was home so much more than he used to be, not making all of his lectures for some time now, staying in, with me. For the first time in a long while, I was alone, out and about, actually feeling myself relaxing for a change—coupled with exhaustion. And then she saw me, and I could see on her face just how bad I looked.

If you lose that amount of weight in that short a time, there's a slackness to the skin, a person within a person, almost. But factor in the stress, the lack of laughter, my poor health and well-being, and I knew I didn't look myself.

I let her take me home. I let her wash my face. I let her talk on and on about how much she missed me, how much she worried about me, how many times she'd tried to call me but Thomas told her I was busy. But when she tried to make me a sandwich and put some cookies on a tray, I left.

And went back to the Bronx, where Thomas was waiting for me, wondering why in the world I'd been gone so long, and shouldn't I have put on some lipstick if I was going out?

But something happened that day—even though I didn't realize it at the time. Just being in my home, with my mother, had opened the tiniest sliver of a door. She'd wept when she saw me, and she'd wept when I'd left, but she was so grateful to have seen my face, even though it was too thin and sad-looking. She was *happy* to see my face.

And Thomas? He was never happy. He used to laugh, make jokes, and tell funny stories—but that night, as I lay next to him in that fourth-floor walk-up studio where our bed was a mattress on the floor, I realized that his humor always had a slant to it, a dark edge or a mean vibe.

He never thought anything good about anything. There was always an angle, someone wanted something from him, or someone was going to try to screw him over for something, or he wasn't going to be able to get something done because someone always had something more. More money, more power, more connections. Stripped down to the naked truth, he was mean.

I used to think abuse was someone getting hit.

Now I know it's anything that makes you double over with pain, that makes you question anything and everything about yourself that you knew to be true. It's anything that tells you that you're only good *if* . . .

I felt a drop of water splash onto the back of my hand, and I realized that while telling this story, which I rarely shared with anyone, my eyes had filled with tears. Shocked, I looked up to see Chad and Logan watching me, their own eyes filled with sympathy.

"I'm so sorry." I sniffed, snatching up a napkin and wiping my face. "I don't know what happened there. Truly, I didn't mean to go on so."

"You didn't go on, it was—"

"Seriously, I'm so sorry, I never talk about that stuff, it's ancient history." I hurried on, dabbing at my nose, horrified to find that it was running. What the hell was I doing, spilling my guts to two men I just met?

"Natalie." Logan covered my hand with his. "Stop."

I looked up at him through still-teary eyes, shaking my head. "I should have never—"

"Shut the hell up and let two gorgeous men hug you," Chad interrupted, no nonsense. Surprised, I laughed, still wiping my face and knowing I must look a fright.

But I let them hug me. And I realized that sometimes strangers can make for the best company ever.

❧

When Chad and Logan dropped me off at Roxie's a while later, I felt wiped out. Emotionally drained. Wasted.

I hated revisiting that stuff, so I don't know why it all came out today in a blubbery mess in front of two people I barely knew.

I thought about Thomas from time to time, of course. Not intentionally, but sometimes he'd flash across my brain when something about old New York architecture would come up, or someone would be talking about their dissertation.

Or the time I was sitting in a booth behind some couple and the guy started telling the girl that she'd had enough to eat and she shouldn't get dessert, and by the way my mother is coming over for dinner next weekend and don't you think it's time you learned how to make a decent coffee cake?

That time was bad. I had to leave the table to hide out in the bathroom for a few minutes while I got the shaking under control, and then I had to leave the restaurant entirely when I poured a pitcher of water over that asshole's head and was asked to leave by the manager.

But not before I gave the girl all the cash I had in my wallet and my card, and told her to call me if she needed a place to stay for the night.

She never called. I knew she wouldn't. But I was glad I gave it to her.

I stood outside on Roxie's porch now, watching the taillights of Chad's car disappear into the early evening, and took a moment to banish all bad thoughts from my head. I was good at it by now; visualization was the key. I could take about ten deep, cleansing breaths, visualize Thomas's rotten stupid stinking face, and poof! Gone.

I took the breaths. Poof. I opened the front door and let myself in.

"Yo. Rox," I called out, climbing the stairs two at a time. All bad thoughts gone, I was already moving on to the night ahead and seeing my best friend.

She was just emerging from the bathroom clad in a towel, with a plume of steam following her. "Hey, girl, thanks for understanding about tonight. Sorry you had to take a cab over."

"No worries; what happened? Your texts were strange, to say the least. Something about wedding velvet?"

"Kind of. If I didn't think saying the phrase *there was a cake emergency* sounded as ridiculous as I think it does, I'd tell you about how my afternoon went."

"There was an actual cake emergency?"

She nodded. "Mr. and Mrs. Oleson's fiftieth wedding anniversary. She always bakes for him—has baked for him each anniversary for the other forty-nine. But this afternoon her oven quit on her and she needed a red velvet cake like they had on their wedding day. What was I going to do?"

"You're a good egg, Roxie. You're also dripping, by the way."

She looked down at the puddle that was forming and headed into her bedroom. "Come in, I just need to dry my hair and I'll be ready to hit the town!"

"I feel like if we actually hit the town, Bailey Falls may never recover." I snorted, taking a running leap at her bed, displacing pillows right and left.

Roxie slipped into a robe and started combing out her hair. "Your skin looks fantastic. I think it's the mountain air. Or maybe the amazing water. Or it could be the altitude."

"Yeah?" I preened, smoothing my fingers over my cheeks. "That's funny, Olga told me the same thing the other day."

"Who's Olga?"

"Esthetician. She's been sucking my pores for the last five years and she said there was, and this is a direct quote, a sixty-six percent reduction in the amount of *schmutz* in my pores."

"*Schmutz?*"

"Gunk, goo, toxins, pollution—you know, *schmutz.*"

"So this is a good thing."

"This is a great thing." I nodded, sucking in my cheeks and admiring my face in the mirror over her dresser. Then I looked back over my shoulder. "There's a great view of the bed in this mirror. Please tell me Leo and you watch yourselves having sex."

"I won't tell you that."

"That's not a denial, Callahan," I teased, enjoying the way she conveniently covered her face with her hair and began brushing it.

Her voice, however, wasn't covered at all. "Speaking of boning, maybe it's not just the country air that's making you glow. Care to share?"

"Orgasms are great for the complexion, that is true." I sighed, sinking back into the pillows and holding one like a teddy bear.

She laughed, plopping down onto the edge of the bed. "I assume that means that you're enjoying getting to know Oscar in the biblical sense?"

"Honey, there is nothing biblical about what we're doing. Trust me," I said, fanning myself with my hand. Heat was rising to my cheeks from anticipation. When I first found out we were heading into town tonight, I was trying to remain cautiously optimistic. I didn't want to presume that we'd be getting together every time I was in town. And by "didn't want to presume," I mean that was a lie that I couldn't even sell to myself.

I *wanted* to presume, dammit! I wanted to spend whatever time with him that I could. Biblically or otherwise.

"Hey? You with me?" Roxie asked, waving her hand in front of my face.

I laughed. "Sorry, my mind was with a certain dairy farmer."

"I asked how things are going? You seem to be enjoying the Bailey Falls experience."

I was. I couldn't fully admit it to myself, but I was totally drinking the Kool-Aid. Not yet willing to admit how much I was guzzling, I said, "I'm exhausted from today. Your boys wore me out."

"I spoke to Chad earlier. He told me you guys went to The Tube. It's incredible there, isn't it?"

I rolled over, full-blown dreamy sighing.

Like a shark smelling blood, Roxie started circling. "Oh, and Bryant Mountain House?" She flipped her hair back up. "We'll have to make spa appointments there soon. Wait until you see it. Incredible."

"Uh-huh," I murmured, dreamily thinking about the day.

"You know, we could even take a few day trips down to Tarry-town and Sleepy Hollow. Especially the cemetery, it's awesome."

"I love a cemetery," I echoed, mind elsewhere.

"That's what's so great about living here. We're driving distance or train accessible from everything. Great for families . . . very little crime . . ."

"It's a good town, Rox."

"It is, isn't it." She beamed, bouncing happily on the mattress.

"And once my campaign starts running, people will be swarming this place to feel a little of the Bailey Falls Magic."

"Who knows? Maybe if they fall enough under its spell, they won't want to leave . . ." She let the thought float out there while she stood and continued getting ready.

In a fog, I rose and headed into my room. It was a magic fog that was singing all the praises of the town and its inhabitants.

One in particular.

Never a big fan of lying to oneself, I put Oscar and whatever this was between us on the top of the "pros" list for Bailey Falls. I didn't know what would come of the relationship once the campaign was finished. When I went back to the city, would he visit more than just the weekends? Would I? Did he want me to do that? Did he want *me*, beyond the occasional weekend? There was something about being wanted. I'd never wanted to go beyond the confines of my island . . . for anything or anyone. Now, maybe. Possibly.

Not wanting to spend too much time on an existential relationship crisis, I turned to getting ready.

And I had just the outfit. Just in case a certain tall, dark, tattooed drink of water wandered across my path that night.

There are dive bars, and then there are *dive bars,* and this was one of the diviest dive bars I'd ever been in. At the end of Elm Street, *way* down at the end, where the town practically gave up and ceded back to the trees, sat Roxie and Leo's favorite Saturday-night bar. And judging by the amount of cars parked outside, it was all of Bailey Falls' favorite Saturday-night bar as well. Originally called Pat's, it'd been renamed Pat's Nightmare sometime in the eighties, to now be forever known as . . . wait for it . . . Pat's Nightmare on Elm Street.

I'll tell you what, people were pretty funny in the sticks.

Hair metal screamed out of the speakers, peanut shells and sawdust carpeted the gouged wooden floor, and people stood elbow to elbow like sardines to get a cheap beer. If you were very lucky, you were able to nab one of the four tables in the entire bar; those seats were gold.

Luckily for us, we got there just as the mayor and his wife were leaving with a few friends. Leo may have leapt the last ten feet to snatch the table before someone else got it, and now crowded around it were myself, Roxie and Leo, Roxie's mom, and Chad and Logan.

"So, wait, your mom's in town? It's too bad she couldn't come out tonight, too," I said to Leo, yelling a little to be heard since the music was so stinking loud.

"I think this is one place you'll never see my mother in," Leo said with a laugh. "She's not really a bar type. Besides, Polly's staying up at the big house with her this weekend, and they've got their own grandma/granddaughter thing going on."

Leo's family was very old New York, blood bluer than blue, banking dynasty. His family had a large estate on the outskirts of town that went back generations, including a huge old mansion that Leo referred to as the "big house."

"And we've got our *own* thing going on this weekend, if you know what I mean." Roxie leaned against Leo and tugged at the top button on his shirt.

"Yeah, we know what you mean. The entire bar is about to go up in flames from the sexual tension between you two." Chad sighed, fanning himself.

It was true; the amount of sexual energy being generated on that side of the table could have powered a small town.

Just then another pitcher of beer arrived at our table, along with another bowl of peanuts, and the next thing I knew I was standing on the stage (plywood set on cinder blocks) singing the only song I knew in their twenty-song karaoke lineup.

There are songs that are meant to be sung loudly and ac-companied by a PBR and peanut buzz. Songs that make you think you can sing, and that you alone understand the lyrics the way no one else possibly can, and that the only way to do them justice is to leave all self-awareness and good judgment behind.

Which is why when Oscar showed up at Pat's Nightmare on Elm Street, he found me singing at the top of my lungs, finger-pointing and fist-pumping, giving my all to my performance of "Don't Stop Believin'."

To be clear, if this song is on, you turn it up. You stop what you're doing, you roll down every window within reach, you throw every care away, and you give yourself over to the genius that is Journey.

And that's what was happening when I saw Oscar from across the cheering, clapping crowd. You have a choice when you get caught doing something like this—especially in front of someone who's currently blowing your socks off. You can run and hide, or you can sing louder.

I chose the latter. And as I straddled the mike and gave it my eighties all, he grinned wide and wolf-whistled loud, clapping his hands right along with every other fool in that bar. When the song was over, and my voice was still ringing (shrieking) through the air, I dropped the mike, gave a little bow, and strutted off-stage to the screams of the twenty or so applauding locals who happened to be there.

"Glad I didn't miss that," he said as I made my way over to where he was standing by the bar. "That was some song."

"Journey brings out the best, what can I say?" I replied, my eyes appreciatively taking him in. He was easily the biggest guy in the place, but somehow he didn't look intimidating to me anymore. Sure, he wasn't quick to smile, and the scar over his right eyebrow made him look perma-dangerous. I wanted to lick that scar. "How was the farmers' market? Did you sell out?"

"We did." He nodded, his eyes running over the length of my body. "What the hell are you wearing, Pinup?"

"Like it?" I asked, giving him a little twirl. I was feeling a fifties retro vibe when I was getting ready tonight. Off-white skirt with large black polka dots, black turtleneck, wide red belt. The best part? Red stiletto platforms, with an ankle strap and a four-inch heel. When I twirled, the skirt did, too, and revealed one more retro accent.

Garters holding up my thin silk stockings, clipped to a pair of high-waisted black silk panties. The garters he might have seen; the panties were for later.

Based on how wide his eyes grew, and how he gripped the bar until white-knuckled, I'm guessing he saw the garters.

"I just threw on a little something for a night out on the town."

"Out on the town, huh?" He shook his head a little, as though to clear it. "Not really sure that a night at Pat's really counts as such."

"Oh, you'd be surprised," I replied, leaning across the bar and snatching an olive. "Some drinks, some friends, some killer music"—I lifted my chin toward the stage, where someone's terrible version of "Son of a Preacher Man" was screeching out of the speakers. "I'd say it's a great night out on the town."

"How about a great night out in my barn? Maybe even out on the hood of my truck?" Oscar whispered, running his fingers right where the garters were on my thighs.

I choked a bit on my drink, and my heart leapt into my throat. He pressed on the garter, a small, infinitesimal amount of pressure that to anyone else would look innocent.

But we knew better. His thumb was right over the clip that held the stocking up.

He leaned over again, his lips brushing the shell of my ear. "I bet I could roll them down with my teeth. Lemme try, Natalie."

My knees buckled. Thankfully, his big hands were there to catch me.

"Nat, you okay?" Roxie asked, laughing when my drink sloshed over the side of the glass.

"Cheap date!" Leo hollered, waving over the waitress to order another round.

"It's uh . . . the shoes," I lied, holding Oscar's considerable biceps tightly. You know, for support.

Never in my life had a pair of high heels made me wobble. But add the Oscar factor, and the fingers on garters, and I was lying through my teeth.

I had a plan for tonight. I'd decided that if I saw him, I'd be in charge. Before the sex, after the sex, during the sex, I'd drive him wild with need—not the other way around. Yet with just a few words, he managed to make me weak in the knees and flushed in the cheeks. This guy did things to me.

"You can't talk to me like that here," I whispered, brushing my hip against the front of his jeans. I had to regain the upper hand or I'd be naked in a bar in five seconds flat, with Oscar behind me.

I could think of worse things to happen.

He advanced. We were packed into the bar, too many people squeezed into too small a room, but it didn't matter. He found the space, pinning me to the back of a chair behind me.

"I can throw you down onto the bar if I want," he promised. It was just that, too. If I pressed any further, the whole town would be getting an eyeful.

"You wouldn't dare. These are just for you." I slid the hem of my skirt up enough to draw his eye down. "You wouldn't want anyone else to see them, would you?"

His nostrils flared and my favorite eyebrow raised.

"Get a room!" someone called out, and the fog lifted. We were giving the bar a show, with part of my thigh exposed and Oscar's giant hand gripping the fabric of my skirt.

He turned, seeking out the jackass who just poked the bear. When they made eye contact, the guy took one look at him and bolted for the door. Oscar made a move like he was going to go after him but I pulled at his belt. Not that it would hold him in place if he really wanted to kick the guy's ass, but the little effort made me feel better.

"Let it go," I said.

He grunted. Such an Oscar thing to do, but the sound of it nearly gutted me. He ran hot all the time and it was something that I was drawn to.

"Caveman," I murmured, running my hands over his shoulders, feeling the muscles bunching beneath his shirt.

Slowly, he turned, and practically growled, "I need a beer."

"Make that two." I smiled, pulled him down to me, and kissed him.

It was supposed to be quick, but something snapped when our lips touched. He pushed while I pulled, and we crashed somewhere in the middle.

The catcalls and whistling egged us on and then his lip was between my teeth.

"I'm done here," he barked, pulling out his wallet. He threw money onto the table and grabbed me around the waist, lifting me off my feet and damn near right out of my come-fuck-me heels. I glanced back over my caveman's shoulder to a bar full of people applauding and Roxie cheering louder than anyone.

I could only giggle in the most excited way, clapping my own hands along with the town.

I had a feeling the heels were about to earn their name . . .

❧

The cool air blew against my overheated skin when we walked out of the bar. I half expected Oscar to press me up against the side of the building, but he didn't, keeping a strong grasp on my waist as I hovered a foot above the gravel, his long strides eating up the lot with determination.

He didn't even speak on the way to the truck. He held open the door for me to crawl inside but was mindful not to brush against me.

Did I bend over too far when climbing in? Of course.

Still nothing. It was like a barrier went up the second we left the bar. Oscar got moody sometimes; it was part of his charm in my eyes.

He closed the door, moving with purpose around to his side. I slid my skirt up my thighs to give him a full view of the garters when he climbed in, and after he started the truck he peeled out and raced down Main Street.

Still . . . nothing.

I wasn't misreading the situation. I could see the prominent outline of his dick in his jeans. He was totally hard but not making a move.

Leaning over, I pushed the armrest back and slid across to the middle of the seat, close enough to feel the heat coming off him in waves. I took his hand, held it, and waited. Interlocking our fingers, I moved his hand to my knee and then slowly slid it up to my thigh while spreading my legs slightly in the dark cab.

It was what I was feeling, and what I knew *he* was feeling. The little sparky static from the hosiery, the goose bumps covering my leg, the shiver I got when he finally hit the garter.

"You know, there's something I can't stop thinking about," I said, spreading my legs farther.

"What's that?" he asked, his voice strained, his hand on my thigh growing hot.

I flattened my hands on the hem of my skirt and slid it up slowly. Oscar's jaw ticked in the moonlight.

"Us fucking in your truck. Pretty sure you mentioned that."

When we slowed to a halt at the stoplight, I plucked the garter clip between my fingers and pulled it up. His eyes slid to the little black fastener and watched as I released it with an audible snap against my skin.

My hips bucked from the zip of pain. Oscar released a grunt that came from the back of his throat. It was thrilling to watch his knuckles turn white from strain. The hand that stayed on my thigh was clenched in a fist as if he were deliberately trying to *not* touch me the way we both knew he wanted to.

"Mmm, Oscar, what are you thinking?" I asked, running my hands down my chest before unhooking my belt and sliding the hem of the turtleneck up over my breasts and exposing my bra.

His hand flew to the steering wheel, and he held on so tight that I swear I heard the plastic crack beneath his palms.

I twisted in the seat so my head was leaning against the passenger door, lifting my feet up onto his lap and parting my knees. When I inched the skirt up higher he got a great view of my new panties and exactly what the garters were for.

He growled, and I felt the rumble of his chest right between my legs. I sat up enough to pull the sweater over my head before unclasping the front of the bra.

"Fuck," he whispered, and looked into the rearview mirror before giving the truck a hard turn to the left. "Hold on," he said, dropping his hand once more on my thigh and sliding it on home.

Finally.

He didn't even bother shutting off the ignition before he flung his door open and dropped out of the car. I barely had time to blink before he grabbed my ankle and pulled me unceremoniously to the edge of the car, my legs hanging out of the driver's-side door, my head conking prettily on the steering wheel.

He was unzipped in a flash, a condom rolled on before I could even rub my head. Oscar took my ankles and placed them on his shoulders, ballooning my skirt, then kissing his way down to my knees while he stroked himself.

"Please," I begged, pulling at my nipples beneath the bra cups.

"Not yet," he whispered between kisses.

One finger ran from my belly button to my panties and back up, each time getting just close enough that I thought, *Here we go!* He was making me crazy, driving me wild, with the sheer insanity of what we were doing and where we were doing it.

When I finally couldn't take the teasing anymore, I reached down and slid my panties to the side, the chill sending a shock through my body.

"That's my girl," he purred, taking the head of his cock and placing it just *there*. Just enough that my eyes rolled back in anticipation.

There was something so dirty about all of this but I didn't care. Here we were . . . *somewhere*. Lord knows who might come pulling up alongside. He couldn't even take off my panties before he slipped inside and moaned into the darkness.

He held them off to the side with one hand, the other holding my ankle near his lips, where he peppered kisses against it in time with his thrusts.

Oscar wasn't moving fast, but he wasn't slow, either. His movements were measured. He was painstakingly taking his time and not just letting loose.

"I could fuck you like this all night, Pinup," he said, slapping my ass with his free hand.

"Yes. Please," I chanted in time with his thrusts, and something snapped in him. His hips slammed into me, the truck literally rocking while he fucked me.

"Touch yourself," he begged, reaching forward to pull my bra down, fully exposing me to him. "I love watching the way your body moves when I'm inside you."

Holding on to my boobs, I pinched my nipples. He liked to watch. I filed that away for later.

"You like this?" I asked, biting my finger coyly.

"I love this." And he drove into me hard, hitting spots that were making me climb high, so high, wound tight and strung out.

"Fuck, Oscar, that's it!"

He wasn't sure and steady anymore. He was erratic, fired up and frantic to make me come. "You make . . . me . . . crazy," I panted, loving the feeling of him losing control.

Just as I was about to come, he slid both hands to the clasps on the garters and snapped them. "Give it to me."

I did. Jesus Christ I did, crying out his name on the side of the road, while he chased down his own orgasm, pumping deep inside of me, his own cries matching mine in the dark night.

It was not lost on me that I'd added my own sounds to the country soundscape . . .

Chapter 15

After the scene in the truck, there was a similar scene in his bedroom, this time with the two of us ping-ponging off the walls as we each tried to gain the upper hand, ending up on his bed with first me on top, then him, then finally me once more, with him spinning me at the last minute so he could watch me ride him in reverse, the better to *watch that great big ass bounce on my dick . . .*

Well, he had promised that would happen.

And then we collapsed. I've never faulted a man for being deep into the z's ninety seconds after really good sex, because I do that, too. All that beautiful tension, all that wonderful energy that's trapped inside and then goes shooting out into the universe . . . it can be tiring.

But when Oscar fell asleep after the second round, I was unable to sleep. This was becoming a problem.

It was too quiet—so quiet you could literally hear a pin drop.

I stayed in bed for a long time, listening to his deep, even breathing as he slept. I wrapped myself around him, seeking the comfort and warmth that often leads to a great night's sleep. I nestled against his side, throwing a leg over and draping an arm, resting my head on his powerful chest.

Didn't work.

I tried wrapping him around me, rolling to my side and dragging him with me, forcing the spoon of the century when his deadweight arm fell across me, and I tucked it around me, his powerful hips nuzzled against my bottom, cocooning me in Oscar . . . and reminding me of a position we'd yet to try but that I was dying to. That led to some rather colorful daydreams, but as far as sleep?

Didn't work.

I kicked a leg out from under the quilt, then an arm, then finally rolled over again and hung my bum over the side—but nothing was working.

Too. Fucking. Quiet!

An hour later and I was propped up in the bed, Oscar snoring away next to me looking adorable and full of restorative z's, and I was playing solitaire on my phone while catching up on my favorite celebrity Twitter feeds.

An ad popped up for a new game involving sheep counting, and it gave me an idea. I quickly pulled up the app store, typed in *sound machine,* and there were literally hundreds of white-noise downloads, just waiting for me and Mr. Sandman.

Let's see, what have we got?

Whispering Meadow? No.

Twilight Sunset? Not.

Rain on Tin Roof? Under the subset of Rain, also including Rain on Umbrella, Rain on Car, Rain on Vinyl Tent. Nope, not a one. But now I had to pee.

After scurrying to the bathroom and back, I quickly dove back under the covers, and finally stumbled upon some appropriate sounds.

Cityscape. *Now* we're talking.

You had your Restaurant Sounds, your Before the Theater Begins, Central Park Joggers, and the very intriguing New York City Streets.

I downloaded it, settled back against the pillows, and listened with a satisfied grin as the sounds of cabs honking, doors shutting, trucks rumbling, people chatting, and far-off sirens wailed. I grinned as my city enveloped me in the country, and I finally laid my head gently down to sleep . . .

Until Oscar sat straight up in bed, scrambling for the bat he kept next to his nightstand, and crashed to floor, bat held over his head and ready to do battle.

I peered over the side to where he was just as he peered up over the bed, the two of us knocking skulls and further confusing him.

"What the hell is that!" He rubbed his head, looking wildly around the room. "Is there an ambulance outside? And a . . . is that . . . it sounds like people clinking glasses?"

"It's New York City Streets—an app?" I answered, sitting cross-legged on his side of the bed, rubbing my own quickly forming goose egg. "You know, background noise for sleeping?"

"Why would anyone need background noise to sleep?" he asked, still holding the bat.

"Stand down, Oscar, it's okay," I soothed, tugging him back up onto the bed by his arm. "It's too quiet; I needed something to listen to, to help me fall asleep."

"That's ridiculous. How can anyone sleep through that racket?" He slumped back into bed, the bat hitting the floor. "How can a honking car help you fall asleep?"

"It's what I'm used to." I yawned, tucking the covers up and around us, curling into his side. "Just close your eyes, you'll get used to it in no time."

"I doubt that," he huffed, and I could hear his eyes rolling. But he did take a moment to look at the way my naked breasts shone in the moonlight. "So, you're sleepy, is that it?"

I turned onto my side, facing away from him, and slid the covers down to expose my equally naked backside. "I could be persuaded to stay up a little bit longer, since you're awake now."

Five seconds later I felt his hand slide up my thigh, toward my hip, then back down, smoothing it across my skin and along my bottom. Ten seconds later I felt his warm body curving against mine as I arched my back, smiling into my pillow.

The sounds of my sighing and his groaning were mixed in with doors slamming, cabs honking, and glasses clinking.

New York comes to the country.

And *in* the country . . .

✒

"Tell me about this one."

"Slipped on a patch of ice one winter, went down on a rock, sliced my arm open."

"And this one?"

"Gutting a walleye on a fishing trip when I was thirteen—the pocketknife slipped."

"And I've been dying to ask you about this one right here." I swept my fingertip across his eyebrow, feeling the small white scar there.

Sunday morning at Oscar's meant lying around in a big old antique iron bed covered in layers of quilts and blankets, feeling the sun shining in through old rattling windows, and playing Connect the Scars on his beautiful, scarred naked body. I'd been playing this game for a while now, and was nowhere near running out of scars.

"Hairbrush."

"Hairbrush? How could a hairbrush give you a scar on your eyebrow?" I laughed, settling back against his leg. He was sitting with his back against the headboard, sheets puddling low on his waist while I faced him, his propped-up legs acting as my headboard.

His hand closed around my ankle, his fingers gentle and soothing on my skin. "I pissed off my brother Seth, he threw the hairbrush, next thing I know I've got blood seeping through my hands and my brothers are all running down the hall screaming for my mom. Seth ran the opposite way to hide in the barn, convinced he'd killed me."

"How old were you?"

"I was eight, he was ten," Oscar said, smiling at the memory. "I'd been teasing him all night about finding Cindy Montgomery's school picture folded up in his wallet."

"What were you doing in your brother's wallet?"

"That's exactly what he asked me, right before he threw the hairbrush." Oscar laughed. "Ended up in the emergency room, with eight stitches. And this scar."

"I think it's sexy," I whispered, crawling up his body and perching with one leg on either side of his waist. "It was one of the first things I noticed about you. Now tell me about the big one."

"The *big* one?" he asked, lifting his hips up into mine with a suggestive grin.

"The big scar on your knee," I said, looking over my shoulder at the mess of white lines and scar tissue there.

"Oh, *that* big one." He sighed, running his hands through his hair until it almost stood on end. "You don't want to hear that story."

I smoothed his hair down, petting and patting it back into shape. "I asked, didn't I?"

"Surgery. Blew out my knee. You hungry? I'm hungry." He lifted me off his lap with one mighty bicep, his strength unfathomable, and climbed out of bed. He seemed uncomfortable.

"How'd you blow out your knee?" I asked, lying back against the pillows as he started to get dressed. He looked around the room, spied a pair of jeans thrown across a wing chair (I'd thrown them there last night in an effort to get at the goods), and he stabbed his legs into them quickly.

"In a game. No big deal, shit happens. I'm gonna go put on the coffee; come on down when you're ready." He dropped a quick kiss on my forehead, then left, pulling on a T-shirt as he went.

Huh. Snuggled under the still-warm covers, I wondered what in hell had just happened. I could hear him banging away down in the kitchen. Coffee grinder, water running, cups clinking.

I slipped into one of his T-shirts and found a pair of heavy woolen socks that I could pull up over my knees. The floor was chilly, and as I peeked out of the window over the bed, I saw a thick layer of frost across everything. Fall was most decidedly here, and winter was not far off.

A match scraping on sandpaper told me he was firing up the old Franklin stove in the kitchen, and I knew it'd be warm down there soon. After sweeping my hair up into two pigtails, I headed down the back stairs that led into the kitchen.

"So, what kind of game?" I asked, watching him taking out what looked like everything from the fridge at once.

"Eggs okay with you? I can make toast," he said, juggling a package of bacon, a carton of eggs, and some potatoes.

"Eggs are fine. What kind of game?" I asked, tugging at my shirt to pull it down a little lower.

"Football," he said, his face hidden from me in the pantry. "Do you know how to make biscuits?"

Football—of course. A bunch of pieces clicked into place. The physique. The coaching. The scars. The smashed knuckles. The overall beefiness.

"You played football? For how long?" I asked, sitting down on a step, tucking my legs up under my chin.

"Forever. Biscuits?" He looked at me over a bag of flour.

"Hmm?"

"Biscuits. Know how to make them?"

"Hell no. I'd scorch the earth if I tried to cook something."

"I thought you went to culinary school with Roxie."

I snorted, resting my chin in my hands. "Sadly, going to culinary school and being good at culinary school are not the same thing. Ask Roxie to tell you about the time I burned water."

"You can't cook? Like, at all?" he asked, assembling everything on the counter.

"No, not all women can cook, you know," I replied, arching my eyebrow toward him. He didn't respond, too busy beating up on some eggs. "Do you get the *Times*?"

"Should be on the front porch. I think I heard it hit the door earlier."

I stood up, brushing off my behind. He whistled at me, and I flashed him as I walked away. Was it a coincidence that I heard what sounded like six eggs cracking all at once? Or was my ass just that sweet?

I peeped through the lace curtains on the front door, and did indeed spy the Sunday *Times* sitting on the welcome mat. Wincing at the sudden guilt that washed over me that I wasn't at brunch (well played, Ma, I'm ninety miles away), I wrapped a throw blanket around my shoulders and darted outside to snatch it up. Brrrr, it was really cold this morning! Seeing my breath puff all around me as I bent down, I almost didn't see the basket by the front door, with a red-and-white-checked cloth tucked in and a note addressed to Oscar. Grabbing the basket and the paper, I headed back in.

"The *Times*, and something else," I announced, setting them down on the counter. He looked up from the bacon, saw the basket, and then looked at the newspaper.

"I get the financial section first," he said, returning to the bacon.

"Um, okay," I said, picking up the basket and dangling it off one finger. "Don't you want to know what this is?"

"I know what it is," he answered, and went back to his bacon. Silence in the kitchen.

"Shit, I want to know what it is, too!" I said, sitting down on the stool across the island from where he was, looking everywhere but the basket.

"A hundred bucks says it's muffins," he said, nodding for me to go ahead and open up the basket. I lifted up the corner of the red and white checks.

"They are muffins," I said, looking back up at him. "What are you, on some kind of muffin delivery?"

"You could say that. Try one, they're delicious. Pumpkin is my guess," he said, nodding me forward.

"Yeah?" I asked, picking one out and sniffing it. "I'll be damned, it is pumpkin." I bit off a corner, then swooned. "Ah mah guh thih ih hayvon."

"Told you," he said with a laugh, flipping the bacon with tongs and impressively stirring a panful of eggs at the same time.

I chewed, then swallowed. "Sign me up for this delivery; these are the best muffins ever." I took another monster bite.

"I'll tell Missy you liked them," he said, an amused look on his face.

I stopped midchew. "Meffy mah dees?" I sprayed pumpkin

crumbs everywhere, and didn't even care. I scrambled back to the basket, opening the note that was pinned to the outside.

Thanks for everything Friday night, you're the best.

Missy
XOXO

My mind reeled, rolling back to Friday night. Whoa, wait a minute. He didn't leave me to go to—

"Whoa, whoa, whoa, hold on a minute here. You left me to go see your ex-wife, and then you knowingly feed *me* her *thanks for the Friday-night fuck* muffins? What the *hell*?" I picked up the note and read it aloud with the most sickeningly sweet voice I could muster. "*You're the best.* Come on, why doesn't she just say, Hey ex-husband, thanks for the penis, thanks for visiting my vagina, here's some fucking awesome muffins?"

"She bakes me muffins all the time—"

"Oh, is that what they call it up here?"

"Is that what they call *what* up here? What are you talking about?"

"Well then, what the hell did I do last night: *churn your butter*? You better not have *whipped her cream*, or so help me God, I will—"

"I fixed her hot water heater."

I froze. Then blinked. And glared.

"What the hell kind of sick sex act is that?"

"Did you smoke crack when you were outside?" he asked, the bacon now smoking and the eggs a curdled mess. Even not directly touching it, I can ruin a meal.

"Did you or did you not leave me Friday night, after fucking my brains out, because your ex-wife called?"

"Yes."

"And she baked you muffins just for fixing her water heater?"

"Yes."

"I don't buy it."

"Her water heater's been on the fritz for the last year. She doesn't want to buy a new one unless she has to. So when it goes out, she calls me, I come over, I fix it, and she bakes me muffins as a thank-you."

"Oh," I said, sitting back down on my stool. Oh.

"What the hell was that about churning my butter?"

"Never mind. So nothing happened with you and Missy Friday night?"

"Nope."

Shit. "Well, don't I feel like an asshole."

"You should," he said, lifting the pan of burned bacon and dumping it in the trash. The eggs followed.

"I'm so sorry," I said. "I'll clean the pans. Maybe we can go grab some breakfast in town?"

He looked at me for a moment, really looking at me. I tried a half smile, which coaxed one from him.

"You're a bit loony—you know that, right?" he asked, reaching out and grabbing a handful of pigtail.

I grinned. "Comes with the territory."

          ✑

We did go into town for breakfast. Tucked into the last empty booth at the coffee shop, we ordered up a big mess of waffles based on the waitress's recommendation.

"These are special, the last of the blueberries for the season till next year."

"Then that's what we're having," I said, not bothering to open my menu.

"Done," Oscar agreed, handing back his menu as well. "And coffee, lots of coffee."

"I'm not surprised. The way you two were carrying on at Pat's last night, you should need some caffeine." She raised her eyebrows at the two of us, and went off to put our order in.

"You think the town's talking about us?" I asked, looking around the busy restaurant. There were definitely some interested looks being thrown our way. And we had been a little ridiculous last night.

"Do you care?" he asked, leaning across the table and picking up my hand, then kissing it slowly, his lips just barely brushing the backs of my knuckles.

"Do you?" I breathed, already knowing the answer. Oscar did what he wanted, when he wanted, and really didn't care what anyone thought.

His answer was in fact another kiss, leaning across the table and giving me one hell of a lip smack.

"You're determined to make us the town topic, aren't you?"

"People are gonna say what they want to; I can't stop that," he replied, a teasing look in his eye. "Besides, they're always trying to figure me out. It's been that way since I moved here; best to keep them guessing."

"How long ago was that?" I asked, enjoying the warmth of his hand in mine.

"Hmm, five years now? Six?"

"And where were you before that?"

"Dallas."

"Is that where you grew up?"

"Nope," he said, chewing on his bottom lip. I noticed he did this when we were talking about something he didn't really want to. "Cream?" He gestured to the silver pitcher that a busboy had just set down on the table, along with our coffee.

"Please," I nodded, tearing open a sugar packet and adding it to my cup. "So you didn't grow up in Dallas. Where were you before Dallas?"

"LA."

"You lived in LA?" Holy shit, my country boy in Los Angeles was hard to envision.

"I didn't live in LA, I just went to school there. I didn't like Los Angeles much."

"What school did you go to?"

He chewed his bottom lip again. "USC."

A lightbulb went off. "You played football there, didn't you?"

He nodded. "Full-ride scholarship."

I squeezed his hand. "That's incredible!"

He squeezed it back, then let go. "It's not that incredible." He looked out the window, watching the clouds. "Looks like we might get rain today."

"Wait a minute, you went to one of the best colleges in the country on a full-ride scholarship and you say it's not that incredible?"

He shrugged. "I come from a football family. We all played, all my brothers."

"Did any of them go pro?" I asked. Finally, a reaction on his face. He blushed and smiled sheepishly. "*You* played pro football?"

He shrugged once more. "Dallas."

My head exploded. "You played for the Dallas Cowboys?" My shriek caused several to look our way, and he winced.

"Could you not yell, please?" His expression was guarded now, closed off somehow. "Yes, I played pro ball."

"How long?"

He didn't answer for the longest time. When he did, his voice was quiet, and harder than I'd ever heard it. "Six and a half."

"Years?"

He shook his head. "Games."

I remembered our conversation from earlier, all the scars. The broken fingers, the busted elbow, the blown-out—

"You blew out your knee playing, didn't you?"

He sighed, a sigh that seemed to go on and on and carried such a heavy load. "Yes," he finally said through gritted teeth. And when he met my gaze, those piercing gray-blue eyes were full of so much hurt.

"Here we are, waffles for everyone!" the waitress chirped cheerfully, setting down two platters of waffles studded with enormous blueberries, pulling a container of syrup out of her apron pocket.

Oscar nodded his thanks, poured on the syrup, and then started eating. The conversation was over.

❦

After the quietest breakfast ever, he looked at his watch and swore. "I'm late for practice, want to tag along?"

"Sure," I said. I knew he had kids' football today, I just hadn't known if I'd be invited along. He paid quickly, and we headed out into the sunshine for a short walk over to where the kids were starting to gather. As we walked he stayed quiet, but he held my hand. That meant something.

Once there, he deposited me with some of the players' moms on the bleachers, threw me a woolen blanket he'd grabbed from the truck, kissed me quickly on the forehead, then headed out to his team. I watched as he greeted his players with real joy, the first I'd seen since we'd started talking about something that he clearly didn't enjoy discussing.

I watched him tease his players, slapping a few on top of

their helmets, chasing a few others, truly in his element. Ignoring the stares I was getting from some of the moms who doubtless enjoyed the view of Oscar each week while their sons played, I pulled out my phone and did the modern-day-dating equivalent of asking around.

I Googled Oscar Mendoza.

And in three seconds I had access to everything about him. He grew up in Wisconsin on a dairy farm, the son of a former professional football player and a high school English teacher. Oscar's entire life seemed to have revolved around football, and he'd been poised to be the next big thing ever since he started playing. Originally coached by his father, he then played for a highly competitive secondary school, eventually being selected for All County, All Region, All State, and, his senior year, selected as a High School All American. Sought after by all the major football schools in the nation. Played three years as inside linebacker for USC. Picked third in the second round of the NFL draft by the Dallas Cowboys.

Taken out of his seventh professional game when he was injured. Spent the next year rehabilitating his knee after surgery for those injuries. His contract was dropped when he failed to regain the speed he'd once had, and his football career was over at twenty-three.

Oh, Oscar.

I stopped reading and watched him coach his team the rest of that morning, not wanting to know the rest of his story until he was ready to tell me. When practice was over, I walked out to him on the improvised field in the middle of the town square, a million miles away from where I'm sure he intended to end up but seemingly happy. He looked up from his clipboard with a genuine smile, also seeming happy that I was here, with him, in his world. As soon as I could, I wrapped my arms around him and kissed him. Just once, soft and sweet. And when he kissed me back, he lifted me against him, his arms so tight around my waist, the autumn sun dancing around us, and I felt very happy to be here with him.

When we got back to the truck, he threw his gear inside and looked at me expectantly. "Feel up for a walk?"

"Sure," I said, letting him slide his long arm around my shoulder and tuck me into his side. We headed down Main Street, turning right on Elm, and walked with what seemed no real direction, no real hurry. Just walking. We went right again on Maple, right on Oak, then finally right once more on Main, having walked all around the town square. He started talking when we made the next turn onto Elm.

"Football was everything in my family—you should know that first."

I exhaled, relieved that he was trusting me enough to tell me his story, and pleased that he wanted to. I tightened my hold on his waist, my hand resting along his hip under his jacket, warm and cozy.

"Football. Got it." I nodded and looked up at him. The sunlight was encircling his head a bit like a halo.

"My father played football—never was a star, mind you, but played in the NFL for almost five years. Third string for Indiana, then half a season in Detroit, and he played out his last season close to his family home in Green Bay. When his contract wasn't renewed, he moved us all to the farm and worked with his father at the dairy they owned."

A family of dairymen; interesting.

"But football was still part of his life, all of our lives. I played, my brothers played, he coached, and if we weren't out working the cows or milking them in the barn, we were on the field."

"Sounds like fun," I replied when he seemed to stall in his story.

He nodded with a faraway look. "It was. As we got older, it wasn't as much fun. I loved football, loved the game, the sport, the community, all of it. But if you were good, and I was, it could take over everything else. That's what happened for me and my brothers. Everything became about training, everything became about the game that weekend, what plays we could have run better, what block could have been harder, what tackle should have been a sack. We literally ate and slept and breathed football. When the season ended, we kept on drilling at home, year-round."

He paused somewhere in the middle of Oak Street, scrubbing at his face. "He wanted us to have that edge, to be better than anyone else. It started to not be so fun anymore."

"Did you ever want to quit?" I asked, and he shook his head immediately.

"Not an option—quitting is never an option. Eventually, it became just such a part of everything that it seemed normal. We were a football family, and that's what we all did. Even my mom—she ran the boosters, organized bake sales when we needed new uniforms, all that."

"Family business," I mused, and he squeezed my shoulder.

"That's exactly right. My older brother, he ended up getting a partial scholarship to a regional school there in Wisconsin. He played for four years, and that was it. But me, I started getting scouted when I was a sophomore in high school. I was really good, and my family knew if it was going to happen, it was going to happen for me."

"Were you still working for the dairy?"

"Yup, football and cows, that was literally my life."

"And Missy," I said quietly, knowing that by now in this timeline, she'd made an appearance.

"And Missy," he agreed. "She was as much a part as every-thing was back then. She was a cheerleader, she was right here for every game, on the sidelines or with my parents. We used to sit out back at nighttime, in one of the pastures, and talk about what things would be like when we were older. I'd play profes-sional, I knew that now, and I knew I'd be afforded a life that I couldn't turn down. No one from a tiny town in Wisconsin whose only other prospect was a lifetime at a dairy wouldn't go for it guns blazing."

I kept quiet, sensing that there was a turn coming in this tale.

"My knee started acting up my senior year at USC. At first I thought it was nothing; we all got banged up pretty good each game. My knee held, we were winning games right and left, and it was all starting to fall into place. After graduation, I got drafted, Missy and I got married right after that, and we were off for Dallas. To this day, I've never seen my dad more proud."

He chewed on his lower lip, lost in thought.

"And then?" I prodded, and he cleared his throat.

"And then it was just how life was. We bought a house, we started talking about kids, I was playing, it was all good. Then my knee started getting really bad, but I thought, I really thought, I'd be able to stick it out. But . . . seventh game of the season, I was driving hard and the turf was loose. I went one way, my leg the other, and I could literally hear my knee pop. Worst pain I've ever felt."

"Oh, Oscar." I sighed, leaning my head on his strong arm, feeling the power that was still there, humming beneath the surface. So strong.

"Anyway, that was it. I had the surgery, went to rehab, tried liked hell to not see the signs that were so clear, but in the end it was obvious, I was done."

"I bet that was rough."

"You know what?" His expression lightened surprisingly. "It

was rough, but it was kind of a relief. I couldn't play anymore, so I could actually breathe for a bit, think about what else I wanted to do. Neither one of us wanted to stay in Dallas; big cities were never our thing. So we went home. I'd saved most of my signing bonus, and money went much further in rural Wisconsin than it did in the big city, so we went home and started over."

"And that's where the cheese comes in?"

"Exactly. I knew an old guy who lived in town, made cheddar. He used to buy his milk from our dairy, and I'd been interested in the process. I started working with him, learning the business, and when Missy and I talked about what we wanted to do with the rest of our lives, we started thinking about where else in the country we might like to live. She'd always wanted to live somewhere different—and it's crazy when an idea takes hold, how fast things can change."

I shook my head. "It's not crazy, it's just you. Anyone who can overcome an injury like that is tough. You're determined as hell, Oscar. I'm not at all surprised you figured out a way through it."

He blushed a bit, shrugging his shoulders. "Anyway, that's how we ended up here. There was a farm for sale, there were several outbuildings on the property for me to get my cheese-making thing going; it was almost too easy. But once we got here and settled in, things changed."

"Between you and Missy?"

"Yep. Away from family and friends, away from everything we'd always thought we'd do together, we started to . . . I don't know . . . drift apart, I guess? Not right away, but luckily it happened before we had any kids. So when the split came, it was clean."

"And she didn't go back home."

"Oh no, she loved the area. She lives in the next town over, as you know. I admit, I didn't get to know many people here when we first moved. You might have noticed I tend to be a little . . . standoffish?"

"Noooo," I mocked, and he kissed me on top of the head.

"But then the cheese started coming together, literally and figuratively, and I'd invested the money I'd earned well enough to really give it a go. And there we are."

"And there we are," I said, stopping on the sidewalk. We'd walked around the town square nearly enough times to wear a path in the concrete. I wrapped both arms around him, leaning into a hug. "And your family?"

"They're back home. They do their thing. My dad's grooming my nephew to be the next Brett Favre."

"Who?"

"Oh, Natalie." He sighed and hugged me back just as tightly.

So now I knew the story of Oscar.

I spent the rest of the day with him, helping him move the cows around, enjoying the day, kissing him whenever I could manage it. And when he kissed me good-bye at the train station that night, it was all I could do to not throw my arms around him and stay another night.

He was under my skin now.

Chapter 16

Back in the city, I worked my ass off, spending ten hours a day in the office, focusing my attention on work to keep my mind from wandering to what was waiting for me just a train ride away. But I had work, and work I did.

The T&T campaign was coming along marvelously, sharp and witty and exactly how I had envisioned it. Dan had made a few suggestions about how to beef up the coverage a bit, including some witty copy that would play really well on the radio ads the client had agreed to purchase.

The best part of the week? My friend Clara was in town, working on a hotel remodel in the Flatiron District. She traveled all over helping to rebrand hotels, specializing in historic hotels that were on the verge of going under. Sometimes it was as simple as bringing in a new manager, changing out some staff, or brightening up the rooms, but sometimes it was a complete overhaul. That was the case with the Winchester, a pre-WWI hotel that had hosted presidents and kings, movie stars and countless starlets. It had fallen on hard times, and in a last-ditch effort the family that owned it had hired Clara's firm to try and rebrand it for the new batch of stars and starlets.

"You should see the dining room—heaven! It's still got the original windows, hidden behind miles and miles of awful draperies, but the windows are still there." Clara was sipping her sparkling water, hands flashing about as she talked a mile a minute. Clara moved almost constantly, her sleek runner's frame seeming almost incapable of keeping still. Running ten miles a day four days a week (on the fifth day she'd push herself to fifteen if she had a race coming up), she competed in marathons and triathlons around the globe. She traveled a lot, was always on the move, although her schedule had been slowing down of late, as she took more projects that seemed to be based in the United States than abroad as was her norm.

Which was fine with me, because it meant I got to see her more often. And now that we had Roxie firmly ensconced in upstate New York, we were even all planning a weekend get-together just as soon as we could pin Clara down. Which was proving almost impossible.

"Mom and I used to have lunch in the tearoom at the Winchester when I was a kid," I reminisced, thinking back to the wintry Saturdays we'd spend together. "I'd always order the French onion soup, which used to come in these fantastic earthenware crocks, all bubbly and cheesy. I'd always burn the hell out of my tongue because I couldn't wait, but it was soooo worth it."

"Shit, Natalie, if I had a nickel for every story I've heard like that, I'd have a lot of nickels! They still have those bowls; I found a bunch of them in a storage room. Trying new things is good, but when you have something you're known for, like the onion soup? You never take it off the menu."

"So will the new Winchester Hotel have onion soup again?" I asked.

"Hell yes," she answered, raising a glass in salute. "When the tearoom reopens for the Christmas season."

"My favorite time of year." I sighed, thinking of the department store window displays and crowds, tourists and natives alike. "Do you know where you'll be this holiday?"

"Not sure yet; there's a hotel in Colorado we've been in talks with. Over a hundred years old, same family for generations, but really struggling. If we get it, I'm asking to go there."

"You know you're always invited to our house; my parents put on a killer holiday party."

"Mm-hmm, I know," she said, her eyes moving around the restaurant, not quite lighting on anything in particular. She never liked talking about family, or holidays. I only knew the little bit I did know from the few times she'd been pickled enough to talk about it. From what Roxie and I had been able to figure, her childhood hadn't been a happy one. Never knowing her father, she'd been removed from her mother's home early for reasons she didn't talk about, and she'd bounced from one foster family to the next. What was amazing about Clara is having that kind of start in life could have broken her, but instead she'd struck out on her own as soon as she turned eighteen.

She'd won a scholarship to the Culinary Institute both Roxie and I attended freshman year, and like me, she realized quickly it wasn't her cup of tea. But she stuck it out until the end of the year, and then applied for financial aid at a traditional four-year school in Boston.

The three of us had kept in touch through the years, and it was nice having us all on the East Coast again. I invited her year after year to holiday parties with my family, but she always politely declined.

"You know I appreciate the invitation, right?" she asked now, her voice quiet.

"You know I'll always ask, right?" I answered with a question of my own.

She smiled. "One day I'll say yes."

"Perfect!" I said, patting her hand and changing the subject. "So, this guy I've been fucking—"

The waiter who'd discreetly been trying to peek down my dress all lunch dropped his tray of drinks.

Clara just held her head in her hands and laughed.

❧

I walked back to work after lunch, with kisses and hugs from Clara and a promise to come over for dinner next week sometime when she was back in town. I'd picked a restaurant only a few blocks away from the office, and I took the long way back so I could walk a little longer. I wasn't quite ready to go back to work yet. I was restless, I could feel it in my bones.

Oscar had been slowly driving me mad this week with his texts. His first came in Sunday night, before I'd even gotten to bed. Once again, I'd caught the last train home from Poughkeepsie, and was just turning the key in my front door when my phone buzzed in my pocket. Standing in the entryway, I read his text and his words made me flush scarlet almost instantly.

My bed still smells like you.

The next bubble was even better.

I still smell like you.

But the last bubble was my favorite.

Get your great comma big
ass back up here, Pinup.

I did love a guy who didn't need a thigh gap.

The texts continued all week, some flirty, some dirty, all designed to drive me crazy. We talked each night around nine, him going to bed so much earlier than I did since the cock crowed before dawn. Thank goodness that on weekends, he had some of the local 4-H kids come around to take care of the animals, affording him a rare Saturday or Sunday morning sleep-in.

Sleep-ins that I'd gotten to take advantage of the last few weekends. But I couldn't possibly go up again this weekend; there was no reason to. I had what I needed to get started on the Bailey Falls campaign, and my mother would put out an APB for me if I ditched brunch again. Still, when he started telling me all about the Halloween harvest festival that was going on that weekend . . .

"I can't, I just can't! I've spent the last few weekends up there as it is, my city needs me! I can't disappear again," I teased, lying on my bed with my feet propped up on the headboard Thursday night, listening as Oscar made a case for why it was imperative that I get my great comma big ass back up there this weekend.

"I've even got people covering my stall at the farmers' market this weekend. That's how big this festival is," he replied, his voice extra low and sexy tonight. Maybe it was just that it'd been four days since I'd had a hit of Oscar, and my body was literally craving it.

"You're not going to be in the city Saturday?" I asked, disappointed. I'd planned on stopping by, going through our normal "Brie" conversation, pretending I didn't know him at all but just still had a crush, but making sure to wear something extremely low-cut to torture him with.

"Nope, I'll be at Maxwell Farms Friday night helping them

get set up, and will probably spend all Saturday there. Leo's setting up a corn maze."

There was a new club opening in Gramercy that I'd been invited to, two dinners with friends I hadn't seen for a few weeks, and a fund-raiser for a friend of my mother's on a yacht on the Hudson. All places at which I'd planned on making an appearance.

But nowhere on my island was there a corn maze.

As I turned onto Forty-eighth Street I saw a subway poster advertising Grand Central as the weekend getaway hub.

No, universe! No, no, no! No weekend getaways. No taking the train. No going back to Bailey Falls for the weekend just for a corn maze.

But it wouldn't be just for the corn maze . . . there'd be dick involved.

I packed an overnight bag that evening, and this time instead of asking Roxie to pick me up at the Poughkeepsie station, I asked Oscar. He agreed instantly, and then spent ten minutes describing exactly what he planned to do to me in his truck on our way into town. To be fair, some of them couldn't realistically be done while driving, but it didn't really matter . . .

❧

Friday evening, I walked off the train platform and headed for the parking lot, knowing Oscar would be waiting there for me. But instead, he surprised me by actually sitting inside the station, in the beautiful old lobby. For a second, I had an overwhelming urge to drop my bag and go running across the lobby, throwing myself into his arms, and letting him spin me silly while laying a big wet kiss on me. I walked quickly toward him, fighting the urge.

He met me halfway, walking rather quickly himself, and did

indeed spin me around while giving me the biggest kiss of my life. The only deviation from the Disney version in my head was that one of his hands was splayed across my ass.

"Wow," was all I could manage when he finally set me down.

"Was that too much?" he asked, the grin on his face unstoppable.

"Hell, *I'm* too much," I replied, my grin matching his. "That was just right."

He scooped up my bag and wrapped an arm around my shoulders, guiding me out to the parking lot.

"So, I've been thinking about all those things you wanted to do to me on the way home, and I think I figured out a way you can do them and not get arrested—or both of us splattered across the road."

"Natalie, listen, I—"

"There's that old turnoff, right by the old state highway? Roxie said it used to be one of the roads up to Bryant Mountain House, but it isn't used anymore. So I was thinking we should go use it."

"We can definitely do that, but not—"

I hurried toward his truck, eager for the weekend to start. "Come on, let's go. If I sit next to you, I can slip my hand inside your jeans and lean down to— What the *hell*?"

Missy was sitting inside Oscar's truck.

"Hi, Natalie." She waved. I waved back, looking at Oscar with questions all over my face.

"Her car broke down," he said as he stowed my bag in the back of the truck. Opening the passenger door for me, he had the decency to blush slightly. Considering what I'd been saying as we walked up, and knowing full well she must have heard my indecent proposal, a slight blush shouldn't be enough. And did he look amused?

"My car broke down," Missy echoed like a parrot. She patted

the seat next to her. She'd slid into the middle seat, positioning herself between Oscar and me.

That would make road head a bit harder . . .

I grabbed hold of the door and stepped up gingerly. I was wearing new four-inch Bionda Castana fringed leopard booties, and while walking a mile over cobblestones wouldn't give me pause, climbing in and out of trucks wasn't what the designer had in mind. A large, steady hand landed on my behind, supporting me—and also engaging in a little grab-ass where prying Girl Scout eyes couldn't see.

Whatever.

"Hello, Missy," I chirped. I settled myself in the passenger side, feeling enormous next to the tiny ex-wife who was riding next to my guy.

Was he my guy? The proposed road head said yes. Maybe?

Oscar climbed in at that moment, and the two of us positively dwarfed Missy.

"So, are we giving you a lift somewhere?" I asked her.

Score one for me, with my specifically chosen use of the word *we*.

"Oh yes, when Oscar came to help, he suggested we come pick you up on our way to the auto shop. He arranged to have my car towed there for me."

Score two for the Girl Scout for managing to not only use *we* to her advantage, but slip in an *our* for good measure.

"Well, Oscar's good like that, isn't he? He'd never leave a woman stranded on the side of the road." I smiled through my teeth, to make sure she knew I had them.

She showed me her own toothy smile. "He's sweet, looking after me the way he does."

"Hopefully you'll bake him some more muffins." I smiled back just as sweetly. "I loved the last batch—they were great for breakfast."

We drove across town toward the shop where Missy's car had been towed, tension thick inside the cab. I wasn't mad; what kind of a guy would he be if he left her stranded on the side of the road?

On the other hand, what kind of ex-wife was she, calling only Oscar when she had honey-do's to be done? She'd had her chance; it was my turn to have *my* honey done.

On the third hand (work with me), I was hardly in a position to be thinking about Oscar in any way but a fun weekend thing. This wasn't my territory, there was no reason to be pissy.

On the fourth hand, if no one was at fault here and it was just three people who didn't truly bear anyone any ill will, then this was just silliness and I could be the bigger person.

"So, Natalie, I was planning on making another batch of pumpkin muffins this weekend, but if you're here, maybe I should whip up my low-fat bran cookies instead. Lots of fiber, not so much sugar, better for us girls when we're watching our figures."

And with my fifth hand, I'd slap the shit out of—

"Natalie doesn't need to watch her figure." Oscar sounded amused, but his voice held a note of warning. My grin was so wide it could have pulled in neighboring planets.

Now tell her not to bake you any more muffins! No more muffins!

"You know I like those blueberry ones you make, with the maple drizzle?" he asked, and Missy beamed triumphantly.

I stared out the window. *Who cares? She can only bake him muffins.* You *get to watch him eat them naked.*

While I might not be his future, I was his present, and she was his past. Once she shut the hell up about blueberries and climbed out of this truck, I'd be the one fucking his brains out.

My grin was back.

∽◦∾

At the garage, Oscar went inside with Missy to make sure every-thing was sorted out. A new battery was being installed, so once he knew she'd be on her way, Oscar said good-bye and returned to the truck.

I said nothing when he climbed in. And I said nothing when he pulled out, heading down the road. The silence pressed in on both of us, begging to be noticed.

Finally, he looked my way. "You okay over there?"

"Mm-hmm."

He chewed on that a moment. "Is that a loaded *mm-hmm*? Like when a woman says *mm-hmm*, but it means the opposite of *mm-hmm*?"

"Mm-hmm," I answered, letting my eyebrows do the rest of the talking.

"Look, I'm sorry I surprised you like that. That isn't how I planned to start this weekend. But she was stranded—what was I supposed to do?"

"You did the right thing, of course," I said, turning to face him. "But do you always have to be the one she calls? Doesn't she have someone else to fix her water heater or take her to get her car fixed?"

"Why wouldn't she call me?" he asked, looking genuinely cu-rious. Oh, bless his heart.

"I'm just saying that not all exes are on such good terms."

"It would be better if we were nasty with each other?" he asked, and I had to shake my head. Damn him and his common sense sometimes.

"Of course not. It's actually refreshing to see two people who used to be married still be good friends," I said, choosing my words carefully. "I just wonder if that's all she wants—friendship."

"Missy? And me? Oh no, she doesn't want that any more than I do. And I don't," he said, shaking his head. Oh, bless his heart twice.

He turned off the main road, heading underneath the archway for Maxwell Farms.

I looked at him, then looked back at the sign. "What are we doing here?"

"Remember, I told you, I'm helping Leo get ready for the Halloween festival tomorrow."

Dammit, I had forgotten. All those thoughts of potential road head, then commonsense ex-wives, and I plum forgot.

I looked at the fine mist of rain sprinkling down, then looked at my four-inch booties. Dammit. I really need to start packing more—ugh—practical shoes.

Turned out that most of the work we'd be doing was in the barn, which was great for me and my booties.

Roxie was there, and she gave a surprised shriek when she saw me. "What are you doing here? Did I know you were coming? I've been baking damned pumpkin pies for three days for this festival, so it's quite possible I forgot you were coming. Yes, Polly?"

Leo's daughter was tugging at her shirttail, holding up a mason jar.

"Oh crap. I mean, not crap! Ugh, that's three, isn't it?" Roxie asked.

Polly laughed delightedly. "Yeah—twice just now, and the one about the pumpkin pies." She held out the mason jar while Roxie rummaged in her jeans pockets.

"I've got fifty cents, that's it. Natalie, you got a quarter?"

"I think so. What's this for?" I asked, digging through my purse. I handed over a quarter, then looked at her expectantly.

Polly said, "I started a bad-word jar, because Roxie is so bad about not saying bad words. I've got almost fifteen dollars already!"

"That's all? I'm surprised it's not more," I said, watching as Roxie dropped the money into the jar.

"Fifteen dollars just this *week*!" Polly told me.

"That makes more sense," I agreed, digging back into my purse. "Here you go—here's a dollar in advance, for the next four."

"Awesome! That'll take us through the rest of tonight, I bet!" Watching Polly tease Roxie was pretty great, and I could tell by observing the two of them it was enjoyed by both. "But Oscar never has to give me money for the bad-word jar."

"Nope," Oscar said with a stoic look on his face. "Unlike these ladies, I'm a gentleman."

I snorted. "A gentleman who talks about my ass every chance he gets."

Oscar's eyes danced as he held his laughter in check, especially when I started to hear a jingle jangle from the pipsqueak.

"Ante up, Natalie," Polly said, shaking the mason jar.

"Ante up? Where does she hear this stuff?" I asked Roxie.

"My mother is teaching her poker."

"Take it out of my dollar, tiny person. Okay?" I said, and she nodded before rushing off. "I just got hustled by a seven-year-old."

Leo came out of the crowd and snuck his arms around Roxie's waist, and I pointed a finger at him. "Your daughter just took almost two bucks from us."

"You must have been swearing," he replied, planting a kiss on Roxie's neck. "Can I borrow this big guy a minute?"

"Borrow whoever you want, but I need you back in the big house in twenty minutes to move your mother's chairs into storage. She'll kill me if anything gets on them." Roxie squealed as he kissed her a little more.

"But wait—back to this right here," she said, pointing at Oscar and me. "When did you get here? You weren't planning on coming up, were you?"

"I wasn't, no," I said, feeling the color coming into my cheeks.

"I'm gonna go help Leo, let you two hens squawk a bit," Oscar said, seeming to hesitate for a split second, then leaning in to plant a quick kiss on my forehead before walking away with Leo.

Feeling my skin tingle where his lips had just been, I smiled, watching the two of them head into the barn, Oscar punching Leo on the shoulder as he clearly teased him about what just happened.

I could feel eyes on me, and I turned to Roxie, whose grin was even wider than her eyes.

"So . . . ?" she asked, and I could feel my blush deepen.

I crossed my arms in front of my chest. "So?"

She studied me carefully, watched as I got redder and redder. "I never thought I would see the day—"

"Shut up."

"—that Natalie Grayson, hater of all things country—"

"Shut. Up."

"—would fall in love with a country boy."

Fall in love? Whoa.

"Shut. Up. *Now*," I said, heading toward where all the action seemed to be, setting up the stalls for the next day.

"Seriously, Natalie, come back here! Hey!" Roxie yelled as I walked faster. Not easy; with each step I was sinking farther and farther into the wet grass on the way to the barn. She caught up to me fast. "I was just teasing."

"I know, I know," I said with a heavy sigh. I turned back toward her, basically pivoting on my left heel, which was stuck thoroughly in the mud. "I just— I don't really know what this is yet. So let's not go making a big deal, okay?"

"It's a big enough deal that you're up here every damn week-end all of a sudden. I'd say you're pretty smitten."

"That's a good word for it," I said, watching the scene below. The big stone barn, people everywhere laughing and chatting like they'd known each other for years, pockets of kids running here and there, and in the middle of it all, trying to hold at least six pumpkins in his arms at once, was the guy I was smitten with.

Smitten. Kitten. Mitten. Why did all those words remind me of something warm, and cozy, and safe?

And as I watched Oscar helping out, noticing his quiet strength, his way of staying inside the group but on the edge, I knew I was smitten for sure. Anything more than that, I just didn't know.

Frankly, anything more than that scared the shit out of me. I always got out of things way before smitten kittens started up.

"When did you know?" I asked Roxie, who was watching the same scene focused on the guy running the show. "I mean, that you . . ."

"Loved Leo?" she asked, her face going soft. "I started falling for him when he first brought me walnuts." She bit her lip for a moment while she thought. "But I knew I was in love with him when I saw him with his daughter for the first time."

"How did you know?"

"That it was love?"

I nodded my head.

"Because it scared me to death. And that was new for me."

Roxie had a lot of the same thoughts about love as I did, although hers stemmed not from a Thomas but from a Trudy. After spending her childhood watching her mother jump from guy to guy to guy, always falling in love and then crashing hard when the inevitable breakup occurred, she'd grown up determined never to fall in love.

That is, until Leo. Then all bets were off.

I watched as Oscar stacked pumpkins around the jack-o'-lantern-carving booth, his body so big, yet moving so gracefully. He set another bunch down, then searched the crowd, looking for . . . me?

Our eyes locked across the yard, and even from this distance I could see the sweetness in his gaze. And the heat.

Smitten. Mm-hmm.

Chapter 17

Halloween in New York City means traipsing up and down the back stairwell to go trick-or-treating on all the floors of your apartment building. Telling jokes to the doorman in return for candy. Riding the subway with no fewer than seven men dressed in dirty brown trousers and red-and-green-striped sweaters, six of whom are officially dressed as Freddy Krueger.

Halloween in the country is made for a horror movie. Rustling leaves, phantom wind blowing through bare scraping trees, cornstalks that beckon like creepy fingers, and roads where headless horsemen ride.

Everyone said it was safe, sure. People who knew all about the secrets of the Hudson Valley, and who keep them. *Don't worry, there's nothing to be scared of.* Unless you strayed too close to the edge of the cornfield. Honestly, if I met one person named Malachi, I'd be back on that train in two seconds flat.

So I was very happy that the Halloween festival started in the daytime, where everything was light, bright, and cheery, full of happy people celebrating the harvest like they always had. Maxwell Farms was the center of the cheery, and after all the work we'd put in the night before, it was like a Martha Stewart magazine come to life. A Martha Stewart magazine with damn good-looking farmers.

It was one of those perfect fall days: the air was crisp and clean, the leaves were fantastically bright, the sky so blue it made me squint to look up. And into all this bright and beautiful clean, I hobbled across the barnyard with Oscar, clutching his elbow.

"You should have let me put some ice on that before we left."

"Ice wasn't going to help," I muttered.

Oscar's big hand smoothed down my back, light as a feather. "Ice will help with the inflammation, Pinup. You overtaxed your muscles."

I looked up at him, almost as tall as the sky itself. "*Who* overtaxed my muscles, Caveman?"

"You did," he replied, an amused glint in his eye.

"I certainly didn't throw myself all over the bed this morning," I grumbled, heat flaring through me as I thought back to a few hours ago.

"I put you on your knees, Natalie," he whispered, his voice lowering. He lowered, too, dipping down so that his mouth was just a blink away from my ear, his words dark and delicious. "I'd hardly call that throwing you all over the bed."

A shiver rolled through me, down to my hips, hips that still felt how firmly his hands had grasped me as he did indeed put me on my knees. He'd held me so firmly, in giant warm hands that wrapped around my curves, fit neatly into the small of my back, and pressed me down onto my hands and knees, and tilted my pelvis up so he could thrust inside in one powerful stroke.

I shivered once more. "Whatever. Who threw who, who pushed who, the point is—"

"The point," he interrupted, planting a kiss on the side of my neck, "is that you need ice. Sooner, rather than later."

I stood still, looking up at him. With the sun highlighting the little bit of auburn in his hair, his thick chestnut and mahogany hair waved around his face, still mussed from my hands. This guy, this man who resembled some kind of island god that women should be surrounding with tikis and praying to for increased fertility, had just kissed me on the neck in front of half the town . . . and I loved it.

And I knew that I was falling for him in a big way. Whole heart, full butterflies, threatening to burst out of my chest and skywrite my feelings for all the world to see.

This was moving beyond a crush. This was moving beyond a toss in the hay and a grapple in the truck. I was feeling the feels. Which made me so very nervous . . . but I was rolling with it, dealing with it.

But right now, I was only feeling flannel. In my hand, curling into a fist as I tugged him down to me, those lips too full and luscious not to be kissed. I kissed him, and he kissed me, and before I knew it his hands were around my waist, careful of my sore back but still warm and pressing along my singing skin. We kissed slow, and sweet, and deep and scorching, until I felt nothing except every point of contact between us.

And yes, that included the impressive erection against my stomach.

Suddenly, over the quiet sighs from me and the low grumbling groans from him, I heard something else. Something much higher-pitched and—giggling?

"Ew," a tiny voice said from somewhere much closer to the ground. I pulled my lips away from Oscar's to investigate. Polly was standing next to us, and Roxie and Leo stood nearby with gigantic grins.

"Don't say *ew*, kid." I laughed, dropping one more kiss on Oscar's mouth. "You'll give him a complex."

232 of ALICE CLAYTON

"What's a complex?" Polly asked.

Leo scooped her up and planted her firmly on his shoulders. "Let's go check out that corn maze, huh?"

And with my hand engulfed in Oscar's large one, we did just that.

We spent the day together, enjoying all the activities. I entered and won a jack-o'-lantern-carving contest, capturing the exact skyline of lower Manhattan from memory across a pumpkin sky. Polly and Leo ran the three-legged race and lost spectacularly, coming in so very last they were almost disqualified. Roxie easily beat out the competition in the pie contest, and people were fighting to get the last piece of her classic vinegar cream pie, which sounds terrible but was fucking unreal.

But my day in the country was complete when I watched Oscar compete in the butter-churning race.

There are no words. Scratch that. There *are* words. And some of them are . . .

Pumping.
Up.
Down.
Hands.
Wrapped.
Around.
Wood.
Cream.
Splashing.
Tongue.
Poking.
Out.
Concentrating.
Rhythm.

Thrusting.
Sweating.
Eyes.
On.
Me.
The.
Entire.
Time.
Is.
It.
Hot.
Or.
Is.
It.
Just.
Me?
(This is Roxie . . . it's not just you.)

If it was possible for someone to spontaneously combust from watching a grown man churn butter, then I'd be the first to do it.

After he won, I managed to tug him behind the stone barn afterward and cop a few good feels, enough skin to tide me over until tonight, at least, when I planned on riding my champion until I'd brought him right across the finish line.

The day was perfect, one that if you could watch from above, could pull back to a wide camera shot and observe, you'd think you were watching an ad for the New York Tourism Board, or at the very least a small-town council's print ad in a regional magazine. Shiny, happy people—and now we were dancing.

No, really, there was even a square dance in the middle of all this Martha Stewart meets Norman Rockwell visual perfection.

While my sore back kept me from allemanding left and promenading right, Oscar and I did manage to sneak in a slow dance when the bluegrass band played its own version of Patsy Cline's "Crazy." We swayed back and forth under the October sky, eyes seeing only each other, his hands trying his damnedest not to be full of my sweet ass. Every few bars his hands would start to slip down, and I had to remind him that we were on display here, with kids everywhere.

We saw every stall, visited every booth, chatting with everyone I'd come to know in the few short weeks since discovering this wonderful town. Eventually we nabbed a picnic table, filled it with Leo and Polly and Chad and Logan, and Roxie and I headed to a stand to grab hot dogs for everyone.

"You two seem cozy," Roxie said, bumping my hip on the way to the hot dog stand.

"We do, don't we?" I replied, feeling my cheeks creak as I grinned for the thousandth time that very day. "I gotta admit, it's pretty great."

"That's obvious." She jumped into line right before a gaggle of junior high kids beat us to it. "So where is this headed?"

"Can it, Callahan."

"Shut the fuck up with your can, this is me. Give me the deets please."

"The deets are that it's an impossible question to answer. Besides, who says we have to decide where it's heading right now? I'm heading in the direction of the biggest hot dog I can find." This placated her for a moment, and we moved up another space in line. But then she simply couldn't resist . . .

"At least tell me something about his hot dog," she said, shooting me a conspiratorial look.

"It's in the direction of the biggest hot dog I can find," I repeated.

"I knew it! I fucking knew it!" she cackled, squeezing my arm. "Sometimes it's like God handed out great bodies and beautiful faces, but then absolutely nothing in the trouser department, and it's just the worst! And Oscar is so beautiful, I was afraid for his trousers."

I laughed in agreement. It was rare that someone so blessed above was so blessed below. And some of the least attractive guys could have the most talented cock out there. But not often did the two converge. And I was beyond delighted to have that convergence occur between my thighs.

I leaned in close. "Be not afraid of his trousers, for it is good and we are well met."

"I love when you go all Middle-earth on me," she said, just as I heard one of the kids behind us ask—

"What the hell are trousers?"

"I think they're some kind of old-timey pants," one of the other ones answered.

She caught my eye, and we silently agreed to keep the rest of our conversation trouser-free as long as we remained in line.

"Three hot dogs, please," I chirped to the guy behind the counter.

"How d'you want them?" he asked, gesturing to the array of condiments.

I had no idea. When in doubt, go bold.

"One with just mustard, and put everything on the other two." I grinned as I watched him pile them high with all kinds of goodies, thinking that Oscar seemed like an everything kind of guy.

Once we were headed back I looked up over the hot dogs I'd procured for my man, and his eyes met mine. Pure heat burned across the barnyard and made my pulse once more go crazy fast.

Then my gaze shifted a smidge to the right, and the heat

turned to fury. Because seated next to Oscar, sandwiching herself right in the middle of the bench, was none other than ex-wife Missy, looking decidedly wifelike as she set a tray of hot dogs right in front of my guy.

"Oh, sister, did you pick the wrong seat," I seethed, and Roxie looked where my eye daggers were landing.

"Oh boy," she muttered, and tried to step in front of me. "Take a breath, Nat. Just—"

"I'm calm," I said through my teeth as I continued toward the table. "Perfectly calm."

So calm, in fact, that when we reached the table, I stepped up onto the bench between Leo and Polly, stepped up on top of the table, stood in front of Oscar with my tray of hot dogs and smiled down sweetly at Missy.

"Thanks for saving my seat, Missy."

I set my foot down between them on the bench, turning at the last minute to place my posterior directly in her face, then wiggled down into the space she suddenly had to vacate.

Across the table Leo, Polly, Chad, and Logan were all staring back at me with dropped jaws, and behind them Roxie shook her head with a tightly drawn mouth.

Oscar, however, looked like he was trying very hard not to laugh.

"Hot dog?" I asked brightly, setting the tray down in front of him.

"Looks good," he answered, running a hand along his jaw and failing to conceal his laughter miserably. "Which one is mine?"

"The two with everything," I replied with a grin, picking up his bottle of beer and draining half in one draft. "Thirsty."

I felt an insistent tapping on my shoulder, and though I at first tried to ignore her, it soon became clear that she wasn't going away.

"Yes, Missy?" I asked in my nicest voice, turning toward her.

"Oscar doesn't like his hot dogs like that," she chirped, looking over my shoulder at the tray.

"Sorry?"

"Oscar never gets anything but mustard on his hot dogs."

"You don't say," I answered, trying to keep my cool. Who the hell did she think she was? Ex-wife meant *ex-* on having a say; *ex-* on being a know-it-all; *ex-* on weighing in on anything about Oscar.

She looked carefully at the tray in front of him, cataloguing everything that was wrong with the wieners. She raised a critical eyebrow, cocked her head to the side, and through tiny pursed lips said, "And he hates onions. Did you know he hates onions?"

I let a smile creep across my face—the smile I used for creepy guys on the subway and men who make fat jokes. Part Stepford, part demon, all New York City Don't Mess With Me. "How would I know he doesn't like onions? We've been too busy fucking."

Leo picked Polly up and spirited her away from the table, shaking his head in the same way Roxie had, while Polly giggled something about needing a larger piggy bank.

Chad and Logan stopped cold, their mouths full of hot dog.

Roxie was frozen, too, but the O shape of her mouth was more resigned than surprised.

Missy's eyes filled with tears, first the edges, then spilling into the center, blending with her now visible mascara to make mud.

Oscar's hand settled on my shoulder. And it felt . . . different. Could a hand feel disapproving? I turned and saw his face—and holy shit, that eyebrow was beyond disapproving.

Missy climbed out of the seat and took off for the barn. I

caught the image out of the corner of my eye, and it wasn't lost on me that her hands were over her eyes.

How is she managing to navigate, then?

Inner snark, it's time to stand down.

Now Oscar was standing up—and looking down at me with an unidentifiable expression. Confusion? Hurt? Shame?

Disappointment.

"Oh come on," I muttered as he squeezed my shoulder, then took off in a slow jog in the same direction as Miss Missy.

"How is this . . . but why would he . . . but she knew that . . . and I didn't mean . . . but she's always around and . . . son of a bitch." I slumped onto the seat I'd claimed so dramatically and studied the hot dogs. "How was I supposed to know he didn't like onions?"

"Because you've been too busy fucking?" Logan said.

I looked up to see them all watching to see what happened next, and I slouched farther into the table, chin in hands.

Logan exchanged a glance with Chad. "You okay?"

"Am I way off base here? I mean, it's weird, right? That she acts like she's—"

Three mouths spoke at once.

"Still in love?"

"Wants him back."

"Would love to have that hot dog back inside her bun."

"Wow," I said. "I'm glad it's not just me."

"Totally not just you, sweetie," Chad said, patting my hand. "Those two are like the poster children for how adults should behave after a divorce—"

"—if one of those adults is still totally in love," Logan finished.

"You don't have to say it like that," Chad admonished him. "Natalie's clearly upset here, and I think we need to make sure that—"

"Oh, make sure nothing. She's a big girl, and she knows what's going on. Didn't you see that *Dynasty* moment just now? She annihilated Missy; it was—"

"Oh, you two stop," Roxie said, turning to face me. "It doesn't matter what we say about Oscar and Missy. What does *Oscar* say about him and Missy?"

"Not much. We haven't really talked about it," I admitted. "I guess we should, though, right? I mean, that's what grown-ups do . . . I think."

"Don't ask me. I'm still not sure if I'm an official grown-up yet, although being listed as a second emergency contact at Polly's school made me feel about ten feet tall—and scared to death. But also kind of . . . honored, that Leo entrusted her to me."

I sat quietly for a moment. "You really are an official grown-up."

She nodded. "God help us all."

We threw away the hot dogs and went off to find Leo and Polly. I got a stern glance from Leo, a high five from Polly (who then got a stern glance from Roxie), and a big handful of nothing when I went to find Oscar.

He was nowhere to be found.

❧

Grabbing a ride home with Roxie after we helped Leo clean up a bit, I tossed and turned on the guest room bed, clad in one of her T-shirts, since my weekend bag was in Oscar's truck.

Where the hell was he? I'd texted him twice, but he didn't answer. Never one to chase what doesn't want to be caught, I gave him his space. But I still wondered where he was . . . and what he might be up to.

This, this right here, what I was feeling—confused, unsettled, unsure—was why I never got in this deep this fast. And I was in *very* deep. I had it bad for this guy, and I didn't see that going away anytime soon.

Ugh. I flopped over onto my stomach. The biggest T-shirt Roxie had was snug across my hips, and most certainly my breasts.

I flopped back over onto my back. I sat up, punched my pillow repeatedly, lay back down, sat back up, then flipped once more onto my stomach and starfished. Just as I was finally getting settled, there was a knock at my door.

"Nat?" a quiet voice called.

"Yeah?"

"There's a good-looking dairy farmer at the front door. Go see what he wants." Then Roxie's footsteps went back down the hallway toward her room.

It was after 2 a.m., for pity's sake. Curious to know what he had to say, I threw off the covers, slipped into a robe, and padded down the dark back steps to the kitchen, then let myself out onto the porch. Shivering in the cold night air, I was grateful for the thick woolen socks I'd pulled on before going to bed.

Standing in a puddle of moonlight, rocking back and forth on his heels, Oscar was watching the front door. Nervous? Still disappointed? The moonlight wasn't bright enough to tell, but something was clearly on his mind.

A board in the porch creaked, and he whirled in surprise.

"Hi," I said.

He looked at me, taking in my robe and socks. And said nothing.

"You woke me up out of a sound sleep, Caveman. What's going on?" I didn't want to let on that I was losing sleep over what had happened.

"I wanted to talk to you," he finally started, taking a step toward me on the porch.

"Talk to me about what?" I asked.

"About what happened tonight." Step. "With Missy." Another step.

"Oh. That." I made myself sound like it hadn't affected me in the slightest that he'd left me to go chase his ex-wife to wipe her oh-so-convenient tears. "Yeah, let's talk about that." So much for unaffected.

"What Missy said, about the way I like my hot dogs, was . . ."

Rude. Assuming. Territorial.

". . . true."

I blinked at him. "True?"

He nodded. "She's right. I don't like relish. And I don't like onions."

My hands were suddenly on my hips, and my right foot was tapping furiously. "Fine, Oscar. You don't want my relish and my onions, then just say so."

"I just did, actually," he said, his eyes watching my foot tap.

"So Missy knows everything there is to know about you, and I know nothing."

"She was my wife, Natalie," he said softly, and something very small and almost foreign to me, way down deep inside, twisted over at hearing those words. "She knows I sometimes like chocolate chips in my pancakes. She knows I'm terrible at folding laundry but that I love to iron my sheets. She knows that when I'm sick, I like to have the ginger ale swished up to get rid of all the bubbles."

"If you woke me up in the middle of the night just to list all the wonderful things Missy does, this really could have waited until the morning."

"And she makes great muffins," he continued as if I hadn't

said a word, looking at me with the faintest hint of amusement.

"Tell me again why you divorced her?" I asked sweetly. "She sounds like the one who got away."

"What's wrong with two people staying friends after they divorce?"

"It's weird," I answered promptly.

"It's weird?"

"Yeah, it's weird. You're supposed to, I don't know, hate each other, and be bitter and angry, and fight over things like coffee tables and salad spinners."

"What's a salad spinner?"

"It's a bowl that you put washed greens in and— Oh stop it, that's not what this is about!"

"You brought up the salad spinner, it must be something pretty amazing if I'm supposed to be . . . what did you say? Fighting over it? Along with a coffee table?"

"You. Are. Infuriating." I spat each word out slowly and clearly, not wanting him to miss them.

"Missy used to tell me the same thing."

I launched myself at him, threw myself on this giant man with his giant shoulders, and literally tried to take him to the ground, my sock-clad feet sliding on the cold wooden planks. My hands struggled to land a blow, to do anything other than hang pitifully from his enormous shoulders, while he simply braced himself and let me tantrum in midair.

When he began to chuckle, I *really* lost my cool. "Don't you dare laugh at me, you motherfucker! I can't believe that you'd laugh at me, after what you did to me tonight at that stupid hoedown!" I swung wildly at him, missing by a mile.

"Okay, that's it," he grumbled, grabbing me across my middle, throwing me over his shoulder like a sack of potatoes, and starting across the lawn. "'Night, Roxie, sorry about the noise," he called out.

I looked up to see her hanging out of her bedroom window and waving merrily at the two of us.

"Thank goodness, now I can go back to sleep," she said good-naturedly, starting to close the window. "It used to be so quiet out here in the country."

He carried me over to his truck, kicking and screaming obscenities. Opening the passenger side, he dumped me inside, then closed the door. As I continued to yell at him, he stood outside the door until I'd exhausted every insult I could think of, which was a lot.

"—until it falls off and rots!" I finally finished, panting. The passenger-side window was almost completely fogged over, but I could see his shape through it, just waiting it out.

I rubbed the tie of my robe over the fog, making a clear spot. He leaned down to look through, his eyes twinkling in the moonlight.

Sonofa— "Let me out."

He said something, but I couldn't understand the words.

"What?"

He pantomimed rolling down the window, and I rolled it down a crack. "Let me out," I repeated.

"I'll let you out when you calm down."

"I really don't take orders well. You should know that about me," I said, seething.

"Duly noted." He smiled that damn killer grin. "You ready to talk like normal people now?"

"Define normal."

He thought a moment. "How about we just shoot for no more yelling?"

I pondered. "Deal. Can I get out now?"

He shook his head. "I'd feel safer with the steel door between us for a little while longer. But maybe you could roll the window down a little more?"

"I can hear you just fine," I mumbled, but rolled it down all the way. When I looked up, his face was mere inches from mine.

"With the window up, I couldn't do this," he whispered, then kissed me slow and sweet. When he pulled away, my lips wanted to follow, but I kept them safely inside the truck. "So you're really this pissed off about onions?"

"I—" I started to yell, then clamped my mouth shut tightly and tried to think about what I wanted to say. "I was pissed off that your ex-wife couldn't wait to tell me you didn't like onions. And believe me, we're talking about that. But what *really* pissed me off was that you left, and you never came back. You left me there alone—

"You weren't alone—"

"I *felt* alone."

He was silent outside the truck. I was silent inside the truck.

"I'm sorry that I left, and I'm sorry that you felt alone," he said after a moment. "But you really hurt Missy's feelings."

"I don't think that—"

"Let me finish." He waited, and when I nodded, he went on. "You think divorced people should be arguing about things, but I think the opposite. We'd been friends since we were in seventh grade. We dated all through high school. She went with me to USC, and when I got drafted she was cheering me on in the front row. She was with me in Dallas, she was with me in the locker room the day my knee gave out, and she was next to me the entire time I was in rehab, training to get strong again."

Shit. That was the definition of history.

"So why wouldn't we be friends after we were no longer married?"

"Why aren't you still married? It sounds like you two were perfect for each other." I hated that my words came out as sharp as they did, but I had to know.

"Do you want the same things you wanted when you were seventeen?"

I flashed on that tiny apartment in the Bronx, cooking for Thomas and flinching when he told me I was a fat slob. Yet I'd stayed. I'd wanted it.

"No," I said vehemently.

"We fell out of love—it happens. But just because we didn't make it as a couple, I'm supposed to hate her?"

"She sure doesn't hate you," I mumbled, and suddenly there was a hand under my chin, tipping my head upward. And warm gray-blue eyes, staring deeply into mine.

"Is she a little dependent on me? Maybe. Maybe I've let her get too dependent. But it doesn't bother me, and it shouldn't bother you. There's nothing but friendship between Missy and me. That's it."

I started to say something, but wisely bit my tongue. Because those eyes were burning into mine, almost in a hypnotic kind of way, and I wanted to see what he'd say next. Oscar was a man of few words, so when he used them, I liked to hear them all.

Good thing, too, because what he said next . . .

"In case you haven't noticed, my attention is focused right now on one woman only. And she's pretty much got me twisted up in knots, in all the best kinds of ways."

"Twisted?"

"Mmm-hmm," he breathed, his hands curving over mine on top of the window, his breath puffing against my face as he lowered his head down toward mine. "All twisted up."

"Twisted up like . . . head over heels?" I asked, holding my breath. He thought a moment, then kissed me on the tip of my nose.

"Exactly like that."

Oh. Shit. But as I waited for something like panic to set in, something else entirely happened. Warm fuzzies bloomed outward from my belly into my hands and feet, currents zipping out and back again. I tugged his face farther through the window.

"Don't leave me again, okay?" I whispered, and he nodded, dipping his head down, running his nose along the side of my face, nuzzling into the crook just below my ear.

"Can I please get out of the car now?" I asked, sitting up higher on the seat, curling my legs underneath me and in the process, flashing him my thighs as my robe rose higher and higher. He started to nod again, but then thought better of it.

"How about I just take you home?" he murmured, beginning to drop tiny kisses all along my jaw, sweeping back along to the hollow of my neck. I shivered, and he took that to mean yes, yes get in this truck and drive me the hell home.

And he did.

I climbed all over him in the truck, sitting on his lap, straddling his lap, laughing as he drove while looking over my shoulder, right hand on the wheel and left hand fumbling under my robe. I kissed his neck, bit his ear, sucked on his jaw, and got my hand halfway down his jeans before he turned into his driveway and pulled me out of the cab and onto him. His hands were everywhere as he picked me up, this time not over his shoulder but tangled across him like he was wearing a Natalie sweater, legs wrapped around his middle, arms wrapped around his neck, my robe dangling from my elbows with my T-shirt up around my neck.

His eyes were wild as he devoured my skin, almost tripping up the front porch steps in his need to get me inside . . . to get me inside. And when we saw the basket of muffins nestled next to the front door, he kicked it aside, the front door banging open wide.

He fucked me on the stairs in the entryway, with his pants around his ankles and my panties torn from one thigh. He fucked me with the front door wide open, with the truck lights still on and the driver's-side door still hanging ajar, the radio still turned on.

And the muffins stood alone, cold and untouched.

Chapter 18

$\mathcal{I}$ stayed in Bailey Falls all day Sunday, and Sunday night as well. I'd planned to get back into the city and get some laundry done, see my parents, get some work done, see some friends, but man oh man, when a guy like Oscar looks at you from across the room, and wants to figure out exactly how many times he can make you come by his tongue alone . . . time tends to stand still.

So I took the early train Monday morning, raced to my apartment, threw on the first clean anything I could find in my closet, and made it to work only an hour late. Well. Ninety minutes.

I walked quickly into my office, keeping my head down to sneak in under the radar, but when my coworker Liz saw me, she shrieked, "It's not an urban legend! Natalie has returned!"

So much for under the radar.

"Hey, Liz, how's it going?" I replied, smiling and nodding and trying like hell to get into my office quickly. There was something stuck to my back that had been itching the entire way uptown, and I'd been scratching since Twenty-second Street. I slipped out of my jacket, tossed it across the back of my chair, and waved her in.

"You've been spending so much time on this account I feel

like I never see you anymore," Liz said, looking at me pointedly.

"I know, it's been crazy! But the campaign is coming along really well. You know how it is, really want to capture the essence of the small town, blah blah blah."

"Speaking of blah blah blah, I heard a rumor that one of the campaigns up for grabs today is Wool, that cute little shop over on Madison that sells those insanely expensive sweaters? If it happened to come to me, I wouldn't be opposed to it, if you know what I'm saying . . ."

"Shop on Madison, shop on Madison, have I been there?" I asked, trying to picture which one she was talking about. Shops tended to open and close so quickly in Manhattan; no one could afford their rent very long if their store wasn't performing almost immediately.

"Sure, sure, remember we went there right after it opened? You hit on the sales guy who tried to sell us woolen dickies and ended up meeting him for a drink that weekend?"

"The guy with the ears, right?" I dimly remembered riding a beautiful face with unfortunately large, floppy ears. I'd felt like I was on a ride at Disney World.

"Exactly, the guy with the ears. And his boss is the guy with the pitch, so when it comes up, if you could be looking in my direction, that'd be ever so groovy." She blinked at me so innocently I couldn't help but laugh.

"Ever so groovy?"

"*Partridge Family* marathon yesterday. I was this close to getting my hair feathered."

"Jeez, I would have had to friend-divorce you—or at least take you to my salon. Which reminds me, I'm pretty sure I missed my last appointment with Roscoe."

"Whoa, you missed an appointment with Roscoe? Hairstylist to the stars Roscoe?"

"That's the one, and he gets pretty testy if you no-show on him. I've been avoiding my email all weekend; I just know I got one of those 'sorry we missed you, but no one does this, so thin ice and all that' emails," I replied, scratching my back again. I did feel bad. Roscoe had been doing my hair for years, long before he became the stylist everyone was trying to get an appointment with. I also didn't tell her that the appointment I'd missed had been the second in a row . . .

"I would kill for an appointment at his salon, and you're blithely missing yours—what a life!" Liz said, shaking her head. "So, you'll be on the lookout for that pitch today? Wool?"

"Why are you asking me? You know Dan decides that," I said, twisting in my seat, trying to find the itch that just wouldn't stop.

"Yeah, but you're Dan today."

"Pardon?" I asked, half listening to her as I grabbed a pen and tried to use that on my back.

"Dan is out sick, so you're running the meeting today. Did you know that your dress is on inside out?"

"What are you talking about?"

"He sent an email last night saying that he's out with the flu, and you'd be running things today and possibly tomorrow—"

The air left the room.

"He attached all the accounts for you to review—"

My entire body went rigid and cold.

"—and if you could make sure that Wool job goes to me, but don't make it look like it was mine all along, you know, that'd be awesome . . ."

It was strange, being able to breathe with no air in the room. And I was breathing. Heavily.

"And you should fix your dress since the meeting's in five minutes. See you in there . . . boss." She winked and was gone.

No worries. No worries at all. I could cram a day's worth of work reviewing these accounts into five minutes.

Actually, four. Because my dress is on inside out.

∽

Bad week. Bad, bad, *bad* week.

Liz got the campaign she wanted, because I didn't have a clue who else to give it to. I'd missed the email that Dan had sent the entire group, as well as missing the email that he'd sent just to me Sunday afternoon. In this age of smartphones and everywhere Wi-Fi, it simply wasn't possible to lie to your boss about not getting an email. Unless you weren't checking your email because you were too busy.

But when the tongue and the coming and then the fingers and the screaming and the oh my, that was unexpected but awesome, can you do that exactly the same way again . . . Things like phone chargers tend to go by the wayside.

So I refocused. I spent the week getting caught up on the work that was beginning to slip. Phone messages were falling through the cracks, my in-box was beyond full, and I might have missed a deadline on the T&T campaign.

Word got back to Dan that I'd been unprepared for the Monday meeting, and I had to sit in his office when he returned and listen to him artfully ask me questions designed to find out if anything was going on outside of the office that might be affecting what was going on inside of the office. Nothing had officially happened, except for one slightly late deadline. But I'd always delivered everything on time or early, and I was never behind on emails or phone calls. He seemed reassured—but there might've been a hint of *What the hell is happening to my* number-one *account exec . . .*

I buckled down, worked twelve-hour days, and by Friday I was back on top of the pile, work completed ahead of schedule. I hadn't realized just how much I'd fallen behind, which for me was unheard of. Technically nothing was really late, because I routinely had my work done ahead of schedule. But for me, I felt very behind.

Oscar and I had been texting some throughout the week, in the few moments when I surfaced. I tried to keep my focus on work entirely, which was so hard to do when my mind kept flying up the Metro North to a town where leaves were crunchy underfoot, jack-o'-lanterns gave way to November pumpkin and squash arrangements, and my handsome farmer was sending me messages like:

I miss your mouth

I miss your taste

Get your great big comma
ass back up here so I can
bite it

Oscar was coming in for the whole weekend—a first! Technically he came into the city every Saturday—but this time he was spending the night.

Friday night I stayed at the office until nine thirty, then finally headed home. There was a new club opening that I'd RSVP'd to, and a birthday party being held at one of my favorite restaurants uptown. But by the time I climbed the subway steps, all I wanted to do was soak in a tub. And eat Malaysian takeout, which I did at eleven, while soaking in that tub.

The delivery boy said he'd missed me.

⇜⇝

Saturday morning dawned clear and cold, the stiff wind making my coat swirl as I made my way down Fourteenth Street. I'd told Oscar I'd arrive early, and my feet burned to skip across the market when I caught sight of his booth.

Carefully carrying two coffees, I moved through the throngs of early marketers to cut in line at Bailey Falls Creamery, which was already about twenty deep.

As I searched for Oscar, nodding to the salesgirls I'd actually come to know by now, I felt my skin begin to tingle. I smiled even before I turned.

"Thought you were coming early," a deep voice said.

"Oh, I came early. At home, in my bed, alone," I purred. "You should have been there—I was magnificent."

His eyes narrowed as he imagined exactly what I'd been up to this morning. It was true, too. I was wound so tightly in anticipation of seeing him I'd taken care of business twice before heading to the market. I needed to take the edge off, but it'd only made me more excited to see him. Even now, as he stepped closer to me, I could feel my body begin to hum at having him near.

"I believe it," he whispered, leaning down to place his mouth next to my ear. "I came all over my hand this morning, thinking about seeing you today."

I shivered. He quivered. And all around us, people waited to buy cheese.

The day was long, but fun. I stood behind the counter and helped him take and fill orders, listened to his regular clients sing his praises, and watched Oscar shake off the compliments as though they meant nothing. I'd come to realize that he was genuinely shy and reserved, which sometimes came across as . . . well . . . being an ass.

"You need to be nicer to your customers," I whispered, after one particularly uncomfortable moment.

"I'm nice," he insisted.

"You're dismissive and rude," I insisted back.

"I don't want to get to know my customers. Why is that rude? They like my cheese; I like making it and taking their money," he said, tugging on my apron string. Thank goodness he didn't insist on the hairnets when at the market. "Where is it written that to sell cheese I also have to be best friends with everyone here?"

"It's just good business, Oscar. Plus, you're adorable when you smile."

"I'm adorable?" he asked. Six foot six inches, covered in tattoos and scars, with hands as big as a boule and arms as big as tree trunks. And now with the same menacing look he used to give me when I'd approach him to buy his Brie.

"Yeah, you kind of are," I grinned, tugging on his apron string.

Without meaning to, and most certainly without wanting to, he grinned back. Then he realized how adorable he might be, and away went the smile. He turned to the first person in line, an attractive woman in her fifties who was looking like she was shopping for more than Camembert. "What do you want?" he growled, and I had to turn away to stifle my laugh.

The woman looked head over heels. I knew the feeling.

I spent the day making change and wrapping up orders, chatting with the customers since Oscar wasn't, asking them questions about what they liked and what they loved. Sort of informal market research. I went on a coffee run with him just before lunch, and found myself pressed against a giant bale of hay over by the free-trade sustainable green coffee roasting booth, getting felt up through my apron as he stole kisses.

When it was time for lunch, we headed down to the south end of the market to get sandwiches for everyone from the guys who owned the local salumeria. Salami, prosciutto, mortadella—they piled everything onto enormous sandwiches made with some of the best bread in town. As we waited for our Italians on French with everything, he slipped his arms around me from behind, under cover of my apron, leaned his head on my shoulder, and whispered filthy, naughty things into my ear as he slid one hand into my panties to find me wet and wanting.

I was so close I nearly let him get me off in front of a hundred hoagies.

And as the day wound down, I noticed that every time Oscar walked past me or reached around me to grab something, he made sure to grab something else. His hands rubbed my bottom every chance he got. I loved it. I may have even stuck my butt out on purpose to make sure it was in his way.

Finally the last customer paid for his cheese, the market was officially closed, and the stalls started coming down. Thank God, because the sexual tension that was pinging back and forth could have lit up an entire city block. It hadn't gone unnoticed by his team, which could have been why they had the booth broken down and loaded onto the trucks in record time.

As we said good-bye to everyone, he took my hand, which was also lost on no one, and steered me in the direction of his truck.

"Today was fun," I said, leaning into his arm. His hand was warm in mine, his fingers laced solidly through mine, his thumb tracing the inside of my palm. I knew these tracings. They were the same ones he drew on my back, or on my front, or on my thighs, or on my bum, before and after he loved on me. For someone who didn't let a lot of people in, he seemed to love to touch and to be touched. I sighed contentedly, tucking my other hand into his arm, nuzzling his flannel shirt. He smelled clean and sweet, with a touch of barn and clover.

"Fun?" he asked. "You've been to the market before—every week, like clockwork." He looked down, his eyes teasing.

"Damn straight. I had to get my Brie."

He grinned, not buying it for a second. "Only the Brie, huh?"

"Certainly not for the conversation," I replied, earning a swat on the butt.

"Thank God you did. Watching you walk away, and getting to see that sweet ass every week—mmm, woman, the thoughts you gave me."

"Tell me," I said, looking up at him.

"Tell you what?"

"What you thought about me, before we met."

"You mean before you scared my cows and then attacked me in Leo's barn?"

"Yes. Before the luckiest day of your life, what did you think of me when you saw me, stumbling and stammering each Saturday?" I stopped in the street, turning into him as throngs of people pushed past us like water breaking over a boulder.

"Well, you know I loved your ass," he began.

I rolled my eyes. "It's a great ass, a sweet ass, a beautifully perfect, great, big ass—this we know." I slapped at his chest. "But did you think anything else?"

"I wondered what made you so nervous."

"Maybe I was just the nervous type. Ever think of that?" I teased.

"No way. I watched you sail through the market each week

like you fucking owned the place. You only got nervous when you got to my line."

"Wait, what?"

"You don't think I noticed you before you got in my line, Pinup?" he asked, sweeping a piece of hair back from my face. "Each week you'd come in from the east, buy your coffee, stop at a few other booths, and then you'd come see me. And you'd strut through the place like a peacock, tits up and out, secret smile on your face, knowing exactly what you looked like and enjoying the shit out of the attention."

My mouth was hanging open.

"And then you'd come see me, and the swagger was gone, and you'd roll on those gorgeous ankles a little, and it was like you'd disappear. And I always wondered why."

"Because you're so beautiful," I answered, slipping under that spell I always felt with him. I wasn't tongue-tied anymore, but there was still something kind of magical about him that would never go away.

"*You're* beautiful," he countered—and just like that, his lips were on mine. Slow and sweet, he kissed me like we were in a meadow all alone, not a care in the world. When in truth, we were surrounded by hundreds of people on a crowded city street in Manhattan. People with shopping bags banging into my shins, tourists with camera phones pointed up crashed into us as they tried to capture their New York City experience. And people from the neighborhood, just out to enjoy their Saturday, were grumbling for us to get a room, take it inside.

But it didn't matter. Because when that man kissed me, it was magic. And I was 100 percent under his spell. When he finally pulled his mouth away from mine, I could see how hungry he was.

"How far is your place?"

"If we drive your truck, we'll spend an hour looking for a parking space."

"If we do it your way?"

"We'll be home in ten minutes."

He bent down and nipped my neck. "Ten minutes, then."

I got him there in eight.

                                  *

As soon as I closed the front door he pressed me up against it, holding me there with the strength of his body as he kissed me fast and furious. He bared my breasts quickly, ripping my shirt and scattering buttons. With his mouth closing around one nipple and his left hand teasing the other, his right hand unsnapped my jeans, tugged down the zipper, and shoved inside.

I'd been turned on all day and cried out at his touch, gasping when his fingers found me, stroking and petting, his thumb rubbing my clit and working two fingers inside me, already soaked. My back arched, trying to get closer to him, my hips riding his fingers.

Panting and chanting, I came hard and fast, my legs trapped inside my jeans, unable to do anything but ride the orgasm, totally at his mercy.

Before the first one ended, he was already chasing a second. Kneeling in front of me, he slipped my heels from my feet, pausing to admire the four inches of red leather Prada I'd been prancing around in all day.

"You wore these to tease me today, didn't you? Don't lie," he chided, tugging my jeans over my hips, watching my breasts bounce, having been liberated from my white lace bra only moments earlier.

"I wore these for *me*. I love these shoes, and I love what happens to me when I wear them."

"And what is that?" he asked, pulling my jeans off and sliding his hands up the inside of my thighs.

"When I wear shoes like this, I get fucked," I whispered, trailing my fingers over my breasts, the tips still sensitive from his mouth and his teeth.

"And how do you like to get fucked?" he asked, slipping his hands underneath the bands on my hips, pulling my panties down along my legs, nuzzling the outline of where they had just been.

"Hard," I moaned, as he kissed the soft mound just above my clit—his favorite pillow, he'd once told me. "And filthy."

His lips found mine, spearing me with his tongue, licking and sucking, burying his face as my back arched once more. Lifting his head, he circled my clit with his tongue, still so sensitive but so receptive to everything he was doing. He knew my body like his own. "Tall ceilings."

"What?" I panted, confusion clouding through the delicious things he was doing.

"You've got tall ceilings," he told my skin, his hands sliding up the backs of my legs to grab my ass, pushing me harder into his face.

"Ten feet. They don't make them like this . . . oh Christ . . . anymore," I managed with a groan as he lifted his face once more. "Stop doing that! Get back down there."

"Hold on to my shoulders," he said, and before I knew what was happening, I was airborne. Oscar lifted me straight up into the air, pushed me up against the door once more, and wrapped my legs around his shoulders. Now, eye level with his favorite pillow, he grinned.

"Hold on to something," he instructed.

My head was practically bumping the ceiling. As I scrambled to get my fingers latched on to the thick crown molding, he held me in place and fucked me with his tongue until I was shaking.

While I was seeing stars, he gave the insides of each of my thighs a bite, then slid me down his body, took us both to the floor, setting me on top of him, legs astride.

"Get my zipper, would you?" he asked, lying back with his arms tucked behind his head, a giant grin on his face.

"As you wish, Caveman," I replied gleefully, unzipping and bringing him forth. He groaned as I stroked him, marveling once more at how perfect he was, how perfect he felt in my hands. I still felt a little dizzy, but he was so very hard and so very ready, and I really did deserve another . . .

I lifted up, positioned him at the center of the world, and sat down, hard. We both gasped, me from feeling him stretch me inside, so big, so thick, so exactly right. I lifted my hips just a little, squeezing him from inside as he hissed and I got to watch his eyes close in bliss.

He bit down on his lip, his hands squeezing my hips, urging me to move, to do something, anything. But still, I waited.

I wanted to move. He wanted me to move. And I waited. I waited until I was almost panting, almost out of breath from sheer want and need. And then I threw my head back and began to ride.

I rode him long and hard, exactly the way *I* wanted to. My hair had come unpinned, and it spread out all around me, hanging down long in the back, and I could feel it tickling my backside. Could he feel it? Could he feel it as it danced along his thighs, as I gave myself over to everything I was feeling, to that moment where everything boiled down to feeling him deep inside?

His hands were everywhere. On my hips, encouraging deep thrusts. On my breasts, rolling my nipples, cupping and kneading and mmm, pinching. On my ass, slapping and squeezing and grabbing handfuls of me, pushing me faster and faster, higher and higher.

His eyes wandered over my naked skin, thrilling to the sight of my breasts bouncing and my hands running lightly over my body.

And he smiled as I rode him. He told me how beautiful I was, how gorgeous I was, how good I tasted, and he used dirty, filthy words like *those fucking tits* and *come all over my cock* and *that sweet cunt.*

And when his thrusts came faster and harder, he guided my hands down to where we were joined and told me to touch myself, to make myself come just I had that morning, with my fingers imagining his cock.

And when I came, *he* came. Just like that.

∾

"We missed dinner."

"How's that?"

I bumped my hips, causing him to lift his head from my tush. "We missed dinner—I had a reservation at Mateo's."

He looked at his watch. "How late are they open? We could run right now." He laid his head back down, not motivated to move anywhere anytime soon.

I smiled at the sight of him, his head on one cheek and his hand rubbing the other. He really did love my bum. "You can't just waltz into Mateo's; their reservation list is a mile long. I made this weeks ago."

"Weeks ago? We didn't know each other weeks ago."

"True, but I still made the reservation. It's new, incredibly popular, and everyone is dying to eat there."

He nibbled on my thigh. "So you were going to go to this place tonight even if I didn't come into the city?"

"As you said, I didn't know you weeks ago. Now that I do—Ow!" He'd bitten down a little too hard.

"Sorry," he murmured, kissing the spot softly. "Doesn't matter, take me somewhere else."

"Where do you want to go?"

"Somewhere that tells me something about you."

"Something about me, hmm?" I thought for a moment. "Oooh, dumpling crawl!"

I was up and off the floor in five seconds flat, leaving him naked and repeating the words *dumpling crawl* while I hauled ass to my bedroom to change into something warm. "Come on, get dressed!"

Moments later we were outside on the stoop waiting for the cab, and he was still trying to figure this out.

"I've heard of a pub crawl—anything like that?"

"It's exactly the same, except it's dumplings."

"We're crawling for dumplings?"

"Yes."

"As in, chicken and?"

"As in dim sum."

"What?"

"Oh just get your ass in the cab." I pushed him into the waiting car and told the driver, "Canal and Eldridge."

Seated in the back of the cab, Oscar glared at me. "You're bossy."

"And you love it. All cavemen secretly like to be told what to do now and then. And after these dumplings, you'll do anything I say."

"You sure are building up these dumplings."

"By the end of the night, you will swear you have had the tastiest thing ever in your mouth. And that's saying something, considering where your mouth was an hour ago."

He snorted as the cabdriver tried to make eye contact with me through the mirror, and I stared him down.

Mateo's would have been really nice: elegant and chic, incredible food and wine, likely even romantic. But with Oscar in my city for the first time, I realized a dumpling crawl through Chinatown was exactly right. It was a nice night; not so cold that we'd freeze walking through the streets, but chilly enough that I could break out my new Burberry. Once altered for my size, the claret-colored cashmere Chesterfield coat, with the single-breasted detail, was a lovely way to handle the chilly night in style.

Plus, the gorgeous man on my arm made the only shivers running up and down my spine purely sexual in nature. And now that we were in Chinatown, out and about with everyone else who'd had the same idea, I was glad we did this instead of dining at some expensive restaurant.

Normally I'm a big fan of the expensive and the fancy, but I loved me a dumpling. The cheaper the better, and I knew every nook and cranny in Chinatown.

"This place looks . . . wow," Oscar said, shaking his head as we approached the first stop, Lucky Dumpling. Most of the stores were already shuttered for the night, but the lights and the line were humming at Lucky. "I wouldn't have picked this place. It looks like—"

"A hole in the wall?" I steered him around a display of "Chanel" umbrellas. "It literally is. And you don't ever want to see the alley."

"So we're here because . . . ?"

"Because of *that*." I sighed as a couple passed by us, the guy balancing four containers of dumplings while the girl shoveled them into both of their mouths.

He looked skeptical, but when we got closer and saw how long the line was, he became more intrigued. And when I finally popped that first pork dumpling into his mouth, salty and crackly on the outside from the hot wok, soft and chewy on the inside, the first thing he asked was, "Did we get enough?"

Four dumplings for one dollar. We got enough.

We spent the evening crisscrossing the streets of Chinatown, popping in and out of noodle houses and dim sum palaces, cheap and cheaper, better and best. We sat at crowded tables with other diners, traded stories about where they'd been and where we should try next. He ate piles of handmade noodles at Lam Zhou, ate mountains of shrimp-and-chive dumplings at Tasty, and had a religious experience with a pork bun at Nice Green Bo. He tried soup dumplings for the first time, biting into the hot little pocket and sucking out the hot broth, dipping the rest in vinegar and pronouncing it the best thing he'd ever tasted.

Which was followed up quickly by a searing kiss and assuring me that it was just a figure of speech and that I was still the best thing he ever tasted.

Until the firecracker shrimp showed up.

Chinatown gained another convert that night, and we finally headed back to my place at midnight, full of amazing food and cheap beer, having spent less than fifty bucks between us.

Cheapest date in Manhattan.

"I think I'm overstuffed, and not in a good way," I whined as we went up the steps. "I've got a food baby." I rubbed my belly in soothing circles. "I wonder if you can do Lamaze breathing for too many dumplings."

Oscar was also stuffed. I'd warned him to stop after that last bowl of noodles, but he'd ordered a second. Big guy, big appetite. But everyone had a limit, and we'd both officially passed ours. "I wonder if that breathing works on guys as well," he groaned, patting his still-perfectly-flat belly.

"It couldn't hurt." I turned the key in my lock. "You want coffee?"

"I can't ingest another ounce," he said, helping me with my coat and hanging it up, and then his. "I'm glad I've got the kids taking care of the cows tomorrow morning. I'm in no shape to drive back tonight."

"Good, then I get you all night to myself." I tucked myself into his arms and let him hold me for a moment, swaying a little back and forth just inside my door. I was suddenly struck by the hominess of it, the comfort of having someone's arms waiting there for you when you got home, with a quiet hello and an on-demand snuggle.

I snuggled deeper as he ran his hands up and down my back, soothing and sweet. I could hear his heart beating through his clothing. Thud *thud*. Thud *thud*. Thud *thud*.

"I'm officially old," I said softly.

"How's that?"

"I've got this beautiful man in my apartment, and all I want to do is hug him and fall asleep. We're officially old people."

"Speak for yourself, Pinup. I could be up for some banging."

I snorted, lifting my head to see his tired face grinning down at me. "Up for some banging? You must write poetry when you're not making cheese."

He slowly moved his hips back and forth a few times, in the

most pitiful way possible. "Okay, I give. Too many dumplings. Sleep now, bang later."

"Poetry, I tell you. Sheer poetry," I teased as we walked toward the bedroom, scooping up his duffel bag on the way.

"I'll give you poetry," he said as we moved through the apartment, turning off lights as went. "Roses are red—"

"Oh man."

"Hush, I'm creating a masterpiece here," he said, tucking his chin into my shoulder as we walked. His breath was warm against my ear, tickling pleasantly. "Roses are red, violets are blue. I'm too tired to bang, but that's okay because she is, too."

"Bra-vo." I clapped.

"Quiet, there's a second part. Roses are red, violets are blue . . ." We were in the bedroom by now, and with his hands on my hips he turned me around, his arms snaking around my body, pulling me snugly against him. Dropping a kiss on the tip of my nose, he continued. ". . . I made her come seven times before we went out to eat dumplings, so there's that—and something that rhymes with blue."

I smiled. "I can't really argue with that."

"You shouldn't argue, it's a poem."

"It's a great poem."

"All great poems are based in truth."

"Truth?"

"Seven times, Pinup." He grinned proudly. "Seven times."

I laughed, pushing him down onto the bed. "We're going for eight next time."

❧

We undressed, brushed our teeth, climbed into bed, and fell asleep immediately.

Well, almost immediately. Twenty minutes after I fell asleep I was awakened by his grumbling about it being too loud, and how could anyone sleep in this damn city?

I rolled over, cued up the Sound of the Country app I'd downloaded in anticipation of this exact event, put in my earplugs, and let my guy fall asleep to the sound of freakin' crickets . . . just like in the country.

Give me sirens, horns honking, and drunk people walking home any day of the week.

⁓⁓

Dawn came early and swiftly. And so did I. Did you think he wasn't going to go for eight? Oh my, yes he did, and before the sun was even fully up.

I could get used to getting up early on Sunday mornings if this was the wake-up call. My toes pointing and back arching, he thrust into me from behind, spreading me wide, stroking me with his fingers as he drove deep. He made me say his name over and over again, made me come over and over again, then finally collapsed against me, pulling me on top of him in a tangle of tired limbs and messy hair.

Afterward, he kept murmuring *eight* with a look of pure male satisfaction. Rolling my eyes, I snuggled back into his side to catch a few more z's.

But by nine, he had to go. Football practice, he said, and with more kisses and a promise to spend the night again next weekend, he was gone. And I had a brunch to get to.

When I pushed open the door at my parents' townhouse, Todd said, "Oh boy, are you in trouble."

"Hello to you, too," I replied with a frown. No Mom yet. No Dad. And . . . did I smell something burning? "How bad is it?"

"Four brunches in a fucking row?" He looked at me incredulously. "Did you suffer some kind of brain injury up there in the sticks?"

I sighed. "I'd better go ahead and get this over with."

"One day when I have kids, I'll tell them about their brave Aunt Natalie—the aunt they never got a chance to meet," he said, taking my coat with all the ceremony of a general sending a soldier into a final battle.

As he walked away whistling taps, I faced the kitchen with foreboding. I'd broken the cardinal rule of this family, and not even my father was going to believe the brunch-skips were all work-related.

I took several steps forward, cocking my head and listening for signs of anything that could be taken as a good omen, that my parents were in a good mood this morning, and that other than some good-natured ribbing they'd be glad to see me, hand me a bagel and schmear and the lifestyle section of the *Times*, and everything would go back to normal.

Then I heard my mother tell my father that if he burned another bagel, she'd use the paring knife on something he really didn't want unattached from his body.

Oh boy.

I stepped on a squeaky floorboard right outside the kitchen and then froze, wondering if they'd heard it.

My mother's footsteps rang out across the kitchen floor, sounding like she was trying to crash her heel through to the cellar below. Each stride sounded familiar, and not in a good way. I knew the sound of those heels well.

She was wearing her Chanel pumps. Pumps reserved for serious moments, like when I'd been caught smoking in eighth grade and she was called to the headmaster's office. Moments like when tenth-grade Todd and his twelfth-grade girlfriend got caught with their pants down in our attic, and my mother had the girl's parents over to discuss why this could never happen again. Pumps reserved for board meetings, for social functions with people she didn't like but was required to play nice with . . . and funerals.

The swinging door to the kitchen flew open, and there was my mother. Smiling. Which was the scariest part of all . . .

"Natalie, so nice of you to show up. Care to tell us all about this cheese maker you've been running around with?"

Here it comes . . .

Chapter 19

I lasted two days. Then I couldn't stand it anymore. I knew when Roxie held her cooking class, I knew Oscar went to it, and I knew I could get up there, get to class, get a quickie in afterward, and be back in the city by midnight.

"Holy shit!" I squealed to myself as I sat on the train, nearly bouncing off the walls with the excitement of sneaking off to the country for a midweek tryst with my . . . boyfriend.

Officially I was writing this off as market research, just another way I was going above and beyond on the Bailey Falls campaign to make sure I was highlighting everything that could bring in revenue for the town.

Hee-hee-hee . . .

Every other time Roxie hosted one of her Zombie Pickle classes, I'd been busy and hadn't had a chance to come up and take part in the class. I wanted to take the class because it was another way to spend time with my new friends and check out my best friend in action . . . and see my caveman.

Zombie Pickle class started out with just her and her boys (Leo, Chad, and Logan). She wanted to teach people how to do things in the kitchen that everyone's grandmother knew how to do, but that most young professionals didn't have a clue how to do. Canning vegetables. Making jam. Cooking from scratch with a little bit of fun and love. As well as knowing how to make pickles so that if the zombie apocalypse ever hit upstate New York, Bailey Falls would be able to weather the storm as long as someone kept planting cucumbers.

Her classes were a hit right from the beginning. Everyone from teens to the retired was heading to the diner for the classes and spreading the word on social media.

When I'd decided at the last minute to come up for class, Oscar was thrilled at the prospect of getting a little midweek nooky.

Roxie was less than thrilled. "It's not that I don't love you; it's that kitchens don't love you," she said as I raced across town to Grand Central to catch the train.

"Oh, come on, I'm not that bad—"

"You have burned water, Natalie—that's as bad as it gets. Don't you dare ruin my class."

Point taken. I'd have to be on my best behavior.

The diner was filled by the time I arrived. Roxie waved when I walked in, standing near the only empty station.

"Your apron is hanging on the back of the chair and everything you need is here," she explained, pointing to the table and giving me a "this is a terrible idea but we're going to try it anyway" smile.

I looked around, wondering which station I should go to, when I heard a low voice chuckle behind me. "Hey, Pinup."

I turned with a smile, almost tripping over myself to kiss him hello. Towering over his work space, surrounded by little glass bowls and measuring cups, was Oscar.

He chuckled, deep and sexy. Judging by the heat present, he was thrilled to see me. His eyebrow quirked up as he gave me a very thorough once-over, and he licked his lips when his eyes reached mine.

How scandalous would it be if I just pushed him down on top of the counter and had my way with him in front of the class?

Roxie cleared her throat and banged a wooden spoon on a pot to get everyone's attention.

"Tonight, in case you couldn't tell by the ingredients, we're making banana nut muffins! It's something that a bunch of you requested."

Great. I raised an eyebrow at Oscar, knowing that his ex-wife kept him swimming in muffins, and he tried not to laugh.

Roxie was moving on to the next step. "If you'd prefer a loaf pan instead of a muffin tin, I've got a few pans up here. Anyone?"

My hand shot up. Oscar looked over, but I brushed off his silent question.

Roxie tossed me the loaf pan and I got to work buttering it while everyone else was lining their muffin tins. Oscar's and Leo's big hands were struggling with dropping the tiny paper liners into their trays, but they seemed to be enjoying the experience. Everyone was, actually.

Roxie walked through the class, offering tips and praise. "Very good, guys. Louise, try a little less butter. Elmer, you don't need that many liners in the same tin, they'll never bake that way. Looks good, Oscar."

While I was still greasing the pan, she moved on to the next step. My hands weren't cooperating and I fumbled over the flour measurement, spilling some of it onto my station.

"What are you doing?" Oscar whispered to me, watching me make a mess.

"Having fun," I whispered back through my teeth.

During the banana-mashing process, I dropped an earring into the macerated mush and had to fish it out with a toothpick.

When it came time for the whisking, I splattered not only myself with the batter, but poor Elmer in front of me.

"Stop laughing," I snapped at Oscar and Leo.

"I'm so sorry," I apologized to Elmer, handing him another paper towel.

Roxie, busy with a teenager who was having a hard time measuring out the right amount of mix per cup, looked over at me and mouthed, "You okay?"

I just nodded and kept mixing the lumpy mess in my bowl. The bananas were stinky, and was it supposed to be bubbling?

"If your mix is ready, pour it into the tins and we'll get them in the oven. Holler if you need a hand."

I turned the bowl over the loaf pan and waited. The mixture oozed out slowly, dropping into the pan in a congealed glop.

"I'm pretty sure it's not supposed to look like that, Pinup," Oscar said, poking it with a wooden spoon.

"It's fine," I said, slapping the spoon away with my own. "I've never been a big fan of baking. Or cooking. Or grilling."

I brushed past him, taking my pan to the kitchen. Roxie joined me, waiting until the room was clear before asking, "How're you doing?"

She looked down at the pan and didn't have to ask again. "I'm sorry. I shouldn't have kept pushing you to come to one of these. It's just that everyone has fun, and I wanted you to—"

"Rox, it's fine. I'm having fun, and now having experienced it, I have a new angle for my campaign."

"Zombie Pickle class will be part of it?" she said, surprised.

"Yeah, it might not be the front page of a travel brochure, but it's definitely included."

As our boys joined us, Oscar kissed me sweetly on the cheek, then his eyes went wide and he pointed to the bank of ovens. "Rox, you got a problem there." The oven that contained my loaf pan was pouring smoke out of the front.

"Shit! Grab the extinguisher just in case." She donned two pot holders while running over.

It wasn't as bad as the smoke made it seem. Apparently my loaf pan was too full and overflowed onto the floor of the oven. She pulled out the pan and dropped it onto the counter, and waved off any smoke that her exhaust fans didn't get.

My banana nut bread was neither banana-y nor nutty, but it was very much misshapen and inedible.

"Good thing I hate bananas," I joked, feeling a pressure in my chest when Oscar looked over.

"Remind me to keep you away from my grill," he said with a laugh when he poked the bread brick. "I can't believe you're this bad at cooking."

A lump formed in the back of my throat. "I told you I was this bad. I just wanted to try something new." The last time I'd tried to cook for someone, anyone, was Thomas . . . Ugh. Not going there.

"Natalie, I'm just teasing you," he said, leaning in to kiss my cheek. "Not all women can cook."

Logically, I know he didn't mean anything by it. But I wasn't feeling logical right now: I wanted to have cute muffins like everyone else. I could have tried harder, I could have listened better, but—

Fuck that. Natalie Grayson wasn't a Susie Homemaker. And I wasn't ever going to be.

"Don't worry, I'll share my muffins with you," he offered, draping his arm over my shoulder. He looked proud when Roxie pulled his tray out of the oven.

They were perfect. For all the screwing around he and Leo

did throughout the class, they managed to not fuck it up. The muffins were light golden brown and smelled fantastic. Had Missy taught him how to bake?

Jealousy wasn't something I liked to experience. Add in my failure of the evening, and I was downright cranky. And what was this other feeling, making the backs of my eyes burn? Suddenly I wanted to be at home, in my apartment, ordering takeout and not feeling all the feels.

"You know what, I'm not feeling that well. I think I'm going to head back into the city."

Oscars eyebrows rose. "Now?"

"Yeah, can you run me back to the station? I can be at home and in bed by eleven. Do you mind?"

"Well, no, I mean of course I want you to feel better, but I thought that we'd get a chance to—"

"Not tonight. I need to go home," I interrupted, not sure why I needed to so badly, but home right now sounded like a better place to be.

His disappointment spoke volumes, and part of me really wanted to explain. But how could I when I didn't know exactly what I was feeling? It was hard enough figuring out my own shit, let alone having to worry about how he might take it.

As I gathered my things, Roxie handed out the trays labeled with the students' names. It was little touches like that that I wanted to make sure I included.

As she hugged me good-bye she said, "We can make something else next time you're in town."

"I'll pass," I said firmly, and kissed her on the cheek. "This class is fucking fantastic."

She nodded thanks, looking like she wanted to ask me what was going on, but knowing me well enough to leave it alone.

Oscar drove me to the station, I kissed him good-bye, and

was back in my bed by eleven as promised. Though I didn't fall asleep for a long time . . .

∽◯∽

Over the next week I thought about what had happened at the cooking class, and I wanted to do something to make it up to Oscar. And I think I knew just the thing . . .

"It's just like babysitting," I told Roxie over the phone.

"It's a hundred percent *not* just like babysitting."

"But it *could* be—it's just a matter of rebranding it."

"Then call Clara to babysit your boyfriend's cows! She's the rebranding expert."

"First of all, Clara can't babysit cows; she doesn't have the necessary skill set. Second of all, I resent you insinuating that she's the only rebranding expert around—I'm an expert, too. Third of all, he's not my boyfriend."

"Not your boyfriend—that's hilarious!"

"Fourth of all, I'm not asking you to babysit Oscar's cows; I'm asking your boyfriend to do it. So Oscar can spend the entire weekend in the city with me."

I held my breath and waited. We'd been texting all day about this, and I'd finally called her to see if I could work some magic this way.

It was Thursday afternoon, my desk was covered with All Things Bailey Falls as I worked on the Hudson Valley campaign, and all the pictures of fall leaves and glacial lakes and down-home family fun were making me horny.

In my head, that sounded better . . .

I'd woken up this morning with the brilliant idea of asking Oscar to come into the city a day early and spend the entire weekend with me. A real New York weekend.

Oscar didn't have the same kinds of responsibilities a regular boyfri— Er . . . guy would have. It wasn't as simple as canceling a tennis match or theater tickets; Oscar's plans involved other people each weekend. Not to mention bovines.

So I was trying to get Roxie to help me smooth the way before I broached the subject. Since Oscar's herd seemed to enjoy pasturing over on Maxwell Farms occasionally, maybe they could have a weekend getaway, too?

Oscar would have the final say, of course, but my analytical mind liked to always present problems with solutions, getting out ahead of any possible no's in order to make it a yes. Or at least a very firm maybe . . .

Because when it came to firm, I needed it. Bad. I'd been strung out in orgasm withdrawal all week, and if I didn't get some this weekend . . . well, then . . .

"Just talk to Leo, see what he says. If he says no, then fine. But if he says yes—"

Roxie laughed. "It's not like watching somebody's dog for the weekend, Nat. It's a little bit bigger deal."

"Yeah, but all you farmers are tight up there, helping each other out all the time and all, right? Don't the Amish always get together, raise each other's barns and such?"

"We're not Amish."

"Semantics. Say you'll do it," I commanded, pounding on my desk with my fist, trying to be as forceful as possible. "I need to get laid."

Intern Edward walked in during that last part, turned beet red, and walked right back out again.

"See, I may have just contributed to a hostile working environment. Someone needs to step in and save me from myself," I whined.

"Oh, shut up already, fine," she snapped, and I gave myself a fist bump. "You owe me. Next time I'm in town, you're taking me to any restaurant I choose."

"Done."

"And you're paying."

"I figured." I grinned, doodling pictures of cows on my scratch pad, and drawing little hearts around them. "Now when I ask Oscar to spend the weekend, he'll see how responsible I am."

"You do that. And the next time I talk to Oscar, I'm going to ask him if he's your boyfriend. He usually comes into the diner for lunch on Wednesdays . . . Maybe I'll just pop on over and see if he feels chatty."

I sat up straight in my chair. "You wouldn't."

"You know I would."

"Don't you dare—"

"Gotta go, I'm feeling the sudden urge to have a tuna melt," she cackled, hanging up the phone.

"Sonofa . . ." I muttered, dialing her back immediately. Of course she didn't answer. Or when I called her again ten seconds later. Or answer the nine texts I sent her over the next five minutes, each one laced with increasingly creative obscenities.

"Natalie, you got a minute?" my boss, Dan, asked, sticking his head inside the door.

I looked up, sighed, and put down the phone. "Of course. What's up?"

"Remember that gourmet food store you worked with last year?"

"Brannigan's? Sure, they just opened their fifth store—in Chicago, I think."

"There's a sixth store now, in San Francisco."

Huh, I'd missed that in the trades. "Wow, good for them."

"You still in contact with their marketing team?"

"Yep, want me to reach out?"

He nodded. "If they're in San Fran, they'll be expanding again. If they do that—"

"—they'll need a new marketing strategy. I'm on it." I cleared a spot on my desk and started making notes. "I'll reach out to Sara; she's heading up creative over there now."

"Perfect, keep me in the loop," he said, walking back out of the office, pausing just before he left. "What happened to your usual stacks? What gives?"

I was known for having multiple, very neat stacks all over my office. It was how I kept the creative and analytical parts of my brain together. Spread it all out so it was easier to see, but the stacks were always squared off.

I looked around. It was messier than usual. "Just keeping all the plates in the air. They'll be back in their stacks before I leave today; no worries."

"Who's worried?" he said.

Still, I made a mental note to tidy up a bit while I pulled up Brannigan's website. They'd updated it recently; it had a great new look. After running a mom-and-pop gourmet store here in the city for forty years, the actual mom and pop had retired, passing along their pasta and escargot empire to their kids. The "kids" had turned the business into something new and exciting, which was rare in this niche market. They'd opened a second store in the city, then branched out to the outer boroughs with a flagship in Park Slope over in Brooklyn just when the neighborhood was becoming the most fashionable place to live in in New York City. A fourth store had opened in Philadelphia, and then Chicago. Oh yeah, and now San Francisco.

I looked through my client files, shot off a quick email, and was on the phone with Sara by that afternoon. I'd spent the interim pulling stats on some of the brands and vendors they featured in their stores, and noticed they seemed light on . . . cheese.

An idea began to take shape.

After the usual pleasantries were exchanged, congratulations on all the success (due in no small part to the fantastic campaign my team had crafted for her before they began expanding), I told her that of course Manhattan Creative Group was looking forward to working with them again in the future and that when they were ready to begin the next phase, we were ready to launch them into every major city in the country, making them a household brand. And I might have mentioned, several times, this wonderful new cheese maker from the Hudson Valley, the next big foodie scene in the culinary world . . .

By the end of that call, I'd not only secured a firm commitment for future advertising business with our firm, but planted several seeds about Bailey Falls Creamery, and had arranged to have some of their best cheeses sent to her and her team at their corporate offices in Midtown.

I'd tell Oscar the good news once I knew his cows were being babysat. And after I knew the outcome of Roxie's conversation with him, about whether or not he was my boyfriend . . .

The outcome came that night when I got a text from Roxie.

Leo will babysit your boyfriend's cows. Pretty sure
no one has ever said that
before. Welcome to life in
the sticks.

I texted back:

Brilliant! I'll tell Oscar
he's free and clear to

spend the weekend with
me. I thank you, and my
future orgasms thank
you.

You're welcome. To both of
you.

So? What the hell did
he say when you asked
him?

Number one: I said he was
your boyfriend first, so I get
bragging rights.

Wait, did someone else
say it?

Your boyfriend said it, too.

There was a long pause . . .

Hello? Are you still there?

I'm lying on the bed,
kicking up my heels and
squealing into my pillow!

Why the hell isn't there a
pom-pom emoji? Here you
go—closest I could come up
with. 🏈

That's a football

Well, they shake pom-poms
at football games. And he is
Mr. Football . . .

I love you.

I know you do. Gotta go.
I wonder what kinds of
snacks you buy for a cow
sleepover?

I set the phone down, still feeling giddy that I had a boyfriend. And then, not too long after, felt the first pangs of *Holy
shit . . . do I have a boyfriend?*

∽

I was indeed able to convince Oscar to drive into the city a day
early, and I didn't even have to try that hard.

"What good is it having employees if you can't trust them to
do their job on their own once in a while?" he'd said, then told
me that one of his interns from the culinary school had already
stepped up and was in charge of bringing in everything they'd
need at the market on Saturday. He was well and truly off the
clock, for the first time in a long time.

And I was ready to show him another side of my Manhattan.
The glitz, the glamour, the secret nighttime hot spots, and the
members-only clubs that I belonged to. It was the side of Manhattan you see on television and reality shows. I'd run in those

circles since I was a kid, and I couldn't wait to show Oscar. And to show him off a little—let's be honest.

My absence from the social scene over the past month had been noticed. And I was aching to get out and about, eat some gorgeous food, drink some fabulous wine, go dancing at the hottest clubs in town, and shake my ass all over my city.

My plans were 100 percent derailed when Oscar showed up at my apartment Friday night, took one look at me in my replacement thigh-high Chanel leather boots with the four-inch heels, growled "Fucking hell, Natalie," dropped his duffel bag, threw me over his shoulder, and took me straight back to the bedroom.

Did I forget to mention I was wearing only the boots, a brand-new apron I'd had designed with Bailey Falls Creamery emblazoned across the front, and a long string of pearls?

Yeah, it really wasn't fair of me.

He fucked me for three solid hours, and then we ate Moroccan takeout at 11 p.m.

I kept the boots and the pearls on the entire time. The apron went by the wayside.

We didn't see the outside world again until Saturday morning, when we headed to the market. I'm sure New York missed me, but I wouldn't trade that night for the world.

❧

"So, about tonight."

"Tonight? I thought we'd have another night like last night, but if you want to go out, I could be talked into those dumplings again," he replied, dropping a kiss between my neck and shoulder, to the dismay of the woman at the front of his line. The dismay was shared by the next woman, the woman after that, and the man after that. I understood; I'd been in that line only a few weeks before.

But back to tonight. "No, no dumplings. And yes, obviously last night was incredible," I said when he moved my apron strap over and dropped one more kiss just below my ear, making me go all shivery. "But tonight, we're going out."

"I still can't believe you had these made for everyone." He gestured at the rest of his team, now proudly wearing the new aprons. He wasn't sure about them at first, wondering why in the world he needed to wear an apron that said Bailey Falls Creamery when he was standing under a sign that said the same thing, but eventually he acquiesced and slipped it over his head with a sheepish look. "So, where are we going tonight?" He handed an order of cheddar to the next customer with his usual "strictly business" expression.

"How would you feel about going to the opening of a new art exhibit?"

He looked back at me while handing over a wheel of Brie. "What, like paintings?"

"No, it's an abstract exhibition—a photographic study of New York City trash cans juxtaposed with large-scale plastic installations, designed to represent man's overarching reach toward industrialization, and its impact on the environment with its waste."

The entire line had fallen silent, as had Oscar's team, listening to what I was saying with confused looks on their faces.

"It's garbage art?" he asked, looking beyond skeptical, then noticing that the line had stopped. "Here's your cheese," he grumbled, handing over a package and putting the line back in motion again.

"I can't describe the work as well as the artist; you'll have to ask her for her explanation." I sighed, rolling back and forth on my ankle.

He instantly spotted it. "Why are you nervous about going to see garbage art?"

"Because the artist is my mother," I squeaked.

"You want me to meet your mom?"

"And my dad? Is that too weird?" I said, pulling at my apron.

It *was* weird, it was totally weird. Why was I doing this? This was too much too soon, and it was suddenly very warm in this stall.

Oscar studied me carefully, and I wondered what he was thinking. Would he say yes? Would he say no? Would he order me out of the stall? Would he run screaming in terror at the idea of meeting my parents? What the hell was I thinking? I never did this!

"Okay," he replied, turning back to his customers. "What do *you* want?" He always accentuated the *you,* making it sound like the customer was somehow putting him out.

"Wait, so, you'll go?" I asked, breath moving back into my lungs.

This was happening—this was really happening! The budding panic was gone the instant he said yes, and I realized how very much I wanted to introduce him to my world and my family. This. Was. *Happening.*

He turned toward me with a grin. "Sure, no big deal. Not sure I have anything to wear, though. I didn't bring anything fancy."

"We can go shopping after we're done here!" I squealed, giddy over the idea that my boyfriend and I would be stepping out on the town tonight. "I can call Barneys or Bergdorf's and have them set some things aside for you—"

"Can we go to Macy's? The one that has the parade?" he

asked, his face lighting up. "We always watched the parade every year, before the football games started up. I've always wanted to go there."

He was smiling. Even at his customers. And between orders, he actually began to . . . whistle.

Macy's it is.

⚬

We took the subway to go shopping, something he'd never done before.

"We can just take my truck, no biggie," he said, gesturing to where it was parked behind the stand.

I shook my head. "It'll be faster this way, and we won't have to worry about parking. Besides, no one drives in the city."

He looked around at all the traffic with raised eyebrows, then turned to me with a "tell me that again" expression.

"Seriously, look again at those cars. They're all cabs, Uber guys, or private drivers. It's much faster to move underground," I replied, taking him by the hand and leading him toward the station on Thirty-fourth Street.

They had a helluva men's department at Macy's, and within an hour we had him outfitted in a nice oxford shirt, a new tie, and a jacket. He refused to buy new pants, though. "Jeans are fine. I always see guys in jeans in those fashion magazines," he'd said.

And I agreed. He looked damn fine in jeans.

Back on the packed train afterward, we stood front to back with the other Saturday shoppers, our bags and bodies jostled about with everyone else. I spied someone with a Brannigan's bag, and I realized now was as good a time as any to give him my good news.

Turning to face him in the tiny space I'd created, I beamed

up at him, tucking into the spot below his arm, where he was holding tight to the bar above. "I have news for you, mister."

"Oh yeah? What's that?" he asked as he looked down at me.

"Ever hear of Brannigan's?"

"Sure. Gourmet food store, expensive food for fussy people. They just opened a new store in San Francisco."

Stifling an eye roll, I leaned up on tiptoe to press a kiss on his chin. "I wouldn't call Bailey Falls Creamery fussy, would you?"

"I don't get it," he said, confusion on his face.

"I know the woman that heads up their marketing, and I touched base with her a few days ago. I might have mentioned a certain creamery in the Hudson Valley that was making some pretty great cheese."

"Oh?"

"I also might have sent over a sampling of my favorites to their offices."

"Oh."

"And she might have sent me an email this morning telling me how batshit crazy everyone went over your cheese, especially the Brie." I smoothed out his jacket, patting his chest as I went. "And you know how I feel about your Brie."

He was silent.

"So anyway, she asked me who was in charge of your marketing, and I told her that there was a very good-looking farmer who handled most of that, and if she was interested I could put her in touch with you, and—"

"Wait, hold up. What did you do exactly?" he asked, his face not angry but not happy, either.

"I didn't *do* anything, other than put someone with the fastest-growing gourmet foods franchise in the country in touch with one of the best local cheese makers I know."

He was silent again, his eyes distant.

"The best, but not the most chatty," I mumbled.

I didn't get it—why wasn't he excited? Before I could say anything else, tell him more about what an incredible opportunity this was, how people would slaughter a Camembert for the chance to get their product in front of a company like Brannigan's, he caught my chin, tilting my face up to look at him.

"I appreciate what you tried to do here, and I know why you did it. But no thanks."

I gaped up at him. No thanks? No *thanks*? Who said no thanks to something like this? I must not have explained it well enough; he must not know what—

"And I know what a big deal this is, if that's what you're thinking."

"How'd you know I was thinking that?" I asked, amazed.

He smiled, a little sadly. "I've gotten to know you pretty well, Pinup. I can see when you're working something over in that pretty head of yours."

"But if you know what a big deal this is, then why don't you—"

"I just don't," he said, his jaw clenching. "I just don't," he repeated, as if there wasn't any more to say about it.

I had more to say about it—lots more. But before I could launch into my pitch, the train slowed. "This is our stop, right?" he asked.

As we exited the train, he shuffled his bags all into one hand so he could hold mine. Our fingers fit together the same, he traced the same design on the inside of my palm with his thumb—but I couldn't help but think something had changed.

∾∽

And it continued to change as the night went on. Things seemed relatively okay when we were back at my place. He wolf-whistled at me when he saw my dress for the evening, a heather-gray wrap dress that clung in all his favorite places. And he ran his hands across those places. "Tits and ass, baby—that's what makes me a caveman," he quipped, his hands full. I chuckled and swatted at his hands, begging off to finish my hair.

"Your ass could make *me* go caveman," I quipped back as he got dressed for the evening. Oscar in country clothes was always a sight, but Oscar in city clothes? Mercy. Hair slicked back a bit, loose of its usual tie, it just dusted the tops of his shoulders. His powerful build was even more dramatic in the tucked-in button-down and the "fancy schmancy" jacket, as he called it.

He was beautiful.

But somewhere between the laughing over the tits and ass, and the walk down to the town car when it pulled up, he was withdrawing. There was a tension between us that had never been there before.

A strange sense of almost not knowing what to say, when we'd always had plenty to talk about. When I opened my door to get out of the car—a habit that Oscar was slowly breaking me of—he made sure to get there before I got out, but his usual head shake and "Woman" had an edge of frustration, rather than teasing.

Dinner was quiet, and increasingly awkward. I took him to one of my favorite spots, a little French bistro that I typically reserved for special occasions. When the maître d' took my coat, beating Oscar to it, Oscar rolled his eyes. When the same man pulled out my chair before Oscar could, Oscar may have growled. And when the manager came over to greet me, dropping kisses on both cheeks and saying how long it had been since I'd been by and how much he'd missed me, Oscar quietly steamed in his chair.

Once given the menu, however, he no longer steamed quietly.

"What the fuck kind of food is this?" he asked, his voice loud enough to make the people at the nearest table look over in alarm.

"It's French," I replied, my voice even and cool, and quiet. "Country French, specializing in Provençal cuisine."

"I don't know what any of this is," he replied, arching his eyebrows as he read through it. "It's all in French; how is anyone supposed to know what they're eating?"

"I felt like that the first time I came to a French restaurant, too," I agreed, smiling a little to show him I was on his side. "My mother taught me a few French words so I could figure out a few things on any menu. Once when we were in Paris, I thought I was ordering chicken, but I got—"

"When we were in Paris," he muttered, closing his menu and setting it back down again.

Now I was the one who had the raised eyebrows, unaccustomed to being interrupted, especially so rudely. But before I could say anything, our waiter appeared, looking at us expectantly. I quickly scanned the menu.

"I'll have the *blanquette de veau,* with a glass of the Château de Chantegrive."

"*Certainement, bon choix,*" he replied, looking at Oscar now for his selection.

Still reeling from his rude comment, I let him order on his own, not wanting to offer any assistance. As it turned out, he didn't need it.

"Cheeseburger. Fries. Bud Light." He glared up at the waiter as if daring him to challenge his obviously-trying-to-be-difficult order.

To his credit, the waiter's eyes merely widened slightly, then he nodded his head. "*Certainement*."

Oscar's eyes now met mine across the table—challenging me next?

"I'm sure it'll be delicious," I said, my tone icy.

"I'm surprised he took the order. I was expecting a fight," he said, smirking a little.

"The service here is impeccable. No one would ever argue with a customer." I sighed, placing my napkin on my lap. "But if it's a fight you're wanting . . ."

"I don't know what you mean."

"Oh please, you're spoiling for a fight." I leaned across the table, my voice a low whisper. "What the hell is your problem? Is this because of the Brannigan's thing?"

He just pointed at the waiter who had brought our drinks. He set them down quickly, obviously sensing the tension at the table.

Once he walked away, I leaned in. "Well?"

"Well, what?"

"Jesus, you're so stubborn. It is about Brannigan's, isn't it? I know you didn't ask me for help, but I—"

"I didn't ask you for anything," he said, cutting me off. Then he drained half of his beer in one draft and looked at me, daring me to say something.

I wasn't playing this game. No way.

I smiled sweetly, ending the trajectory of the conversation. "So, Roxie told me that Polly ate so much of her Halloween candy the other night they've had to hide it and dole it out so she can't OD on it again. Isn't that funny?"

I was determined to save this night . . .

⮠⮠

Stepping out of the car in front of Gallery O, I saw the usual photographers, movers and shakers in the art world, simpering debutantes with their equally simpering hedge fund manager boyfriends, blue-blooded matronly art patrons paired off with good-looking young hipsters, society hangers-on, and, in the middle of it all, actual artists.

I heard a sigh behind me, and when I turned to see Oscar, he was looking at the entire scene disapprovingly.

"You ready?" I asked, looping my arm through his as he came to stand next to me.

He grimaced, then forced a smile. "Sure thing."

"You sure?"

"I love it when people ask me the same question twice," he replied, looking like a man about to walk into the dentist's office for a root canal.

I dug my nails into his arm as we walked past the photographers, here to snap a few shots for Page Six. "Play nice, please."

"Oh, you want me to play?" he asked, a devious grin now making its way across his face. "Okay, let's play."

I saw my mother coming through the crowd, smiling and nodding and shaking hands, and I squashed every single thing I wanted to say: that I wanted to wipe that smug grin off his face, ask him what the hell was the matter, why was he being such an ass, and where was this all coming from?

I squashed, I centered, I smiled.

"Mother!" I called out.

She caught my eye and beamed. She looked radiant. Dressed head to toe in all black accented with a bright lime-green scarf wrapped around her shoulders, she looked like some beautiful exotic bird. Some artists were notoriously shy, but my mother thrived under the spotlight and loved to show people her latest piece.

And behind her, as always, was my father. Strong and solid, anchoring her crazy with his sensible, he was always content at her side.

"Natalie, I was hoping we'd see you here," she cooed, slipping an arm around my waist and hugging me close.

"Of course, I wouldn't have missed it. Looks like you've got quite a turnout already!"

"Crows, they're all crows! Just here for the free food and drink, and to pick pick pick apart my work."

"Which she secretly loves," my dad chimed in, sharing a secret smile with me.

"I do, I really do," she agreed, dropping a kiss on his cheek. They both realized there was a man on my arm at exactly the same second, and I stifled a grin when I watched them both tilt their heads up slightly to take in his height.

"Oh, and this must be the man who's been keeping my daughter out of town so much lately. Oscar, isn't it?" My mother offered a hand, which Oscar took. Her eyes widened at the size of his paw.

"Yes, ma'am, it's nice to meet you, Mrs. Grayson. Looks like quite a show here tonight."

"It really is such a spectacle," she said, looking him up and down, taking the time to catalogue each feature. "And this is Natalie's father."

"Mr. Grayson," Oscar said, shaking his hand firmly.

"I'm Al; that's Anna," my dad replied, taking it to a first-name basis already. An interesting development.

Then someone from the gallery came outside and asked my mother if she had a moment.

"Oh goodness, I've got to go—a few interviews. Will we see you later, Oscar?"

"I'll be wherever Natalie is, I expect," Oscar said, smiling smoothly.

I smiled and nodded, and as the two of them whisked away and melted into the crowd, I looked around for other faces I knew.

"I've got to make the rounds and say hello to some people. You with me?"

"Sure," he said, "I'm with you."

And he couldn't have been more wrong. All night long as I introduced him to people I knew—some friends from school, some friends just from the party scene—he was more and more rude. At first it was little things: not listening when other people were talking, staring off into space when I was asking him a question to bring him into the conversation; but then it began to get worse. He was muttering snide comments under his breath, commenting on everything from the hors d'oeuvres to the photographers and finally my friends. I don't know if they heard it, but I did, and it was enough.

Not that my friends didn't have plenty to say about Oscar, too. Rich people don't say what they're thinking right out loud, but it's right there on their face, in their eyes. They asked the right questions: where is your farm, how long have you been making cheese, how long have you been making Natalie (a particularly rude one asked by someone I went to high school with and never particularly liked); nothing openly hostile.

I'd gotten so used to party small talk that I barely heard it anymore. But Oscar heard everything, and it was not sitting well.

Finally, after circling around and making nice with everyone I needed to, I knew it was time for a drink.

"I'll be right back," I muttered, starting to head off toward the bar.

He caught me by the arm. Gently, of course, but still . . . "Where are you running off to?"

"Getting a drink. I'll be right back." And I left.

Was I rude? Maybe, but I needed a breather. This shit was getting complicated and I didn't like it. I wasn't sure quite what was going on with him tonight, but I didn't like how I was feeling.

When I finally made it to the front of the crowded bar I blindly asked the first bartender I could find for a double vodka, straight up.

And when he handed me my drink, and I finally looked up to hand him a tip, I found myself looking into the coldest brown eyes I'd hoped to never see again.

"Thomas." My voice caught in my throat, barely a breath, but he heard it and smiled. My skin crawled.

"Hello, Natalie, it's been a long time."

I instinctively tugged at my dress, pulling it a little higher across my cleavage, a little lower across my bottom. "What are you—"

"—doing here? What the hell does it look like? I'm serving the masses. There are so many drunk women here tonight I might get lucky." And he waggled his eyebrows at me.

I was frozen. As the familiar scent of his cloying cologne reached my nose, it was all I could do not to burst into tears right then and there. How could he still do this to me, after all this time?

I'd sacrificed everything for this man: gave up my family, gave up the time in my life when I was supposed to be the most free and adventurous, gave up my dreams.

I wanted to say something worthy of who I was now, one perfect, cutting sentence that would eviscerate him for what he'd done to me. But no words could ever bring back all that he had taken. So like before—I walked away.

And walked right into Oscar, who was pacing at the edge of the crowd, looking at his watch like he couldn't wait to get out of here. And when I saw him, saw the irritation he still so clearly felt with me and at being here, in this world, my world, and hating it, it all became very clear.

I'd sacrificed everything for a man once. I'd never do it again.

✑

Neither of us spoke in the car on the way back to my place. I should say, neither one of us spoke actual words. There was sighing, there was restless movement, there were lips bitten and tongues bitten, for that matter, and none of those things were done in the usual Natalie and Oscar fashion.

The car pulled up in front of my place, and like a shot, Oscar was out of the car and around to my side, as though refusing to let me get the jump on him again. I was angry. I was angry at how I'd handled things with Thomas, of course, but more important, I was angry at how Oscar had been behaving all night. I knew how to compartmentalize Thomas and would deal with that later. But I hadn't built up any defense against Oscar.

I'd never thought I'd need to.

I stormed past him, clicking up the steps to my apartment while he slammed the car door shut behind me. I turned the key in my lock as if the door had done something personally to me. I sort of wished it would, so I'd have an excuse to break something.

What the hell was happening? Hours ago, we'd been making out behind the stall at the farmers' market, hardly able to be near each other without wanting to bang our brains out. Now there was this horrible tension, like waiting for a balloon to pop.

I heard him come in behind, heard him shrug out of his jacket and felt his hands near my neck, ready to help me out of mine. I whirled on him suddenly, no longer willing to pretend I wasn't angry.

"What the hell is happening?" I demanded. "I mean it, Oscar: what the hell?"

"You want to talk about this now?" he asked, tugging my coat off and hanging it carefully next to his.

"I think we'd better, don't— Hey, don't walk away from me!" I shouted as he walked toward the kitchen.

Spinning on his heel, he held his hands in the air as if to say no big deal. "Just getting a drink, baby. That's all."

"Don't fucking call me baby. I hate that. You never call me baby," I sputtered, still standing in the entryway, getting angrier by the second.

"What do you want me to call you? Honey? Sweetie? Tell me exactly what you want to be called, so I can make sure to address you correctly." He disappeared around the corner and I could hear him opening the fridge, the ice tinkling in the glass.

I stomped down the hall. "What's that supposed to mean?"

He poured a scotch, then waved the bottle around dramatically. "It doesn't mean anything. Why does *everything* have to mean something?"

"It doesn't, normally. But when someone's acting like an asshole, then yeah, things tend to mean something."

"An asshole?" he asked, raising an eyebrow.

I shook my head in surprise. "You don't think so? '*What do you want to be called, tell me exactly what you want to be called so I can*'—what did you say?—'*address you correctly*'? *Asshole* works, but I'm thinking *jerk*, *dickhead*, and straight-up *motherfucker* sound pretty good, too."

"You're pissed at me," he said.

"You're damn right I'm pissed at you. Your behavior was totally out of line tonight. First at the restaurant, and then at my mother's art opening. I think out of line is an understatement."

"Your mother was nice. Your father, too. But the rest of those people?" He tossed back the rest of his scotch. "*They* were all assholes."

"I'm sorry?" I asked, fire creeping into my face.

"I'm sorry, too. Your little social circle is filled with jerk-offs."

"You don't even know them. How can you make judgments about people you just met?" I asked. "I've known some of these people for years. Maybe they're not close friends, but I've spent time with them. We see each other at all the same parties, all the same restaurants, all the same events. Maybe they're a little snooty at times, and a bit judgmental, but . . ."

Huh. Some of them were assholes, actually. But still, they were *my* assholes. Wait, that sounded terrible.

I changed course. "Oscar, I know you like to say what you want, when you want, at the exact second you have a thought. But sometimes you have to take a minute and think about what you're saying, and if it's necessary, and are you hurting anyone when you say it!"

"It hasn't been a problem yet," he answered.

I slammed my hand down on the counter. "It *is* a problem if I can't take you out without worrying if you're going to be an asshole!"

"Ahhhh," he said, setting his drink down and taking a few steps closer. "That's what this is about: not knowing how the guy from the sticks is going to behave at one of your bullshit cocktail parties."

"Is that what you really think of me?" I whispered, feeling tears spring to my eyes.

"Why'd you talk to Brannigan's about me? Tell the truth, now."

"I already told you: because I wanted to help you! They're one of the fastest-growing brands in the country, and they can put your product on shelves in cities all over the place. Why wouldn't you want that?"

He slammed *his* hand on the counter. "Because I don't need that! I don't need to be on everyone's shelves, I don't need to be 'in,' and I don't need some rich girl in Chicago to tell me that my cheese is good. *I know* it's fucking good. Why does Bailey Falls Creamery need to be a household name?"

I blinked, surprised by his vehemence. "What's *wrong* with being a household name?"

"*I* was supposed to be a household name! Me!" he yelled, pounding his chest. "And I didn't want it! I didn't want it then, and I don't want it now. What the hell is wrong with everyone these days? Everything has to be bigger and brighter and better—when is it *enough*?"

"No one is saying that it has to be that, Oscar. I only thought that—"

"All my father wanted from me was to be a famous football player. Always number one; coming in second wasn't an option. I got drafted for the National Football League, Natalie—and the first thing he said when it didn't happen until the second round was that he hoped when it was my younger brother's turn, he'd go in the first round." He paced around the kitchen, getting wound tighter and tighter. "Do you have any idea how proud I am of what I'm doing now? I love what I do. We're making some money, sure, but people *love* that fucking cheese. It's really good, and that's saying something."

"It *is* really good, and you know how much *I* love it, too. But for God's sake, Oscar, sometimes it's okay to let someone help you. I can put your product on shelves across the country: why wouldn't you want that?"

"Because I don't. And that should be enough for you."

I dug my hands into my hair, closing my eyes in frustration, trying to understand.

"And if that's not enough for you, then maybe *I'm* not enough for you."

What? My eyes snapped open, not sure what I'd heard. "What are you saying?"

"Come on, Natalie—where is this going? Huh?"

I felt punched in the gut. "Wait, hold on. We're deciding this *now*? What do you mean, where is this going? We're having fun, we're enjoying each other—what's wrong with that?"

He nodded, crossing the kitchen toward me, reaching out with one hand. "Yeah, we are, and it's great. But come on, you live in the city; I don't. I'm not moving here. For me, everything is in Bailey Falls."

"Sure," I nodded dully, feeling nothing now except the warmth of his hand. "Sure, you've got the cows."

"I've got my life," he corrected, "and you've got yours. Unless you'd consider . . ." He trailed off, his eyes hopeful.

"Unless?"

"You'd consider moving upstate."

And there it was.

Move upstate, giving up everything else, uproot everything I know and love and worked my ass off to get—sacrifice it all, for a man.

Tears spilled over, sudden and hot, and then there I was, hands shaking, taking him into my arms and telling him no, no, I can't *do* that.

Because no matter what, that was the one thing I'd never, ever do again.

And then he's kissing me, kissing my tears away and telling me he understands, and then he's picking me up and wrapping his arms around me and taking me back to the bedroom and he's loving me, and he's loving my body and he's peeling off my dress and he's making me naked and warm and his hands are running all over my perfectly imperfect body, and he's so warm and he's so tender and he's so gentle and his body is so incredibly strong, and maybe it's strong enough and maybe he's strong enough and maybe he's strong enough for both of us, and maybe I could just consider that maybe, possibly, I could think about this some more . . . But then no, no, no I can't do that because I can be strong, too, and I can be strong on my own and for myself, and oh yes, oh no, and now he's loving me so hard because he knows I can take it, and so sweet because he knows that I need that, too, and it's too much and not enough all over again . . .

He left that night, driving back upstate. He didn't tell me he loved me. He didn't need to.

I knew.

Chapter 20

But I didn't know what would happen next. Was it over? Were we over? Did it have to be all or nothing?

I didn't know these rules. I knew men, but I didn't know what happened when people were invested. This was beyond me.

I didn't talk to Oscar for three days. No texts, no calls, no contact of any kind. In the past few weeks, we'd chatted almost every day. Sometimes it was a quick call to confirm what train I was on. Sometimes it was a stolen moment to tell him about something funny that had happened at work. Sometimes he'd call right before he went to sleep. And though he didn't use flowery words, when he said, *"Sweet dreams, Pinup,"* it was better than almost anything.

When I woke up Thursday morning still with no call or text, I felt . . . alone. Really alone.

I was usually surrounded by laughing, smiling, chatting people—at work, after-work cocktails, nights out on the town, weekends filled with brunches and lunches and clubs and parties. And this week had been no exception. I'd worked my ass off, spent time with friends I hadn't seen in weeks, and kept my social calendar full.

So why was I feeling so alone?

No Oscar.

And I didn't like it one bit.

Thursday afternoon I bit the bullet and called him myself, no longer waiting for his call.

"Hey," was his answer when he picked up.

"Hey to you," I said, my voice already tense. "How've you been?"

"Good. Busy but good. You?"

"Good," I said, twisting a lock of hair around my finger. "I haven't heard from you once this week."

He sighed. "I haven't heard from you, either." He had a point. "I was meaning to call, it's just been—"

"Busy, I know. I've been busy, too."

More silence. I'd never felt the need to fill the silence before, but this felt awful. "I got a rough cut of the first Bailey Falls commercial; it's looking pretty good. Still needs a lot of work and the music will be different, but it's going in the right direction."

"That's great," he said softly.

"Yeah. I can show you this weekend, if you want. You can get the gist of it from—"

"This weekend?"

"Well, yeah. I mean, I figured I'd see you," I replied, my voice getting higher than I would have liked it. "At the market, at least."

"I won't be there this weekend."

"You're not coming to the market?" I asked, disbelieving.

"Now that it's winter we only come in once a month, and we're not scheduled again until after Thanksgiving."

"Oh," I whispered, my finger twisting in my hair so hard it was starting to hurt. "So, when will I see you?"

"It's a busy time right now, even though it seems like it would slow down when winter comes. I've got repairs I put off all summer; the cows are getting ready to come indoors for longer than they're used to, and lots of prep needs to happen for that; it's just—"

"Busy." I deliberately lightened my tone. "Yeah, I've got tons of work blowing up, too. I've got some new campaigns I'll be working on soon, with the Bailey Falls job winding down. Yeah. Lots to do."

"Yeah," he said. He sounded a little . . . sad? "Anyway, I've got to go to football practice now. The kids have been winning all their games, and now's the time to put a little more pressure on them so they don't slack off."

"Oh, sure. Well—"

"Talk to you later, Natalie," he said, and hung up.

I had chosen this. I had made this decision. I couldn't be the woman he needed. He needed a muffin maker, a clothes washer, an all-in kind of girl who would be willing to give up a part of herself to be there for him. I could not, would not, do that.

Willing myself not to cry, I flicked on the fan in the corner, drying my eyeballs until I could go back to work.

I talked to Oscar two more times that week, twice the week after that, and then it was an entire week before I spoke to him again. Not once did he mention trying to get together.

When I talked to Roxie one night, she told me he was crankier than ever, barely speaking when he was in town.

That's how it goes, I suppose.

I worked back into my routine; well, part of my routine. I didn't go out nearly as much, but that was okay. I couldn't conceive of meeting anyone new. Flirting with a guy seemed unappealing at best, gross at worst, and the last thing I wanted was to pick up a random guy. I worked a lot. I talked to Roxie,

I talked to Clara, and I spent more and more of the weekend at my parents', needing some familiarity while I worked myself over.

Did I make the right decision? Could I have considered, just considered, the idea of trying to make things work with Oscar?

"You sure as hell could have tried," a voice said, and I blinked, confused.

"Huh?" I turned around on my perch in the window to see my mother standing there, holding a teacup.

"Should you have considered the idea of making things work with Oscar? Yes. The answer to that is yes." She shook her head at me, handing me the cup. "Drink this. It's green tea, you need the antioxidants."

"Sorry, I didn't know I—"

"Said it out loud? You did; you've always said things out loud when you're working yourself over."

"I do?" I'd never heard this before.

"Sure; your father's the same way. When he's in a pickle, he poses questions to the wall sometimes, trying to work his head around a problem. Me, I just throw some paint at a canvas and work it out that way."

I sipped at the tea. It was December, and I was spending a Saturday night at my parents', watching the first snow fall outside on Perry Street.

Saturday night with my parents. How the mighty have fallen.

"He wanted me to think about moving."

"I figured."

"To Bailey Falls."

"I figured."

"To the country, Ma."

"I know where Bailey Falls is. The question is, do you want to go?"

"And sacrifice my career and life for a man? You always told me that was the worst thing a woman could do."

"Wrong."

I exploded from my chair. "What? Are you trying to make me crazy?"

"I think you're halfway there already, dear daughter. Now drink your tea and listen to me."

I sat.

"I always told you that the worst thing a woman could do was sacrifice her career for a man—"

"Exactly."

"—but I don't think you'd *have* to sacrifice your career to have this man."

"He's got cows."

"Sure, and they're just ninety minutes from where you're sitting right now. You don't think you can make it work when you're only ninety minutes from the man you love?"

"The man I love, I—" I sputtered.

She laid a hand on my knee, patting gently. "Now listen up good, Natalie. You've been in love once in your life."

"And we know how that ended."

She shook her head. "You were never really in love with Thomas. You thought you loved him, because back then you thought you were unlovable. And a good-looking man came along, saw a possible weakness, and he preyed on that and on you. I don't blame you for thinking you were in love with him, but I'm here to tell you that it wasn't love. What you feel for *Oscar* is the real thing."

"But I can't give up my job! I love my job!"

"And you're great at it. You know that, and the people at MCG know it, too. You don't think they'd work with you if you wanted to work from a home office a few days a week? And maybe Oscar could spend some time in the city every now and again?"

My heart started racing. I could see the possibilities, the maybes. "But wouldn't I be sacrificing too much for someone else?"

"Do you love him?"

Oh sweet Christ on a cracker, I think I really do.

Now I just had to find out if he still loved me.

Chapter 21

It's beginning to look a lot like Christmas . . .

No shit.

Everywhere you go . . .

Nothing wrong with your eyeballs.

Take a look in the five-and-ten . . .

Done.

Glistening once again . . .

You're darn tootin'.

With candy canes and silver lanes aglow.

There *were*, in fact, candy canes at the five-and-ten. And though I didn't see any silver lanes aglow, I did see an oddly compelling display of silvery chain saws hanging in the window of the hardware store.

Ever seen *It's a Wonderful Life?* Remember the part when George Bailey runs screaming down Main Street, tossing out Merry Christmases to everything that would stand still?

Main Street in Bailey Falls during the Christmas season looks just like it. Maybe Frank Capra had this little town in mind when he created Bedford Falls . . .

Though my heart will always skip a beat when I see the holiday windows at Bloomingdale's, the tree at Rockefeller Center, and the wreaths in every window at Bergdorf's . . .

There is nothing prettier than this damn Hudson Valley town at Christmas. There, I said it.

Roxie picked me up at the train station in Poughkeepsie, and when we hit Main Street in Bailey Falls, I fell silent. It was still two weeks until Santa popped down the chimneys, but the town was ready. Each storefront was ringed with tiny white twinkle lights, each lamppost wrapped in red-and-white ribbon, looking like a legion of candy canes marching down the main drag. Beautiful evergreen wreaths, studded with pinecones and deep-red bows, hung from the signpost that hung out over the sidewalk over each store, and big old-fashioned globe lights, the outdoor kind with all the colored lights, were strewn across Main Street every twenty feet or so, supporting equally as bright signs that proclaimed Merry Christmas, Season's Greetings, and Happy Holidays.

The town common was dressed with a large Christmas tree, thirty feet tall and bedecked with tinsel and ribbon and crowned with an enormous gold star that you could see twinkling from all over town. And as we drove past, as though cued by some kind of celestial production designer, it began to snow.

"Oh," I breathed, marveling at the beauty taking place just outside my car door.

"I know," Roxie echoed, her own face glued to the window as we took in the winter wonderland around us. "I can't believe how long it took me to realize it."

"Yeah," I said back, in equally as dreamy a voice. "The hot farmer you're banging had nothing to do with it."

She laughed. "Okay, you got me there. Of course, you know something about that, too."

"This town has some kind of pull. Did you hear Clara is

heading up to Bryant Mountain House?" Knowing how much trouble the resort was having keeping the rooms full, Roxie and I had dropped Clara's name several times and the family had finally bitten, calling her firm in Boston and hiring her to come up and help them figure out how to turn the place around.

"I know! I can't wait!" She flipped on her wipers, because the snow was really starting to come down. "Archie isn't too happy about it."

"Archie Bryant? He seemed nice enough, why would he be opposed to Clara coming in to help out?"

"Eh, he's a bit of a stickler for how things used to be, how they've always done things up on the mountain." She air-quoted. "I'm sure it'll be fine; Clara can charm the pants off anyone."

I thought about Archie. Good-looking yes, but there was something a bit remote about him, maybe not standoffish, but with an edge of that trademark East Coast Cool.

Then I thought about Clara. A tiny little spitfire, she was used to kicking ass and taking names, bringing everything up to code and shipshape as quickly as humanly possible, all the while looking like six feet of woman scrunched into five feet of awesome.

I chuckled to myself, thinking about those two rattling around the old Mountain House. My chuckle quickly faded when Roxie pulled into a parking spot half a block from the old barn at the edge of town, where the party was being held tonight for the new commercial viewing.

I swallowed the lump that had unexpectedly shown up to the party as well. "Here we go."

❦

The snow dusted everything with fluffy powder by the time we made it to the barn. There were cars parked everywhere, and from the noise inside, it sounded like the entire town was there. Roxie had some cakes to drop off, so she waved me on in while she went in search of a rolling cart to bring everything in from the car.

Tonight we screened the Bailey Falls commercials I'd created. In all the years I'd been in advertising, I'd never actually been to a "premiere" party for one of my campaigns. Usually they took place in a very dry and boring conference room, the clients screening it while we explained the buy-in and the target markets.

Not in Bailey Falls. As I walked into the barn, it was like walking into a wintry wonderland. Combining the premiere with the annual holiday party, they had gone all out. Roxie once told me that her hometown would hang bunting from *every fucking place you can think to hang bunting.* I think the same can safely be said about twinkle lights.

Soaring overhead high into the rafters, each beam was wrapped entirely in white twinkle lights. Lighted stars, lighted wreaths, even a few lighted balls were hanging from the ceiling, bathing everything in rich, warm, sparkly gold.

And across the entire back wall, interspersed with the seven (count them, seven) Christmas trees, were the photographs from the campaign. I grinned when I saw them, feeling pride at what we'd created.

Each picture showed a different slice of Bailey Falls life. Swimming in one of the beautiful mountain lakes. Fishing in one of the cold, clear streams. Walking down the same Main Street I'd just been on, covered in fall leaves and soaking up the sunshine. Eating at one of the locally owned restaurants, white-water rafting, dancing under the stars.

And the last few pictures featured some of the best scenery around. There was Leo, filling farmshare boxes while laughing. I remember that shot: Roxie was standing just off to the side and promising to harvest honey if he'd just make this easy and smile for the camera. And there were Chad and Logan, holding hands as they took their own walk down Main Street, making it a truly family-friendly town for all. And the last picture?

Oscar. With his cows. Not smiling, because come on, it's Oscar. But *almost* smiling. One corner of his mouth was curved up, like he was in on something no one else was. Arm slung around one of his pretty cows, with the enormous barn behind him. The Hudson Valley. Where the food is pretty, and so are the farmers.

I stared at his picture, remembering.

The first time I'd met his cows, how I'd tried to run away.

The first time I'd visited that barn, how he'd made me shiver.

The first time I'd traced his tattoos, run my fingers over them and then later my tongue.

The first time I'd fulfilled my secret dream of making cheese . . . and realized it was much harder than it seemed. And stinkier.

The first time I'd realized I was falling for that stupid farmer.

I was smiling, looking at these pictures, thinking about the possible life I could have here . . . if he wanted it, too.

I needed Oscar. I wanted Oscar. And I also . . . you know what? I really missed him. Beyond the sex, beyond the obsession over my ass and watching it bounce, beyond the showers and the barns and the sweet, sweet love on the stairs, the man made me laugh. I *missed* him.

Where the hell was that man?

"Hey, Natalie! The pictures look great; we can't wait to see the commercial!" Roxie's mom, Trudy, and her boyfriend, Wayne Tuesday, danced by, literally rocking around the Christmas tree.

"Good to see you! Have you seen Oscar?" I replied, trying to act like a normal person, though I was all butterflies inside.

"Haven't seen him, sweetie; I'm sure he'll be around. The whole town is here!" Trudy waved as she danced past.

Good lord, when did the dancing start? While I was going inside myself for a feelings check, the Christmas party hop had officially begun.

I smiled and nodded at people I'd actually gotten to know on my weekend trips up here, people who smiled and nodded back, welcoming me, accepting me as one of their own, even though I'd only been here for a short time.

A couple danced past, seeming lost in each other, dreamy happy and—holy shit, was that Missy?

It was. She caught my eye around the same time I realized it was her. I watched her face change, working through surprise, acceptance, and then . . . hope?

It was hope. She offered me a cautious smile, one that I returned. That done, she returned her gaze to the man she was dancing with, and I took a deep breath.

"Hey, pretty girl!" Chad called out as he and Logan danced past. "Why so glum? Your pictures look gorgeous!"

"Not glum, just, have you seen Oscar?"

They exchanged knowing glances.

"No, but if he's not here yet, he'll turn up soon. Get yourself a drink; try the eggnog. Mr. Peabody made it and it's filled with hooch," Chad said.

"Eggnog. I'll give you some fucking eggnog," I grumbled, searching through the crowd. It shouldn't be so hard to find a six-foot-six-inch-tall man, but still no sign of him. "Sonofabitch," I continued—and heard a telltale rattling sound behind me.

There was Polly, wearing a Christmas sweater and shaking her swear jar, which was festively festooned. "You swore, Natalie. Please put in a quarter."

"You're like a little curse ninja, you know that?" I said. "Who're you here with?"

"Daddy brought me, but he's helping Roxie bring in the cakes." She winked, and started talking out of the side of her mouth a little, very 1930s gangster. "And you know what that means."

I'd been burned like this before. "What *does* that mean?"

She shook her head and rattled her jar. "I don't know, actually. It's just what I heard Uncle Chad say one time. Quarter, please."

"Kid, you're bleeding me dry." I dug in my purse for a quarter. "That's all?"

"You said a quarter."

"Yes, but you usually give me a dollar, in case you say something else."

"Well, I'll try and keep my mouth zipped tonight."

"You can try . . ." she muttered, walking away while shaking her jar to the tune of the music.

"Little hustler," I said under my breath, and I heard a low chuckle behind me.

Every part of me turned on. I could feel it, feel him. My skin tightened, my hands clenched, my heart burst, and my teeth chattered. I slowly turned, and there he was.

Tall. Beautiful. Hair artfully pulled back in that leather tie, looking effortless as usual. It was Oscar, my caveman.

Wearing the ugliest Christmas sweater I'd ever seen. Red and green, covered in running reindeer, it was too tight across his chest and too long in the arms, and absolutely hideous.

"Wow," I said, taking in the riot of colors. "That's some sweater."

"Missy made it for me; she knits me one each year," he said with a shrug, watching my eyes carefully for any sign of jealousy.

I realized with a start that there was no jealousy here. I didn't have to worry about Missy, even if she did still love him. Which, based on her dance partner and the way she was gazing at him, seemed like less of a possibility than before. If the world had more relationships end as amicably as theirs did, it'd be a much happier place.

"That's truly sweet," I said sincerely.

He stepped closer to me as the Christmas lights twinkled all around us. "Everything looks really great, Natalie. People have been saying all night long how impressed they are, and how Natalie Grayson is the best thing to happen to this town in a long time."

"That's kind of them," I answered, taking a step toward him as well. "I have to admit, I'm pretty impressed with the way things turned out campaign-wise." I stepped closer. "But not so much with how things turned out . . . with us."

His eyes widened for a split second, the tiniest bit of hope showing before he got his emotions in check. "Well, the deck was kind of stacked against us, I suppose."

Taking one more step, and a chance as well, I reached for his hand. "What if I told you I could unstack that deck?"

"What are you saying?"

I took a deep breath, looked into his eyes, and told the truth. "When I was seventeen, I fell in what I thought was love, with a very bad man. He told me things, made me think certain things about myself, about my body. He turned me against my friends, against my family, and by the end I was willing to sacrifice everything for him, because I thought that's what love was. And that I wasn't worth anything. And when it ended, I had to get away and rebuild everything that was left of me."

His eyes flared hot with anger on my behalf, for things that had happened long ago and he could never change, but wanted to anyway.

"I was lucky to find myself again, to come out the other side of it. But something got lost in the process, and it made it impossible for me to fall in love again. Until you."

His mouth parted, wanted to say something, but he held it back.

"I do love you, Oscar. I love you so much, but I can't give up who I am and my entire world just to be with you." I squeezed his hand. "But I would like to try a compromise."

The smallest of smiles curved his lips. "A compromise, huh? What does that mean?"

"It means that I'm going to start working from home a few days a week. I've already talked to my boss, and while we're still ironing out the details, he knows that it's in his best interest to let me have this."

"Home office?"

"Mm-hmm, and funnily enough, Chad Bowman knows the guy who owns that old store on Main Street—the one with the empty top floor that's just waiting for someone to open up shop."

His smile grew. "You don't say . . ."

"Hold on there, Caveman: you've got a part to play in all this, too. I realize you've got responsibilities here that aren't so mobile. And I can work with that, provided that you agree to spend weekends with me in the city when the market is running weekly again, as the cows allow. I'm willing to work with you on this because I know how much you love my apartment, and I know how much you love the bed in my apartment."

"It's a good bed."

"And speaking of beds, we'll need to make some changes at your place. I'm willing to bet your last dollar that Missy picked out every piece of furniture and country cow art in that house, yes?"

"Yes," he said, the grin getting larger by the minute.

"Luckily for you, I happen to know all the best furniture

designers in Manhattan, and we'll be taking advantage of the discount I get. Just nod, Oscar."

He nodded, looping one finger through my belt loop, tugging me closer. "Any other compromises I need to agree to?"

"I hate that sweater."

"Okay."

"Lose it."

He tugged it off over his head, revealing his bare chest, threw it onto the table next to us, his scarred eyebrow raised in challenge.

There was a round of applause at the impromptu strip show, and as I looked around I had to laugh, seeing Roxie and Leo and Polly, Chad and Logan, Trudy and Wayne, Elmer and Louise, Mr. and Mrs. Oleson, and every other person I'd gotten to know over the last few months.

Roxie pointed above our heads; I looked up, and there it was.

"Mistletoe," I whispered, and he laid an enormous kiss on me, lifting me up out of my shoes, to the sounds of Bailey Falls' approving applause.

"I love you, Pinup," he murmured, crushing me against his naked inked chest.

"Turns out I really, really, love you, too, you fucking caveman."

He kissed me again, this time to the sound of Polly's swear jar shaking.

Epilogue

My girl clung tightly to my hand as we walked down the street. It was really cold; it wouldn't get above freezing all day. I liked the cold: it made her stick closer to me. Her arm was either through mine or around my waist, clinging tight.

Natalie had moved to Bailey Falls. She hated when I said that, said to keep my voice down or she'd lose her New York card. Technically, she hadn't really moved. We were figuring it out. But the town was ecstatic to have a "highfalutin big-city advertising whiz" ensconced on Main Street. And while she'd never admit it, she quite enjoyed being consulted on whether or not The Jam Lady's new labels should be a pinkish beige or a beigey pink and how that might impact her overall sales trajectory . . .

Until the spring market started up again, it was hard for me to come into the city every weekend, so there were some weekends when we couldn't see each other. But come March I'd be in town every Friday through Sunday. She was campaigning hard for Monday too, which I'd told her was next to impossible but that didn't stop her from pleading her case. Which I encouraged her to do, since she typically wore her thigh-high boots and nothing else whenever she attempting to sweet talk me into anything. I really should tell her sometime that I was pretty sure one of my volunteers could cover Monday mornings occasionally but then again . . . she looked fucking fantastic in those boots so . . .

For now, she typically spent Monday night through Thursday morning in Bailey Falls, taking the morning train back into the city. Sometimes I could convince her to stay over one more night. It didn't take much; my girl was lost when my mouth was on her. Which was as often as possible, and would be even more if I had anything to say about it. There was nothing I loved more than making that woman come under my tongue. Unless it was watching her walk away, that great . . . big ass bouncing. I loved to make it bounce.

I loved everything about her, plain and simple. She was a nightmare in the kitchen, a dream in the bedroom, and bossy as all get-out, but she was my girl and we were figuring it out.

I'd be coaching the local high school football team next fall, and Natalie was keen to be in town for all my games. Not sure if she realized that would mean giving up Friday nights in the city, but we'd work on it. I was getting to know the city beyond the market, and it was growing on me. I'd never enjoy those cocktail parties that she'd dragged me to a few times, but I'd go. For her.

"This is it," she said, stopping in front of a tall brownstone, its warm lights shining out into the snow-covered street. My girl was taking me to brunch.

She was nervous, I could tell. Everything that had to do with us, figuring out what kind of couple we were, made her a little nervous. She'd been hurt really bad before, and I understood why she was gun-shy. She could take all the time she needed; I wasn't going anywhere.

"My parents are so excited you're coming today. I told you, right?" Her voice was full of excitement as she clung to my hand.

"You did," I answered, leaning down to drop a kiss on her forehead. Before we could go up the steps, her father threw open the front door.

"Get in here, it's freezing outside! Oscar, how are you? I saw your cheese in Brannigan's the other day—the big store over in Brooklyn. They even had the new one—what's it called?"

"Pinup." I grinned, resting my hand on my girl's backside as she walked up the steps before me. "It's called Pinup."